For Lovers Only

Also by Alex Hairston

SHE CREEPS

For Lovers Only

ALEX HAIRSTON

KENSINGTON PUBLISHING CORP.
http://www.kensingtonbooks.com

DAFINA BOOKS are published by

Kensington Publishing Corp.
850 Third Avenue
New York, NY 10022

All Kensington titles, imprints and distributed lines are available at special quantity discounts for bulk purchases for sales promotion, premi-
ums, fund-raising, educational or institutional use.

Special book excerpts or customized printings can also be created to fit spe-
cific needs. For details, write or phone the office of the Kensington Special
Sales Manager: Kensington Publishing Corp., 850 Third Avenue, New
York, NY 10022. Attn. Special Sales Department. Phone: 1-800-221-2647.

Dafina Books and the Dafina logo Reg. U.S. Pat. & TM Off.

ISBN-13: 978-0-7582-1884-1
ISBN-10: 0-7582-1884-2

First Kensington Trade Paperback Printing: June 2008
10 9 8 7 6 5 4 3 2 1

Printed in the United States of America

For
Margaret Hairston
and
Kim Hairston

Acknowledgments

Thank you!!!

Lots of Love,

Alex

Part One

Love's in Need of Love

Chapter 1

The beginning of the end.

At 3:45 AM, Joel was awakened from a peaceful deep sleep by his girlfriend Renee's annoying tossing and turning. Their bedroom was shrouded in grayish-black darkness, and the soft glow of pale moonlight seeped in from behind the curtains and partially closed mini-blinds. As soon as Renee stopped moving, Joel was out again, his mind completely at ease. Drowsiness had filtered out any remnants of stress or aggravation.

All of a sudden Joel was awakened again because Renee's tossing and turning was quickly replaced with moans and groans. In an airy tone Renee softly whispered, "Ooh . . . ooh. Ah, yeah."

Then she whispered another man's name. His stomach dropped, flooded with acid and then felt as if it was bound in a giant knot. All kinds of wild sexual thoughts bounced around in his cloudy and confused mind. His imagination began to get the best of him. An image popped in his head of a big, black, sweaty NBA-lookin' brotha totally dominating Renee in bed.

Within seconds Joel dismissed his crazy perverted thoughts because he wasn't trying to kill anybody or have an argument at this time of night over his overactive imagination and insecurities. This was more about Renee's subconscious thoughts, secret dreams and hidden desires. Joel just took a deep breath and made a quick mental note of the name *Robert*.

As always, Joel's optimism began to overtake his sense of uncertainty. He could rationalize anything and everything. He tried with everything inside of him to convince himself that there was a possibility that Renee could have been dreaming about him. And instead of whispering another man's name, she could have mumbled something as simple as, *stop it*. Then again, he was pretty sure that he had heard the name *Robert*.

In no time, Joel worked himself up to a state of disbelief, staring into the darkness thinking, *I know she didn't just call out another man's name in my bed. Who the fuck is Robert?*

Renee began to fidget between the sheets. Joel felt her legs spasm. Her moans became louder and increasingly sexual. At first Joel was under the impression that Renee was in the middle of a passionate wet dream and he could excuse that, however he quickly realized that she was wide-awake and in the midst of masturbating with another man on her mind. What she was doing was without a doubt inexcusable. In the back of his mind, Joel knew that Renee had to have been cheating, but his forgiving heart refused to believe his judgmental mind.

It was awkward as hell for Joel to be awoken like this, especially since he wasn't Renee's motivation or at least playing an active role in making her moan. Joel felt an internal rage and again he thought, *Who the fuck is Robert?*

Joel was about to confront Renee, but he decided to hold back the anger that raged within because she wasn't finished with her little show.

Renee continued fidgeting and going through mini-convulsions between the sheets. He couldn't believe his ears or understand why Renee was doing all this while lying next to him. She knew that Joel wasn't a heavy sleeper. After a minute or so, Joel realized that Renee didn't give a damn whether he was a heavy sleeper or not. He just lay there with a big throbbing hard-on, listening to Renee please herself.

Renee was driven by what Joel considered an intense case of SSD, selfish sexual desire, and that made him feel more useless than he had ever felt in his life.

Joel had nothing against masturbation because he thought it was natural. He had masturbated plenty of times, but he considered what Renee was doing an insult to his manhood because more than likely she did have another man on her mind.

Joel was boiling mad. They hadn't had sex since the huge argument they had three weeks ago, yet Renee had the audacity to lay next to him pleasing herself instead of involving him in the fun. Joel was convinced Renee's stubborn ass still held a grudge and just didn't want to give in to him after their big blowout. He lay in bed, cold and angry, while Renee experienced pure ecstasy.

The thing that pissed Joel off the most was that he had no idea that Renee masturbated. They had been together for two years, and she always said that her mother raised her to believe that it was a sin to touch herself in a sexual way. Joel could see that was a bunch of bullshit.

Renee's breathing intensified. Her entire body trembled and then she mumbled something totally incomprehensible—it sounded like she was speaking in tongues.

Joel's tired eyes widened in the darkness. Renee was going for multiple orgasms and Joel was beginning to feel like he was trapped in the middle of an erotic nightmare. He wanted so badly to join in on the fun, she was driving him crazy, but his stupid male pride wouldn't let him interrupt for fear of rejection, because Renee was so into having a real soul-stirring and self-satisfying experience.

Finally, Renee was done. She really got her thing off. Joel lay still in the darkness and complete silence of their bedroom for a few minutes. He was too shocked to move or even take a breath.

Renee shifted to her left side, reached over to the nightstand and sipped from her bottled water. She lay back down, turned her back to Joel and cuddled up with her favorite pillow. She was oh-so-satisfied, and acted as if Joel wasn't even lying next to her. He was less than a foot from her physically, but emotionally they were worlds apart.

Chapter 2

After Renee's little episode, Joel lay in bed analyzing their relationship, as if there were really something to analyze. So many different emotions filled his heart and mind. The time had come for him to confront Renee and possibly end things for good. All of a sudden Joel felt Renee scoot her thickness—that soft round naked ass—against his thigh.

All those emotions that filled his heart and mind began to fill his penis. He regained his big throbbing hard-on from earlier. This time it wasn't going to go away so easily. There was only one cure for Joel's weakness and he was no match for Renee's feminine strength. She was much too powerful to resist.

For Joel and most men, sex is much more than a want or a need. Sex is a biological urge or demand that sometimes needs immediate attention.

Before Joel knew it, he had cuddled up behind Renee and began to caress her soft warm body. He had almost forgotten how good she felt, and he had totally forgotten about Robert.

Joel asked, "Renee, you 'sleep?" She didn't respond. He felt somewhat discombobulated because the blood from his brain had been rerouted and flowed directly to his penis. Joel rephrased his question in hopes of getting a response. "You awake?"

Still feeling the effects of her multiple orgasms, Renee moaned, "Mmmmmmm."

Joel kissed her on the back of her neck. She grabbed his hand and gently placed it between her thighs. Joel could feel that her warm pussy was still soaking wet.

Renee could feel Joel's throbbing hardness pressed against her naked ass. Passion was ignited. She turned around and kissed Joel on his lips. The sexual excitement within Joel grew. For the first time in weeks Joel felt wanted, needed and strongly desired.

When Joel tried to return the same attention, Renee grabbed his hands and said, "It's okay. Relax and let me do you. I know it's been a while."

Joel didn't say a word because he was too afraid of wrecking Renee's flow. He thought, *Lord knows, this girl hardly ever shows any kind of initiative when it comes to sex. I'm just gonna enjoy the moment.*

Renee touched Joel's dick and set his entire body on fire. He soon realized that there was definitely something different in Renee's touch and her actions, but at that moment she made him feel too good to even care. He wasn't able to process his thoughts properly because he was too caught up in *sextasy.* Renee was completely and deeply stimulating. The allure of instant sexual gratification had Joel's mind stranded on the border between sanity and temporary insanity.

Renee began to create a variety of warm wet pleasures with her mouth. She kissed and sucked Joel's neck the same way she used to do when they first met. Then she kissed his chest and rippled abs. She surprised him with a few bites here and there.

Renee focused that same attention down a little lower. She began to lick and suck the shaft of his dick as if it was her favorite hard chocolate treat.

Right in the middle of giving Joel a blow job, Renee said, "What was I thinking . . . letting all this good dick go to waste?" She went right back to satisfying him with her mouth.

Renee wasn't really used to or typically good at giving head, but she started feeling very adventurous. She attempted this new and fascinating deep-throat maneuver until her gag reflex reminded her that Joel was a lot larger and longer than she could handle.

The sound of Renee gagging turned Joel on even more. He admired Renee's creativity and thought that all she needed was a little more practice—daily practice.

Both of Renee's hands caressed a different part of Joel's body, or worked together along with her mouth to create the most intense pleasure she had ever made him feel. As she climbed on top of Joel, Renee couldn't believe how hard his dick was. Her pussy began to crave the sensation of feeling his hardness inside of her.

But Renee didn't slip Joel's dick inside of her right away. Instead she let the passion and anticipation build. She just played around by sliding her wetness up and down his hardness, stimulating her swollen and excited clitoris at the same time.

Joel kept his hands down by his side exactly where Renee had placed them. She grabbed his dick and slowly slid it deep inside of her inch by inch until it pressed against her cervix and beyond. She held her position for a few seconds, enjoying a momentary sensation of pressure in a few of her most sensitive spots. Right after that, the ride began.

Renee yelled, "Ah, yeah! I love it! Feels . . . so . . . good! Does it feel good to you, too?"

Joel replied, "Yeah!"

This was kind of weird for Joel because they never talked during sex. Renee was never one for comments during sex or talking dirty in general. A few screams, grunts, whines, moans and groans were the only way they usually communicated during sex.

Renee was in charge, feeling good and saying stuff like, "I'm gonna put it on you good. Take this pussy . . . take it!" Renee began to ride a little harder and a little faster. The bed squeaked and creaked. "Who got that whip appeal, baby?" With more intensity she asked, "Huh? Who got that whip appeal? Who . . . got . . . it?"

Joel didn't say anything. Renee's aggressive commando-take-charge approach threw him off a bit. He lay there thinking, *What the hell?*

Renee repeated, "Who got that whip appeal, baby?"

She started putting it on him real good. Resistance was futile. Joel grunted, "You! You do! Ah! You got it! You got it!"

Joel must have said the right thing because Renee began to ride him ten times as hard and as fast. She broke it down, started winding and grinding her hips better than an ATL stripper and then made her booty clap loudly as she slammed her ass against him.

They fucked like it was the weekend. Usually when Joel wanted sex from Renee on a weeknight he had to hear about how tired she was and about how early she had to get up for work the next morning. Renee would promise to hit him off on the weekend and most times she didn't keep her promise. Renee must have been really horny, because she had forgotten that this was a Wednesday night.

Joel thought about how enthralling and strangely erotic it was having sex in dense darkness. He thought about how easily the eyes could begin to play tricks on someone. When the eyes played tricks it was almost like being with someone else— it made a lover faceless or gave them almost any face someone would like to see.

That's when it hit Joel. He carefully considered all of the sexually pleasing things that Renee had done to him. The way she took charge, her touch, the kisses, the deep throat maneuver and her overall sexual energy were all fueled by someone else. She was with Joel physically, but mentally she was with Robert. Joel felt as if Renee was rehearsing or doing things to him that she probably had already done to Robert. Although Joel's sanity had returned somewhat, he was still out for sexual gratification. It was a male thing. In addition to that, it had been so long since he had had sex and things felt too good to stop.

Renee reached her climax first and automatically assumed that they were done. She was so exhausted that she really didn't seem to care whether Joel had reached his climax or not. Joel knew the deal and laughed to himself because Renee had no idea what he had in store for her. As far as he was concerned they were far from being done. To Joel it was just time for a position change and time for him to take charge.

Renee assumed a submissive position in the center of the bed. She was on all fours facing the headboard. Having Renee in this position really turned Joel on. He was about to give it to Renee from behind. He had a big long dick and was a master at deep penetration. He loved doing it doggie-style on the bed, on the floor or anywhere.

At first Renee bucked back, throwing her ass at Joel just how he liked it. That's when the name *Robert* popped back into Joel's head and made things get a little rougher. Joel had one hand on Renee's left hip to help guide her and the other on her right shoulder to help thrust his dick deeper inside of her. Joel was extra aggressive trying to make sure Renee never thought about another man or whispered another man's name in their bed again.

With tons of confidence Joel asked, "Who's got the whip appeal now?"

Right away Renee screamed, "You!"

"Am I whipping it on you good?"

"Yeah! Oh, yeah!" She couldn't really think about anything else because Joel's dick felt so good to her.

"Who's pussy is this? Tell me!"

"It's your pussy!"

"Say my name!" Joel hit Renee's ass with a nice steady rhythm and shouted, "Say . . . my . . . name!"

She shouted, "Joel! Ooh, it's yours! It's all yours!"

Renee held her position on the bed as Joel lowered his feet to the floor. Standing was all about gaining better leverage, thrusting in and out. Joel's erection hardened, strengthened and his thrusts became more forceful. He grabbed a handful of Renee's long, glamorous honey-blond hairweave and wrapped it around his hand forming a fist. He pulled it, making her arch her back and giving her ass just the right lift.

He pulled again.

This time Renee yelled, "Ow! My hair! That shit hurt!"

Joel didn't apologize. He kept pounding away like a machine.

Renee was used to Joel being rough, but she could tell that this time was a little different. Joel was really enjoying himself and just kept going and going.

Renee moaned louder, hoping that her excitement would make Joel hurry up and come.

Beads of sweat poured down Joel's face, chest and back. Although his breathing quickened and his muscles began to tense up, his body continued to move with machine precision, pounding and pounding away. Joel was caught up in three very intense emotions: pleasure, jealousy and anger.

Renee continued to moan, "Awwww! Awwww!"

Renee found herself getting wetter. By now she was really enjoying Joel and started bouncing all of her thickness right back against him like she did earlier. He gladly returned the favor by sending forceful shock waves throughout her body. It was a challenge to see who would come first.

Joel said, "Feels . . . so . . . damn . . . good!"

Renee closed her eyes and yelled, "Oh, God! Joel, you feel so good! You . . . gonna . . . make . . . me . . . come!"

Joel let go of Renee's hair, gripped tightly around her narrow waist with both hands and moved in and out of her as fast and as hard as humanly possible.

He asked, "You like that? Does it feel good?"

"Yeah! Awwww! Ooh! Ooh! Yesssss!"

Renee lowered her head and bit down on their Ralph Lauren comforter, trying to muffle her moans. She knew that their neighbors all around their apartment building could hear her. Joel knew it too, but he couldn't care less.

Joel said, "It's okay. You can moan and scream for me as loud as you want. I wanna hear . . . need to hear you."

"Mmmmmm! You . . . tryin' . . . to . . . kill . . . me!"

Finally Joel felt himself about to come and it made him fuck even faster. Within minutes, he gave in to the rush that led to a powerful release. After he came he felt an immediate urge to hold Renee really tight. Insanity had crept back into the picture. He thought of Renee and Robert. But this time Joel began to show Renee a much gentler side by kissing, caressing and hopefully making her fall back in love with him and only him. Joel was sure that Renee could see that he was more than enough man for her to handle and all the man she needed.

They both were literally finished. They lay there sweaty and gasping for air. As soon as they drifted off to sleep their annoying radio alarm clock went off, playing the theme song to Tom Joyner's morning show. Although the loud music echoed throughout their bedroom, neither of them moved. They remained cuddled up in a spoon position.

Joel was awake and thinking about everything he had just experienced.

He whispered in Renee's ear, "Baby."

"Huh?"

Joel really didn't want to do it, but he just had to ask, "Who's Robert?"

Chapter 3

Renee acted as if she didn't hear Joel's question. He felt himself getting angry, but remained composed. He sat up in his king-sized bed and hit the snooze button on the radio alarm clock.

Birds sang a variety of songs outside of Joel and Renee's bedroom window. Traces of sunlight pierced their way through tiny gaps in the mini-blinds. With every passing second the morning sun's brightness intensified. The darkness was gone and now it was time to shed some light on the truth.

Joel said, "I asked you a question. Who's Robert?"

A puzzled expression covered Renee's face. "What?"

Frustration moved throughout Joel's body and found its final resting place in his head. He placed his hands at his temples and said, "I hate when I ask somebody a simple question and they play dumb or act like they didn't hear me." He paused. When no response came, he said, "See, now you're playing dumb. Who the fuck is Robert?"

Joel's typically cautious approach was out the window.

Bright eyed and surprised, Renee asked, "Why are you cursing at me?"

"Because you know damn well you heard me and understand perfectly well what I asked."

Renee threw the covers off of her and sat up looking for her slippers. "I don't know no damn Robert."

Joel yelled, "I heard you say his name last night!"

Renee found her slippers and then quietly slipped into her robe. As she fastened it she said, "You need to calm down 'cause I don't have a clue what you're talking about. And judging from your expression, I can see that you don't really know what you're talking about either."

Joel jumped out of bed naked and wrapped his towel, still damp from his shower the night before, around his waist. "Come on. Cut the bullshit. I know there's somebody else. No need to hide it anymore. We're both responsible adults. Well, at least I am. Maybe I'm not meeting your needs."

Renee sucked her teeth and rolled her eyes. She walked into the bathroom and sat down on the toilet. Joel noticed that Renee unconsciously broke her typical morning routine. Usually she would take a good look at herself in the mirror first, but this time she didn't. Joel figured that Renee wasn't in the mood to see the guilt in her eyes.

Renee looked at Joel and said, "It's too early in the morning for this. You need to stop being so insecure. You're always trying to interrogate somebody. That's nothing but your guilty conscience."

Joel stepped into the bathroom. He confidently looked at himself in the mirror and prepared to shave and brush his teeth. "Yup. That's why you can't even look at yourself in the mirror and exactly why you're always checking up on me. I swear to God that there isn't anybody else in my life except you. You're guilty and you're dying to get some dirt on me to help take the heavy load off your conscience."

Renee was pissed because she hated when Joel scrutinized her actions and more than that she hated to be chastised like a child. She got off the toilet and turned on the shower. Out of habit she closed the bathroom door. She looked at Joel and said, "I don't know what you mean."

Steam from the hot shower quickly filled the bathroom, fogging up the mirror. Joel thought that Renee was rude for not considering the fact that he was using the mirror. He wiped a line of fog from the mirror, but within seconds it steamed up again. Since he couldn't see, shaving was definitely out of the question. He decided to brush his teeth first.

As he put toothpaste on his toothbrush he said, "Since you don't know what I mean, then I'll tell you. I mean stuff like our big argument a few weeks ago. When I came home and you were in here looking crazy, color-coding my damn cell phone bill with different highlighters based on numbers that were or weren't familiar to you. That was some ridiculous shit. I'm not a child and you're definitely not my mother." He began brushing his teeth.

Renee sarcastically said, "If I was your mother you wouldn't talk to me like this, would you?"

With his mouth full of white foamy toothpaste, Joel mumbled, "What?"

Climbing into the shower Renee looked at Joel and said, "Nothing. Just forget it."

Joel spat the toothpaste from his mouth and then yelled over the noisy shower, "That's exactly what's wrong . . . communication! Act like a responsible adult for a change and speak up. Your unspoken words are the ones with the most meaning. When your words are left unsaid, your actions speak loudest. Your actions from last night told me a whole lot about you." He shook his head in frustration because he felt like Renee was ignoring him. He yelled, "I know about you and that punk-ass Robert and you know I know."

The steam and noise of the shower were too much for Joel to compete with for the moment. He decided to give Renee a few minutes alone to think about what he had just said. After relieving his bladder he headed back into the bedroom.

When Renee was finished in the bathroom, she quietly stepped back into the bedroom.

Joel was calm and very clever. He knew how to get what he wanted out of Renee—all he needed was the right approach. He looked Renee directly in her eyes, gave her a pleasant little smile and calmly asked, "Does Robert make you happy? Does he truly make you happy? Does he fill your heart with joy and make it overflow? That's all I need to know."

Renee's bitter expression gradually changed. She felt warm inside and lit up on the outside with an undeniably radiant glow. She battled like hell to control her emotions and facial expressions. Joel watched closely as the corners of her mouth seemed to spasm. Within seconds a bright smile emerged. Joel couldn't believe what he was seeing. Just as quickly as Renee smiled, her eyes began to water. Tears streamed from her eyes. She was as beautiful and as messed up as sunshine on a rainy day.

Renee was absolutely unpredictable. She sighed and then put her right hand up to her mouth for a few seconds to help compose herself. She wiped her tears and said, "Robert is one of my co-workers. I said his name last night trying to get a re-action out of you."

Joel was so shocked by Renee's open admission that he felt like he had just stepped into the twilight zone. He grimaced and said, "Okay, you got a reaction. Why are you crying now?"

Renee made a face that told Joel that she was still holding back the truth. She took a deep breath and said, "I'm crying because of all of the hurtful things you said. You made me sound like such a bad person."

Another round of tears began to pour from her eyes. This time Joel wiped them away. With a hint of sarcasm he said, "Poor little misunderstood Renee. Look at you . . . still lying. Always bending, contorting and redirecting the truth and the blame. Where's the truth? It must be hidden under your tongue or somewhere in the back of your mind. It might hurt me, but just think about how much you're hurting me by lying. C'mon, I know you better than you know yourself. Are you fucking Robert or what?"

Renee yelled, "No!" She stared at Joel for a few seconds. "Since you wanna know the truth so badly, then here's the truth." She paused again to collect her thoughts. "Things did get a little heated and out of control between me and Robert once, but that's it."

Joel raised an eyebrow. "Exactly how heated and out of control did things get between you and him?"

Renee appeared to be somewhat embarrassed, but Joel could see that a huge weight had been lifted off of her. She turned away from him and started to talk to his reflection in the bedroom dresser's mirror. "A couple of kisses and some light fondling—that's all."

Joel spoke to her reflection. "That's more than enough, don't you think?"

Renee stood in front of Joel nude. She finished drying off with a pink towel and then slipped into her fancy underwear. "I know and I'm sorry. You were right. You win. I am a bad person. Hope you feel better knowing the truth."

"Nope! I don't feel any different because I knew your ass was lying the whole time. And this isn't about winning, losing or who's right or wrong. This is about us and this stagnant and troubled-ass relationship of ours. Things won't ever be the same between us regardless."

"What do you mean by that?"

"We had something special in the beginning, but now it's completely gone. I have no idea what happened."

Renee sat down at her vanity and started styling her hair. In a real nonchalant manner she said, "I know exactly what happened. We happened, and time revealed our true selves. Now, here we are two-and-a-half years later."

"Yup, and this is as good as it gets."

"That's sad, but it's not all my fault."

"Who cares about whose fault it is? You went out looking for attention from another man and had the audacity to call out his goddamn name in my bed. See, I'm really getting pissed now. The more I think about it the madder I get."

"I was wrong for saying his name in our bed. But you can't

even see your own faults, and you're too self-righteous to even ask why I did what I did."

Renee attempted to turn the blame on Joel. He picked up on her trick and shook his head in disbelief. He laughed. "You're right. I didn't ask, but I was about to." Joel put on a fake melodramatic voice and asked. "Why? Why, Renee? Is Robert's dick bigger than mine?"

Renee replied, "Typical male response. It had nothing to do with dick size. It's about how he treats me compared to how you treat me."

"Whoa, that's funny. You just said how he *treats* you. Don't you mean how he treated you? I mean, since things only got a little heated and out of control once."

"There you go analyzing me again. I see Robert at work on a daily basis, therefore *treats* was used in its proper tense, thank you."

"Well, how exactly does he treat you?"

Renee answered calmly, "With respect and very gently. He isn't all rough and overly aggressive like you."

Joel burst out laughing. "Shit, sounds like you and that nigga did a lot more than get a little heated and out of control. And listen to you, talking about I'm rough and overly aggressive. What about your damn whip appeal last night? I bet you whipped it on him, too."

"When it comes to me and Robert, you can say and think whatever you want. And give me an f-ing break. I didn't hear your ass complaining last night about, as you call it, my damn whip appeal."

Joel had reached his boiling point. "You're right. You know what? I don't have time for this anymore." Joel paused and took a deep breath. "So, I'm gonna say that this right here, is officially over. We're done! Consider your walking papers signed and authorized, so you can step any time you get ready."

"Don't make me laugh. I hope you don't think it's over because you said so." Renee laughed out loud. "As far as I'm concerned, it's *been* over!" She sucked her teeth and threw her hand at Joel. "I don't have time for this either because you're making me late for work."

"Go ahead to work. And you better tell that bitch Robert that I figured y'all out."

"He doesn't care about you or what you figured out."

Joel squinted with anger. "Hold up, he actually knows about me? Because if he knows about me and is messing around with you . . ." He stopped himself, changed his thought process and let out a heavy sigh. He shook his head and said, "That's all right because you aren't even worth going to jail over. I'd be in jail and the two of you would probably be up in here calling out each other's names and shit."

Renee used her usual sarcasm and carelessly added insult to injury. She shrugged her shoulders and said, "I wouldn't doubt it."

Joel's anger level and blood pressure peaked, and then quickly dropped back down within normal limits. With a straight face he said, "I hate you."

"The feeling is mutual." Renee held up her left hand and paused. She felt her emotions getting the best of her. There was a tiny burning sensation in her nasal passages and a stinging in her eyes that made them water. "No, I'm not gonna sit here and say that I hate you, because I sincerely love you. I love you, Joel."

This was the same dramatic breakup scene that had been repeatedly playing in Joel's mind—the same scene that he had been trying to avoid for months. He hated when emotions flew high between him and Renee. He felt her words *I love you*, right in his heart making him realize that he loved Renee. After all that had happened, he stood there wondering why he still loved her so much. His mind raced. He began sifting through the sands of time, searching for something meaningful to hold on to. Sadly, everything just seemed to be slipping away. Hundreds of short but significant moments that he and Renee had shared flashed through his mind. These were happy moments he had pretty much forgotten. Joel knew they would never have the chance to experience anything like those moments again.

Although Joel was hurting and felt betrayed, he hid his emotions and said, "*You love me?* You need help."

"No, Joel, you need help trying to understand me better. I'm a woman with a new opportunity."

Joel laughed. "Take advantage of it then." He looked up at the ceiling and jokingly added, "God, please give me strength and guidance to keep me from killing this crazy-ass woman."

Renee sighed loudly. "Thanks to you I've basically been forced to take advantage of my new opportunity, because we don't have a future together. All we've had for the longest time is convenience. Well, this is very inconvenient for me now."

Joel's demeanor changed because he started to take Renee's words seriously. "Don't say that. I don't believe you."

"I need a husband and you're not willing to step up and put a ring on my finger."

Joel pointed to her right hand. "What's that right there? Looks like a ring that I bought for you and put on your finger."

"I'm talking about a wedding ring and not this friendship ring. I'm twenty-five and you're twenty-six. I think we both need a little more than a friendship."

"All right, I respect that and I ain't even mad at you. Now I see where you're coming from. Finally, you sound like a responsible adult. I understand you perfectly. Effective communication has taken our relationship to another place—looks like we've finally arrived and reached the end of the road."

"I guess so," Renee said sadly.

Joel tried to lighten up their situation a bit by saying, "I wouldn't mind getting married, but we both know damn well we'd end up killing each other right after our honeymoon. It would be all downhill from there."

They both had to laugh at that.

Renee said, "That's true. The pressure alone from trying to

make a marriage with you last beyond the honeymoon would be enough to kill me."

"Me too. Damn, girl, you had me feeling sad enough to cry, but fuck that. I'm not that weak and life is too short to be sad." Joel glanced at the alarm clock. "Look at the time. I gotta shower and get outta here. Just believe me when I say that you'll never find anybody as real as I am."

Renee had the nerve to ask, "What about me? Am I real?"

Joel frowned and reluctantly agreed. "Yeah, you're real."

Renee read Joel's facial expression and said, "A real phony, huh?"

"You said it, not me. Keep it real with me and I'll keep it real with you. Haven't I always said that?"

"Yeah, that is one of your sayings."

"Seriously, I gotta get going." Joel misread something in Renee's eyes as a sign of hope. He was already thinking about how good the make-up sex was going to be. "So, can we talk about this later this evening after work?"

Renee looked at Joel like he was out of his damn mind. She rolled her eyes and gave him a quick and simple reply. "Sure," she lied.

Joel was so used to arguments that he almost acted as if nothing had happened. "Oh yeah, I love you, too."

Joel caught her off guard with his last statement. She smiled and her voice cracked as she said, "I love you." It was painful to say those words again because she had already figured out what was next for them.

Joel and Renee embraced tightly as if this was going to be their last time together and neither of them wanted to let go.

From the start Joel knew that he and Renee were opposites, but he strongly believed that opposites did attract. As he held Renee, he closed his eyes and saw an image of two opposite puzzle pieces. He could see how well they complemented each other. He knew that if the pieces were the same they would never have made a connection. The only problem was that over time the pieces started to wear out and began to take on different shapes. The connection wasn't the same and the pieces no longer fit—permanently disconnected.

Joel and Renee had changed too much to be together. Renee's embrace loosened. Joel got the subtle hint that it was time to let go.

When Joel arrived at his apartment after work that evening it looked like a hurricane had hit the entire place. He knew that his apartment hadn't been burglarized because his computer, plasma and LCD TVs and other expensive electronic equipment were untouched. He knew that his apartment had been struck by Hurricane Renee.

Joel figured that Renee played hooky from work and removed most of her belongings. He saw that she had removed everything except for a bunch of gaudy pieces of fabric that she called evening gowns, some old ugly multicolored knit sweaters, two pairs of dusty hooker boots and a few pairs of worn-out high-heeled shoes with broken straps.

The thing that shocked Joel most was finding Renee's door key on the bedroom dresser. That wasn't all. Attached to the key ring was Renee's one-and-a-half-carat diamond ring. Women hardly ever returned rings, and Joel saw this as Renee's arrogant way of saying that she no longer needed his friendship or his ring.

For some strange reason, Joel felt empty and found himself drawn to the one who hurt him most. Maybe it was the fact that someone else wanted Renee. Was Robert really willing to marry her? The whole thing made him wonder if Robert saw something in Renee that he couldn't. Maybe Robert brought out something special in her that Joel couldn't.

The most embarrassing thing was that Joel thought that he and Renee would sit down that evening to actually try and work things out one last time. Joel knew that somehow he had to shed his indecisiveness and try to get the message through his thick skull that there was nothing left to salvage when it came to his relationship with Renee.

Joel understood that he had created a concept and had fallen in love with a woman who never really existed. Renee was never the woman Joel made her out to be. Everyone has the tendency to build people up and make them into someone greater than they could ever possibly be.

He was bitter because Renee cheated on him, but for some unexplainable reason he still wanted her. It's hard as hell for a man to admit to something like that. He hated Renee, but at the same time he loved her so much. She had disappointed Joel, even though he knew their breakup was inevitable.

Chapter 4

Joel and Renee met at an upscale nightclub in downtown Baltimore called Club One, two and a half years ago. He picked Renee out of a crowd of women, offered to buy her a drink and he'd been paying for that drink ever since.

In public Joel and Renee were the type of couple who appeared to be in love one minute and the next minute, in private, they were completely at war—volatility at its finest. The simplest thing would set them off and lead to an argument with lasting effects.

Joel and Renee knew for a while that their relationship had been stuck in neutral. All of their possibilities had already been maximized and completely exhausted. They couldn't see a promising future together whatsoever. The weird thing was that for the longest time they just couldn't break up. They had developed a fragile bond based on convenience. Instead of breaking up they used to act as if nothing was wrong and did crazy stuff like fantasize about their jacked-up future together. They joked about their ghetto-ass wedding day even though neither one of them wanted to marry the other.

Renee craved attention from day one and Joel basically went along with just about everything she wanted. For example, the time Renee casually mentioned that she wanted a diamond ring, one that she and Joel both refused to label an engagement ring. Renee automatically referred to it as a friendship ring. To Joel calling it a friendship ring was a weak but appropriate title. He temporarily lost his mind and bought that ring, but he swore that he had no intention of marrying Renee. Buying that ring was more or less about going through the motions in a strained relationship and trying to keep his girl happy. In reality, Joel viewed that one-and-a-half-carat diamond friendship ring as a small price to pay to keep Renee's big mouth shut.

Fortunately there was never any talk of kids or accidental pregnancies. They were always extra careful when it came to involving a new and innocent life in their messy relationship. More proof that they didn't intend on anything too serious or long-term.

Things between Joel and Renee weren't always bad. When they first hooked up he knew that she was a high maintenance type. She told him that it took lots of effort to keep up her Beyoncé appearance. What guy wouldn't want a beautiful celebrity-lookin' chick on his arm? If it meant kicking out a little cash to get Renee's hair and nails done, then Joel was fine with that because she made him happy and happiness meant everything to him.

Renee had her own cash flow. She worked as a disability claims processor for the Social Security Administration. Joel's first impression of Renee was that she was a glamorous well-educated sista with a decent career. He was incredibly impressed. Here was this Howard University graduate, no kids, career-oriented, low debt-to-income ratio and a slammin' body that any man would love to have. When Joel seriously thought about it he knew that some serious drama had to come along with this one: Renee was too good to be true.

Like most beautiful overconfident women, *Getting Over* was the name of Renee's game. The thing that bothered Joel most was that she used her looks to get whatever she wanted from him and her body to get whatever else was left. In the beginning Joel was just plain ole pussy whipped. Renee had the whip appeal for real. She had him wrapped around her little finger and eating out of the palm of her hand from the moment they first laid eyes on each other.

After dating for six months, Renee asked if she could move into Joel's cozy little one bedroom apartment located in the Owings Mills section of Baltimore County. Renee was in Joel's life, in his heart, so he thought why not his apartment. Being the accommodating type of man that he was, Joel welcomed Renee with open arms.

Joel was a graduate of Morgan State University and now a fifth grade social studies teacher with a pretty decent income. He automatically assumed that with their combined incomes, he and Renee were about to be elevated to a new socioeconomic level. He thought their relationship was moving in the right direction—he was delusional. The excitement and initial steady flow of great sex often has that effect.

He felt that the best way he could get to know Renee was if they tried living together. He assumed from her personality and general appearance that Renee would be an absolute pleasure to live with—even though he never had the opportunity to see Renee's old apartment on a real functional level. When they met she had most of her belongings boxed up or lying in huge piles all over her apartment. Renee blamed the clutter and confusion on the fact that she was in the process of moving. Joel believed her because he thought there was no way a fine-ass woman like Renee could purposely be living in a junk pile.

Joel's apartment was full of art and imported furniture. His place could have easily been featured in a magazine. When Renee moved in, it slowly began to resemble an obstacle course. Organization was important to Joel, but he eventually got used to having tons of makeup and other beauty supplies all over his bedroom and bathroom. He couldn't get used to tripping over expensive high-heeled shoes, designer handbags, and blow-dryer and curling-iron cords.

When Joel said something to Renee about the condition of his apartment, her response was, "I'm still getting settled in."

He frowned and said, "It's been almost a year now."

Renee was very squeamish about doing housework. Cooking and cleaning were at the bottom of her list of priorities. Renee and Joel ate out every weekend and at least two to three week-nights per week. Joel's money was going fast with Renee living with him. He was paying most of the bills. In the meantime, Renee's money was going even faster because of her incessant shopping habits and mandatory monthly spa treatments. She was a broke-ass wannabe who was in love with an upscale or celebrity lifestyle. All she knew was running up to New York to Bergdorf Goodman and Saks Fifth Avenue for fashions by Prada, Gucci, Dolce & Gabbana, Manolo Blahnik and Marc Jacobs.

Joel almost lost his mind when Renee suddenly traded in her reliable little red BMW 325i for a brand new fully loaded white Cadillac Escalade. He thought that getting that expensive oversized SUV was nothing but a power move. Renee loved to pull up next to his black Jeep Cherokee and look down at him. From that point, Joel knew that there wasn't any way he could possibly marry Renee. Relationships are supposed to be give and take, but from Renee's end it was all take. She was a parasite and too superficial.

A stupid little voice in Joel's head said, *Don't give up on Renee. You can change her.*

Instead of changing Renee, Joel felt himself changing. He never imagined enduring so much drama from any woman. Renee continued to change into a complete phony. She lied to all of her friends about investments she supposedly had and how much money she had been saving up to buy a huge new house in Prince George's County. Renee wasn't saving jack. Joel was the only one with investments and he had been saving for a house long before he met Renee.

Renee began to show personality traits that Joel never knew she possessed. At one time Renee was cute and affectionate, but that side had taken a backseat to her psychotic side. She had turned into a rebellious child—it was her way or no way.

She became temperamental, unreasonable and very argumentative.

Renee used other couples to gauge her relationship with Joel. She would say things like, "Tim and Nicole just bought a new house in Howard County. We need to hurry up and get ours. Jajaun bought Pam a diamond ring, I need one, too. Did you see Kia and Rick's new Lexus truck? People are starting to notice that your Jeep is getting old. It's time to trade that in because I can't be seen in that thing. We'd look real nice in a Mercedes-Benz 500 SL."

Joel wasn't cheap, but more like frugal. He was in his midtwenties and already saving money for an early retirement. At the rate he was investing and saving money, wealth was definitely in his future. And then there was Renee and all of her friends, the compulsive shoppers. They were broke as hell, but their dumb asses would do just about anything to look rich.

Before long, Renee was living paycheck to paycheck, acting as if the instant-wealth fairy was going to appear any day and grant her a wish for everything her money-grubbing heart desired.

Joel admitted to being a fool—a fool in love. He knew that his biggest problem was being stuck on stupid and trying to make things work between him and Renee. He considered Renee a well-educated woman who lacked common sense. To him there was a big difference between a well-educated woman and an intelligent woman. A well-educated woman had been taught—supplied with the knowledge she lacked. On the other hand, an intelligent woman is naturally equipped with knowledge and common sense and really knows how to apply herself in real-life situations.

Before long, communication between Joel and Renee had drastically changed because of mutual suspicions of cheating, jealousy, boredom, and general lack of interest. The romance factor was at absolute zero—gone. Their sexual relationship was shaky at times, but remained their common link. Everything around them was falling apart. The only thing they were building was an impenetrable wall that separated them even more. They both realized the relationship's downward spiral had gained too much momentum to be stopped. A breakup was inevitable, and they were too distracted and too stubborn to try to stop it.

Some days Joel felt like he was dying inside. He had lost his sexy best friend and lover of more than two years. Now the woman who slept next to him every night was more like a beautiful stranger with an unpredictable personality that made her ugly.

For months Joel sensed that his relationship with Renee was coming to an end. For some reason his heart and mind only wanted to hold on to the highlights from the past and the few remaining good qualities she possessed.

He wanted to beat Renee to the punch by ending their unstable relationship as soon as possible, because he didn't want her to have the last word or the last laugh. The crazy thing was that for a while Joel was way too comfortable and attached to actually do anything like carry out the dramatic breakup scene that had been repeatedly replaying in his mind.

Chapter 5

Breaking up is hard, but starting over after a major breakup can be even harder. Joel tried to rebound and get back on the dating scene. He let his best friends Greg and Dave talk him into going back to Club One, the same nightclub where he met Renee. Joel had known Greg and Dave since elementary school. They went to the same church and played sports together from recreation leagues, AAU to high school. Joel respected Greg and Dave's opinions even though he knew they were professional bullshitters. Greg was a bus driver for the Mass Transit Administration and Dave was a Baltimore city policeman, which meant these two worked closely with the public and met women all day long. They were single and planned to stay single. On the other hand, Joel was a serial monogamist looking for love and a decent relationship.

Whenever Joel went to Club One he was traumatized because all he could see was haunting images of Renee everywhere he looked. It was so bad that he could even smell her scent flowing through the air. The last time he went to the club he left without telling Greg and Dave. They were so busy mackin' that hours had gone by before they even noticed.

Two-and-a-half years is a long time to be with one person, and in that time Renee had become a major part of Joel's life. In a way, she was part of him. It had only been a little over a

month since Renee walked out of his life. Not being able to
hear her voice was strange and not seeing her was even stranger.

Joel's job was really the only thing keeping him going and
now that the school year was coming to an end he wasn't sure
where to direct his attention.

Occasionally he experienced difficult days and this was one
of them. He sat at his desk in an empty classroom, missing
Renee and writing a poetic piece from his random and free-
flowing thoughts. Joel wondered if Renee would have understood him better if she could have read his thoughts.

Renee,

*Open your eyes . . . really open them. Free your heart and
mind for a minute. My eyes are open . . . I can see and feel the
beauty within you. Can I speak to your mind? I'd like your
heart to listen too. I hope you feel me on this. If I could take a
beautiful journey into your mind, would you allow me inside?
What would I find? Would I find the real you, the one I fell in
love with? Would I find myself? And if I found myself would I
like your perception of me? What I'm really asking is, if I could
see myself through your eyes, would I like what I saw? Would I
recognize my image or would I appear as a distorted picture of
the man I used to be? Could you still see me if I were invisible?
Did you really see me when I was in your presence? Would you
know me now? If I ceased to exist would my image still linger in
your mind? If I couldn't speak could you still hear my voice?
Can you hear me now? Do you ever speak to me in your mind
and if so, what do I say? If your heart spoke to me could I deci-
pher the message? Would I wanna hear what it had to say and
would it still speak the language I once loved to hear? Can you
see and hear me now? Do you ever dream of me? Ever have
daydreams . . . wet dreams or any kind of dreams about us?
Whatever makes you smile. Can you smile for me? Are you smiling on the inside right now? Do you ever wake up in the middle
of the night and hold your pillow, wishing it was me? If your
pillow could talk what would it say? Would it tell me of the*

times it was soaked with your tears and how it soothed your pain and gently caressed your head in my absence? Can I speak to your body? Does it miss me? Can you still feel me, like I still feel you? Can you really hear me or should I bring my lips a little closer? Do you think I still know every inch of you? I'm still talking to your body. I miss your hips, your sexy dips and all of your lips. Damn, can I make you smile on the inside and come on the outside? Can I take a journey inside you? Submerge deep within your soul . . . a soul like no other I've ever known. Are you afraid? Can I go there? I wanna take you there and together we can drown in intimate emotions. I wanna feel you. I want you to feel me. I'll cry . . . you'll cry and together we can stand the pain, share the pleasure, and face any fears. As we stand here at the threshold of fantasy and reality, can I take that journey, that journey inside you? But before we do anything, can you please tell me where we went wrong?

LUV4U,
Joel

Someone knocked at Joel's classroom door. He looked through the door's tiny glass window and saw Mrs. Betty Kelly, the school's stiff and often uptight principal staring at him. Because she was always busy and extremely task oriented, Joel feared that she had something for him to do. Mrs. Kelly was traditional in every sense, from her clothes to her demeanor. If they made a television reality show about her life it would be called, *Lifestyle of a Prudish Principal.* She was really sweet, but unfortunately her job as principal automatically made her unpopular and the natural enemy of everybody in the school.

The students and some of the faculty at Mary E. Rodman Elementary referred to her as Smelly Kelly because of the unmistakable odor of her cheap perfume, Burly Betty because she was morbidly obese and Funeral Face because of her thick layers of dull makeup. Someone needed to come up with a name for her wicked synthetic auburn wig.

Joel wasn't in the mood for talking at all. He took a deep breath and put on a fake smile. "Come in."

As soon as the door opened Mrs. Kelly's scent rushed inside, filling the air before she even stepped one foot inside of Joel's classroom, making him sneeze.

Mrs. Kelly gave Joel a rare smile that made him expect to see her makeup crack. "Hi, Mr. Davis. God bless you."

"Thank you."

"You must have some type of seasonal allergy."

Joel played it off and said, "I don't know. Guess it's just something in the air."

"Could be, you never know." She paused and said, "In case you're wondering, I just stopped by to thank you for another successful school year. You already know you're one of my favorite teachers and you never cease to amaze me."

Joel was surprised. Mrs. Kelly's words relaxed him a bit. He was about to pour on the bullshit and spread it nice and thick. "You're definitely my favorite principal. I wouldn't be able to do half of the things I do around here without you."

Mrs. Kelly deliberately took a seat right next to Joel's desk. "Awwww, thank you. Our fifth graders really looked like distinguished young ladies and gentlemen during today's closing ceremony. Didn't you think so?"

Joel always got distracted, focusing on her dull makeup and drawn-on eyebrows when they were face-to-face. Catching himself he said, "Yeah, they really did look distinguished. Michael Stevenson's speech was outstanding. I had to take a minute to explain to him what it meant when people said he was articulate and spoke eloquently. He didn't know whether people liked him or were criticizing him."

"That's cute. Good thing you told him what those words meant. I'm surprised he didn't snap and go upside somebody's head first. His mother must have medicated his little behind a couple of times this morning."

Joel almost liked this side of Mrs. Kelly. He laughed and said, "Check you out making jokes. I don't know about the medication part. All I know is that Michael made me real proud up there today. He didn't even seem nervous."

"That's because you worked extra hard with that young man and everyone is extremely pleased with his progress. I already called Mrs. Winston at West Baltimore Middle and told her to keep a close eye on Michael for us."

Joel thought to himself, *That poor little boy was marked for life.* He hated the fact that Michael would never be able to escape his troubled past and get the fresh start he deserved. Most of the time Joel's colleagues meant well, but they had a tendency to do more damage than good to their students' reputations.

Joel said, "I'm sure he'll do just fine over there."

"He certainly will." Mrs. Kelly looked at her watch and asked, "What are you still doing hanging around here?"

"I'm just about to get outta here. I was putting the final touches on something I was writing."

"Honey, work is over. You better enjoy this temporary freedom while you can."

Joel laughed and said, "Yes, ma'am."

"So, what do you and your girlfriend have planned for the summer?"

A solemn expression covered Joel's face and there was little he could do to hide it. "Nothing special." He shrugged his shoulders and said, "Probably nothing at all. I dunno. What about yourself?"

"My husband and I are heading out to California in a couple of weeks to visit our oldest daughter and her family."

"Sounds nice."

"Well, I don't know about you, but I'm going home." Mrs. Kelly stood and said, "Give me a big hug." As he stood, she put her arms around him and said, "As always, it's been a real pleasure working with you. You're such a positive role model for all of our students, but especially for our young men. Hard to believe you've been here for three years already."

"I know." Joel struggled to get his breath back as their hug ended. "It's been a real pleasure working here and I'll continue to do my best." He was blown away by Mrs. Kelly's kindness. "Have a great summer. Don't forget to send me a postcard from Cali."

"I'll do that, and pick out a nice refrigerator magnet for you too."

Joel managed a smile. "Thanks."

Mrs. Kelly was about to exit the room, then suddenly turned around and asked, "Mr. Davis, I mean, Joel. Something is bothering me. I don't mean to get in your business, but are you okay? You seem really sad."

Joel put on another smile and said, "I'm fine."

"I've been part of this faculty for twenty-one years now and I've seen it all. I can tell when someone is having relationship problems. If that's the case and you need someone to talk to or someone to just listen, I'm here for you."

"I appreciate it, but I'm fine."

"You can talk to me openly without having to worry about other people around here knowing your business or gossiping about you. Whatever you say to me stays with me . . . I promise. It bothers me seeing you like this. You're like a son to me."

Mrs. Kelly seemed so sincere, compassionate and genuinely concerned that she quickly put Joel at ease.

"I usually don't discuss any of my business at work. But since you put it like that, Renee and I broke up a little over a month ago. What gave me away?"

"The sadness in your eyes. It looked like your mind had drifted off somewhere else when I mentioned something about your girlfriend."

"Like I said before, I usually don't discuss my business at work, so please don't repeat any of this because I'm really a private type of person."

"So am I. I'll respect your privacy, okay?"

"Okay."

"You just better keep your head up." Within seconds

Mrs. Kelly's face lit up with excitement. "Let me tell you something."

"What?"

"An angel just whispered something in my ear."

Joel laughed. "What did it say?"

Mrs. Kelly couldn't stop smiling. "This is such a blessing. The angel said, hold on and don't you worry 'cause help is on the way."

Joel hunched his shoulders and said, "Wonder what that means."

"I know exactly what that means. Is it all right if I share what we just discussed with one other person?"

He looked at Mrs. Kelly like she had lost her mind. "Who?"

"My niece. She's right around the corner in my office, dying to meet an attractive professional young man like you. I know the two of you would make a lovely couple."

He felt lightheaded and disoriented. He looked at Mrs. Kelly and thought, *Hell no!* He struggled as he asked, "Your . . . niece . . . meet . . . me?"

Joel instantly imagined someone younger who closely resembled Mrs. Kelly, with a face covered with dried pancake batter-lookin' makeup, topped off with a synthetic auburn wig and the same cheap overpowering fragrance.

Mrs. Kelly grabbed him by the arm and pulled. "C'mon."

"Where are we going?"

"We're going to meet my niece."

Like a fool Joel yelled, "Noooo!"

"You're coming with me."

Mrs. Kelly actually pulled, pushed and nearly dragged Joel's five-eleven, one hundred ninety pound frame down the hall with her five-three, three hundred twenty-five pound self.

Mrs. Kelly asked, "Do I have to drag you around the corner too? You know I will."

Joel was laughing so hard that he cried. "All right. Hold up a minute. I'll do this if you give me time to get myself together. We both look real crazy right now. I've never seen you act like this before, but I like it. You've got me cracking up. I had no idea you were this wild or so strong."

"Nobody around here takes the time to get to know me better. I'm always in a good mood, especially when the school year is over."

"Your job must be stressful as hell."

"You don't even want to know." Mrs. Kelly paused for a second. "Look at you trying to change the subject. Stop acting so silly and shy. I'm serious about you meeting my niece. I'll pick you up and carry you if I have to."

"I know you will, but that won't be necessary. I promise I'll walk the rest of the way."

Mrs. Kelly exhaled loudly and said, "Thank God. Look at me. You've got me all out of breath and about to have a heart attack."

Joel straightened out his clothes and said, "I'm sorry. I really wanna meet your niece now."

"Well, what was the problem at first?"

"Immaturity on my part. Plus, I wasn't really trying to meet anybody new. I was thinking about contacting a couple of my old girlfriends to see what they've been doing and see if they were interested in hooking up again."

Mrs. Kelly frowned and threw her hand. "Ugh! That's not the way to go at all. Been there, done that."

Joel smiled and said, "I've been there, but I didn't do all of them."

Mrs. Kelly thought she had missed something. "What?"

"Put it like this, too much information and not enough time to explain."

The sound of somebody approaching stole their attention for the moment. They listened closely as a pair of high-heeled shoes tapped to a certain kind of sophisticated cadence on the school's industrial tile flooring. That was a sound Joel loved to hear.

Mrs. Kelly took a quick peek around the corner and said,

"Oh look, here comes my niece, Asia, right now. When you meet her you'll forget all about your old girlfriend."

When he made eye contact with Mrs. Kelly's niece, she reminded Joel of Renee. Her intricate hairweave of long blond spiral curls, big expensive Coach handbag, stilettos, manicured fingernails and toenails, and the annoying way she popped her gum all sent up a huge yellow caution flag. She seemed too artificial. After a quick introduction to Asia, Joel automatically shut down because he knew that he wasn't interested in her. No chemistry whatsoever. Then he thought, *Whoa, hold on a minute. She's got a cute face, nice ass and some big titties—good. But she doesn't smile enough and I don't like this strong hoochie vibe she's got going on. All I'd do is end up using her for sex. Hmm, that might be nice. But I'd hate to dog this girl and then have to deal with her and Mrs. Kelly.*

Asia didn't initiate much of a conversation and didn't strike Joel as being too intelligent. Her physical appearance was fine, but she didn't stimulate his mind at all. He was looking for a total package. In reality, Asia was okay, but was forced to pay the price for looking too much like Joel's ex. He wanted the real thing or nothing at all. Thinking about Renee and looking at Asia was like comparing McDonald's to Burger King, Coke to Pepsi and Beyoncé to Ciara.

Asia only made matters worse by trying to act more glamorous than she really was. She began to come off as goofy. Every move she made ended with an awkward pose. It was obvious that she had been watching too many reruns of *America's Next Top Model* and was emulating what she saw. Joel laughed to himself because the only thing sophisticated about Asia was the way her heels had sounded when she first walked around the corner. Joel could tell that they had very little in common and the last thing he needed or wanted was a carbon copy of Renee. Too much work.

Meeting Asia left Joel feeling severely discouraged and disappointed. He wasted thirty minutes of his life trying his best to humor Mrs. Kelly and her ghetto-fabulous niece.

Asia said, "It was nice meeting you, Joel. Here's my number." She handed him a colorful business card with her full name, *Asia Kelly—Model & Fashion Designer.* It had a notation above her number, *Available for fashion shows*, *photo and video shoots.* She said, "Check out my page on myspace.com whenever you get a chance. Just type in my screen name, *Holla at this model chick* and you can find me."

It took everything inside of Joel not to burst out laughing. "Aight, Asia. It was nice meeting you too."

"Don't forget to *holla at this model chick* when you get home."

Joel felt that strong urge to laugh again because Asia sounded so silly. His eyes got big and he said, "Wow, I don't even know what to say."

Mrs. Kelly sensed that Joel wasn't interested in Asia, but she was determined to make something happen. She said, "Joel, you forgot to say that you were gonna call Asia and you forgot to give her your home and cell numbers."

He pressed his lips together really tight, scratched the side of his face and fidgeted with his ear. "I . . . I don't really use my home number anymore. The best way to get me is on my cell."

As soon as Joel handed Asia his cell number Mrs. Kelly snatched it from her hand and whipped out her cell phone. She dialed the number and within seconds Joel's cell phone rang.

Joel and Asia stood there with puzzled looks on their faces.

Mrs. Kelly acted like one of her students and said, "Oh, all right. I thought you were trying to play my girl."

Joel just shook his head and walked away laughing. He went back to his classroom to pick up his belongings. He loaded the last few boxes of paperwork and supplies in the back of his Jeep Cherokee and headed to the beltway to claim a spot on what looked like the world's largest parking lot. It was a hot muggy day and traffic was bumper-to-bumper. In front of him was a giant display of assorted bright red brake lights as far as the eye could see. Joel intentionally turned off his cell phone and thought about how tough it was going to be to find an intelligent, attractive woman with goals and interests similar to his. He knew that finding someone compatible meant more than just finding a woman with a heartbeat, a warm body and good sex.

Chapter 6

On the way home Joel listened to a local talk radio show. The call-in topic was about ways to heal after bad relationships. The heat, the traffic congestion, the fact that nothing seemed to be going his way, and some of the call-in guests heightened Joel's frustration. One guy called in and talked about how his previous relationship made him lose track of who he really was and how he had lost sight of the world around him. His ex was just that consuming. He described himself as a decent hardworking black man trying his best to find love and the secret to making a relationship work. The caller said that just before his relationship ended, he resembled a clown walking a tightrope without a safety net, doing backward flips and jumping through narrow rings of fire, while wearing gasoline drawers. After all that, his ex still wasn't impressed and wanted him to do more. This particular call really hit home. Joel knew exactly what this guy was going to say before he even finished his sentences. He was basically telling Joel's story.

During the rest of the ride home Joel thought about how his story went back a lot further than Renee Monique Rhodes. He was born in Baltimore, in a working class African-American community. He grew up on a quiet street lined with old row homes and huge shady trees. Kids played ghetto games on the sidewalks and in the street.

As a child, Joel promised to never break his parents' hearts. They always showed him and his older brother Shawn unconditional love. Joel's father, Theodore Davis, was without a doubt one of the most abrasive, easily agitated and hotheaded individuals anyone had ever met. When he got mad he appeared to be larger than life and scared his kids half to death. He worked two full-time security jobs to keep the lights on and food on the table. Joel's father rarely had a traditional day off from work. His off days usually meant he only had to report to one job. A regular eight-hour shift was an easy day to him. Joel and Shawn didn't have real father-son relationships with their dad. The little time they did have with him consisted of a lot of lecturing, complaining, yelling and outrageous demands. Soon after all that came the beatings. Joel could never forget the beatings. One thing Joel could say about his dad was that he made time to attend church with his family. He always seemed to be a God-fearing man, a quality Joel undoubtedly inherited from him.

Joel came from a strict Christian family. His mother, Mary, was a homemaker and a dedicated Sunday school teacher. She was old-fashioned in every sense. Everybody knew that Mrs. Mary Davis wouldn't be caught dead or alive wearing pants or makeup. She mostly wore her hair in a bun. Skirts, dresses and her natural effortless beauty were the norm for his mother. She recognized and respected her husband as head of their household. It was hard to find anyone as easygoing or as proud as Mrs. Davis. Most of her time was spent cooking, cleaning and making sure that Joel and Shawn stayed on the right path. Mrs. Davis taught her boys to have the utmost respect for women. She even found time to teach her boys about the birds and the bees, constantly reminding them that premarital sex was a sin. She was the only person Joel knew who could recite the Ten Commandments word for word and in order.

Although Joel had both parents at home, he gave his mother most of the credit for molding him. She tried her best to raise

Joel and Shawn to be well-mannered and respectable men. Their father taught them right from wrong at an early age. Once he laid down the law that was it. If they did wrong their mother would instantly report it to their dad. When their father got home from work he'd wake them up in the middle of the night if he chose to, and would whip them from head to toe with a belt—and sometimes the buckle, depending on what they had done.

No matter how hard parents try to guide their kids and keep them on the right path, they should never forget that their kids have minds of their own. Shawn knew the consequences for disobeying his parents, but he did what he wanted to do anyway. He started hanging out with the wrong crowd during his senior year of high school. Within the first few weeks of school he was doing stuff like smoking and selling marijuana. Peer pressure can be vicious. At the time, Joel was a junior at the same high school and was too involved in wrestling and playing on the varsity basketball team to consider doing anything related to drugs. Joel was strong, quick, agile, and had plenty of stamina. A local trainer noticed how athletic he was and introduced him to boxing.

While Joel was busy with sports, Shawn was busy getting into drugs. He actually brought weed into their house. Shawn was living fast and going out of his mind trying to impress people, mostly girls, by being a fake thug. Joel and Shawn lived in the hood and all, but the only thing they knew about the streets was what they heard from classmates or saw on television. Eventually Shawn learned the streets for real.

On the other hand, Joel wanted to be different. He knew that every poor young black man from the ghetto didn't have to be a thug or drug dealer. There were a few straight-up good kids in the hood and Joel was one of them. Nobody bothered him. Guys approached him occasionally, trying to recruit him to sell drugs. No words from Joel were ever necessary. He would give them a certain look, and then shake his head. The fearlessness, or a degree of hardness in his stare, made them leave him alone. From that point on everybody knew that Joel was focused on making something positive out of himself. He carried himself with respect and received plenty of it in return.

One afternoon, Joel was in his parents' basement working out when he smelled something strange. He followed the scent and found Shawn sitting near their washer and dryer blowing smoke out of a tiny vent.

Joel said, "Yo, what you doing? Why you bringing that stuff in here? You better do something with that before Momma gets back from the supermarket."

Shawn was so high that all he could think to say was, "Boy, if I ever see you smoking this shit I'm gonna kick your little ass."

Joel thought that was Shawn's way of telling him not to smoke weed, but in reality that was his way of telling Joel to stay the hell away from his stash.

Joel never told his parents that he caught his brother smoking weed in their house because they would have killed Shawn. Months later, Mrs. Davis found a big shoe box full of cigar tobacco and empty Phillies Blunt boxes under Shawn's bed. He was emptying the tobacco from the cigars and filling them with weed to make marijuana blunts. By the time she figured out what was going on, Shawn was already snorting cocaine. Joel felt that if he had told on Shawn right away, then maybe things wouldn't have progressed like they did. Their mother punished Shawn and their father beat him, to no avail. The boy was so messed up and strung out on drugs that he didn't hear half of the things they said. He was absolutely immune to any form of parental disciplinary actions. Joel's parents were forced to seek professional help for Shawn.

While most of Shawn's classmates were graduating from high school he was sitting in central booking. He was charged with possession of a deadly weapon and possession of a controlled substance. Joel's big brother broke their parents' hearts and shattered their dreams when he was sentenced to five years in the Baltimore city jail.

Joel and his parents were at all of Shawn's court dates. Mr. and Mrs. Davis spoke up for Shawn. Everybody in the courtroom eventually got tired of hearing his parents say things like, "Shawn could've . . . Shawn should've . . . Shawn would've." His mother cried, "He's my baby and I love him! God knows he's a good boy!"

It was sad that Shawn had to learn life's lessons the hard way. Things were completely different for Joel. By learning from Shawn's mistakes, he avoided making certain fatal mistakes of his own.

By the time Joel's senior year rolled around his parents were harder on him than ever. They were in his corner, by his side and had his back at all times. They flat out refused to allow Joel to become a negative statistic. Having a strong, hardworking father around definitely made Joel's life easier. Mr. Davis eventually recognized some of his wrongs when it came to how he raised his boys and made subtle changes.

No matter what Joel and Shawn did, their parents were always supportive.

Joel ended up breaking his parents' hearts a different way. All of his mother's lectures about avoiding premarital sex fell upon deaf ears when he started getting attention from countless girls in his neighborhood. With his Christian beliefs firmly planted in his mind, Joel fought sexual temptation on a daily basis. He got involved with a few girls, but out of all of the girls who sought Joel's attention only one was truly able to tempt him sexually and stole his heart.

There aren't any words in the English language to describe how special true love really feels. Love is meant to be mentally and physically uplifting, spiritually soothing and comforting beyond anything imaginable. Joel found true love at the age of eighteen when he hooked up with Nia Thomas, the pastor's daughter. The most beautiful, intense, and exciting feeling Joel had ever known happened the day he lost his virginity to Nia.

People suspected that Joel and Nia were dating, but no one

suspected that these two squeaky clean, God-fearing kids were actually having sex. Joel was just about to start his freshman year at Morgan State University when Nia told him that she was pregnant. Nia only told one other person, her best friend Tonya, and that's when Joel and Nia's world began to fall apart.

When word got out that Nia was pregnant with Joel's baby, it caused a major uproar and embarrassment for both of their families. Joel's parents were stunned and heartbroken. Now they had two sons who had disappointed them. They feared that Joel was headed down the wrong path. His parents feared that he wouldn't be able to attend college and instead would be forced to work in order to support his girlfriend and baby.

Nia's parents were more concerned about their reputation in the community. They were so outraged and disgraced that they acted impulsively and forced Nia to get an abortion. They quietly moved her down South to attend college under the watchful eye of her relatives. Joel never even got the chance to say goodbye. Both families failed to take into consideration the emptiness, hurt and deep sadness that Joel and Nia dealt with. Although Joel and Nia were heartbroken, their lives were redirected and they were able to focus more on pursuing their educations. They stayed in contact for a few years, but eventually pursued other interests and other people.

Certain things that Joel experienced as a teenager made him a better person. Other experiences affected his outlook on love and relationships for years to come.

Chapter 7

When Joel arrived at his apartment something led him directly to his bedroom. There were two messages on his answering machine. He immediately pressed Play, and the first message began, "What's up, Joel. It's Dave. Me and Greg are heading down to Club One around eleven tonight to meet up with some fine-ass honeys. We even got one for you. Stop acting all antisocial and shit. Get back at me if you wanna go. I'll probably hit you back on your cell. Hopefully you'll have it on. Peace."

The answering machine beeped and the next message began. "Hi, Joel."

Joel's heart stopped. Acid burned his stomach. He hadn't felt that searing sensation in weeks. He was too young and healthy for an ulcer and unprepared for an unexpected reminder from his past. It was his ex-girlfriend, Renee. For Joel, it felt strange thinking of her as his ex. Today marked six weeks, two days and eleven hours since Renee walked out of his life without a decent note or a phone call.

Joel paused Renee's message. He needed a quick distraction. He picked up his iHome audio system remote control. He hit the power button and began to listen to the smooth and relaxing sounds of Miles Davis as he took off his Kenneth Cole shoes and Brooks Brothers suit. His neatly pressed clothes were already laid out on his bed.

After showering, Joel put on a pair of khaki shorts, a short sleeve button-down Ralph Lauren Polo shirt and a pair of brown leather Cole Haan sandals. His outfit mirrored his demeanor—simple and cool.

Joel pressed Play again and Renee's message continued, "I'm sure you already know who this is." She laughed nervously. "Oh my God, this is so hard to do and I can't believe I'm calling you like this. I've rehearsed what I wanted to say in my mind a thousand times, but I still won't get it right. There's no real way to say I'm sorry. I was gonna call you on your cell, but I was afraid you might answer. It's easier this way. In case you were wondering, I'm okay. Thanks for calling my mother last month to check up on me. I mean . . . I don't know what I mean. Sorry things had to end the way they did. God places certain people in our lives for a reason. Now, I understand. You helped prepare me for where I am right now. I know who I am and exactly what I want. You made me a better person and I love you for that. Thank you. If we ever cross paths again I hope you'll greet me with a smile and a warm embrace because we will always be friends. I wish you all the best and I know there's a special woman waiting out there for you somewhere. Have a blessed life. Oh yeah, I almost forgot. I left a few things behind on my side of the closet. Feel free to donate them to Goodwill. My sister Cheryl will probably be giving you a call because she was interested in my old shoes and boots. Okay, Joel. Be blessed."

Like a fool Joel started speaking to the answer machine, as if Renee could actually hear him. "Wow! That's it, huh? Your message seemed so genuine and straight from your cold heart, you little slut!"

Joel was pissed because he knew the real reason Renee was calling was to let him know her sister was interested in her old shoes. Then he thought the real reason she called was to rub her happiness in his face.

Before Joel could even take a moment to calm down his doorbell rang. The ring was so quick and faint that he almost ignored it. Within a few seconds there was a knock at his front door. The knock sounded hesitant and kind of unsure. His first impression was that it may have been a child. Joel raced to the door. He was in such a hurry to get rid of whoever it was that he didn't even look through the peephole.

Joel opened the door and in an instant he let go of two-and-a-half years. He thought, *Renee Who? What? When? How? And most of all, Why?*

All of his ill feelings dissolved. The past was behind him. He was staring his future directly in the face and she was smiling beautifully right back at him. Joel absolutely loved what he saw.

Time seemed to be at a complete standstill, allowing Joel and the brown skinned beauty who stood in front of him the opportunity to conduct thorough surveys of each other before their first words were exchanged. His mind raced, etching significant and sufficient details about this angel. Her gleaming almond-shaped eyes expressed an obvious hint of attraction that her glowing smile quickly confirmed. Joel attempted to draw her in deeper with a gaze that conveyed an unmistakable signal of mutual attraction.

In a soft friendly tone she said, "Hi, my name is Erin McKoy and I just moved in across the hall in 2D."

First impressions are long lasting and have a powerful influence when it comes to sparking the flames of passion. Pure chemistry is a key component of physical attraction. Pheromones filled the air and permeated Erin and Joel's senses.

Joel extended his hand, taking Erin's soft hand into his. He gently caressed her hand, looked down at their connection and immediately saw Erin as an extension of himself. They shared the exact same mahogany skin tone.

"Hi Erin, I'm Joel Davis. Welcome to the building."

Erin maintained eye contact. With her hand still locked in Joel's sensual grip she said. "Thank you. It's nice to meet you, Joel."

"It's nice to meet you too. I guess you want your hand back, huh?"

Erin liked the feel of Joel's hand. "Only if you're ready to let go."

Joel smiled and said, "Umm, not really, but I'll let go as long as you promise not to go anywhere."

Erin gave Joel the prettiest and brightest smile he'd ever seen and said, "Okay."

Joel slowly let go of her hand. "You know what?"

"What?"

"You're without a doubt the most beautiful thing I've seen all day. Thanks for making me smile."

Erin blushed. "Thank you." She acted as if she wanted to return the compliment, but instead she cleared her throat and quickly changed the subject. "The mailman accidentally left some of your mail in my mailbox. So I thought I'd bring it to you." Erin handed Joel his mail.

He looked down and said, "Thanks. It's been hot and muggy all day. You wanna come inside for a cold drink?"

Erin was typically shy and felt that she had already been forward enough. It had taken a few minutes for her to build up the courage just to knock on his door. She didn't think that it was appropriate to come inside so soon. With apprehension she said, "No, I'm fine." She quickly picked up on the look of disappointment in Joel's eyes. She needed a way to restore his faith. "I need to run back downstairs and bring in a few boxes . . . *three huge boxes,*" Erin said with a little sly grin.

Joel caught the hint. He licked his lips and asked, "You need any help?"

"Sure."

"Are you ready for me to grab those huge boxes right now?"

Erin quickly replied, "Yeah, if I'm not interrupting anything."

Joel felt inside his front pocket to make sure he had his keys. The last thing he needed was to be locked out of his apartment. He shrugged and said, "I wasn't doing anything at all. I'm ready."

"Thanks a lot. The boxes are down in my car."

Erin led the way downstairs and out to her car. Joel thought that she was really cute. At first glance he usually knew whether he was interested in a woman or not. He knew how far he'd like things to go and things he could actually envision himself doing to her and allowing her to do to him. Erin possessed a lot of important physical qualities that Joel found attractive in a woman. She had gorgeous facial features, like an even glowing skin tone, dark expressive eyes and a cute little button nose. She had shiny black shoulder-length hair with plenty of body. Joel thought that Erin's soft voice and pleasant easygoing personality were a nice touch. She seemed dainty, practical and somewhat subtle—yet very appealing. There was something so right about the way she looked in her form-fitting pink T-shirt. Joel loved the way she moved in her denim shorts and the way they fit. He just couldn't take his eyes off of her perky breasts, narrow waistline, shapely hips, thighs and her sexy apple bottom.

When Erin and Joel got outside they noticed that the sky was full of ominous-looking clouds. Daylight was quickly fading. The wind had kicked up a little and it wasn't as muggy as earlier. The weather had been hot and humid all week and now a major storm was brewing.

Erin said, "Looks like we got a temporary break from the heat and humidity."

Joel looked at her and thought, *Hopefully, things are about to heat up between us*.

He said, "Yeah, but we're about to be hit by a major storm system."

"I'm praying that the storm won't last too long because I have a moving company delivering my furniture and other belongings tomorrow morning. I was just kidding when I said huge boxes. All I have right now are a few small boxes filled with fragile things I didn't really trust the movers to handle."

Joel laughed and said, "Uh-oh. So, you're gonna trust me, a total stranger with a minimal amount of moving experience to handle your most delicate possessions in the world?"

Erin smiled. "Yeah. I can just look at you and tell you're good with your hands, and judging from the way you gripped my hand earlier, I'm sure you know how to be very gentle."

Joel couldn't hide his smile. "I like you already. You've got me all excited about you moving into the building . . . right across the hall, too."

Erin flashed her contagious smile again and said, "Sounds fun and convenient, right?"

"I'm not even gonna lie. Yeah, it does sound fun and convenient. Oh, in case you were wondering, I'm single."

"I already know. Ms. Benson from downstairs gave me the scoop."

"Dag, that old lady is like a reporter from *Eyewitness News* sometimes."

"No, she wasn't like that. She was just being friendly. We happened to end up at the mailbox at the same time and started talking. She filled me in on everybody in the building."

"I bet she did all that within two minutes."

"Pretty much. Actually, she filled me in on everybody in something like ninety seconds or less." A tiny look of skepticism came over her face. "Maybe you're right about the *Eyewitness News* thing."

They laughed.

"Hopefully she didn't say anything too bad about me? But then again, whatever she said couldn't have been too bad because you were brave enough to knock on my door."

"Brave? Shoot, I was scared half to death knocking on your front door."

"Oh yeah, I could tell. You rang the bell and knocked so softly that I was about to completely ignore you."

"Just for that I won't tell you everything Ms. Benson said about you. Anyway, a girl has to keep something to herself."

"That's cool because I know she told you some good stuff."

Erin twisted her lips. "Yeah, she might have said that you were a pretty boy with a muscular body and she might have called you a good catch."

Joel beamed with confidence. "Really? I don't know about the pretty boy part, but I do have a few muscles here and there. I dunno . . . I might be a good catch. Somebody may have mentioned that to me before."

"Is that right?"

Joel smiled. "Yeah. You *don't* have a boyfriend or anything, do you?"

"No. Just a roommate."

"Male or female?"

"Female."

"Good!"

"Her name is Kenya. She works for NSA, you know, National Security Agency?" Erin asked as she unlocked the trunk of her car.

Joel reached into the back of her little gray Mitsubishi Eclipse and pulled out two boxes and she grabbed the other. He said, "Yeah, I know a lot about NSA. I remember that Will Smith movie, *Enemy of the State*. Kenya must be a real serious kind of girl."

"Actually she's a nut, but really sweet. That's my girl. I forgot about *Enemy of the State*. It was pretty good—real informative. Made me think about how easily the government can tap into someone's life and even ruin them if they want. I don't even associate Kenya with creepy government people like that."

Erin and Joel headed up to her apartment carrying the boxes. Joel asked, "Where's Kenya now?"

With a slight grin, Erin asked, "What, you need her help with those little boxes or something? Don't tell me you're getting tired already, muscle man."

They both laughed.

"No, I'm all right." Joel paused for a second and said, "Girl, I can carry you and all these boxes if I wanted to."

"Psssss, yeah right." She laughed and said, "Nah, I believe you." A curious expression appeared on her face. "I'll have to keep that in mind."

Joel smiled and said, "Look at you. I mentioned carrying you and these boxes and all of a sudden you look like you're thinking about something real sexy."

Erin laughed. "You're crazy."

"No, I'm good at reading facial expressions."

Erin bit her bottom lip, looked at Joel out of the corner of her eye and said, "All right, maybe a little something did cross my mind real quick. You are a hottie."

Erin always presented herself in a respectable manner. Her last relationship ended on a sour note because of her prudish sexual nature. She was a good girl, far from being promiscuous. This time she really wanted to step her game up to the next level. She was kind of interested in a hot intense hookup with Joel without titles or strings attached. She had never in her life been so flirtatious with a guy she had just met.

Joel felt a rush of excitement. "Thanks. See, I knew I saw something. Don't be embarrassed . . . I like that."

"Boy, stop playing. You made me forget what I was saying."

"Something about Kenya."

"Oh yeah. She called me a little while ago. She'll be calling back to check in again soon. Anyway, NSA sent her away for two months of intense training."

Joel gave Erin a silly suspicious look. "What kind of intense training?"

"I don't know. That's all she's allowed to say. She can't discuss her job in detail. I have no idea what her exact job is. All I know is that she took some self-defense and weapons qualification classes and now she carries a gun and a badge."

"I'm impressed. And who do you work for—the FBI, CIA or Secret Service?"

As Erin unlocked her front door she said, "No. I work for the Baltimore County school system. I'm a third grade language arts teacher at Winands Elementary."

"For real?" Joel asked as he stepped inside of Erin's apartment and followed her to the kitchen.

"Yeah. Don't I look like a teacher?"

"None that I ever had, but I'm sure I don't look like a teacher either. I teach fifth grade social studies at Mary E. Rodman in the city."

"Oh my God. You're a teacher."

"Yep."

Erin entered the kitchen and set her box on the counter. She turned around and said, "You're not gonna believe this, but Mary E. Rodman is my old school. I mean, I actually attended school there from kindergarten to fifth grade."

Joel set his boxes next to Erin's and said, "Me too. This is a small world. I grew up in the Edmondson Village neighborhood."

"So did I."

Leaning against the counter Joel asked, "Why don't I remember you from around the way?"

After talking to Erin a little more, Joel found out that they grew up four blocks from each other, but had never met until this evening. Erin's family moved from the old neighborhood the summer before she started high school. Her parents divorced earlier that year and her mother struggled like hell to take care of her daughters. Erin was the oldest of three girls and had become an intelligent career-oriented woman with a bright future ahead of her.

Erin showed Joel around her two-bedroom apartment, which smelled of fresh paint with a tiny hint of commercial carpet cleanser. It didn't take long to tour her empty apartment. She quickly described how she planned to hook the place up after the mover delivered her furniture.

When Erin and Joel were finished looking around they stood in the living room near the patio doors, talking. They seemed to click on all kinds of levels. They both had majored in education and had graduated from local historically black colleges—Erin from Coppin State and Joel from Morgan State.

Joel asked, "So, what made you decide to become a teacher?"

"I was always a teacher's pet."

Joel laughed. "Oh no! One of those, huh?"

"Yeah, I was kind of nerdy. At an early age I fell in love with books. Something amazing happened the first time I stood in front of a blackboard; it felt like I was in the spotlight."

"I know, that all-eyes-on-me feeling."

"Yeah. I can't even describe how good it felt standing there writing in pure white chalk on a blackboard and seeing my words stand out so clearly and brilliantly for everybody to see."

"Wow. I've never heard anybody describe their first experience writing on a blackboard so passionately. I think I'm probably more passionate about the first time I erased a blackboard than my first time writing on one. I loved erasing my teacher's writing."

"Are you serious?"

"Yeah. That just goes to show how differently men and women think."

"I guess you're right, but let me finish telling you about why I became a teacher." Erin got her thoughts back on track and continued. "I love being around kids. I love learning and always had a natural ability and desire to teach. It's so exciting helping to mold young minds. Every day I feel like I've helped someone. To me it's the most rewarding career. Now what made you become a teacher?"

"I always wanted a career with a hefty salary, bonuses and summers off." Erin gave Joel this you've-gotta-be-kidding-me look and then he said, "Nah, I'm just playing. I definitely didn't become a teacher for the money. I wanted to rewrite the rules of exclusion and help make certain opportunities available for underprivileged kids. A lot of top-achieving students come from low-income communities."

"I know, because we're proof of that."

"True. But in too many cases there are needy kids with the least amount of resources available and it's my responsibility to help them."

"You're so right. We need more men like you." Erin paused for a second and with a look of adoration she said, "Wow, you're handsome, intelligent and you stand for something real . . . I like that."

Joel smiled. "Thanks, I appreciate you saying that. But more than anything, I stand for kids that remind me of myself back when I was in school. I had bad experiences with teachers when I was growing up. I only had a few teachers who were passionate about teaching. Most of them used the same cookie-cutter lesson plans from year to year or they taught directly from the same outdated textbooks. They were never willing to adapt to the changing needs of their students. I always wanted to show kids that learning could be fun and exciting. I'm flexible and know how to use different approaches to learning. I try to personalize learning and make it interactive. History has always been my favorite subject, especially anything dealing with the Civil War. You can ask me anything about the Civil War, from Fort Sumter to the Appomattox Court House, and I guarantee you I'll know the answer."

"I believe you, and I can tell that you're one of the passionate ones, like me. I agree with you one hundred percent. Plus, I think students really admire male teachers, especially black men because brothas are a rare sight in schools."

"That's true."

"So basically, your desire to help the underprivileged and your experiences with bad teachers made you want to become a teacher."

"Yeah, that's exactly what motivates me. I used to hear my teachers tell students, 'I got mine and you got yours to get.' I hate that saying because it shows arrogance on the teacher's part and belittles the kids."

Erin agreed. "I had teachers say that crap my whole life, but that probably motivated me to strive a little harder to be better than them."

Joel said, "I see your point, but a lot of kids get discouraged and end up quitting because they feel that teachers like that are against them."

"Yeah, that happened to a bunch of kids we grew up with and they ended up stuck in our old neighborhood."

"I know exactly what you mean." Joel paused for a second and then redirected the conversation. "It's hard to believe that we grew up in the same neighborhood and went to the same elementary school. The fact that we never met before is crazy."

"I know."

Talking about the old neighborhood gave Joel a new energy. He said, "We have to know some of the same people. Do you remember a guy named Arthur Washington?"

"I dunno."

"You had to have seen him before. He looked like a little strong-ass midget. They called him Baby Hercules or Big Pee Wee."

Erin laughed so hard she almost choked. "Oh yeah. You're talking about the little bodybuilder with the big head and short thick stubby legs who hardly ever wore a shirt and jogged around in those freaky little shorts. Who's that, your brother or something?"

"Heck no!" Joel doubled over laughing. "Aw man, you're trying to joke me."

"I was just trying to catch you off guard and make you laugh, that's all."

Still laughing, Joel said, "That was funny though. I mentioned Big Pee Wee because he stood out more than anybody else and I figured you'd remember him. It's rare that you see a crazy midget jogging around the hood in Speedos, and once you've seen it you never forget it. And if you grew up in Edmondson Village, then you have to remember the block parties."

Erin nodded and smiled. "Every summer, I remember."

"And you gotta remember Daddy Milton's Snowballs."

Erin playfully tapped him on his arm. "Oh yeah. I had one

of those things almost every day during the summer when I was a kid. Oh my God, they were so good! Wish I had one now."

"Remember the marshmallow topping?"

"The marshmallow topping made the snowballs even more delicious and was worth the extra money."

"Yeah, Daddy Milton had everybody walking around looking silly with white stuff around their mouths."

Erin laughed, then caught her breath and said, "One day, me and my sisters were wearing our little matching pink-and-white short sets and new tennis shoes. Boys were trying to talk to us. I thought I looked real cute walking around until I looked in the mirror and saw dried up marshmallows all around my mouth and on the tip of my nose. My sisters let me walk around like that and didn't say a word."

"That's funny. I wish I could have seen you." Joel paused for a few seconds because he was having a flashback. "Hold up, I remember you now. You have two younger sisters and all of y'all used to look just alike."

"Yeah!"

"You lived right across the street from my old church. I used to see you and your sisters all the time when I was in the church's front yard."

"Don't tell me you were one of those little bad-ass church boys who used to yell and throw rocks at us."

"No. At least I don't think so." Joel made a strange facial expression. "On second thought, I probably was one of those little boys. I'm sorry. I was like eight years old back then. I didn't know any better. Little boys are dumb. I'm sure that was just our way of telling you and your sisters that we liked y'all."

"Uh-huh. Tell me anything." Erin gave Joel a playful but stinging slap on his arm.

"Aw! You're really gonna hit me when I tell you this. I just remembered something else."

Erin put on a silly frown. "What?"

"Didn't you and your sisters sing, 'We Are Family' back when we were kids at one of Mary E. Rodman's talent shows?"

Erin laughed. "Oh, no! You're not supposed to remember stuff like that." Erin hid her face. "Yeah, we did sing, 'We Are Family.' That was so embarrassing. Our mother thought we were going to be the next successful girl group on the scene, but all we did was make fools of ourselves."

Joel laughed and said, "Y'all looked real cute. I swear, I loved your performance."

"Thanks, but I know you're lying. You probably thought I was ugly back then and that's why you never tried to get to know me."

"No, it wasn't like that at all. It's hard to get to know everybody in a huge neighborhood. And you weren't ugly at all. If anything I was intimidated by your beauty, but now I can't get enough of you."

Erin smiled. "All right, you redeemed yourself nicely." She sighed. "It was so much fun back then. I miss the old neighborhood. I remember how we used to have stores on almost every corner. Back then the corner stores were black owned."

"That was way back when they had real penny candy. Then all of sudden the black store owners sold their businesses to the Koreans. I have to admit that some of the Korean store owners kept their shelves stocked a lot better than some of the black store owners."

"That's true. I hated when they ran out of any of my favorites." Erin looked like she was really into their conversation. "I used to love eating pumpkin seeds, Jolly Ranchers and Now & Later candy."

"Yeah. How about eating a bag of Utz Bar-B-Q flavored potato chips with a pack of butterscotch Tastykake Krimpets and then washing them down with a cold bottle of pineapple soda?"

"Mmmm. Growing up in the city was the bomb. I know you used to go to Mondamin Mall to that store called Somethin' Good. They had the best candy apples and cotton candy."

"Yeah, but I really used to go to Mondamin to get a cheese-steak with everything and fries from that place on the second level."

"Mmmm. And then stop by the Great Cookie for a little quarter-pound bag of snickerdoodle cookies."

"You're making me hungry."

Realizing that they were both starving and didn't have any other plans, they stood in the hallway of their three story apartment building for a few minutes, trying to decide exactly where they wanted to go for dinner. Erin had a quick and simple solution. She had the taste for a Meat Lover's pizza from Pizza Hut with a large order of fries from McDonald's.

Joel said, "No, I can do a lot better than that. Let me take you out for a nice seafood dinner at the Inner Harbor. We can go down to Legal Sea Foods or Phillips."

"That's okay. I really have the taste for pizza and fries. This is such a spur-of-the-moment type of thing. We can do seafood tomorrow if you don't have anything planned."

"I'm free to hang out with you whenever."

"Don't get me wrong. I'd love to go downtown for dinner, but don't forget about the weather. I'd hate for us to get caught out there in the middle of the storm. We should just grab a quick bite to eat."

Joel agreed, and they rode in his Jeep Cherokee to pick up their food. On the way to Pizza Hut Erin's cell phone rang. It was Kenya. Joel listened in on a couple of minutes of what seemed to be carefully coded girl talk. When Erin started telling Kenya about him, then she had his full attention. The excitement in her voice made Joel feel good. She gave Kenya a detailed and very flattering breakdown of his physical appearance. She actually described him as looking *yummy*. Then she went into specific details of how she and Joel met. Joel could tell that Erin and Kenya were close because Erin pretty much gave Kenya a minute-by-minute breakdown of nearly everything she experienced that day. Erin even told Kenya exactly where she and Joel were and how she planned to spend the rest of the evening with him, if he didn't mind. Right after that Kenya was dying to talk to Joel. They were introduced by cell phone.

When Erin first handed Joel her cell phone he was kind of reluctant to speak, but he and Kenya talked as if they had known each other for years. Kenya came across as very pleasant and somewhat flirtatious. Joel thought that it was weird and tried not to pay too much attention to Kenya. To him it was very stimulating meeting and connecting so fast with two friendly, energetic and intelligent women. Somehow everything just seemed to click.

After a few minutes or so Joel's overactive imagination took over. He started imagining Kenya profiling him on a government computer as they spoke, doing an in-depth background check to make sure her friend wasn't dealing with some weirdo-psycho-stalker type.

Joel handed the cell phone back to Erin. As they entered the restaurant, they placed their carryout order and sat down in a booth.

Erin and Kenya continued talking. Erin didn't want to seem rude so she soon cut her conversation with Kenya short. Erin asked Joel if it would be okay if she took a picture of him with her camera phone to send to Kenya. At first that kind of raised his suspicion and damn near confirmed his notion of the background check, but then he had to laugh at himself. He agreed to the picture and within a minute or so Erin was showing him a text message from Kenya saying,

Gurl, your new man is fine—a real yummy yum yum. Show Joel da pics in ur phone's gallery.

Erin and Joel laughed.

Then Erin showed Joel pictures of her and Kenya having fun. The pictures ranged from being very silly to serious. Erin had used the camera's special effects feature to make some of the pictures appear more animated and artistic. As Joel looked at the pictures he thought that Erin and Kenya were two very attractive women.

After showing Joel the pictures, Kenya called Erin back.

Kenya started having an anxiety attack after speaking with Erin and Joel. She was incredibly homesick and she wanted to hang out with them so badly. She was down to her final week of training and Joel promised that the three of them would go out for dinner that following Friday night to welcome her back home. Kenya promised to leave Erin and Joel alone for the rest of the night. They both knew that Kenya couldn't and wouldn't stop calling. They told her that she could call back a couple more times throughout the night just in case her anxiety level got too high.

Joel was glad that the interference from Kenya had ceased for the moment. He looked at Erin and asked, "So, what do you like to do for fun?"

"I like to read African-American novels. I like going to the mall. It's not really about shopping every time, but it's a social thing too. I like going to the movies, checking out new restaurants and traveling. I like going to parks for walks or hiking. I'd love to go camping one day. I'm always open for new things. I like to dance, but I'm not big on clubbing. What do you like to do for fun?"

"I like going to sporting events with my buddies, Dave and Greg. I'm not big on gambling, but Atlantic City is my quick getaway for fights. I love boxing, college basketball, the NFL and the NBA. I like to work out at home or at the gym. I like going to concerts. I love going out to eat. I'm big on traveling and I'm even fine staying at home watching a movie."

"Interesting. I like sports and working out too."

Joel asked, "What qualities do you look for in a boyfriend or husband?"

Joel's question made Erin's eyes widen. "Whoa. I had to duck because you threw some titles at me with that question."

"Is that a problem?"

"No," she lied, and put on a sugarcoated smile. In reality one of the last things she wanted right now was a boyfriend or a husband. All she really wanted was a friend who could show her a good time. When it came to a relationship, her intention was to move along as slowly as possible because she knew that her heart and mind weren't ready for another major upset. Erin had just gotten out of a stressful relationship two months earlier. She didn't know how to tell Joel her true intentions because the look in his eyes told her that he was looking to settle down with the right woman as soon as possible. She threw him a hint and said, "I like patience. That's a good quality."

That definitely sounded like a subtle hint to Joel. "Patience? That's it—one word?"

Erin smiled. "That's all I need to say. I already see everything else I'm looking for in you, so there's no need for a long, drawn-out description. Now, what do you look for in a girlfriend or wife?"

Joel decided to throw a subtle hint of his own. "Honesty."

Erin got his hint and laughed out loud. "Honesty. That's it—one word?"

"That one word goes a long way." With a bit of sarcasm in his voice he caught himself mimicking Erin when he said, "I already see everything else I'm looking for in you, so there's no need for a long, drawn-out description."

Erin burst out laughing and said, "I like you."

Joel touched Erin's hand and then their fingers slowly intertwined. "I like you, too. You seem to be a good girl with the right amount of oomph."

There was a definite connection being made. They shared a good amount of similarities. There were of course their subtle differences, but there was also enough healthy friction to spark a lot of interest and passion in their eyes.

Erin and Joel left Pizza Hut with a large Meat Lover's pizza and headed over to McDonald's drive-thru. Joel ended up ordering two super-sized fries and Cokes. They hurried back to his apartment while their food was still hot and fresh. Before going up to Joel's apartment, Erin grabbed her overnight bag from her car.

After washing their hands, Erin and Joel headed straight to his kitchen. Joel grabbed a couple of paper plates, paper towels and a plastic container of grated parmesan cheese. Erin picked up the salt and pepper shakers along with a giant bottle of Heinz ketchup. Joel told Erin to relax and make herself at home. She kicked off her shoes and picked a comfortable spot on the floor in front of Joel's chocolate leather sofa.

Chapter 8

Erin glanced around Joel's apartment. She loved the Afro-centric décor that featured original paintings and sculptures from West Africa. There were several pieces of imported furniture situated around the room—tables and chairs that varied in size and shape, which complemented each other nicely. The furniture was art and some of the art was actually furniture. Erin looked at the bookshelves lined with hundreds of books from almost every genre. She felt right at home as she took in the warmth and beauty of the contrasting earth tones.

"This is a really nice place you have."

"Thanks."

Erin surprised Joel when she suggested that they sit on the floor to eat. He clicked on his 42-inch plasma TV and joined her on the floor.

Erin combined their super-sized fries onto one plate. She was very meticulous about how the fries were placed on the plate, making sure they were all lined up in the same direction. Next, she carefully sprinkled an adequate amount of salt and pepper on them. She was starting to rub off on Joel. He poured a pool of ketchup onto the other plate, forming a near perfect circle. After all that thorough preparation with the fries, Joel quickly dashed the grated parmesan cheese on the pizza and they ended up eating it straight from the box.

Erin said, "The pizza is really good."

"Yeah. So, I guess you're not really big on nutrition."

"Not really. Kenya is the one who's big on nutrition. She makes sure that we follow a health-conscious diet. I've been eating just about everything since she's been gone and haven't gained a pound."

Joel laughed, "But in the meantime you've probably been clogging up your arteries like crazy."

"Yeah, I have to die from something. Food makes me feel so good—why not die happy?"

"That's true. I read a bumper sticker the other day that read, *Eat healthy, exercise daily and die anyway.*"

Erin sipped her Coke and laughed at the same time almost causing her to choke.

Joel and Erin were down to their last morsels of pizza and had only a few fries scattered on the plate they shared. Joel poured two glasses of white wine and they continued sitting on the floor with their backs resting against Joel's sofa. He flipped channels back and forth between the melodic videos on VH1 Soul and the smooth sounds of the R&B digital music channel.

Joel looked over at Erin's duffel bag and asked, "What's up with that bag you grabbed from your car?"

"Nothing. That's my overnight bag."

Joel smiled. "Where do you plan on sleeping tonight?"

Erin quickly replied, "My apartment. I got a sleeping bag across the hall."

"I got a king-sized bed with fresh clean linen on it—right down the hall. You can have it and I'll sleep out here on the sofa."

The modesty in Erin made her say, "No, we just met and I can't even begin to consider sleeping over here. Plus, I can't put you out of your own bed."

"You're such a good girl. You can't even hide your wholesomeness—you're oozing with it and I respect that. But can I corrupt you tonight and make you do some things you normally wouldn't do?"

Erin felt herself get a little turned on. She blushed and said, "No."

"Grab your sleeping bag and stay over here if you'd like. Nobody is gonna judge you and I promise to be good."

"Yeah, I bet. I can see one thing leading to another. If I agreed to stay here tonight I probably wouldn't even touch my sleeping bag. I can see us right now, cuddled up in your bed during the storm."

"Ooh, that sounds real nice to me."

"Me too, but I can't commit to anything like that yet. We'll see."

Joel shrugged and sipped his wine. "All right. No pressure."

"I'm glad you invited me over."

Joel smiled, picked up a french fry and said, "I'm glad you're here with me. Sitting on the floor eating like this takes me back to another time."

"And what time would that be?"

"When I was a kid, I used to sit on my living room floor and eat breakfast while watching Saturday morning cartoons. Some mornings I would make a tent using two dining room chairs along with my blanket and sheets."

"Sounds fun. I noticed something about you."

"What would that be?"

"You tell a lot of stories about when you were a kid."

"Do I?"

"Yeah, but I understand. I'm the same way. When we're kids we don't really appreciate our childhoods and can't wait to get older. When we're adults we love to reminisce about our childhoods and try our best to stay as young as possible."

Joel smiled. "That's true, but I'm still a kid at heart and I never plan on changing."

"I feel the same way."

"I think we have a lot in common."

Erin combed her fingers through her hair and said, "We do. I think we're very compatible."

There was an awkward moment of silence. Joel couldn't

really think of what to say next. He just stared at Erin and got
lost in the beauty of her brown skin. Out of nowhere he asked,
"Did you notice that we have the same skin tone?"

Erin was about to laugh until she held her arm up next to
Joel's and said, "We sure do. Look at that, the same pretty
brown skin."

Erin looked down at her food and Joel looked down at his.
He was finished. The expression on Erin's face told him that
she was finished and hungered for something else besides
food.

He looked at Erin and could see a change in her. Her modesty was gone. He felt himself drawn toward her and he could
tell that she sensed the same magnetic attraction. Their body
temperatures rose, passion heated up and was about to come
to a rapid boil.

All of a sudden there was a loud explosion of thunder that
echoed all around them. It caused the entire building to
shake. The clouds couldn't hold back the rain any longer. It
seemed as if the sky had cracked and began to spill out a
steady downpour of the heaviest and loudest raindrops Joel
and Erin had ever heard.

The thunder startled Erin and made her move closer to
Joel. A Donnell Jones video came on the TV. They watched
the dark stormy sky through the patio doors, as lightning created what appeared to their eyes as a split second glimpse of
daylight. Heavy raindrops beat against the windows and rooftop.
The wind blew so hard that it whistled.

Erin cuddled up even closer. She found comfort in Joel and
the most perfect spot to rest her head between his muscular
chest and shoulder. They were so close that they basically
breathed each other's breath. Joel ran his hand up and down
Erin's leg. He loved the way her feminine curves felt, along
with her soft warm body pressed against his.

With his strong affectionate arm around Erin, Joel inhaled
deeply, taking in her shower-fresh scent and said, "You feel
and smell so good."

Erin was in a dreamlike state when she said, "So do you."

Joel whispered, "There are so many things that I like about you." He slowly ran his fingers through Erin's hair. "Your hair is really pretty and I love your almond-shaped eyes." He traced her perfectly arched eyebrows with his thumb. "Look at your cute little nose. And your kissable lips."

Joel grabbed Erin by the chin, guided her to him and planted a gentle kiss on her lips. He took his time kissing, nibbling and sucking her lips. Things got wet and wild when he slipped his tongue inside.

Their tongues danced—moved with passion and grace. Their hands moved from their faces, to the backs of each other's necks and then to different body parts.

After a couple of minutes Joel eased back a little to try and gauge Erin's reaction. Her reaction was off the meter. They both appeared to be breathless.

Chapter 9

With a surprised, love-struck expression, Erin said, "Oh my God, did that just happen?"

Joel played it cool. He had completed the first stage of corrupting his good girl. "It happened. Did I offend you?"

Erin's panties were so wet. Joel could look at her and see that she was getting hot, but he just played along, acting like he didn't notice a thing.

Erin shook her head and said, "No, you didn't offend me. That kiss was soooo nice. Trust me, the last thing I am right now is offended."

Joel smiled and said, "Good. 'Cause I wasn't about to apologize for kissing you. I think we both wanted that."

In a seductive tone Erin said, "Mmmm . . . you're right. No need to apologize."

"I didn't really think you were offended. That was a nice kiss. Your lips are so soft."

"Your lips are soft, too. I love the way you kiss. You really know how to work that tongue of yours."

"I felt yours working, too. You haven't seen nothing yet. I'm definitely interested in sharing some more intimate experiences with you."

With a little apprehension in her voice Erin asked, "Tonight?"

Joel heard the apprehension in Erin's voice and saw it on

her face. "It's okay. Tonight is all about us getting to know each other better."

Erin sighed. "All right. I just don't want to lose your respect. I'm not the type to give it up on the first night, you know?"

"I figured that. I can tell that you're the nice wholesome type . . . exactly what I'm looking for. I'm not just out for sex. If it happens, fine. If it doesn't, fine. Either way, I'm really enjoying your company."

Erin didn't want to spoil the mood or disappoint Joel. She sipped her wine and then gave him a quick peck on his lips. "You're so sweet. Do you think you'd respect me if I gave you some tonight?"

Joel's eyes widened. "Without a doubt. Why don't we just let things happen naturally?"

"Sounds good to me."

Erin had a quick flashback of her ex. She could still hear him complaining about her not being freaky enough for him. He constantly complained and criticized her. She blocked out her thoughts and focused on Joel and the unlimited possibilities of their new friendship. Erin needed a fresh start and a sexy new approach. She ignored the consequences and got caught up in the excitement of the moment—the here and now. It's strange how experiences from the past can dictate actions and reactions in new relationships. Erin hoped to get the sexual validation from Joel that her ex never gave her.

The next thing Erin knew she had moved her empty wine glass aside and straddled Joel.

They kissed again. Their tongues danced to a different rhythm. This time Joel's tongue followed the graceful choreography of Erin's tongue. Her kiss was welcoming and comforting, and gave Joel an intense feeling of closeness and acceptance. Erin had a deep longing for a nice fulfilling sexual episode and so did Joel, but he also yearned for love and commitment. Erin wanted to be free like the wind and remained commitment-shy.

Joel stroked her hair and face. "Look at you, so beautiful. I want you so bad."

"Shhh. I know . . . I feel the same way. Kiss me. No need for words."

Within seconds something amazing happened. Their lips spoke in a warm wet way. Through that kiss Joel was able to express himself without words and that same kiss allowed Erin the chance to feel and comprehend exactly what he meant. In return, Erin kissed Joel so deeply that he could taste her thoughts. Every kiss was more sensual and more arousing than the previous.

So many thoughts flowed through Joel's mind. He thought, *I wanna make love to you. Erin, you feel so good to me. Help fill this void. I wanna make you mine.*

Erin thought, *Heal these wounds. Satisfy my soul. Help me find intimacy. Validate me. Make me feel good!*

The steady downpour continued. Along with the wine they drank, the rain had a lulling and spellbinding effect. At the same time the sound of the falling rain was naturally stimulating and added something special to the ambiance, heightening Joel and Erin's attraction.

Joel tilted Erin's head back. The sensation of his lips as they delivered wet kisses to her neck made Erin hot. The tip of his tongue made her even hotter. Joel slowly moved his attention down to Erin's breasts. He lifted her pink, formfitting T-shirt and exposed her pink lace bra and ample cleavage. Joel began to squeeze her breasts and play with her perky nipples through her bra. Everything felt so good to Erin that she eventually took her T-shirt off. Within a few minutes Joel found himself reaching around and unfastening her bra.

Joel's moist tongue slowly circled Erin's areola and then he teased her erect nipples with the tip of his tongue. He began to feast on her breasts, sucking her mounds like an overgrown baby boy. Joel gently nibbled with his teeth and pulled her eraser-sized nipples with his lips.

Erin unbuttoned Joel's shirt, revealing his perfectly sculpted body. She massaged his muscular chest and tight abs. She teased and tantalized every inch of his exposed skin with her fingertips and fingernails. She kissed him and brought her hands up to Joel's mouth to play with his soft, luscious, full lips. He sucked her fingers. They kissed again, but this time Erin's fingers were between their lips, slipping inside of both of their mouths. Erin pulled away slowly, sucking Joel's bottom lip. She quickly moved in again to kiss his eyelids, cheeks and chin.

Erin even kissed and nibbled on Joel's ears. She continued to straddle him with a slow grinding motion. Erin whispered in his ear, "I can feel how big and hard your dick is."

"Let me feel how wet you are."

In an airy tone Erin whispered, "Not yet."

She drove Joel crazy, kissing the most sensitive part of his neck. She moved back a little and began to lick his chest and suck his nipples. Joel was turned on more than ever. He was more than ready to come out of his shorts.

Joel looked into Erin's eyes and felt the urge to kiss her again. This time he led their tongues to a passionate slow dance. At this point they completely ignored the raging storm and music video playing in the background. After a few minutes, Erin's eyes were fixed, and overflowed with a beautiful expression of sensuality and an openness that told Joel that she was ready and willing to fully surrender her body to him. He silently thanked God.

The whistling winds had gained a lot more momentum. Fierce gale-force winds roared like a runaway freight train. Lightning flashed, followed by rolling waves of loud and violent thunder. All of that commotion eventually stole Erin and Joel's attention. Their faces expressed the same look of shock and concern. Within seconds the TV screen went blank and the indoor and outdoor lights shut off, turning the room nearly pitch black. They were sitting in darkness listening to a raging storm, but not even a blackout could reduce the heat or smother the flames of passion that burned between them.

Joel said, "Give me a second and I'll be right back."

"What are you doing?"

"We need light."

Erin shook her head and said, "No, we don't need *any* light to do what I wanna do."

Although Joel liked what he heard, he looked at Erin and sounded really sincere when he said, "I want and need to see you . . . every inch of you. This is our first time together and I don't wanna miss a thing. I'll be right back, okay?"

Erin smiled and said, "Okay."

Joel jumped to his feet. He grabbed his flashlight, a book of matches and blanket. Then he lit six candles that were already situated around his living room, one of which was a huge apple-melon scented candle. Within seconds the darkness was made beautiful by the shimmering illumination of candlelight. Joel looked over at Erin and could see a glow in her eyes. She smiled at him with desire in her eyes and he returned the same type of smile.

Joel asked, "Better?"

Erin replied with her soft voice, "Yeah. Much better."

"I'm not finished yet."

Joel spread out the blanket in front of Erin. She eased her way into the center. He went to the kitchen and returned with his little battery-powered boom box. He pressed Play, and out of nowhere Maxwell began singing a sweet love song. Since the power to the air conditioner was off, Joel decided to crack the patio door slightly. Instantly, a refreshing breeze rushed inside, carrying the distinct scent of falling rain. Now everything was perfect to continue their night of soulful passion.

Erin stood up and walked toward Joel.

As they embraced she said, "This is really nice."

"I know. You need more wine?"

"No, I'm fine. My little buzz came and went already. Now all I need is you."

Joel caressed Erin's face with both hands and gave her a deep passionate kiss. He controlled her head movement the entire time they kissed. That kiss brought back that sweet look of surrender in Erin's eyes.

She said, "Joel, I want you so bad."

"I want you, too," he whispered. "Can I taste you?"

Erin looked surprised, showed a little smirk and asked, "Huh?"

"You know exactly what I mean."

Erin felt the rush of a warm tingling sensation between her legs. She smiled and stepped back in a slow, seductive manner. She maintained her sensual eye contact with Joel as she began to slide her denim shorts down, revealing pink lace low-rise panties.

Joel said, "I like that. Turn around, so I can really see what you look like in your panties." Erin turned around and he said, "Your ass looks so good. Look at your little phat booty, girl. Make it bounce." He stepped in closer from behind and pressed his hard dick against Erin. He cupped her firm bare breasts with his hands while her erect nipples poked out between the index and middle fingers of both hands. He whispered in her ear, "Bend over."

Joel stepped back a bit. He palmed, stroked and then spanked Erin's firm but still soft enough to wiggle and jiggle ass. Joel liked what he saw so much that he had to kiss it. He gave Erin a spine-tingling experience, kissing and licking her up and down her back.

Joel lowered Erin down so she was lying on the blanket. He licked around Erin's navel, skipped over her panties and introduced his mouth to her inner thighs. He made his way down Erin's legs to her feet, and sucked her toes. He had a foot fetish going on. Erin felt her heart pounding faster and faster, preparing for takeoff. Joel made his way up her legs and teased around her bikini line with his tongue.

Passion and anticipation mounted.

Pleasure moved in waves.

Joel's tongue moved in straight lines and then small circles.

Erin's cell phone rang. She knew that it was Kenya calling and so did Joel.

Joel said, "Phone's ringing."

Erin was damn near breathless. She sighed, "Uh-huh."

"Answer it."

"No."

"It's okay. Answer it."

Erin reluctantly picked up her cell phone and said, "Hello."

Kenya automatically started running her mouth.

Joel's whole intention was to tease Erin while she talked. He slid her panties over to the side and brought his tongue closer—zeroing in on her erogenous zone. He moved her panties down slowly, revealing a neatly shaven strip of pubic hair. Erin held her phone in one hand and covered her eyes with the other. She bent her knees and spread her legs, exposing just about everything she was made of. Joel decided to give Erin a little sample of what she had been dying for.

Joel massaged Erin with his hands. He moved his fingertips slowly up and down and between her moist labia and gently touched her clitoris. Her juices began to trickle a little more and glistened in the candlelight. Erin shuddered when he introduced his tongue down there, following the same path as his fingers.

All types of heavenly sensation flowed throughout Erin's body as she peeked down between her legs and caught a glimpse of Joel pleasing her with his tongue. All Erin could manage to say as Kenya spoke to her was, "Mmm-hmm. Um-hmm." Her senses seemed to heighten with every touch and stroke of Joel's tongue. Erin tried to compose herself as much as possible.

Kenya bombarded Erin with questions about her and Joel. "Am I interrupting? How was dinner? Where are you right now? Is Joel right there? What are y'all doing? Let me speak to Joel."

Joel continued to work his tongue. This time when Erin tried to speak, she was forced to take a deep breath between every single word. Her voice quivered, "Call . . . me . . . back . . . girl . . . I . . . gotta . . . go . . . bye." She pressed the End button and dropped her phone on the floor.

Erin moaned, then screamed, "Oh my God! Joel! Kiss me . . . lick me . . . love me with your tongue. That's it baby, make me come!"

Chapter 10

Joel was very attentive and it was absolutely astounding the way he used his slow, gentle but masculine touch to seduce Erin. He received great pleasure from pleasing her. He was so caring and patient that he made Erin feel like they had all the time in the world and she was the only thing that truly mattered. Before tonight Erin had only been with two other men sexually. She definitely had never been with a man so in tune to her body, or a man so blessed with the natural talent and ability to possibly fulfill all of her sexual wants and needs.

Joel's tender tongue slathered Erin's clitoris and labia with warmth and affection. He gently penetrated her with his right middle finger and then doubled the pleasure by inserting his index finger. Joel's fingers explored, located and delightfully stimulated Erin's G-spot. At the same time his left hand tended to her excited breasts.

Erin felt so much pleasure that it made her feel light-headed. Her muscles tensed and contracted. Her toes curled, eyes rolled back in her head, she called God's name a few times and then in an instant she sensed an orgasm mounting like she had never felt before. She felt a powerful release and then completely relaxed. Intense climactic sensations pulsated between her legs. Within seconds the same wonderful sensations radiated throughout Erin's body and created a breathtaking and mind-blowing full body orgasm.

Joel looked up in amazement and enjoyed the beautiful sight that his labor of love had produced. He gave Erin a passionate kiss. After all that attention, she was still hot and bothered. Erin saw a hefty bulge in Joel's shorts and now she felt a strong urge to please him sexually. She touched him and then helped Joel take off his shorts. Erin had a desire of her own and pretty much begged to feel Joel's dick inside of her. All of that goodness and wholesomeness that Joel saw in her had been put on pause.

Erin stroked Joel's hardness for a moment and watched him slip on a condom. She lay on her back with her legs spread, eagerly waiting to receive Joel's love.

Joel's dick was fully erect. He held it by the base to make sure it stayed completely engorged as he moved in closer to Erin. She closed her eyes when she felt the head of his penis penetrate her tight wet opening, which stretched nicely to accommodate his girth. Joel was instantly greeted by her soft supple tightness, surrounded by a very inviting and deeply soothing internal warmth. Erin opened her eyes and gave Joel a long, beautiful, enchanted gaze. She felt that no man had ever deserved her body more. Joel scooted his hands under Erin's ass, giving her pelvis the right tilt. She braced herself, then he plunged every inch of his love deep inside of her. She gasped for air.

The glow of shimmering candlelight from different angles caused Erin and Joel's hot lustful bodies to cast shadowy images of their passion-filled lovemaking on the walls. Their mahogany flesh slowly combined as they melted deeper into each other. In an instant two bodies became one. Joel devoured Erin with kisses as her heart took off, began to soar, and never wanted to come down from the high she felt.

Out of nowhere Erin's cell phone began to ring. It was Kenya checking in on her friends again.

Maxwell's CD provided a continuous mellow musical vibe that filled the room.

The storm raged on, but Erin and Joel were inseparable and totally oblivious to whatever was going on around them.

They remained in a zone as they moved through a variety of different sexual positions. Attemping to be a tantric lover, Joel purposely delayed reaching his climax before Erin reached hers. His goal was for her to come before he did or for them to achieve simultaneous orgasms. He used a combination of concentration methods and rhythmic techniques to help prolong his and Erin's arousal periods, which helped make their love-making more intense and enjoyable.

Joel sensed that Erin was on the verge of another orgasm. He began to concentrate more of his attention on the localized pleasure he felt with his penis.

Erin was lying on her stomach receiving Joel's love from behind. She noticed a change in his rhythm and rigidity. She sensed that he was about to come. Joel slowly slid both hands under her and applied direct pressure to her clitoris. His motion became faster and more precise. Erin loved the new sensations she felt, internally and externally. She moaned and gradually moved her hands down to meet Joel's between her legs.

Erin cried out, "Oh, yes! That's it, Joel. Fuck me good. Fuck me gooood!"

"I love the way . . . you feel . . . so good . . . to me. I want you . . . all of you. I wanna make you mine . . . all mine. Can you come . . . for me?"

"Yes! Yessssss!"

Joel's actions and words summoned the release of deep sensations and buried emotions that had been lost within Erin for a long time. Joel felt a release of emotions within himself as well. Together their emotions peaked into simultaneous orgasms.

Joel lay down and Erin eased her way on top of him, resting her head on his chest. Joel wrapped Erin up in his strong affectionate arms and held her tight. The warmth and closeness that they both felt was amazing. Erin sensed a powerful and blissful surge flow through her body. Her heart felt light, began to flutter, and filled with delightful emotions. She looked at Joel and saw love, nothing but love. She closed her eyes because what she saw frightened her. She wondered why she was falling for this man so fast. She wasn't quite ready for love. But even with her eyes closed she still saw love. It was as if Joel had worked some kind of magic on her.

It was becoming quite obvious that Erin was basically the female version of Joel. They both were intelligent, indecisive introverts, which made them strangely perfect for each other. Deep down, Erin knew what she needed, but never really knew what she wanted. Falling for Joel so fast wasn't part of her plan at all. She was physically and emotionally confused. This sexual thing with Joel was supposed to have been strictly physical. Her initial plan was to meet a new guy, have fun and possibly move on, like guys do. Either she was backward as hell or it was just that being a slut wasn't in her nature. The first guy she happened to hook up with lived in her new apartment building, just happened to be someone really fascinating, compatible and someone she instantly had feelings for—feelings she wished she could ignore.

Erin's other issue was that she didn't want Joel to think of her as being quick and easy. She really wasn't that type of woman at all. This was the first time she ever had to deal with an issue like this. She considered this bad timing. She had planned to experiment for a little while and then meet a nice guy like Joel and eventually settle down. She wasn't ready for Joel at this point in her life.

Slightly winded, Joel said, "Erin, you're incredible. Feels like you just allowed me to go to the softest place on earth. Thank you."

Erin looked at Joel and manufactured a soft smile. "You're the one who's incredible. So incredible that you got my whole body singing, *ooh la-la-la*."

Joel stroked Erin's hair and face. "I wanna keep you singing and eventually make you love me. You know that?"

Erin hid her face the same way she wanted to hide her emotions. She wasn't trying to hear anything about *love* because at that exact moment she was too focused on the pleasures of great sex. To her, mentioning love and sex in the same sentence was like trying to mix oil and water. She had to think of something that sounded agreeable because she definitely didn't want to spoil the mood. With her eyes closed she said, "Keep doing what you're doing and you might be right." She sighed as she began to refocus on how good Joel made her feel. "Am I dreaming? I feel so lightheaded that I must be dreaming."

Joel stroked Erin's nakedness and said, "I feel the same way. All of this is kind of unreal, like a mixture of fantasy and reality. Everything happened so fast. I remember seeing you at my front door. We carried some boxes, had dinner, there was a storm and then we completely got lost in each other. You made me feel something that I can't even explain. I can't thank you enough for sharing your body and so many intense emotions. That means a lot to me."

"I don't know what to say. You're so different, Joel. You're making me feel so much so fast."

Joel sat up, bringing Erin right along with him. "Is that okay?"

"Yeah, it's fine. But it's scary."

"Why?"

Erin explained, "Because we just met."

Joel laughed. "I know that, but something about you just feels right to me. So what if we haven't known each other for a long time. There's no need to be afraid or apprehensive about anything because you're safe with me."

"I believe you. Thank you. You don't know how relieved I am to hear you say that. This is new to me, that's all. With all this happening so fast, doesn't it scare you a little?"

Joel shook his head. "No."

Most women do a thorough assessment of their self-worth after having sex with a new partner, regardless of how long they made the guy wait. Joel was smart enough to know that this was what she might be worried about, and the last thing he wanted was for her to feel cheap. He decided to open up and tell her exactly how he felt about her because he sensed that she may have been regretting sleeping with him so fast.

He said, "Erin, you just don't know how I feel. I've known for a long time that I wanted someone like you, someone who complemented me in every way. I've always wanted a natural, effortless beauty like my mother. That's what I see when I look at you. I've always wanted someone who was nurturing, with an affectionate touch like yours."

Taken aback and blushing, Erin asked, "You see all that in me?"

Without hesitation Joel answered, "Yeah. I see all that in you." He smiled and grabbed her. They lay down again. Erin put her head back on his muscular chest.

She was silent. She still felt confused. Her eyes watered slightly because Joel's words were so touching. He saw qualities in her that she didn't even see in herself. Joel compared her to his mother, and that was what really touched her. That was something she had never experienced. Even though Erin felt close to Joel and was without a doubt falling for him, she wasn't ready to get serious or make a commitment. Although her heart was healing, it was still scarred from her previous relationship. Erin didn't know exactly how to express her true feelings to Joel.

Joel said, "You're so quiet. What are you thinking?" Before Erin spoke, a single tear ran down her cheek. She tried to wipe her face, but Joel felt her tear make contact with his skin before she could move. "Are you crying?"

"No. I'm okay. It's just the way that I'm laying."

"I don't believe that. What is it?"

"It's just that you're so sweet. You compared me to your mother and that's deep. I'm not sure if my heart and mind are ready for someone like you right now."

Joel's eye's widened. "What? You must be kidding. I don't understand what you mean."

"Don't get offended. I didn't mean that in a bad way. I was told that you were a good catch, but damn. You're like instant marrying material. I'm not used to that. It's crazy that we just met and I can already see all that in you."

"I can see all of that in you, too. So, what are you saying? Don't act like this is a bad thing."

"I'm not. I honestly didn't plan on getting into a relationship so fast. It's only been like two months since I broke up with my last boyfriend."

"We're pretty much in the same boat. It's been about the same amount of time since I broke up with my old girlfriend. Do you still have feelings for him or something?"

"No. I was over him before we even broke up. Do you still have feelings for your ex?"

Joel frowned and said, "No, not at all."

Erin laughed. "What's her name?"

Joel paused for a second because he felt weird saying her name. "Renee, but I don't want to talk about her and I refuse to say her name anymore. From this day on I'll only refer to her as blah . . . blah . . . blah because she means nothing to me."

Erin burst out laughing. "You are so silly. That's funny, because I feel the same way about my ex, Zack. He's just blah . . . blah . . . blah to me, too."

"Glad I made you laugh. You feel better now?"

"I'm all right. I just need to make sure my heart is ready for you, that's all."

"I'm sorry if I make you feel like I'm rushing. It's not like I'm forcing love or marriage down your throat already. It's just that a man knows when he meets the right woman. You're the one and I know you are. I saw everything I've been waiting for when I opened my door and looked into your eyes. It was more than a nosey old lady and an incompetent mailman who brought us together. You're like an extension of me. You're my future. I think we make a really nice couple. Look, I'm into monogamy. Being in a stable relationship is important to me. I wanna get to know you better and learn about all of the intricate details of life. I want us to spend so much time together that people begin to mention our names in the same sentence. I remember you saying that you wanted someone who was patient. I'm down for whatever you want. If you want me, then you can have all of me—I'm yours." That made Erin smile. Joel continued, "Whatever you want or need, I can be that."

"Umm, you make that sound so good. But what if what you're feeling passes by tomorrow—then what?"

Joel laughed. "What do you think I'm gonna do, walk away from you and act like we didn't just share something special? What the heck were you expecting, a one-night stand—for me to hit it and quit it—a wham bam, thank you, ma'am? Do you think you made a mistake by having sex with me?"

Erin said, "No. I don't have any regrets. I just have to think, what if things don't work out between us? I'll be right across the hall, forced to see you every day. I can't even imagine watching you bring other women in here after all that we've done tonight."

"That's why I'm offering you the chance to fill this vacancy. I need a woman in my life and I'm not scared or ashamed to admit it. Eventually I do want a girlfriend or a wife, but for now I'd just like someone to cuddle up with whenever." Joel held Erin a little tighter. "Someone I can talk to about anything and everything. Someone to laugh at my jokes and share little inside jokes—someone to eat and sleep with—someone to watch a good movie with—someone I could eventually love and who could eventually love me. All I know is that you seem real lovable and you're definitely a breath of fresh air to me. In time I could see myself falling deeply in love with you. Plus, I can't see myself doing half of the things I've done to you tonight to anybody else. The way I went down on you, I can't just go around doing that to every woman I meet."

Joel had a way with words. He made Erin feel a lot more re-assured. At that moment she seemed to have gotten the vali-dation she was looking for.

She blushed and said, "I hope you don't go down on every woman you meet. On the other hand, it's a shame because every woman should know the pleasures of a tongue like yours. Oh God! Woo! I'm having a flashback right now. I really like you, Joel. You seem to know me so well. You touched me as if you knew exactly how and where I needed to be touched."

Joel smiled and asked, "Really?"

"Stop trying to act like you didn't notice the effect you had on me."

"I may have noticed a little something, like the way I took your breath away, made your body quiver, and how many times you called out for God."

Erin gave Joel a playful punch to his abs. "Don't make fun of me."

Joel laughed. "I'm not making fun of you. I enjoyed you so much tonight that I feel like you could have saved yourself a bunch of money and just moved your butt right in here with me. It's still not too late. I can talk to the lady down at the leas-ing office."

"And what am I supposed to do with Kenya?"

"Kenya is a grown-ass woman. She'll be all right."

Erin laughed. "You are so wrong. I can't turn my back on her. She's been my best friend since freshman year at Coppin."

"I would say that she could move in here too, but there ain't enough room for her. And I know you've heard that old saying, two's company and three's a crowd."

"Yeah right, you're saying that now. Just wait till you get to see Kenya face-to-face, I bet you'll be sweatin' her like all the other guys in Baltimore. She has a really cool and down-to-earth personality."

"You crack me up. I could tell by your pictures that Kenya is fine and all, but the only person I plan on sweatin' is you."

"We'll see."

"When I was doing it to you earlier, I heard your cell phone ringing, but I ignored the shit out of it because I knew it was your girl, Kenya."

Erin laughed. "I knew it was her, too. You're crazy. I can't believe you just said, *when you were doing it to me.*"

"What? You don't like that?" Joel lifted his pelvis off the floor. He started acting silly, gyrating and pumping his hips like a freaky R&B singer. He sang, "*I was doing it to you, baaaaby. And I wanna do it to you again and again and again.*"

Erin bit her bottom lip and blushed. "I didn't know you could sing. I like when you sing it to me like that."

Joel laughed. "Next time I'll say something like when we were making love, or when we were *fucking.*"

Erin laughed out loud and said, "I like that last part even better."

"Oh, now I see. You like *fucking?*"

With a cute smile Erin said, "Yup."

"Well, I call what we did earlier making love. And I want you to know that I held back a lot when we did it. But next time, we're gonna *fuck* and I'm gonna give you all I got . . . do it till you drop. Make you scream my name. Usually, I'm really aggressive. That was just a sample of my gentler side."

Erin's eyes widened as she looked at Joel. "You said you held back. You're playing, right?"

"No. Why?"

"You're making me curious. Making me like you even more. Variety is something that I love about life. I hate anything that's humdrum or run-of-the-mill. You're making me want you again and again and again."

It should have been kind of obvious to Joel that Erin was mainly interested in having a good time instead of getting serious so quickly. She wasn't in the mood for all of the expectations, disappointments or the pressures and strains of a committed relationship. She had already experienced all that in her previous relationship. This was her time to have fun and be free.

Joel decided to play it cool and just go with the flow. "Let's take a shower together and head to my bed and see what we can get started in there."

Chapter 11

The wind was still an irritable swirling menace, but the rain had been reduced to a steady drizzle. The power was restored before Erin and Joel moved from their cozy spot on the living room floor. The lights came on, but the TV screen remained blank since the cable was still out of service.

Joel picked Erin up, blew out the candles, closed the patio door and carried her to the master bathroom. As soon as they made it to the bathroom Erin started acting silly. She was so cute that Joel couldn't help but follow her lead. They stood in front of the bathroom sink's vanity mirror completely nude—brown skin on brown skin—posing seductively, pretending to be photographed for *Ebony*, *Jet* or *Essence*.

Joel turned on the hot water. Steam formed quickly and filled the bathroom like a sauna.

In the shower, Erin and Joel kissed, touched and washed all over each other's sizzling hot and insatiable bodies. All of the nakedness, groping and steamy water, along with all of the soapy slippery smooth body-to-body contact made things escalate to the next level. It felt like Erin and Joel were in the middle of a dream. What was supposed to have been a quick shower soon turned into a long, hot steamy sexual encounter. Erin and Joel both had put aside that little talk about *fucking* because they were still in the mood for making love. Erin beckoned and Joel gladly obliged. He grabbed a condom from his medicine cabinet and quickly began to satisfy her request.

Their encounter moved to the bedroom. Erin and Joel were wrapped in matching plush navy blue towels. Joel headed straight to his window. He closed the mini-blinds, turned on both of his bedside lamps, and turned down the bed.

With a dreamy expression Erin asked, "What are you gonna do to me now?"

"Whatever you want done. Do you want something sexual or something sensual?"

Erin smiled and sang out, "*Sensual.*"

"Your eyes are so expressive. What are you thinking about right now?"

"You. You're all I can think about. All I want is you. Can't stop thinking about touching you, kissing you and having sex with you." She smiled. "You look so good standing there."

"So do you." Joel moved closer, kissed Erin and then said, "I got something special for you. I'll be right back."

Joel went out to the kitchen, grabbed a few ice cubes and placed them in a bowl. He grabbed a plastic fork from a drawer. He reached into another drawer and pulled a feather from an unused feather duster.

When he returned to his bedroom Erin was sitting on his bed watching Joel's wall-mounted 37-inch LCD TV.

"I see the cable is back, but I got all the entertainment you need right here," Joel said as he turned off the TV.

Erin looked excited. "You think so?"

"Lay back and let me show you."

Erin lay down on Joel's bed. He climbed on the bed and opened her towel, exposing her body. He began running his hands and fingertips all over Erin's body, familiarizing himself with every detail of her figure. His lips, mustache and goatee lightly grazed up and down her skin. He angled the teeth of the plastic fork and moved it methodically, creating sensations that Erin never knew she could feel. After gently raking her skin and lightly prodding her soft fleshy areas, Joel introduced the feather to Erin's oh-so-sensitive skin. He slowly teased and tickled with the feather, creating a very different kind of soothing effect. Next he surprised her already excited nipples with an ice cube.

As soon as the ice cube made contact with her left nipple, Erin raised her chest, hissed like a snake and said, "Awwww. Cold."

Joel made tiny circular motions around her breast and then blew on her nipple. Before making contact with Erin's right nipple he said, "Don't worry, I can warm it." He comforted her cold skin with his mouth and then did the same thing to her right breast. He took another ice cube, ran it around her lips and allowed her to suck on it along with his fingers. He held the ice cube high, dripped cold drops of water all over Erin and then dried her with his tongue.

Erin said, "Ooh, I like that."

Joel warmed Erin by cuddling up with her between the sheets. He said, "You haven't seen nothing yet."

Erin sighed. "You've got so much energy. Let's just lay here for a while. Your bed is nice and warm. The sheets are so soft. They smell fresher than linen that air dried in a gentle spring breeze."

Joel smiled. "Glad you like my bed so much."

With a puzzled expression Erin asked, "I like your bed and all, but why white sheets?"

"White sheets can be fun, but I can show you better than I can explain. Relax and let me take you away. Just lay here and play along, all right?"

"Okay."

Joel had made love to Erin for hours, and now it was time for more afterplay. He pulled the sheet over their heads, then lifted the sheet with his body, creating a tentlike atmosphere. He moved Erin deeper into the middle of his huge king-sized bed. They seemed to move in slow motion under Joel's flowing white sheets. The softness of his pillowtop mattress added to the effect. When Erin looked around she could see why

Joel liked the white sheets so much. The soft light from the lamps made the white sheets appear even brighter and gave her an instant feeling of serenity. It felt like Joel had taken her away to another world or they were lost in the middle of a soft white cloud.

Erin blushed and said, "It feels like we've gone off somewhere else."

"We have."

Erin playfully asked, "Where are we?"

Lying on his side, Joel whispered, "Lost inside my love. Relax your mind and body, let my love caress you and draw you in deeper. Close your eyes and concentrate on my voice." Erin followed Joel's instructions. "Are you relaxed?"

With her eyes closed Erin answered, "Yeah."

In the same soft tone, Joel said, "Let your body relax completely. This is all about total relaxation. Take slow deep breaths. Inhale through your nose and exhale through your mouth. Each breath is cleansing your soul."

Erin took slow deep breaths just as Joel asked. She felt subtle changes with each breath. Her perception of time and space seem to be altered. Joel was using a relaxation technique called guided imagery.

He whispered, "Your spirit is becoming lighter and lighter. You're completely weightless. You're floating . . . higher and higher. There is no limit to how high you can go. Move your arms and legs, slowly and gently. Remember to breathe slow deep cleansing breaths. Free your mind and allow yourself to feel the softness and subtle sensations flow throughout your entire body."

Erin moved her arms and legs in a slow fluid motion. She felt sensations in the palms of her hands and the soles of her feet. She seemed to be absorbed into the softness and texture of Joel's bed. Waves of pleasure moved through her head and she felt she had never felt more peaceful or relaxed in her life.

Joel continued, "You're gradually coming back down . . .

slowly and softly. No need to rush. Slowly . . . slowly . . . that's it. You're about to land on a bed of white flowers . . . orchids, roses, carnations and lilies. You're there. Now, inhale deeply. Can you smell the flowers and feel the petals against your skin?"

The scent and texture of Joel's bed reminded Erin of a peaceful warm spring day.

"Yeah," Erin said as she smiled and took a soul-cleansing deep breath.

"Open your eyes. How do you feel?"

"Like heaven . . . so relaxed. That was nice. You're really creative. Thank you."

They kissed.

"You really know how to make me feel special. I swear I'm tingling all over."

"You did that. All I did was tap into your mind a little and elevate your sensuality to another level."

"You're trying to make me fall in love with you, aren't you?"

"No. I can't make you fall in love with me, can I?" Joel asked with a curious look on his face.

"It's possible. Falling in love is the easy part. Staying in love is the hard part."

"True, but once I get you there—I'll keep you there."

"I believe you. Can I do something creative with you now?"

"Sure. What are you gonna do?"

"Just listen and play along." Erin paused for a brief moment. "We're underwater and you can't breathe. You desperately need to get to the surface for air."

"What about you?"

"Pretend that I'm not here or you lost track of me and I'm gonna catch up to you. Hurry up and get to the surface. You need to breathe."

"No, not without you . . . I can't breathe without you."

Erin laughed. "Yes, you can. It's okay to leave me. I'll be okay. Swim to the surface."

Joel kissed Erin and moved to the head of the bed. He took a deep breath when he reached the top. He said, "Come up and get some air."

Erin replied, "It's okay. I found a breathing tube."

Joel had no idea what Erin was about to do until she touched him in the right spot. Her touch made his eyes widen and then they slowly settled down. She teased, titillated and tantalized Joel with her mouth, from the tip of his penis, all of the way down the shaft to his scrotum. This was Joel's sample of heaven. Erin licked him like she loved him. She eventually took him inside her mouth deeper and deeper. Joel reached under the sheets and started playing in Erin's hair. A minute later he pulled the top sheet back just enough to see her in action. He couldn't believe his eyes.

He continued playing in her hair, and he said, "Erin! Yeah! Oh, yeah! That feels so good."

He wanted this to last forever, but Erin was in control. She controlled the intensity and she turned it up so high that she knew that Joel wouldn't last much longer. She reached for her towel and positioned it next to Joel. He wanted to slow her down, but he didn't do anything to resist or impede his orgasm.

Joel's body tensed and upon his release he cried out, "Ah yeah! Mmmmmmm."

Erin resurfaced. She kissed Joel on the lips and they wrapped each other in a sweet caress.

Chapter 12

Erin stopped dead in her tracks as she returned from Joel's bathroom. She watched in awe as he slept in the nude with the top sheet partially wrapped around him. She smiled all over because she knew that this was a deep sleep induced by her seduction. The sight of Joel, and most of the things that happened throughout the evening, seemed so surreal. As Joel lay there, Erin thought he looked cute, sexy, strong, and more than handsome enough to be considered fine as hell. She wanted to know more about Joel, exactly what made him tick, his fears, struggles and the obstacles he had overcome. Erin wanted to touch him, but didn't because she figured that her sensual touch might wake him.

Erin's mind went into overdrive because she didn't know what to do with Joel. Thoughts flowed through her mind like busy travelers through Grand Central Station the day before a major holiday. Part of her wanted an exclusive relationship with him, but she knew the love thing would eventually come into play and she wanted to avoid that by all means. She wanted to avoid getting her heart involved and simply wanted to keep Joel on the level of a very good friend with benefits. She had a specific agenda in mind and no matter what, she planned to stick to it. For now Joel was going to remain her friend and lover—at least until her heart and mind were ready to fully accept love in her life again.

The entire apartment was quiet until Erin's cell phone rang. The last thing she wanted was to disturb Joel. She raced out to the living room to answer it. Erin looked at her Caller ID. Just as she suspected, it was Kenya, with another untimely cell phone intrusion.

Erin sat down on Joel's chocolate leather sofa. She inhaled the rich scent of the quality leather and then, with excitement in her voice, she said, "Hey, girl. What's up?"

"What's up with you? Are you okay?"

"I'm better than okay. Are you okay?"

"I'm just okay . . . just regular old okay." Kenya paused for a moment. "I've been laying here going crazy worrying about you. What's going on?"

"Nothing . . . right now."

"Where is . . . um . . . what's his name?"

"Joel. You know his name. He's in his bed sleeping like a baby."

There was an awkward moment of silence. Then Kenya yelled, "Oh my God!"

"What?"

"You fucked him, didn't you?"

"No!" Erin said with excitement, but keeping her voice at a quiet and controlled level.

"You're lying. You're still at his apartment right now, aren't you? Don't even try lying to me 'cause you know I'll know."

Erin laughed. "Ain't nobody trying to lie to you. Since you wanna know everything, Miss Nosey, Joel and I haven't fucked yet, but we did *make love* tonight."

Kenya screamed, "You little slut!"

"Shut up!"

"You just met him."

"Not really. I remembered him from years ago. We grew up in the same neighborhood."

Kenya laughed. "Oh yeah, that definitely justifies sleeping with him on the first night. That wasn't even a real date."

"You need to stop. Hope you're not trying to make me feel

bad because if you are, it's not working. I don't have any re-grets. You know for a fact that I usually don't get down like that, but honestly I feel like I've known Joel forever. I felt him and he felt me way before we even laid one finger on each other . . . before our first words were exchanged. That's how strong our vibe was and still is . . . pure chemistry. You have no idea how good I feel right now. Feels like I won something."

"Well, I guess I'm happy for you and I hope you know what you've gotten yourself into. He lives right across the hall. Do you realize how messy that can be? Do you realize that we signed a one-year lease?"

"I thought about all of that already."

"Before or after y'all got busy?"

Erin quickly mumbled, "After."

"Huh?"

"I said *after*, but so what. You don't know how it happened. Everything was so right. It was romantic."

Kenya burst out laughing. "You're trippin' for real. Didn't y'all have pizza and fries for dinner? C'mon, how freaking romantic could that have been?"

"That's exactly what I wanted for dinner. The romantic part had nothing to do with the food. It was the rain, the music, the atmosphere and *him*. Mmmm. The feeling was so right. Like I said, no regrets. Wait till you see him face-to-face. He's fine as hell. And he's so smooth."

Kenya burst out laughing again. "Obviously. He's so smooth he made your panties slip right off."

"I don't care what you say. I like Joel. He and I have a lot in common. We're both teachers and we look damn good to-gether. Joel is the right height for me. I know you saw a pic-ture of him, but you'll get a better appreciation once you see him in person. He's probably just a tad under six feet tall, with an athletic build. He's real clean-cut with short black wavy hair, a nice little mustache and goatee. His mouth is amazing and I love his voice. You should see his lips and his smile up close. I wanna tell you about his tongue, but I can't."

Kenya begged, "Yes, you can."

"No, I can't."

"You can. I insist."

"Can't. All I can say is that he is the type of guy that we always talked about attracting. He knew things about me that I didn't even know about myself. Joel is the type of guy that knows exactly what a woman needs and how to fully satisfy. Being with him was something like going to the beauty salon and just sitting in the chair without saying a word about how you want your hair done and having your beautician hook your do up better than you ever imagined, and then you walk out looking and feeling brand new. The way that he made love to me was . . . *sensational*."

"You make me sick. I wanna feel like that too," Kenya whined.

"You will . . . one day. When your Joel comes along," Erin said smugly.

"Sounds like he pumped your head way the hell up."

"Don't be *hating*," Erin said, sounding real ghetto-fabulous.

"He must have put it on you real good because it sounds like you're catching feelings already. I thought you weren't looking for love."

"Girl please, I'm not, and don't mention that word to me. I seriously don't know what to do with him. Hopefully, I'll have all summer to figure something out. I'm just kind of going with the flow."

"And what about him?"

"He's ready for a committed relationship already." Erin sighed. "He's so different."

"Uh-huh, see how different he is in the morning. I just wanna know one thing. How was the dick?"

Erin couldn't wait to tell her how good it was, but pretending to sound shocked, she said, "Girl, what's wrong with you asking me something like that?"

"You know exactly what's wrong with me. I haven't had none in a long time . . . that's what's wrong with me."

"Let's just say that his thing was so good that I'm still speechless."

"Did he go deep?"

"Deep enough," Erin replied quickly.

"Shit, how deep is deep enough?"

"He went deep enough to plant his flagpole in unchartered territory. He was so long that I could feel him in my abdomen."

Kenya gasped for air. "That sounds deep . . . and painful."

"Depends on what you like. A little pain in your life once in a while can be a good thing."

"I wouldn't know, but I wanna know. Okay, I want more details. He's long, but is he thick too?"

"Yeah, he's very well endowed. He's so thick that he filled me up on the inside. I could feel the exact shape of his dick and I can still feel him now."

Kenya slipped up and whined, "Ooh, I want some of that. You need to share."

With attitude Erin said, "What? I should be highly offended by you even thinking about something like that. The fact that you said it out loud is insane. I've never shared a man and don't plan on it either."

Kenya fired back, "Hmm, the fact that you're *not* highly offended tells me that you might be interested in sharing."

Erin blushed. "Why do you think you know me so well?"

"Because I do. You know damn well we said that there are so few good men out here that once one of us found a good one we'd share. So, what's up with the threesome now, huh?"

Erin laughed. "All right. I might have said something like that in the past, but I was joking."

"Well, I'm not laughing now. I'm serious."

"I'll admit, Joel is the type of guy that kind of makes me wanna share, but no. Absolutely not. He's too good to share."

"I'm not trying to steal your good thing. I just want us to try something new and this sounds like the perfect opportunity."

Erin's mind started going a mile a minute. She was thinking one thing, but her mouth was saying something else. "I can't.

Anyway, Joel seems like a one woman man, and it's not up to me."

Kenya laughed. "What man wouldn't want to be with two attractive women at the same time? Your good thing can be our good thing. Can't I just have a sample? You're being self-ish."

"Maybe I am. But can you blame me? I've been running on empty for too long and he fills me up in so many ways. I can't get enough."

"I know exactly what you're saying." Kenya said. "I need to experience that same feeling. I'm so stressed right now with this training and all that I feel half-dead. I need something to help me regain consciousness—make me feel alive again. I wish I could have been there with y'all tonight. The three of us would have had so much fun together. I would have turned it into the most passionate ménage à trois ever. Imagine us, you, me and him . . . together. Doesn't that sound stimulating, fun and exciting?"

Erotic images of three bodies engrossed in different sexual positions flashed through Erin's mind. With a hint of indecisiveness in her voice she said, "I dunno."

"See, you know it sounds good. I would love for the three of us to experience something like that together. Run it past Joel and see what he thinks. If you can't make it happen, then I bet I know how to entice him."

Without thinking Erin said, "We'd probably have to entice him together."

"Oh, that's not a problem at all. Do you think he has enough stamina to satisfy both of us?"

"Oh yeah. He's very athletic."

"Do me a big favor."

"What?"

"Can you go in Joel's bedroom right now and take a few quick pictures of him while he's sleeping?"

"Why? You already saw a picture of him."

"I want to see more of him—a lot more. The pictures can be as mild or as provocative as you'd like."

"You're crazy. I can't take pictures of him. That would be so wrong. I'm not really down with this."

"All right. Then forget about it. But I don't see why this is any different than everything else we've shared. We've shared food, drinks, clothes, the same bed, an apartment and the list goes on and on. We almost showered together."

"Where the hell did that come from? Don't even go there. You kill me with your little bisexual innuendos."

"What did I say? That's your freaky mind jumping to conclusions."

"No. I know exactly where you were going. The only reason I even considered jumping into the shower with you was because we were running out of hot water."

With a giggle Kenya said, "Okay, if that's what you think."

"You can't compare sharing a man to the stuff you just mentioned. Find your own man. Shoot, as far as I'm concerned God gave us the same basic body parts, so use what you got to get what you want—just not from my man."

Kenya laughed in Erin's ear. "Well, I guess you told me. But you even said that Joel was the type of man that *we've* always talked about attracting. You know how hard it is trying to find a decent man. I was just thinking that all of us could be happy together . . . sorry. I'm glad you're happy, but you're changing."

"Change is good."

"Not from my perspective."

"What do you mean by that?"

"Joel has your full attention and soon you'll forget all about me. I bet you won't even have time for me when I get back, now that he's in the picture. The last thing I want is for our friendship to be affected and I definitely don't want it to end. If we all hook up like I want, then I guarantee you that things will change for the better."

Erin quickly replied, "Or they could change for the worse. You could be asking for trouble."

"Stop worrying. It's late. I'm gonna let you go now. Just give a little more thought to what I said. And don't forget about the pictures. I'll be waiting. Talk to you later."

"I'm not promising anything."

"I'm not asking for promises. Just don't rule out anything. I miss you."

"Miss you, too. Bye."

Erin pressed the End button on her phone. Her mind was really in overdrive now. She sat motionless on Joel's sofa for a moment, trying to process some of the information she and Kenya had discussed. Erin knew that she and Joel were the two main ingredients in a pot that was just starting to heat up. All of a sudden Kenya wanted to be added to the mix. Words like, *flavor, variety, hot, spicy, sweet,* and *delicious,* ran through Erin's mind. Her mouth watered and then she smiled.

The crazy thing was that Kenya was very manipulative and knew how to stir the pot. Erin just feared that the pot could eventually boil over.

She freed her mind for a minute and returned to Joel's bedroom. If an idle mind is the devil's playground then at that moment Erin's mind was the devil's amusement park. She stood in front of Joel, admiring him again. The white sheets seemed to highlight his flawless mahogany skin. Most of his body was exposed, but Erin made sure that his genitals were covered. Although she knew it was wrong, she snapped three quick pictures of Joel as he slept. She headed out to the living room to view the pictures. She smiled at Joel's pictures as if they were her pride and joy. She considered them tastefully done, even though they were taken in poor judgment. She knew that once she pressed the Send command on her cell phone she was setting something into motion that was risky, unpredictable, and at the same time incredibly sexy and exciting.

Erin had a moment of emotional clarity. Her heart and mind were in perfect harmony because she knew exactly what she wanted to do with Joel. She planned to make him part of a loving threesome.

Kenya couldn't believe her eyes when she received the pictures of Joel. She smiled and was filled with excitement. Within a minute or so she received a text message from Erin that read, *Happy now???*

Kenya immediately replied to Erin's message. *Yes! Yes! Yes!*

Erin called Kenya on her cell. "What do you think?"

"He is sooo fine. Look how he's wearing that sheet. Joel looks like a model for an expensive cologne ad or something."

"I told you he was yummy. And he's a good man with a sensitive heart."

"Stop, you're killing me. You can cut all the romantic bull. I can't wait to meet Joel. Oh my God, I'm getting turned on. Can you imagine us taking turns riding his dick?"

"I dunno. Is that what you want?"

"Yeah. Now give me something else that I really want."

"What?"

"Details. I need hot and juicy details."

"All right, calm down."

Erin began telling Kenya all about the intimate details of her sexual experience with Joel. She was very descriptive. Kenya stretched out on her bed wearing nothing but her panties, and was able to visualize everything that happened between Erin and Joel right down to the smallest detail. With every word, she got more and more turned on. Within seconds Kenya felt the urge to touch herself. She tried to resist, but ended up playing with her breasts. She licked her fingertips and played with her nipples. In her mind it was Joel's hands, wet fingertips and tongue on her. Kenya held her cell phone between her cheek and shoulder while her other hand gradually slid down her abdomen, inside of her panties and into her wetness.

Erin also got caught up in the moment and became so aroused by her own recollection and vivid description that she began to touch herself. At first Erin and Kenya were unaware of what the other was doing. But pretty soon there were brief moments of silence followed by heavy breathing and gentle moans. There had always been an undeniable sexual energy between the two. What seemed so wrong at first, suddenly seemed so right. They enjoyed the hell out of their first session of girl-on-girl phone sex, but more than that, it was like a long-overdue bonding of two kindred spirits.

Chapter 13

The sun was shining brighter than bright. Birds sang while crickets chirped outside of Joel's window. He woke up with a smile on his face, along with an increased sense of optimism and confidence. He was well rested and still felt the wonderful effects from making love to Erin. He felt her leg against his. Joel turned on his side, cuddled closely with her and pressed his morning wood against her warm bare skin. Erin slept like a baby. Joel felt the rise and fall of her torso and synchronized his breathing with hers. He knew that they were in store for a lovely day.

Joel allowed himself to get used to Erin's presence. All he could see, hear, smell, taste and feel was Erin. He was used to falling hard and fast for a woman. His senses were blinded. Joel was intoxicated by the emotions that exist between the stages of like, lust and love.

Since Erin was still asleep one of Joel's other interests summoned his attention. He felt around for the TV remote. He hit the power button and then turned the TV straight to ESPN to watch *Sports Center*. Everything seemed so perfect. He lay there enjoying the contour of Erin's body and watching sports highlights. He thought, *What could be better?*

Out of nowhere Erin's cell phone rang and she jumped up like a wild woman. She had a startled look in her eyes. Her hair was neat on one side and was a pretty mess on the other.

Joel touched her shoulder and said, "Good morning, Erin. Calm down, everything's okay."

Erin wiped her eyes, looked around and then at Joel. She smiled. There was a momentary look of embarrassment on her face because it was obvious that she had forgotten where she was. Last night was like a dream. She hugged Joel, gave him two quick pecks on the lips and said, "I'm sorry. Good morning, Joel. I need to change that horrible ring tone. It scared the hell out of me." Erin grabbed her cell phone and began talking. "Hello." Her hair sent out a quick distress signal and she combed through it with her fingers. "Yes, this is she."

Joel muted the TV and then decided to just turn it off. Erin watched as he got out of bed naked and opened the mini-blinds. Instantly the room was flooded with rays of golden sunlight that resembled warm honey. The atmosphere was sweet, bursting with an effervescent newness. Erin flashed a warm sexy smile and Joel returned it.

He jumped back in bed and began to massage Erin's neck, shoulders and back as she talked on her cell phone.

Erin said, "Ten is fine. Okay. Thank you."

Joel stretched, and asked, "Movers?"

Erin yawned, and said, "Yeah. They'll be here in a few hours. I guess I better get up and get ready." Another distress signal went out. Erin was quickly reminded that Joel had never seen how she looked in the morning. She hid her face with her hand. "I don't want you to see me looking like this. Mornings have a funny way of altering my appearance. My eyes probably look red and puffy. I'm sure I look terrible."

As Joel worked his hands up and down Erin's back he felt her muscles relax. He kissed her between her shoulder blades to let her know that everything was okay. He said, "I don't think you could look terrible even if you tried. You're incredibly beautiful."

"Thank you," Erin said as she gave Joel another kiss.

"You don't know how good you look. I'm kind of glad you don't know because if you did you'd probably be out of control. I can't stand conceited women. I really like your modesty. Please don't ever change."

"Thank you, and I won't." Erin really wasn't paying too much attention to what Joel said. She was more focused on the massage she was getting. As her eyes rolled back in her head she said, "Oh . . . my . . . goodness, your hands really feel nice. I could get used to this—waking up next to a man who looks like America's next top male model and getting a massage without even having to ask."

Joel smiled. "I caught that male model line . . . thanks. This massage is nothing. Wait till I rub you down with some hot oil."

Erin felt that dreamy feeling again. She closed her eyes and imagined how good Joel's hands would feel as they massaged hot oil all over her body. "Mmmmm. I'm ready for that whenever, but I gotta get ready for the movers."

"You've got time. Can't we just stay right here for a few more minutes?"

Erin wasn't trying to budge because she was totally captivated by Joel's touch. "Sure. I'm so used to getting up and rushing. I don't really have to worry about that for a while."

"Me either. I had planned on working at a summer camp, but I'm about to call them and cancel. I've got other plans."

"Are you canceling because of me?"

With hesitation Joel said, "Yeah. But I also need to relax. I'm not hurting for cash. Plus, I'm trying to get to know you better. The idea of spending the whole summer with you is exciting. Do you have anything planned for summer?"

"Usually I teach summer school, but since I was moving I decided to leave the entire summer open to allow myself enough time to get settled."

"That was smart. Since we have all this free time we need to plan a vacation. I had a dream that we went on a cruise. And guess what?"

"What?"

"Kenya surprised us and was on the cruise, too."

Taken aback, Erin turned around and looked at Joel. "Kenya was in your dream?"

Joel smiled and said, "Yeah."

Erin continued staring at Joel. She was trying her best to read him because she wasn't sure whether he was trying to throw a subtle hint that he heard her and Kenya on the phone last night or what. "That's so strange. You've never even seen her in person and she was in your dream already."

"Yeah, but don't worry." Joel paused because Erin's stare became more intense as if she was trying to read his thoughts. "Stop looking at me like that. It's not like I'm trying to get at your friend or anything. I don't even know her." He shrugged and squinted. "To be honest there is something about her that I like—something in her voice, but I can't quite put my finger on it."

"It's called flirtation."

Joel laughed and said, "You're probably right."

"What exactly did she say to you?"

"She said that I sounded nice and mentioned how much she looked forward to meeting me."

"I'm sure it wasn't really what she said, but more like how she said it. She's slick. It's called planting the seed. Your dream is proof that the seed is already starting to grow. I gotta give it to my girl—she's been blessed with the gift of persuasion."

Joel laughed and said, "She's good, but not that good. You can say that she kind of made a lasting impression on me, just from speaking to her on the phone. Her personality seems odd but cute. I could tell that she loves attention. Every time your cell phone rings I think it's her."

Erin felt safe and turned down the intensity of her stare. "I know exactly what you mean about Kenya. She has a way of getting to you. She's not even here and it's like I can sense her presence. I guess that's just how close we are."

"There's nothing wrong with that. I think the two of you are funny—like how her picture comes up on your phone whenever she calls."

"That's nothing. My picture comes up on her phone the same way when I call her. I dunno, me and Kenya might be a little too close. I'm not calling her today."

"No. Don't do that. Please don't change because of me. I don't want Kenya to hate me or to think I'm trying to come between the two of you. I've seen friendships deteriorate over guys. I don't wanna be in the middle of any confusion. Keep doing whatever you'd usually do."

"Okay. But you're absolutely right about friendships deteriorating over guys. Stuff like that does happen. That's a scary thought. I could see me and Kenya being like that."

Joel laughed. "Is Kenya a hater?"

"No, not at all. She's definitely not like that. Kenya and I do everything together and I don't know how she's gonna accept our new friendship slash relationship."

"How did she accept your last relationship?"

"She was fine for the most part. She had a boyfriend too, but after they broke up she seemed really clingy and needy."

"And she's been that way ever since?"

"Yeah."

"She needs a man. She needs one bad."

"Easier said than done. She's really picky and critical of the stupidest details."

"I thought so. Like I said, she's odd."

"You literally have to hook her up with a guy in order for her to date. Every relationship she's ever been involved in was prearranged. She carries a big red rejection stamp in her right hand, ready and willing to stamp a brotha on the forehead with the quickness."

Joel burst out laughing. "Damn that's funny."

"Can you blame women for being so skeptical?"

"Not really. I understand why y'all are like that, but at some point you've gotta give us a break. The new guy can't be held accountable for the mistakes that the previous brotha made, you know?"

"That's true."

"You gotta have faith."

"I've got faith."

"I dunno. You don't seem to have faith in love."

Without hesitation Erin said, "I don't."

"Well, I do. I believe in love whether I can see it or not. Now, that's faith."

"Love is dead."

"Love is alive. It breathes and has a pulse. Remember that faith is confidence, trust and a strong belief in the seen and unseen. Have you ever seen love?"

Erin paused. She wanted to tell Joel that she had seen love when she looked at him last night and was caught up in its afterglow. She saw love every time she looked at him, but she refused to acknowledge it. She laughed and said, "I see what you're trying to do. I'm not falling for your little trick. All right, maybe love isn't dead." Erin made a silly face. "Saying that love was dead was really a negative statement, huh?"

"Yeah, it was. But I'm telling you, love is alive and kickin'," Joel said, as he kicked the sheet off of his legs. "Keep looking and I'm sure you'll recognize love when you see it."

"You're crazy. Enough about love. How about some breakfast? You got anything in the kitchen I can cook?"

"My kitchen is packed with all kinds of food. I'll help you get something started."

"I can handle breakfast on my own. You stay in here and I'll surprise you with something nice."

"That sounds good. You won't get any complaints from me. I haven't had a woman cook a decent meal for me since I moved out of my parents' house. I'll stay in here and get my morning workout going."

Erin gave Joel a peck on the lips and headed to the bathroom with her overnight bag. Joel headed to his walk-in closet and took out his curl bar, dumbbells and space-saving folding treadmill.

Erin showered and came out of the bathroom looking refreshed, wearing a Coppin State University T-shirt. She headed out to the kitchen.

Within fifteen minutes or so, Joel smelled a wonderful aroma circulating throughout his apartment. He began to work out even harder because he could tell that he was in store for a delicious but fattening breakfast.

Erin felt right at home in Joel's clean and well organized kitchen. She planned a breakfast feast that took her a total of forty-five minutes to prepare. In the meantime, Joel worked out so hard that he developed a mild case of muscle fatigue and his blood sugar nearly bottomed out. He showered and then stood in front of the bathroom mirror, brushing and flossing his teeth.

Erin called Joel to the kitchen. He was fully dressed and more than ready to eat by the time breakfast was ready. He made his way out to the kitchen looking kind of dazed from his rigorous workout and lack of food.

He said, "Breakfast smells so good."

Erin looked at Joel closely and said, "Thanks. Are you all right?"

"I'm fine. Just a little exhausted from my workout."

"Poor baby. I thought it was crazy for you to work out before breakfast. I should have given you some orange juice or something. Sorry I took so long."

"No, it's okay. This is how I usually function. But then again, you might be right. I haven't eaten in I don't know how many hours, and didn't take into consideration the amount of energy I used last night," Joel said with a smile.

Erin gave Joel a hug. "And you put your energy to some good use. I'm sure that's what it was then. Sit right here and let me help you replenish your energy. Hope you like what I made."

She set two big plates of food in front of Joel. The first plate contained four plump golden brown buttermilk pancakes covered in melted butter and maple syrup. The second had scrambled eggs, home fries, eight link sausages and a pile of bacon. Erin sat right on Joel's lap and fed him. They sipped from the same glass of orange juice and ended up sharing breakfast just as Erin had planned.

After breakfast Erin and Joel had a little time to kill. They sat on the sofa talking and watching the Saturday morning news. Erin decided to do something special for Joel. She grabbed her overnight bag from the bedroom and returned to the sofa. She had Joel lay his head on her lap while she massaged some vitamin-enriched shea butter into his hair and scalp. Then she brushed his hair as he continued to relax. This was a perfect example of what Joel meant when he mentioned something about a nurturing woman with an affectionate touch.

Erin said, "I'm really enjoying being around you. Last night was perfect."

"I thought so too."

"Sorry if I came off as being a little abrasive earlier when we were in bed talking about love. It's just that I'm a strong-minded woman and I get that from my mother. When we get our minds set on something then that's pretty much it."

"I understand. You weren't abrasive at all. You're just passionate about your beliefs and feelings. I was wrong for trying to make you express something you weren't feeling. For some reason I wanted us to have a love-at-first-sight kind of vibe going. I guess that was more or less a desperate attempt to fill a void."

"What's the rush?"

"I dunno. Maybe it's fear of loneliness. I just think it's time for me to really concentrate on settling down with one woman and eventually finding a wife. I don't want you to think that I'm crazy or anything." He laughed, "I'm a love junky going through withdrawal."

"I never heard a guy describe himself like that." Erin smiled. "Joel, I like you because you seem to be a really open and honest type of guy. You've shown me who you are and what you're about right off the bat."

"That's good to hear. More than anything I wanted to get an

idea of how you felt about love in general, and now I know how you feel."

"Love hurts."

"When I was younger I used to say that love ain't supposed to hurt, but it does. I want you to know that love never meant to hurt you."

Erin felt her emotions kick in. Her voice quivered a bit. "It's weird because my emotional scars run deep. Flesh wounds heal pretty quickly, but when your heart is wounded it takes a lot more than bandages to help it heal."

"Trust me 'cause I know from experience. I wear my scars proudly, like a soldier wears his medals on his chest. I know the pain, darkness, emptiness and abandonment associated with a broken heart. But what I know, more than all of that, is how good it feels to start the healing process and get rid of all of that negative energy."

"I'm getting there, but I have issues," Erin said with laughter in her voice.

"No, *we've* got issues. All relationships do. I felt the need to comfort you because I was worried about you dealing with how fast we slept together and all."

"Yeah, I was kind of stressing over that. You know how women think. The faster we give it up, the less likely you are to stick around."

"I'm not going anywhere. You can blame me for what happened because I didn't wanna wait."

"You wanted yours right away, huh?"

"Yeah. It just goes to show you how strong of an instant attraction I felt."

"I understand. Stop worrying because I'm fine. I was starting to worry about things between us getting too serious too fast, but I'm okay with that now. I feel subtle changes inside already. If you put everything aside, the most important thing is that I want you, and I enjoy being with you."

"And I enjoy being with you. Tell me something. What's your fantasy? Think about it—any kind of fantasy."

"I dunno."

"C'mon, you don't have a fantasy?" Joel smiled. "We all dream a little dream called fantasy."

"I've always dreamed of making love on a beach."

"Okay. We can do that."

They both laughed.

"What's your fantasy? Wait, don't answer. You've always dreamed of making love to two beautiful women at the same time."

Joel smiled and said, "Yeah, what guy hasn't? But that's so unrealistic." He was interrupted by the doorbell followed by three loud thumps. "I got it. Wonder who this is banging on my door like that," he said as he walked toward the front door. Joel looked out the peephole. "It's Ms. Benson."

"I can't let her catch me in here looking like this," Erin said as she jumped from the sofa and hurried toward Joel's bedroom with her overnight bag in hand.

Joel whispered, "Come back. Don't worry, I'm not gonna open this door."

"See what she wants."

Ms. Benson knocked on the door again—three quick thumps. Joel just stood at the door watching her to see how long it would take until she decided to leave. He hated when people dropped by his apartment unexpectedly.

Erin said, "Stop being mean and see what that old lady wants."

Joel held his laugh inside and nodded his head as Erin retreated to the bedroom.

Ms. Benson raised her hand to knock again, but Joel opened the door quickly before her knuckles were able to make contact.

"Oh Lord!" Ms. Benson said as she stumbled backward, grabbing her heart and trying to catch her breath. "You scared the life outta me."

"I'm sorry."

"It's okay. Good morning, Joel."

"Good morning, Ms. Benson. What can I do for you?"

"I'm looking for the young lady from across the hall. You know the one who just moved in."

"Yes, ma'am. I met her yesterday. She told me that you sent her up to meet me. Thanks for doing that. But I haven't seen her today."

"You're welcome. I figured you'd be glad to meet a pretty girl like that." She paused for a brief moment and said, "It was a shame how your girlfriend and her new boyfriend came all up in your place and moved her belongings, out."

Joel felt embarrassed. Then frustration began to set in because he figured if Ms. Benson knew details about Renee moving out then that meant the whole building knew as well. He tried his best to remain respectful. He stood there wishing that he had never opened the front door. He didn't even have a reply for Ms. Benson.

"Are you sure the young lady from 2D isn't home, because I noticed that her car was parked out front, but she's not answering her door."

"It's early. She could be in there . . . sleeping . . . you know? Or maybe she's just not home. Someone could have picked her up or something."

"You're probably right."

"Is there a particular reason why you're looking for her?"

"No, not really. I just wanted to see how she was making out with her new place."

"I'm sure she's all right, but I'm worried about you. Are you all right? It's not even nine o'clock and you're going around on a Saturday morning knocking on people's doors."

Ms. Benson threw her hand at Joel and laughed. "Aw, don't pay me any attention. I don't mean any harm. I get outta my bed at five-thirty every morning just so I can see what's going on."

Joel raised an eyebrow and asked, "Is that right?"

"Sure is. Did you hear about that young man down in 1A?"

"No. But I've got a feeling you're gonna tell me, though."

lowered her voice to a whisper. "He messed
his girlfriend pregnant again. They already got
ing in a one bedroom apartment. Where do
se children are gonna sleep?"

Joel shook his head and said, "I dunno."

Ms. Benson continued whispering, "That woman up in 3C
got a drug problem. If she comes to me begging for money or
I see her daughter begging for sugar with that cup of hers one
more time, I'm gonna have to call both of them out. This
building ain't what it used to be. All of these trifling people
moving in here. When the family from across the hall moved
they loaded their furniture on the back of an old broke-down
pickup truck. You should have seen it. Their stuff looked like
a junk pile all uncovered for everybody to see. Another family
moved into the building next door the same way, using a
pickup truck. Whatever happened to people using U-Haul or
a professional moving company? I tell you, the ghetto has officially made its way to the suburbs. That's why all the white
people moved outta here—they saw this coming. That's exactly why I'm moving back to the city. I'm just waiting to see
how this new young lady is gonna have her stuff moved in."

"Erin looks classy, so I bet she'll use professional movers."

"She didn't look that classy. I think she probably rented a
U-Haul and will have her friends help her move in."

"We'll just have to wait and see. I wanna clarify some of the
things you mentioned a moment ago. I think you're exagger-
ating a little about the people in 1A and 3C. The guy in 1A is
divorced, and only has custody of his two kids every other
weekend, and this is his first kid by his girlfriend. Everybody
knows that the lady in 3C is a recovering addict with over ten
years clean. You know good and well she hasn't been begging
you for money. Her daughter did go around asking for sugar
once and her mother punished her for two weeks for embarrassing her like that. You should be ashamed of yourself
spreading rumors about that nice couple in 1A and that hard-

working single mother in 3C. This building is full of young professionals trying to make a decent living."

"Think what you want. I know what I know because I get my info firsthand."

"You've been misinformed." He paused for a moment and thought about what he was saying. "I dunno . . . I've already said too much and I can't stand here contributing to gossip. I don't want you to misquote me and cause trouble with the other neighbors."

"You don't have to worry about that. Well, I'm sure you'll see the young lady from 2D before I will." Ms. Benson paused to see what kind of reaction she could get out of Joel. He winced. She smiled and said, "Tell her that I came up to check on her. You have a blessed day."

"You too."

Joel closed the door and headed to his bedroom, where he saw that Erin was dressed and looking absolutely beautiful in a bright multicolored sundress and sandals.

With a smile Joel said, "Damn, you look pretty. I like that dress."

"Thank you."

"Where'd the dress come from?"

Erin laughed and said, "It was folded up in my overnight bag. I ran the iron over it real quick and in less than a minute it was ready to wear." She paused for a second. "Oh, I heard most of the stuff that Ms. Benson said. Very audacious is all I have to say about her."

"More like delusional or demented."

Joel's phone rang.

"Go ahead and get that. I'm gonna sneak outta here and make my way across the hall without Ms. Benson noticing. Hopefully she won't see me because the last thing I need is a nomination for tramp of the year."

They both laughed.

"Either way that won't happen. You're grown. Forget about

her. I'll meet you across the hall in a little bit," he said as Erin let herself out of his apartment.

The phone continued to ring. Joel checked the Caller ID and saw that it was his buddy Greg. He answered the phone just before the answering machine activated.

"What's up, Greg?"

"What's up with you? I think you're losing your mind. What happened to you last night?"

"Man, I hooked up with this fine-ass honey. She's moving in right across the hall." Joel was trying to cut the conversation short. "As a matter of fact, I think the movers are here right now."

"Well, I'm glad you've got something going on. Me and Dave thought you were still depressed and damn near suicidal by now."

Joel laughed and said, "Everything's fine."

"I guess we won't be seeing you any time soon since you hooked up with somebody new. We know how you have a problem concentrating on anything else besides your girl."

"Don't even try that."

"You know it's true. The only way I'll see you is by accident or at a couples function."

Joel laughed and said, "All right. Maybe I do get a little consumed, but I'll definitely make time to hang out with my boys."

"Yeah right, nigga. I'll believe it when I see it."

"Shut the hell up." Joel heard someone at his front door and said, "I just heard somebody at my door. I think it's my new girl looking for me."

"You know I'm just playing. I'm happy for you, bro. No matter what, you're still my boy."

"Thanks, Greg. Take it easy. I'll be in touch, aight?"

"Yeah, but you need to stop lying to me and to yourself."

"All right. I'm gone."

"Peace."

Joel hung up the phone and headed out to answer the door,

but before he could make it he saw that it was opening slowly. Joel naturally assumed that it was Erin until he heard a voice that didn't belong to her.

A familiar feminine voice said softly, "Hello, Joel. I'm coming in."

All of a sudden the bright sunlight from earlier was blocked by a cluster of annoying gray clouds. Joel couldn't believe his eyes. He stared at Renee as if she was a ghost, and that's kind of what she looked like. For the first time in years she was without her makeup—barefaced and unashamed. Joel could clearly see that she had trouble in her eyes.

"Oh, hell no! How you just gonna come marching your ass up in here like you own something. You turned in your key the day you walked out and that means you don't belong here. You gotta go."

Strolling into the living room at a snail's pace, looking pitiful and preoccupied Renee said, "Can't you see that—"

Joel rudely interrupted. "Doesn't matter." Renee kept moving toward Joel's sofa. She was about to sit. "Don't even sit down. You don't have time to get comfortable. I have a new friend right across the hall and she'll be back over here any minute. I'm not trying to mess things up because of you. Like I already said, you gotta go."

Joel automatically assumed that Renee had come crawling back because of an argument or breakup between her and Robert. He had no sympathy for Renee whatsoever. The fact that he had just found out from Ms. Benson that Renee had Robert in his apartment the day she moved out didn't help matters much either.

Renee pleaded, "Please, can you just listen?"

"Make it quick, real quick."

"My mother passed away last night."

Joel's heart sank. "Oh no! Renee, I'm so sorry to hear that. Is there anything I can do?"

"More than anything I just need you to be a friend to me right now. Is that too much to ask?"

"I guess not. I feel terrible. You could have told me your mother passed away as soon as you came through the door."

Renee looked at Joel like he was crazy and said, "I tried, but you didn't give me the chance. I'm sure you could see by the look on my face that there was something out of the ordinary going on."

"I'm sorry. But seriously, you're the last person I expected to see walk through that door. Man, I'm really sorry for your loss. Was Mrs. Rhodes sick?"

"These days you don't even have to be sick to die. They think it was a brain aneurysm that killed her, but they won't know for certain until after the autopsy."

"I'm sure this is a lot to deal with. Go ahead and have a seat."

Renee sat on Joel's sofa and said, "Thanks. I still consider this apartment home." Joel gave her a cheap smile. Out of respect for her dead mother he held back his rude comments. Renee could see that things were different. She shifted in her seat and got the conversation back on track. "You can't even begin to imagine how much I have to deal with. I have to go over to Northwest Hospital and break the news to my sister."

"Hospital? What's wrong with Cheryl?"

"She was diagnosed with uterine fibroids and had surgery done yesterday. The bad thing is that she had to have a hysterectomy. Her doctor said that it will take her a couple of weeks to recover. She was already depressed about having to have the hysterectomy and the idea of never being able to give birth again really had her down. Now Momma's death is just gonna add even more stress."

Joel was conscious of every passing second. His thoughts were scattered all over the place. He wanted to show Renee as much sympathy as possible, but at the same time he didn't want her to take advantage of his kindness. He wanted to get across the hall to make sure things were working out okay for Erin. He knew that she looked too damn good to be left alone with a gang of horny movers gawking at her.

Instead of ending things and letting Renee go about her business, Joel continued to be considerate and understanding. He sat down on the leather chair adjacent to the sofa and said, "When you break the news to Cheryl you should have the hospital's chaplain there for added support." He paused for a moment. "How's your father holding up?"

"He's not. My dad is a total wreck."

Joel had to gather his thoughts. He sighed. "I'm sorry to hear about your family's troubles and all, but now that I think about it . . . I really don't understand why you're here. A phone call would have been good enough. Shouldn't you be with Robert? According to your little message from yesterday, things sounded as if the two of you were deeply in love and about to get married or something. You said you knew who you were and what you wanted."

Renee shook her head and said, "Don't believe the hype, Joel. I don't even know why I called you, talking all that bull. Things aren't even like that. I think the novelty has worn off already. Now I know that Robert is more into having a forbidden love affair than a regular relationship, because he has full access to me and only wants me half of the time. What's up with that?"

"Another woman . . . definitely another woman. You're getting played. It's karma. I'm not rejoicing or anything, but that's exactly what it is. I was hoping things were working out for you because I've moved on."

With a sad expression Renee said, "I'm happy for you. I honestly thought I had finally found happiness. The last time I talked to Robert, he called me crazy. Why would he call me crazy?"

Joel paused, while a million reasons why Robert would have called Renee crazy went through his mind. "I found out that you had Robert in here helping you move out. Why would you bring him in here?" He shook his head and said, "No respect."

Renee began to cry. "I'm so sorry for that. I was wrong, and that's why everything is falling apart now. I wanted to talk to you because you know me so well, and you knew my mother. I thought it would be best to tell you in person what happened to her, since I was already in the area. And I just wanted to see you again. I really messed up. I jumped the gun and moved out of here too quick."

"Why are crying like that? Are you crying over your mother or us?"

Renee shrugged. "I shouldn't have come here. I don't know what's wrong with me. Where is my pride?"

"I understand why you're here. It's called closure."

"Yeah."

"There's no need to feel ashamed or embarrassed. Sometimes love has a way of being stronger than pride, and I proved that to you so many times it's not funny."

"I can honestly say that I keep finding myself falling in and out of love with you. Didn't you know I'd come back one day?"

"No."

"My mother's death was some sort of wake up call for me. I thought it was sign, telling me to follow my heart back to you before it was too late." Renee broke down and cried harder than ever. "I keep forgetting that my mother is gone. I almost called her this morning. Her cell phone number is still programmed in my phone. My mind switches from one topic to another and then reality hits so hard and suddenly reminds me that—my mother is gone," Renee said, as she continued boohooing and crying like a baby.

Joel got up, sat next to Renee and put his arm around her. This was his way of offering compassion and forgiveness. "I don't know how much being here with me helps. It might be adding to your stress and anxiety, but I hope this makes you feel a little better. I forgive you for cheating and for walking out on me."

Renee hadn't felt so comfortable or safe in weeks. She rested her head against Joel's head and let out a soft sigh of relief. Within a couple of seconds Joel heard footsteps headed toward his front door. He became so anxious that he wished he could stop time or become invisible. There was a tiny knock at his front door and then it opened. Erin stepped into Joel's living room. She saw Joel with his arms wrapped around a crying woman and she instinctively knew it was his ex-girlfriend, Renee. Her blood was boiling and she had to fight to hold back her emotions. *What the hell was going on?*

Chapter 14

Erin's initial reaction was to bring the drama worse than an ignorant guest on the Jerry Springer show. The sight of Joel consoling another woman was disturbing. But instead of acting real ghetto, Erin decided to use her brain and excellent coping skills. She softened her look of uneasiness and annoyance because she didn't know the cause of Renee's unmistakable sadness. The last thing Erin wanted was to be an embarrassment to herself or Joel. She tried her best not to jump to conclusions, even though all sorts of ideas were already bouncing around in her head.

Erin thought to herself, *God, please don't let another man do this to me again. I don't know if my heart could take another letdown so soon. I have faith in You and Joel. I'm attractive and confident. There's no need for me to act like a fool. There has to be a legitimate reason for this.*

A look of uneasiness was plastered on Joel's face. His eyes were apologetic. He sat motionless, with his arm still draped around Renee. He thought it was best that he act natural because he didn't want to appear guilty. As Joel looked at Erin he was relieved that he didn't see any obvious signs of anger or hostility.

Joel was about to speak, but words flowed from Erin's mouth first. Appearing very poised and polite she said, "I'm sorry for interrupting. I shouldn't have barged in here like that. Joel, I just wanted to see what the holdup was, and to let you know that the movers are almost done. I'll be across the hall."

Joel stood up and said, "Erin, wait. You don't have to go, and you don't have to apologize for anything. It's fine that you felt comfortable enough to just come right in. You're not interrupting anything and I don't have anything to hide. This is my ex, blah, blah, blah."

With plenty of attitude Renee asked, "What?"

"I mean—this is Renee." Then Joel turned to Renee and said, "This is my beautiful friend and hopefully soon-to-be girlfriend, Erin."

Erin and Renee reluctantly exchanged greetings.

Erin flashed a facial expression that said, *Don't mess with me and my man.*

Renee's facial expression said, *He was mine first.*

Joel knew that he had to neutralize the situation.

He said, "Renee's mother passed away last night and I was just trying to console her."

Erin said, "I'm so sorry to hear about your loss. I can't begin to imagine how hard it must be to lose your mother." Erin walked over to Renee and gave her a hug. "I'll keep you and your family in my prayers."

Renee was surprised by Erin's kindness. "Thank you. I know this is an awkward situation for all of us. Please don't be too hard on Joel. He was just being a friend."

"Oh, I'm not worried at all. He's a good guy." Erin smiled and asked jokingly, "Do you think I can trust him?"

"Girl, you don't have a thing to worry about. Joel is so special. You can call him Mr. Monogamy." Her eyes began to water again. "What else can I say? He's polite, considerate, has a good sense of humor and a positive outlook on life. The physical stuff is obvious. He's different from the average guy on the street. I'm sure you could tell that when you first met."

"Yeah, that's what I told my girlfriend last night. He's definitely a special guy."

Renee wouldn't be Renee unless she dug for a little dirt. She tried to act casual and asked, "Erin, how long have y'all known each other?"

Erin replied, "We just met yesterday."

Renee hoped that Erin would have said that she and Joel knew each other a lot longer. She wanted proof that she wasn't the only one who had cheated. She managed to act surprised and said, "Wow! I bet you feel like you've known him for a long time already."

"Definitely. We had this instant connection. Joel has an easygoing personality."

Joel's modesty made him interrupt. "All right. Y'all are gonna pump my head up so big that I won't be able to fit it through that doorway."

Erin said, "You deserve to be praised, because if you were a dog then we'd definitely be dogging you."

Renee tried to cheer up a bit and said, "Uh-huh, real bad. You know how we do."

Joel said, "I believe it."

Renee said, "This is sad because guys are so used to getting bashed that they don't even know how to accept praise."

Erin put her arm around Joel and said, "Poor baby. If you continue to be good to me then I promise to praise you every day."

Joel gave Erin an affectionate hug and a kiss on the lips.

There was an awkward look on Renee's face. Her mouth began to twitch. She felt bad that she hadn't put forth the effort to make things work between her and Joel. Jealousy flared for a few seconds when she sensed the awesome chemistry Erin and Joel shared. Renee could see that physically they clearly made a better couple than she and Joel ever made.

Renee turned toward Joel and said, "It was good seeing you again. I'll call you with the funeral arrangements as soon as they're made. Erin, it was a pleasure meeting you. You're really pretty and the two of you are blessed to have each other."

"Thank you, Renee. I appreciate the compliment. I was

just standing here thinking that you're really pretty. You look just like—"

"I know, Beyoncé," Renee said arrogantly.

Erin was about to say that Renee looked like one of her co-workers, but Renee took things to another level of beauty. Erin tried her best to play it off. Her eyes widened and she tilted her head slightly. "Uh-huh, I can really see it now." She smiled and said, "Go 'head, Beyoncé."

Renee smiled and said, "I really look like her when I'm wearing my makeup. Well, I'm outta here. I still have to head over to Northwest Hospital to see my sister."

With his arm still around Erin, Joel said, "All right, Renee, take it easy."

Erin tightened her embrace around Joel's waist, smiled and waved good-bye.

Renee smiled back, but as soon as she was on the opposite side of the door her smile quickly turned into a frown. Loneliness and despair escorted her to her Escalade. She had thought that she would find Joel down in the dumps and completely miserable. Her real reason for stopping by was to see if she could rekindle something—anything with Joel. Her heart hurt like crazy because deep down inside she knew that Joel was gone forever. She got in her truck and drove away, her vision blurred by tears.

Chapter 15

All of Erin's possessions were officially moved into her apartment. Joel was blown away by how luxurious Erin and Kenya's apartment looked. The last time he was there it was just a blank canvas, and now it was picture perfect. The place had its own personality and identity—warm and eclectic. Erin acted like an anxious mother introducing her precious newborn baby to the world for the first time. She gave Joel a warm but unassuming smile and he automatically showered Erin with praise and admiration for her apartment. She was able to relax a little, but she still felt the need to explain things.

Erin's furniture had an ultra-modern appeal. Joel ran his hand across the custom-designed contoured black leather sofa. He took note of the detail and unique craftsmanship of the wooden cocktail table and matching side tables. He sat on one of the leather armchairs that conveyed style and comfort. What captured Joel's attention most as he looked around the living room was the entertainment console and armoire that was accentuated by abstract sculptures and colorful, exquisite hand-blown glass art.

The movers had completed their job and asked that Erin do a walkthrough, to make sure that her furniture that required assembly was properly done and the rest was positioned the way she wanted. It only took a few minutes for her to give the movers her approval and they headed off to their next job.

Erin showed Joel the rest of the apartment. They started out in the dining area and kitchen and then headed to the bedrooms. Kenya's bedroom was pretty modest, with a queen-sized bed and white lacquer furniture. Naturally Joel found Erin's bedroom to be the more appealing of the two. She had a queen-sized bed with contemporary solid oak furniture. Erin's bed looked inviting to Joel, even though she hadn't put any linen on it yet. She was busy explaining something about the apartment when Joel approached Erin from behind, wrapped his arms around her and planted a kiss on the side of her neck.

At first Erin was really focused on explaining certain details of her apartment, like hanging pictures and maybe painting to add a little color to the walls. Now she couldn't concentrate on anything else except how good Joel felt. His kisses made her so wet that she had to feel Joel inside of her again. He was addictive.

Joel pulled up her sundress and bent her over the bed. He slid her black thong aside. He penetrated her with his right thumb, reached forward a bit with the fingers of the same hand and stimulated her clitoris, using a slow and then vigorous motion. Erin loved how good Joel's hand felt. She moaned, whined and begged to feel his hard dick inside.

Joel had hoped to get in a quickie at some point, and this was the perfect opportunity. He reached in his front pocket, pulled out a condom and slid it on. He tapped his hardness against Erin's ass a few times and then thrust it inside and gave her the fuck she had been looking for.

As they both got closer to finding release, Joel turned Erin around and lay her on the bed. He angled her on the corner edge of the mattress. He penetrated her deeply and used the mattress to make Erin bounce right back at him with the exact force and quickness he liked.

He asked, "You like that?"

Erin screamed with pleasure. "Ah, yeah! Mmmmm. Yeah, I . . . like . . . it . . . rough."

At least forty minutes passed before Erin and Joel finished what had started as a quickie.

The heat and humidity outside had returned with a vengeance. The temperature had reached a scorching ninety-six degrees and the staggering humidity was at one hundred percent by the time Erin and Joel left their building to drive downtown. Heat waves rippled like flags caught up in a steady breeze. When they reached his Jeep, Joel opened the passenger side door for Erin. She hesitated to get in right away because the air was so stifling, but eventually climbed inside with a little reassurance from Joel.

He drove away with the windows down for a couple of minutes, and by that time the air conditioner kicked out enough cool air to keep him and Erin comfortable. As they rode along the beltway, 92 Q premiered a new Jay-Z song. The beat, along with an accelerated tempo and Jay's lyrical flow, made them instantly fall in love with the song. The rhythm overtook them. Without even noticing Joel was speeding, accelerating with tempo of the song and swerving from lane to lane. Joel's reckless driving scared Erin half to death. Her fear of being maimed or dying quickly brought them back to reality.

When Erin and Joel arrived downtown they lucked out and found a metered parking space that was really close to the Inner Harbor. Joel avoided paying the outrageous garage or parking lot rates. Any means of saving a little cash put an instant smile on his face. Erin was happy they didn't have too far to walk because she wasn't trying to break a sweat if she could avoid it.

The sidewalks were lined with people walking in every direction. The fact that the Orioles had a home game made the area even more congested. Excitement was in the air, along with the thick and rich aroma of spices and pit-barbequed meats. Erin and Joel looked and felt confident and comfortable with their arms around each other for the first time in public. The sun beamed down on them as they walked past the Renaissance Hotel and the Gallery Mall on their way to Legal Sea Foods.

Baltimore's Inner Harbor is a lively waterfront tourist attraction and Legal Sea Foods is one the most popular restaurants in the area. Typically the restaurant would be packed with a hungry crowd on a busy Saturday afternoon like this, but luckily there was only a moderate crowd, so Erin and Joel only had to wait a few minutes to be seated. As they stood in front of the hostess station while they waited for their table, classic '80s pop music played in the background like a soft whisper and two flat-screen televisions above the bar were tuned to a battle between the Baltimore Orioles and the New York Yankees.

It was hot as hell outside, but after being inside for a few minutes it felt as if the air conditioner was set to subzero. Joel noticed that Erin felt a chill. Heads turned as Joel switched positions and held Erin from behind. He gave her a simple but sensual kiss that started on her cheek, moved toward her ear and then down her neck.

Joel brought his lips back toward Erin's ear and said, "You look so beautiful and sexy that I just can't help myself." He looked up for a quick second. "I think people are watching us."

She whispered, "I don't care. Don't stop. Hold me tighter. That feels good to me."

"This entire date is gonna be about foreplay. Is that all right with you?"

Erin smiled and said, "Yeah."

Joel continued to tantalize Erin's skin with his lips. She closed her eyes, purred like a kitten and melted from the warm sensations he created. The passion that the two shared was more than obvious and the customers couldn't help sneaking a peek. Some of the men seated around the restaurant looked disapproving, while others appeared to admire his bold public display of affection. The majority of the women who witnessed the passion got turned on, and desired the same type of attention. Everyone assumed that Erin and Joel were deeply in love.

The hostess got their attention and led them to their table. When they arrived immediately Joel pulled out a seat for Erin. She was impressed and gave him extra points for constantly making her feel special and for knowing how to treat her like a lady.

When Joel took his seat the hostess placed menus in front of them. But they didn't look at the menus right away because there was just so much to take in. From his seat, Joel had a perfect window view, where he watched crowds of interesting looking people pass by the restaurant. He looked across the street toward the harbor and noticed the 1854 Civil War ship, USS *Constellation*. Its mast extended high above the Pratt and Light Street pavilions. In the distance he saw a huge new construction site with an enormous crane that was used to build overpriced condos on the southern end of the harbor.

Erin faced the restaurant's interior. She looked around, admiring the restaurant's ocean-themed art deco design. There was a giant mural of an underwater scene on the back wall and two huge arches that were shaped like whale tails that extended from one side of the room to the other.

Tinted windows and dim lighting set the relaxed mood while "Every Breath You Take" by the Police, played in the background. The entire waitstaff was dressed in all black. They zoomed by with clockwork precision as Erin and Joel studied their menus. A few seconds later their waitress, Amy, came over and introduced herself. She was a friendly and energetic all-American beauty with *red* lips, *white* skin and *blue* eyes.

Joel ordered lemonade and Erin ordered an unsweetened iced tea. Amy returned a few minutes later with their drinks then took their appetizer and entrée orders.

Erin said, "For my appetizer I'll have the curry-battered coconut shrimp. For my entrée I'll have the surf and turf, with the three double-stuffed baked shrimp and steamed broccoli."

Amy smiled and said, "Excellent choice. How would you like your steak?"

"Medium-well, please."

Amy turned her attention toward Joel. "For you, sir?"

"I'd like the jumbo shrimp cocktail for my appetizer and for my entrée I'll have the Maryland lump crab cakes with steamed broccoli."

"Another excellent choice. Please don't hesitate to ask for anything else you may need."

Erin and Joel both thanked Amy.

As their waitress walked away Joel asked Erin, "Have you ever been here before?"

"No. I've always wanted to, but never put forth the effort to make it happen. Thanks for making this happen."

They smiled at each other and held hands across the table.

"Don't even mention it. I'm used to coming here in the wintertime. Too bad it's so hot out, because the cream of crab soup is really good."

"Trust me, it's cold enough in here to eat hot soup."

They both laughed.

Joel drank his lemonade while Erin added Splenda and squeezed lemon juice into her iced tea.

Erin said, "I feel so sorry for Renee."

"So do I."

"She seems to be a nice person. I know that her mother passed and all, but I think she came around this morning looking for a little bit more than sympathy."

"She was. I'm not even going to lie, but that's all I was willing to offer her. I think I made it clear that things were over between me and her. Hopefully she was able to find closure. You walking in on us with her crying and seeing me with my arm around her was awkward. I appreciate you being so understanding and not jumping to conclusions."

"No problem. At first I didn't know what to think. When I

saw your face I knew that it wasn't anything romantic going on, but Renee's facial expression showed mixed emotions. I knew she was dealing with losing you and some other kind of tragedy. Would you be as understanding if you walked in on me and my ex in a similar situation?"

Joel made a silly face and said, "Yeah. Of course I would have."

"Seriously?"

"I dunno. Probably not. You know how guys act in situations like that."

"No, tell me."

"Crazy. Mad. Violent. Nah, I'm just kiddin'."

"No you're not."

"Okay. Either I would have been extremely calm or would have completely zapped out on both of y'all."

"I can imagine you being calm, but not zapping out or being mad at all. You know what they say about quiet, easygoing men."

"No, what do they say?"

"We gotta watch the quiet ones because when y'all get mad a completely different side comes out. The other thing I heard is to never underestimate quiet men in the bedroom. This afternoon was a perfect example of that. I enjoyed you so much. I knew you were good, but I didn't know you were gonna put it on me like that. You got buck wild. I'm still weak in the knees."

Joel smiled and said, "You make me act like that."

Erin and Joel cut their conversation short because Amy returned with their appetizers. They sampled each other's shrimp and shared small talk. The more Erin and Joel talked, the more they seemed to have in common. They both admitted to being neat freaks. For the most part, they shared the same political, religious and spiritual views. They were both Democrats. Although they didn't go to church on a regular basis now, they were raised going to Baptist churches. They also had similar tastes in food, movies and music.

Erin and Joel felt stuffed after finishing their entrées, but somehow they found enough room to share a slice of chocolate layer cake. The chocolate was so rich—a natural aphrodisiac. Erin took off her shoes and ran her bare foot up and down Joel's leg. Amy brought the check while Erin fed Joel chocolate cake and used her foot to provide an intimate massage. Erin found humor in the fact that Joel needed a few extra minutes to stand after paying the check.

Chapter 16

When Erin and Joel left Legal Sea Foods they wound up walking across the street to the National Aquarium. Joel got a shock at the ticket booth, because the admission price for two was close to fifty dollars. He was tempted to ask for a discount, but went ahead and paid the full admission price because he didn't want to appear broke or too cheap. More than anything he didn't want to embarrass himself in front of the ticket booth cashier or Erin.

Bright colors and exotic sea creatures set the scene inside the aquarium. Although both Erin and Joel had been to the aquarium numerous times, the exhibits always seemed to amaze them. Erin whipped out her digital camera and took plenty of pictures. She took some candid shots of Joel. A lady passing by offered to take a few shots of Erin and Joel posing together.

As they moved from exhibit to exhibit, Joel stopped in front of a colorful display of tropical fish and asked the question he had been dying to ask. "Why did you and your ex break up?"

Erin watched as the beautiful fish moved through the water with grace and ease. She snapped a picture and calmly said, "That's a long story with a quick and simple answer. He was cheating."

"Why is that usually the case? That's what did it for me and blah . . . blah . . . blah. We had our differences, but the cheating completely did us in."

"Same story with me and blah . . . blah . . . blah. It's funny looking back on it now. I can't even believe I was ever interested in a jerk like that. What did I see in him? We had nothing in common. He constantly complained and belittled me."

"About what?"

"I'm ashamed to say."

"You can tell me anything. I think we're friends now, not to mention lovers."

Erin smiled and said, "True. All right, I'm just gonna put it out there. I wasn't freaky or sexually adventurous enough for him, and eventually he found what he was looking for somewhere else. He loved running the streets and hanging out with his stupid buddies. At first he used them to back up his lies. I suspected he was seeing other women because I noticed that his stories and alibis didn't match his friends'."

"Sounds like he didn't know how to appreciate you. Sometimes it takes the right man to bring out certain qualities in a woman."

"You're definitely the right man for me because you bring out so many qualities in me." She took a deep breath then let it out. "I'm willing to do anything with you sexually . . . anything you can think of."

Joel smiled and his eyes widened. "Anything?"

Erin looked into Joel's eyes and said, "Anything. That says a lot about my comfort level with you and shows how much I trust you."

"I trust you too. You don't have to try to overcompensate to please me. Whatever happened in the past is in the past. If you're willing to do anything sexually, I hope it's not just for my pleasure, but something we both could enjoy together. I'd hate for us to do something that would compromise your trust or comfort level."

Erin said, "Man, you're so considerate and understanding. I know exactly what you mean. I just want to be a little more adventurous and creative. I'm thinking about ways of maximizing our pleasure."

"I like the sound of that."

Erin was thinking about a threesome, but Joel had no idea what she was really talking about. They kissed.

Joel wasn't in a hurry to leave because he was trying to make the most of this experience. He and Erin found a dark secluded spot near the shark exhibit. They did their usual thing and interacted like horny new lovers. As planned, the foreplay continued with hugs, kisses and more sexually charged conversations. They settled down a little at the dolphin show, but the action picked up again inside of the aquarium's tropical rain forest. The waterfalls, trees and exotic wildlife seemed to bring out a different side of them.

Eventually Erin and Joel left the aquarium and headed over to the Power Plant. The huge brick building with its trademark four giant smokestacks sits on the east end of the Inner Harbor. It used to be an actual power plant and now housed the ESPN Zone, Hard Rock Café, Gold's Gym and Barnes & Noble.

Erin and Joel walked through the doors of Barnes & Noble and inhaled the fresh mixed aroma of Starbuck's coffee and brand-new books. People lined the aisles, browsing through the thousands of books. She noticed a poster for an author's book signing and discussion, which had just started on the second level. The book was called, *Do Your Thing Girl ... A Sistah's Guide to Love and Relationships* by Dr. Thelma Rudolph.

Erin and Joel decided to stick around and check out the book signing. They made their way to the escalator. It seemed that a bunch of people were headed in the same direction. As they ascended the escalator, it became more and more obvious that Dr. Rudolph was a celebrity author. They overheard two ladies in front of them say that over the years Dr. Rudolph had been featured on numerous nationally syndicated talk radio shows, BET and TV One to promote her other books. Last week she was on the *CBS Early Show* and *The View*. Like most authors she was still waiting for her career-defining moment to be on *Oprah*.

Erin and Joel walked past the information desk and could see a huge crowd of people both seated and standing near the music section. Then they saw the author, a petite and very sophisticated-looking, forty-something black woman reading words of wisdom. She stood behind a podium talking to a group comprised mostly of young to middle-aged black women with smiling faces, nodding their heads in agreement. There were a few guys in the crowd and even they seemed to appreciate what Dr. Rudolph read.

She read briefly from her book on a number of topics, including: true love and intimacy; communication; getting to know yourself; finding a mate; and getting to know your mate. After reading the last portion, she asked the audience for questions and comments.

The women in the crowd seemed to ask a million questions related to communication. A couple of women commented about their personal experiences and shared relationship horror stories. The majority of the crowd asked questions about true love and intimacy. One woman was about to classify herself in the desperately-seeking-a-man category and asked about finding a mate. The discussion went on for about twenty minutes or so, and then Erin raised her hand and was instantly acknowledged.

She said, "You haven't mentioned anything related to my question, but I'm sure it's covered somewhere in your book. How soon is too soon to sleep with a man?"

Joel's eyes widened and he looked at Erin with this why-would-you-ask-that-question-in-front-of-all-these-people expression.

Dr. Rudolph smiled and said, "Oh, I see somebody might be getting lucky tonight."

Everybody looked at Joel and started laughing. He laughed too, but looked kind of embarrassed.

Dr. Rudolph said, "There is a chapter in the book on when it's appropriate to have sex for the first time. I love that question and that's why I titled the book, *Do Your Thing Girl*. So, go 'head and do your thing, girl." The audience laughed again. "I'm just kidding. Knowing when to sleep with a man for the first time is an individual thing. Only you can decide when it's right to have sex for the first time. We're all different . . . because of customs, traditions and religions . . . just to name a few variables. In the old days—that means the 1960s and before—back then the majority of women waited months, or in some cases until marriage, to sleep with a man. Nowadays marriage isn't so popular and women are jumping right into bed on the first date." Erin looked embarrassed now. "I'm speaking generally, of course. If that's your preference, then fine. However, most relationships that begin that way are instantly placed in jeopardy of failing. The faster a woman gives it up, the less likely the guy is to stick around or to value their relationship. Keep in mind that there is always that rare exception. I know of a wonderful couple that slept together on their first date and recently celebrated their forty-fifth wedding anniversary." The crowd oohed and aahed. Dr. Rudolph continued, "My parents hate when I tell that story because they don't think everybody needs to know their business." The crowd burst out laughing again. Some of the slower people were still looking around asking, "What? What? What did she say?"

Dr. Rudolph mentioned what she called a woman's golden numbers, her age and the number of men she had slept with in her lifetime. "Ideally the number of men a woman has slept with should never exceed her age. Giving up the goodies on the first date tends to throw your numbers off quite a bit, considering that the average single woman between the ages of eighteen to twenty-five goes on three to four first dates per year. Every time a woman sleeps with a man she is giving away a part of herself. That's why we find so many young women who are burned out and have nothing else to give before they're even thirty. I want to share something with you briefly, just to give you an example of the future of sex and relationships in our community. I met a little girl at one of my teen talks and her golden numbers were 13-13. Believe it or not, she was proud of her numbers. She looked at me and asked why should she care about the number of boys or men she sleeps with as long as she doesn't become pregnant or contract HIV. To me that was extremely sad, because the odds are stacked against her and she hasn't even reached high school." Dr. Rudolph paused for a few seconds and sipped from her bottled water. "Before any woman sleeps with a man she should get to know him. I mean, get to know him beyond his name, address, astrological sign, favorite TV show, shoe size and so on. Before getting intimate with a man, she should ask whether there is any history of sexually transmitted diseases. Of course she won't get the truth, but that's why we always use condoms, right ladies?" The women in the crowd all agreed in perfect harmony. "Also determine whether or not he is possibly the jealous, possessive or controlling type . . . this cuts down dramatically on the likelihood of him being a stalker. Make sure he doesn't overreact or is quick tempered. Ask about his parents and siblings to see if there is any family history of violence or abuse. Feel free to ask the following questions: Does he have a criminal record? Does he have a history of verbal or physical abuse against previous girlfriends or other women? How does he handle stress? Even ask yourself questions: Do you feel comfortable around him, or are you walking on eggshells because you're afraid of him? Does he have weapons like guns, knives, or brass knuckles?" A few people in the crowd laughed. "I heard some laughs, but if a man is constantly displaying weapons, that's a hint that he doesn't have a problem using them . . . on you even. If a woman can't answer at least ninety percent of these questions, then it's too soon to sleep with a man."

Everyone really seemed to be impressed with Dr. Rudolph's advice, and how well she was able to simplify everything. Erin and Joel hung around the bookstore for at least another hour listening to her. As she continued giving relationship advice Erin felt more and more convinced that Joel was the ideal man for her. She momentarily shifted the idea of the threesome to the back of her mind. When the discussion ended Erin bought a signed copy of Dr. Rudolph's book.

After leaving the bookstore, Erin and Joel walked along the waterfront holding hands. Erin took a brief moment to call Kenya and check up on her. Kenya was surprised and excited to hear from Erin. They kept their conversation brief and pretty basic. There wasn't any mention of their sexy conversation or talk of a threesome. Kenya's anxiety level seemed to be well-controlled compared to the night before. She said hi to Joel, reminded them she'd be home soon, and that ended their conversation.

As the day wore on into evening, the temperature had become a little more bearable. Erin and Joel decided to rent a paddleboat. They paddled their way out into the middle of the harbor, and then near the piers to get a better look at some of the sailboats, powerboats and yachts. From the water they watched a couple of street performers sing and play their guitars for money.

Erin said, "Even though we're not on a yacht, I think this is really nice . . . very calming and romantic. Being out on the water like this and seeing this city from an entirely different perspective makes me appreciate it more."

"Well, you know going aboard a yacht would probably give you an even better perspective. If you want, I can make that happen too. I know this little boat pales in comparison."

"I'm not concerned about the boat. This is about you and the way you make me feel."

Joel smiled and said, "Watch out, you're starting to scare me. I wish you could see the look in your eyes."

"What? How do they look?"

"You wouldn't believe me if I told you."

"Tell me. What do you see?"

"You've got the look of love."

Erin blushed and said, "Is it that obvious?"

"Yeah, but don't worry, I like it."

"I really like you, Joel. Oh my God, you make me feel so good. I can't remember when I laughed and smiled so much. Thank you."

"You don't have to thank me. You give me the same feeling."

"This feels so right. Initially it scared me, because we seemed to be moving at light speed. Now I realize that maybe this is the proper pace for us."

"What made you realize that?"

"This date. You're really patient. Look at all of the things we've done so far today and there's no telling what we'll do tonight. I've been comparing you to every guy I've seen today and you're without a doubt the best thing I've seen. You have a sexy coolness about you that drives me crazy and makes me appreciate the simple things in life. This is the best date I've ever had."

"I have to agree with you. This has really been a nice date."

"Dr. Rudolph said that we should never seek validation from a man because it starts within. But you validate me and make me feel whole."

Joel smiled. "Wow, I never had anyone tell me anything like that before. I don't even know what to say. That's a major compliment and I appreciate it."

"There's something else that I wanna share with you."

Joel continued to smile. "Go ahead, I'm listening."

"I was hiding or trying to deny my feelings. Hearing those other women talk about their relationship horror stories, and hearing a professional basically describe you when she mentioned the essential traits of an ideal mate—you're intelligent, sexy, sensual, creative, willing to listen and express your feelings—I was sitting there thinking, what more could I ask for? That sounds so much like Joel. I'm not used to a drama-free man who is willing to make himself so available so fast. You seem to have your priorities in order, and you made me feel something special last night. It went beyond a sexual feeling. We're developing a bond that comes from true intimacy, not just sex. I swear I could feel your spirit inside of me. We bonded physically, emotionally and now I have a strong sense of wanting to commit to you."

Joel was speechless, because Erin said exactly what he wanted and needed to hear. He didn't say a word, he just leaned in and gave Erin a long, passionate kiss that expressed every joyous and heartfelt word he wanted to say.

Part Two

Try Tri-Love

Chapter 17

Joel felt more certain than ever that he and Erin could have a successful relationship. They had been together for almost a week and had hardly spent more than an hour at a time apart. At first they spent the majority of their time relaxing at Joel's apartment, but Erin's place required some minor finishing touches before Kenya arrived on Friday. During the first part of the week Erin and Joel painted a few walls and hung paintings. By the time Wednesday rolled around, Erin had her apartment in the best shape possible. She felt more comfortable with her place and invited Joel over for some rest and relaxation. What that really meant was she wanted him to come over to help break in her new bed. Wednesday was so much fun that she invited him over for dinner and a candlelight bubble bath on Thursday.

Shimmering golden candlelight illuminated Erin's bathroom as she and Joel soaked in soothing hot bathwater topped with loads of long-lasting bubbles. They sipped chilled champagne while Miles Davis blew his trumpet in the background to a tempo that was just as soothing as the scented aloe-and-citrus bubble bath. Erin added a few squirts of baby oil to give the water a more pleasing texture and consistency.

Erin lay at one end of the tub and Joel lay at the other end with the faucet right by the side of his face. They repositioned themselves, because he looked uncomfortable and they both needed to feel more body contact. Joel moved to the opposite end of the tub and Erin sat between his legs. She lay back comfortably against his hard muscular body.

The water made their bodies feel silky smooth and irresistible to the touch. That moment was all about stimulating, touching, and kissing. Erin wrapped Joel's legs around her and massaged his sculpted calf and thigh muscles. She arched her back, reached above and behind with both hands to massage Joel's neck. At first his hands roamed, until he felt Erin's erect eraser-sized nipples. He squeezed her breasts with his strong hands and pinched her nipples ever so gently. His hands moved in slow motion up and down Erin's abdomen and then back to her excited breasts. He was tempted to explore the pleasure in her valley. His hands moved downward and massaged Erin's inner thighs with an intense rhythmic motion.

Joel zoned out for a moment and became the slipping-sliding motion of his hands. Erin got lost in the pleasing sensations he created. She couldn't wait to feel the silky smoothness of his hands in and around her vagina. He sensed the anticipation building, because Erin began to shift her body in hopes of making the slightest amount of contact in her erogenous zone with at least one of Joel's fingers. He eventually gave in and allowed two of his fingers to graze Erin's clitoris. He understood her body in ways that no one else did. Joel knew exactly how much Erin yearned to feel the stimulating touch of both of his hands. Minute by minute, he increased the pleasure by using more fingers and applying alternating pressures down there.

Erin said, "Oh my God. That's it . . . just like that."

Joel teased and asked, "Like that?"

In an airy tone Erin said, "Oh yeah . . . just like that. Please don't stop. That feels so good."

Joel was incredibly turned on by Erin's arousal and loved the way she reacted to his touch. He played with her clitoris with one hand and traced her vaginal opening with the other. Her body signaled that it was time to be penetrated. He provided the perfect external pleasure and gradually introduced the internal stimulation she desired. Erin could feel Joel's fingers as they explored and zeroed right in on her G-spot.

She arched her back even more and said, "That's it . . . right there . . . my spot!"

Erin's body shuddered. Joel kissed and sucked the back and sides of Erin's neck. She became overwhelmed with pleasure. Joel was so excited that he came.

Erin's insides tightened, quivered and then tightened again. She moaned loudly. After that came a round of additional body spasms and a lot of heavy breathing. Minutes later Erin and Joel made their way to her bed.

Early Friday morning Erin rose with the sun. She looked and felt beautiful. Getting up early was all about making sure everything was in order for Kenya's arrival later that evening. Joel was awakened by the sounds of dresser drawers opening and closing, along with Erin's sporadic movements at the foot of the bed. He opened his eyes and saw her bent over at the foot of the bed wearing a tangerine-colored bra and panty set. He realized that she was putting clothes away and folding towels and linen.

Erin stood up to fold a towel and noticed that Joel was awake. She smiled and said, "Good morning. Sorry to wake you so early."

Joel yawned and then returned a smile. "Good morning. It's okay. I don't need all this sleep anyway. I don't wanna become lazy."

"That's good to hear. Neither do I. That's one reason I decided to get out of bed so early. You wanna head over to the New Town Diner for breakfast?"

"Yeah, that sounds good." Joel gave Erin a sexy gaze and said, "C'mere."

Erin blushed and walked toward Joel. When she got close enough he kissed her on the lips.

Joel said, "You look so sexy in your underwear."

"And you look sexy in my bed, wearing nothing but that smile."

Joel slapped Erin on the butt and said, "Damn, I love that bounce."

"If you keep reminding me of how much I'm bouncing, wiggling and jiggling back there you're gonna make me feel fat."

"Shoot, there's nothing wrong with being fat as long as it's distributed in all of the right places."

"Is it distributed in the right places now?"

"Yes. God, yes. It couldn't be better."

"You're crazy. Let's see what you think of Kenya when you see her later. She's got some junk in her trunk, too."

"I ain't thinking about the junk or her trunk. All I see is you. Why are you always promoting Kenya?"

Erin shrugged. "I dunno. She's attractive and she's going to be around us a lot. I just want you to know that I'm very secure with our situation. You're a man and it's okay if you look or let your imagination run wild."

Joel laughed and said, "You are so funny. You don't have to prepare yourself for me to start gawking at your buddy. I have a lot of self-control. And you're right, I am a man with a wild and overactive imagination. The only thing that would mess me up is if you and Kenya were bouncing around in front of me wearing matching underwear."

Erin displayed a mischievous grin. "We might have to do that for you."

Joel didn't take Erin seriously at all. He dismissed whatever she said because he thought this was her little way of feeling him out, to see whether or not she could trust him around Kenya. "Uh-huh. I'll believe it when I see it." He shook his head and said, "You're crazy. What else is on your mind?"

"Ah, let me see." She paused as her mind moved away from the sublime and got back to the normalcy of everyday life. "Do you mind if we make a quick stop by Wal-Mart after break-fast?"

Joel laughed. "That's fine with me, but you know good and well that there's no such thing as a quick stop by Wal-Mart. You'll go up in there with one or two things in mind and come out with over twenty items, half of which you didn't really need at all."

Erin laughed and said, "That's not true. All I need are some cleaning supplies and maybe some new bath towels."

"Yeah right, we'll see. I can see the list growing in your mind right now."

Erin and Joel enjoyed a delicious breakfast of French toast, home fries, chicken sausage and orange juice at the New Town Diner. Afterward they headed to Wal-Mart. Just as Joel had predicted, Erin had a shopping cart full of items for every room in her and Kenya's apartment. Being in a family store like Wal-Mart and seeing young couples with their children made Joel think. He saw a woman pushing a little girl in a shopping cart who was the spitting image of her mother. Seeing them, he imagined having a little girl who looked just like Erin. A few minutes later he saw a little boy with his father, picking out a baseball bat and glove. That made him think about his father, and how much he wished they could have spent quality time together like that. Joel's mind began to drift. He thought of his future and at the same time missed his past.

Out of nowhere he asked, "You wanna meet my parents today? I think it'd be a good idea for them to meet the woman I plan on marrying one day."

Erin was stunned, because she had no idea where Joel's mind was. He had a habit of just blurting out his random thoughts, and Erin hadn't quite gotten used to it yet.

She said, "I'd love to meet your parents, but not today. I want to make a good impression so I need a little more time to prepare."

"What are you talking about? They would love you . . . just the way you look right now."

"This isn't my best. I'm a mess, and they'd probably pick up on it right away, especially your mother. You know how mothers are with their sons. She'd probably think I wasn't good enough for you. Plus, my anxiety level is already high enough because of Kenya's arrival. I hope she'll like the apartment, because she agreed to pay rent on a place she hasn't even seen."

"I understand. But I need to head by their house sometime today because I haven't seen or talked to them in a while."

"Well, it's probably best that I don't go. I'm sure that you and your parents have a lot of catching up to do."

"You're right, we do have a lot of catching up to do."

"Y'all don't need me all up in your business."

Joel laughed and said, "All right, I'll go by myself, but you'll be the main topic of our conversation."

Erin thought Joel was joking when he talked about her being the woman he was going to marry one day. She didn't take him seriously. But he was serious—he really wanted her to meet his parents soon. She was the type of woman that was worth showing off to everybody.

Joel arrived at his parents' house a little after eleven o'clock in the morning. The front door was closed and the air conditioner was running. His mother's wind chime hardly moved in the stagnant air. From the front porch he could hear a gospel song called "Jesus Can Work It Out" coming from the kitchen, playing as loud as a live concert. He used his key to get inside. When he stepped inside he smelled the aroma of fresh herbs and spices in the air, and saw his mother standing at the kitchen counter preparing lunch or getting an early start on dinner. She loved to keep herself busy throughout the day. Cooking happened to be one of the things she did best.

Right away Joel noticed that the house was full of sunlight and felt very much alive with the spirit. The music and the bright sunlight were a sign of victory and happiness. Mrs. Davis rocked back and forth, singing her heart out. As soon as she saw Joel's face, she lit up and stopped what she was doing. She turned down the volume on her little boom box and walked toward Joel.

With a smile Joel said, "Hey, Ma. How've you been?"

She greeted him with a smile and threw in a warm, heartfelt motherly hug and kiss on his cheek. "I'm okay. How've you been?"

Joel stepped back and asked, "How do I look?"

His mother looked him up and down. "You look like your old self again. Guess you finally stopped worrying about that ole rotten Renee."

Joel liked the glow he saw in his mother's eyes. He wondered if he was responsible for it, but he didn't want to read too much into it. He simply answered, "Yup. I'm finally over her."

"Good." She started back toward the kitchen. "I was hoping now that school was out you'd find time to stop by here to check up on me."

Joel followed his mother into the kitchen. "I'm sorry. I've been really busy, that's all. That doesn't mean I haven't been thinking about you."

"Good, because I've been thinking about you a lot lately. You want a chicken salad sandwich on whole wheat? If not I can make something else if you'd like. I've got some spaghetti on the stove and some garlic bread in the oven."

"No thanks. I just ate breakfast not too long ago." Joel inhaled deeply and said, "Mmm. The spaghetti does smell good."

"Thanks." Mrs. Davis took a really good look at Joel and smiled again. "Look at you."

"What?"

"You really look handsome. Good to see you looking happy again."

"I've got a new woman in my life now."

In an instant a concerned look covered Mrs. Davis's face. "Oh Lord." She pressed her lips together and shook her head.

Joel frowned and his mother quickly changed her tone. She sighed gently. "I mean, sit down and tell me all about her. Is she anything like Renee?"

"No."

Joel was quickly reminded of Renee's mother's death. He was about to tell his mother about Mrs. Rhodes's passing, but he stopped himself. He hated being the bearer of bad news. The last thing he wanted to do was spoil his mother's bright and cheerful day.

Mrs. Davis smiled as she sat down at the kitchen table. "So, she's nothing like Renee. Oh, I like this one already. What's her name?"

"Erin. She's a beautiful third grade language arts teacher." He looked at his mother's face. He saw that familiar effortless beauty she constantly displayed. That was the same type of beauty that he saw every time he looked at his new love interest. "Erin reminds me a whole lot of you."

His words touched her heart. Mrs. Davis said, "That's sweet. Sounds like a quality woman."

"She is." Joel looked around and asked, "Where's Dad? He can't be at work. I thought he was trying to take it easy these days."

Mrs. Davis closed her eyes and pressed her lips together again. She looked like she was about to lose it, but she took a breath and maintained her composure. "Go 'head and finish telling me about Erin."

Joel looked suspicious. "I will, but is everything okay?"

"No, everything isn't okay." She looked down, then back at Joel. "Your father's gone."

His stomach dropped. "Gone? What do you mean *gone*?"

"He had a problem that he couldn't handle and thought it'd be best if he moved out to deal with it. Now that he's gone, I don't want him back."

"What are you talking about? Can you explain in plain English exactly what's going on?"

"Your father met some young girl at work and completely

lost his mind. She had the nerve to call here to tell me all about them, and how good he is to her and her two kids . . . two little boys."

"What's with that?"

"Don't ask me. She told me some other things that I won't even repeat. I never felt so numb in my life, because I knew the girl was telling the truth. I asked Theo what was going on, and at first that old fool tried to lie. Then eventually he admitted to everything the girl told me." She paused for a brief moment, then said, "We're getting divorced."

Joel couldn't believe his ears, and could hardly think straight. The word *divorced* echoed inside his head. In his mind, he heard a toilet flush and saw everything he believed in—the values and morals—swirling around in a tiny whirlpool and going down the drain. He felt like he wanted to reach inside and grab hold of something, but his father had turned everything into shit. He felt nauseated, because he wanted the kind of long-term loving relationship he thought his parents had. He thought of Erin and wondered if what she said about love being dead was true. It may have been true, because everything he knew about love was based on his parents' relationship, and now their love was gone.

Joel returned to reality and asked, "What? I can't believe this . . . a divorce after all these years? You seem awfully calm."

Mrs. Davis laughed and said, "Boy, that's the least of my worries. I can't make a grown man do what he doesn't wanna do. Theo moved out two weeks ago. I could have balled up and died, but I made a choice. I choose to go on living my life without him."

"I don't even know what to say. I'm hurt and disappointed."

"So am I. We just never know what the future might bring. Theo was probably cheating on me for years."

"Yeah, with that crazy work schedule of his . . . you just never know."

"Hold on, there's more drama."

Joel's eyes widened. "Like what?"

"I let your sorry brother and his girlfriend move in earlier this week. They're so sorry that the two of them are sleeping in Shawn's little twin bed together. They can't afford to buy a new bed. So I told them to take your old bed and push them together, but they're too lazy to do anything productive. I was thinking this morning that you are my everything . . . my reason for living, and I love you."

Joel was blown away by his mother's comment. "I love you, too. Sorry that you have so much on you. Is there anything I can do to help?"

"You're helping right now just by listening."

"I can talk to Shawn."

"Uh, that'd be a waste of breath."

Joel let out a loud sigh and said, "To be honest with you, I had no idea where Shawn was staying. Why would you let him and his girlfriend move in here with you? You must be looking for trouble."

"I just found myself trying to help out because they didn't have anywhere else to go."

"They're using you . . . taking advantage of the fact that Daddy's not around to kick their butts out of here. They wouldn't even have asked to move in if Daddy was still here. Are they paying you to live here?"

"I don't feel right making my child pay to live with me."

"He's a grown man, not a child. And what about his girlfriend, she's not your child. Is she giving you any money?"

"No. Not yet, anyway. The two of them went and applied for social services on Monday."

Joel shook his head and said, "They're using you, and drugs too. How were they making it before they moved in here?"

"That's the same thing I asked. They claimed that they got arrested and all of their assistance was cut off, and now they have to start all over again."

"Do you believe that?"

"You just never know with your brother. That's not all."

"Wow, what else could there be?"

"I hadn't called you for a while because I didn't want to burden you with my problems."

"I appreciate you being considerate and all, but this is too much for you to bear."

"That's not true. The Lord won't put more on me than I can bear."

"At least your faith is strong."

"And that will never change."

Joel braced himself and asked, "So what else is going on?"

Mrs. Davis took a deep breath and said, "I saw my doctor a few days before your father walked out, and she told me that I have cancer in my left breast."

"Oh no." Joel grabbed his mother and held her tight. She held him close like she did when he was a little boy. He felt a stinging sensation in his eyes. As he fought back the tears he silently prayed for the best. "I'm so sorry to hear about the breast cancer, but you're gonna be all right. Plenty of women have battled and survived breast cancer." He tried his best to convince his mother and himself that she'd be fine. "I know you're gonna be all right . . . you just have to be."

Joel and his mother shared the same type of optimism. She smiled and said, "I'm already all right. The cancer isn't that bad. You're the first person I've told. As a matter of fact, I've been trying not to give it too much thought."

"No. That's the worst thing you can do. You need to give this a lot of thought. What about surgery or some type of treatment?"

"I'm scheduled for surgery on Monday at nine o'clock in the morning at Sinai Hospital. They want me there at seven o'clock that same morning. And I'll start chemotherapy shortly after that."

"When were you going to tell me about this?"

"Soon." She paused as she felt her emotions getting the best of her. "I dunno, I'm so tired. And I'm afraid. I'm not afraid of dying. God already told me that this cancer won't be the thing that takes me away from here. I'm just afraid that when

they cut me open the cancer might be worse than they suspected, and they'll have to remove my entire breast and not
just the two lumps. But I don't want you to worry about me.
This is something that I have to learn to deal with on my
own."

"How can I not worry? And you don't have to deal with it on
your own. I'm here for you."

"I'm frustrated and at times disgusted with myself."

"Why?"

"Because I feel like I cheated myself out of so much. I
haven't really lived. What have I done? Nothing. Where have
I been? Nowhere."

Joel felt bad because he knew exactly what his mother
meant. He said, "You sacrificed so much for me, Shawn, and
Daddy. Now it's all about you. If you want to go on a trip to the
Caribbean or somewhere, I'll send you. Where do you wanna
go . . . Jamaica . . . Bahamas? I heard the Virgin Islands are
nice. What about Aruba?"

She shook her head and said, "No. I wanna go to Israel on a
pilgrimage to tour the Holy Land, and be baptized in the Jordan
River just like my Savior."

Joel felt chills run through his body. He instantly agreed to
help his mother finance the trip. He spent a few more hours
with his mother. They talked more—about Erin and about her
trip to the Holy Land—while eating Mrs. Davis's homemade
spaghetti and garlic bread. Joel hated to leave his mother, but
he wanted to get home in time to meet Kenya. Mrs. Davis saw
the guilt in his eyes. She reminded him that he had to go on
living his life with or without her. One of the last things his
mother told him that day was to live life to the fullest.

Chapter 18

Erin's place was immaculate, and could have easily been used as the development's model apartment. The calming scent of an air freshener called Jasmine Breeze flowed through the rooms. Erin rested her head in her favorite spot between Joel's chest and shoulder as they sat cuddled up on her sofa in front of the television watching *Oprah*. The volume was turned down low, loud enough to hear the show, but Erin was also listening for Kenya's arrival.

Joel didn't mention anything to Erin about all of his family's drama. For the moment he tried to clear his mind and put all of those issues on hold. He was good at managing stressful situations. That was one major reason he stayed so healthy. When Erin asked about his family he simply said that everything was all right.

While Joel was at his mother's house, Erin had found time to stop by the mall for a new outfit, a manicure and pedicure. She wore a stylish white off-the-shoulder cotton top with a pair of pink Capri pants. Her fingernails and toenails were covered with a glossy, hot-pink polish, topped with little white floral designs.

Joel appeared to be cool and relaxed in his blue, green-and-white striped Ralph Lauren Polo shirt, long denim shorts and sandals. He turned toward Erin and kissed her on the forehead. That was Joel's way of thanking her for spending so much quality time with him this week. Erin understood exactly what that little kiss meant. She began to feel very sentimental. She held Joel tight, just like she wanted to hold on to these final moments alone with him. Kenya's arrival meant a change, and possibly a threat, to Erin and Joel's relationship. Erin's nervous energy overflowed and quickly made its way from her head down to her stomach.

Joel sensed her anxiety and asked, "Why are you so nervous?"

As her stomach churned she said, "You know."

"Kenya?"

She whined like a little girl. "Yeah."

They both cracked up laughing.

Joel said, "I should be the nervous one. At least she's your best friend. I'm the stranger here. What if she doesn't like me?"

Erin had quickly changed her whiney tone to one that flowed with certainty. "That won't happen. I know she's gonna like you. I can pretty much guarantee it. And I know you're gonna like her."

"I hope you're right."

Erin could hardly sit still. She stood up and said, "I am right. I'll be back."

Erin needed to find a way to suppress her anxiety. She headed to the kitchen to make some fresh-squeezed lemonade. She felt the need to put her nervous energy to work. Within a few minutes or so she began to feel a little better, because her mind was distracted with random sexual thoughts. She imagined how intense and arousing it would be to see Kenya and Joel please each other sexually, while she watched and tried to withstand the urge to be touched by them or to touch herself. She imagined how Kenya would sound when he ate her pussy for the first time and how her face would look the first time Joel penetrated her with his big rock-hard dick. Then she imagined Kenya and herself pleasing Joel at the same time. Her erotic thoughts made her get a little wet and helped to calm her anxiety.

Erin returned to the living room with two glasses of fresh-squeezed lemonade. Joel smiled because that was exactly what he had the taste for. Before Erin could get the words out of her mouth he automatically reached over and placed two coasters on the cocktail table. It seemed that the two of them were almost able to read each other's minds. Erin noticed that Joel had turned the television to BET. *Rap City* was just coming on. He was sitting there watching a rap video that included half-naked girls shaking their asses.

Erin asked, "So, is that what you like?"

The word *like* didn't even begin to describe how much Joel *loved* to see women shake their asses. It was a thing of beauty to him and ninety-nine point nine percent of straight black men. Joel interpreted Erin's question as a cue to turn the channel, but he didn't. Like a typical guy he answered her question without taking his eyes off the television. He downplayed the situation by saying, "Yeah, I like looking at video models."

Erin hit him on the arm. "Oh, *video models*, is that what you call them? I remember when we used to refer to them as something else."

Joel laughed and said, "Don't even say it. They're just providing some entertainment." He sipped his lemonade. Out of respect for Erin and women everywhere he began to channel surf away from the sexist images. He stopped on MTV because he knew Erin would much rather watch a dating show called *Next*.

As soon as a commercial came on Joel began channel surfing again. He stopped on VH1 Soul. A Brian McKnight video was playing. Erin seemed much more relaxed than earlier. Her sentimental mood was gone. She kicked off her sandals, lay down and rested her head in Joel's lap. He let her do whatever she wanted because it felt good to have her head down there. He couldn't wait to see what she was going to do next. She could feel him get harder and harder. Erin turned her face toward his hardness and moved her head back and forth slightly in order to stimulate him a little more. She became really playful and began to nibble on Joel's erection through his shorts.

Erin looked up at Joel and asked in a sexy tone, "Do you want me to suck you off real quick?"

Joel looked excited. He nodded and replied quickly in an airy tone, "Yeah."

Just then the sound of a car pulling up stole Erin's attention. She lifted her head and asked, "Do you think that's Kenya?"

Joel's dick was harder than calculus and trigonometry. He looked down and said, "Nah, I seriously doubt it."

"Let me take a quick peek."

He thought, *Damn. You need to finish what you started.*

They heard a car door slam as Erin made her way to the window. She looked out the window and screamed, "Oh my God, it's Kenya!"

Unable to match Erin's enthusiasm Joel said, "Really."

Erin made her way back over toward her shoes. "Yeah, she's here." She slipped on her sandals and said, "C'mon. We can help her with her bags."

Joel looked down at his erection and said, "Give me a minute. On second thought, I might need more than a minute."

Erin signaled with her hand and said, "C'mon."

She headed out the front door with Joel walking close behind her, trying his best to disguise the bulge in his shorts.

When Erin and Kenya made eye contact they ran toward each other and embraced. It looked like a scene from *The Color Purple.* Joel didn't come down the outside steps that led from the main entrance right away. He took a second to straighten himself out, but it was obvious that he was still aroused. The fact that Kenya was such a delightful sight to behold didn't help matters. Erin and Kenya looked so much alike that they could have easily been mistaken for sisters, or at least first cousins.

Kenya was maybe a shade lighter and an inch shorter than Erin, with the same shiny black shoulder-length hair. They had similar bright smiles and shared the same symmetrical facial features. Kenya's face was oval-shaped and Erin's was a little more round. Another obvious difference was Kenya's breast size. It was at least a cup size bigger than Erin's. Kenya wore a neon orange halter top with a pair of sexy plaid short-shorts blended in a multitude of vibrant summer colors.

As Joel looked at them he realized that he'd never seen the sun shine so bright or had the opportunity to witness such a rich and luminous display of beauty until that moment. He knew that there was something special about this moment, but had no idea that this was the unveiling of part two of his future.

Kenya looked over Erin's shoulder as they embraced, and then she saw Joel. Kenya and Joel shared a brief moment of eye contact followed by an intense, probing stare. They both liked what they saw. They sensed an instant and undeniable attraction. In Kenya's mind she began to sing Joel's praises with an amazing voice that soared to new octaves. Joel read her thoughts and could almost hear that amazing internal voice.

Joel offered a smile.

Kenya accepted his smile and returned one of her own.

As soon as Erin and Kenya's embrace ended Joel took a few steps toward them and said, "Hi, Kenya."

With excitement flowing from her voice Erin said, "Kenya, this is my Joel and Joel this is my Kenya."

"Hey, Joel."

Joel restrained himself because he didn't want to seem disrespectful to Erin or Kenya. Like most guys, it wasn't uncommon for Joel to be a little flirtatious around women he found attractive. For the most part, he was unaware of his flirting because it was an involuntary response to pure chemistry. He really didn't mean any harm.

Kenya and Joel seemed drawn to each other and made things somewhat official by greeting each other with a friendly embrace. Kenya had been waiting for this moment with the same degree of fiery anticipation as Erin.

Kenya pressed her 36Ds against Joel's muscular chest and he seemed to be absorbed deeper into her feminine softness. At the same time Kenya loved the feel of his upper body, but got a pleasant surprise when Joel stepped into the hug a bit more with his lower body. He accidentally pressed his masculine hardness against her.

Kenya's eyes widened when she felt it. She didn't mind at all. She held still and said, "Um, I think somebody's extra happy to meet me."

She attempted to give him a kiss on the cheek, but somehow her lips landed close to his lips. It was completely innocent. The corners of their mouths touched. They were both intrigued by the incidental contact, but didn't overreact. They simply laughed it off. When Joel stepped back the three of them looked down at his erection at the same time.

He automatically looked at Erin and Kenya and said, "I'm sorry."

Erin laughed. Then she quickly came to Joel's defense and said, "It's my fault. I was messing with him right when you pulled into your parking space."

Kenya fanned herself and then smiled. "Don't worry, Joel. I don't mind, but we might have to have you register that thing as a lethal weapon." Before anyone got insulted she said, "I'm just kidding. That was the friendliest welcome I've received in a long time. Thanks."

They all smiled.

Erin and Joel helped gather Kenya's bags from the trunk of her Honda Accord. All of a sudden Joel felt like they were being watched. He looked over his shoulder and noticed Ms. Benson and another nosey old lady looking directly at him and the girls. Ms. Benson and the nosey old lady shook their heads and had twisted grins on their faces. Joel ignored them and continued into the building.

Chapter 19

Erin and Joel were ready to leave, but they allowed Kenya a little time to unwind before going out to dinner. The first thing Kenya wanted to do was to check out her new apartment and she instantly fell in love with the place. She gave Erin her props for picking out such a nice apartment and for her elegant decorating ideas. The new apartment was a lot more modern and spacious than the old one she and Erin had shared. Right after that Kenya was dying to see Joel's apartment. She liked his place too.

Kenya was glad to take a break from her all-too-consuming career. She was a top-notch government employee who was basically forced to live her life as a conformist. When it came to her career, she knew how to play the game for now, but her true self was slowly emerging. If she had it her way she would have had tattoos, a tongue ring and long flowing dreadlocks. Kenya was a beautiful strong black woman who worked in a field dominated by stiff white guys. She could have had her pick of men at NSA, but she wasn't really feelin' white men like that. On the other hand, they definitely wanted to sample her brown sugar. Her preference was black men. She was constantly faced with the same dilemma that too many black women face—the shortage of eligible black men.

Like most women she had a few repressed emotional issues that stemmed from bad relationships. Day-by-day she learned more about love, life, and herself in general. More than anything she just wanted a new and refreshing approach to a healthy and productive relationship. Kenya believed in sex and love without limitations. She had an unfulfilled desire for sexual adventure. That's where Erin and Joel came in. Her attraction to them was different from anything she had ever experienced before. Words like polyamory, ménage à trois, threesome, three-way, love triangle and triad dominated her thoughts.

Kenya had fun messing with Joel because he tried to hide the fact that he was attracted to her. She kept making sexual innuendoes and sexy gestures that said more than a thousand words. Kenya began to play a bizarre game of seduction with her body language, sexy stares, the way she licked her lips and the way she touched Erin and Joel. The sexiest thing of all was the way she touched herself. She had a very subtle way of playing with her breasts and circling her nipples as she talked. Kenya knew that guys were instinctively drawn to the sight of erect nipples.

Later that evening Joel ended up taking Erin and Kenya to The Avenue in White Marsh. The Avenue is an outdoor shopping, dining, and entertainment development with a nostalgic main street appeal. Trees and old-fashioned lantern-style streetlights lined the street. Every Friday night during the summer was usually alive and pulsating with activity. That night was no different. The Summer Sunset Concert Series had just kicked off and featured a reggae group called Unity. A stage had been set up in front of the huge fountain across from the Lowes movie theater.

Music echoed through the night sky and a deep bass beat vibrated and shook the ground. The area was jumping with excitement as people rode up and down the street, people-watching and showing off cars and motorcycles.

Joel planned to take Erin and Kenya to a restaurant called the Red Brick Station. It's actually a restaurant and microbrewery with a fire station theme. When the three arrived they chose to dine outside on the patio, because it was adjacent to the fountain and stage. Now they could eat, drink, sit back and relax, while enjoying the sounds of Unity.

A warm, free-and-easy breeze drifted by as Erin, Kenya and Joel sat outside at a round wrought iron table with a glass candleholder in the center. A tiny flame flickered and gave their faces a golden glow. Joel sat in the middle with Erin on his right and Kenya on his left. Hundreds of stares came their way. Joel appeared to be the luckiest man around because he had the honor of dining with two very beautiful women.

Reggae music drowned out the buzz of conversation that could clearly be heard between songs.

A Drew Barrymore–lookin' waitress walked over to take their orders. Joel ordered a beer sampler for him and the girls to share. The sampler came with seven assorted freshly brewed beers served in four-ounce glasses. Erin and Kenya chose crab dip and boneless buffalo fingers as appetizers for them to share with Joel. Since the girls weren't too big on beer they ordered two strawberry daiquiris. For their entrées they all ordered crab cakes.

Joel stared at Kenya's face until she made eye contact with him, then quickly looked away. He was astounded by the fact that Kenya and Erin looked so much alike. He found himself staring at Kenya again, but this time it wasn't her face that caught his attention. He looked at her breasts and thought, *They're nice and full . . . round and firm, definitely a D-cup. And check out those nipples.*

The music died down for a moment. The band's lead singer took some time to talk about the next song they were about to perform.

Kenya knew Joel was looking at her. She sat back in her seat, acted natural, sighed and then said, "It's so good to be back home."

Erin said, "I'm glad you're back."

Joel asked, "Where were you anyway?" He made a silly

face, changed his tone to a whisper and asked, "Or is it top secret?"

Erin laughed and said, "She could tell you, but she'd have to kill you."

All three of them cracked up laughing. The band started their next song.

Kenya said, "It's not that serious."

Joel looked at Kenya and said, "All I kept hearing from Erin was that you were away for training. She didn't have any other information. Where were you and what kind of training did you receive?"

Erin said, "Dag, Joel, you're nosey."

Kenya said, "No, it's okay. I was in South Carolina for interrogation and polygraph training."

Erin gasped and her eyes widened. "I can't believe you told. Girl, I hope you don't get into any type of trouble."

Kenya laughed and said, "I can tell y'all where I was and the basics about what I was doing, but that's it. I can't go into too much detail because every year I have to go through an in-depth interview that includes a polygraph test, and they review my profile all the way down to my financial records."

Joel asked, "What's that all about?"

"To make sure I haven't done anything illegal or unethical, like selling government information to foreign counties."

Joel asked, "What happens if you fail the interview process?"

"I could lose my job and possibly get sent to prison for the rest of my life."

He said, "Whoa, that sounds like too much stress to deal with. We face our share of stress as teachers. Tell her, Erin, we have to deal with a bunch of bad-ass kids and their ignorant parents on a daily basis."

Erin said, "That's true. Oh my God, let me tell you. I sent letters home and made phone calls all year long trying to inform certain parents of their kids' failing grades. I never saw or heard from these people during the regular school year, but when they saw their kids' last-quarter report cards saying that they had to repeat their grade level, these same people came to the school raising hell."

Kenya sat up and said, "Are you serious? I hate confrontations, especially ones that involve ignorant people."

Erin said, "So do I. I'm glad the school year is over. One good thing about being a teacher is our much-needed summer break. All Joel and I are focused on right now is relaxing and having fun. You better learn to do the same, Kenya."

She said, "I know. I'm taking a four-week vacation so I can hang out with the two of you for a little while."

Joel thought, *Forget that. You're fine and all, but we don't need you under us the whole summer.*

Erin smiled and said, "That's good."

Joel forced a smile that began to feel natural within seconds. He said, "Yeah. We've got a nice long summer break and this reggae music has me ready to take a cruise or fly to an island."

Erin and Kenya agreed that they needed an exotic getaway to the Caribbean. As they talked about vacationing, two servers appeared with the beer sampler, the strawberry daiquiris and appetizers.

Joel said, "Ahhh, right on time."

Kenya said, "I didn't expect the appetizers so soon."

Erin added, "Neither did I. Everything looks so good."

Kenya smiled and said, "Doesn't it. I love crab dip. Thanks for doing this, Joel."

He asked, "What?"

"You know, agreeing to let me hang out with you and Erin tonight. I didn't have anything to do except hang around our lovely new apartment and unpack my suitcases."

Erin said, "Awww, you called the apartment lovely. Thank you, I'm glad you like it."

"I already told you fifty times that I love it."

"Well, I never get tired of receiving praise for something I've done right."

Kenya shook her head and laughed.

Joel was still thinking about Kenya planning to spend time with him and Erin. He was worried that the more time she spent around him the more attracted to her he would become. Out of nowhere he asked, "What's up with you, Kenya? You got a boyfriend?"

He thought, *What the hell am I thinking? Like her having a boyfriend would make her less attractive or something.*

Kenya was focused on her food and her daiquiri. She looked up and said, "No. But don't think I haven't been trying to find one. You know how it is out here for a sistah."

Joel laughed and said, "No, I don't know how it is out here for a sistah. Go 'head and say what's on your mind."

Kenya took a bite of her boneless buffalo chicken finger and asked, "Did you know that seventy percent of black women are single?"

Joel took a sip of beer and asked, "Is that true? Who told you that?"

Kenya said, "Oprah."

Joel laughed and said, "Oh shit, then it must be true. I knew that women outnumbered men, but I had no idea there were that many single black women floating around."

Erin asked, "Will y'all please forgive me if you see me double dipping in the blue cheese dressing?"

Kenya said, "We're not worried about that. I think me and Joel have already been exposed to your germs one way or another."

Erin and Joel laughed and agreed.

Kenya continued the conversation. "Back to what I was saying, you can look around and see how many single black women are out here. The proof is everywhere."

Joel looked around and saw groups of attractive single black women standing near the stage, sitting at tables around him and even riding by in cars. Erin and Kenya pointed out two mixed couples—two black women on dates with white men.

Erin said, "Some sistahs are dating outside of our race because brothas are missing in action."

Joel said, "So, Erin, are you trying to say some brothas are too busy hustling and doing other dumb shit to date?"

"Yeah. Like going to jail or getting killed over nothing. That's why you see all these single black women out here like this. There's a bunch of different reasons black women can't get a date with a black man. Don't get me wrong—brothas are definitely having sex, but dating is another story."

Kenya said, "Black women have it rough. When we think we've met somebody halfway decent he ends up being a married man or a horny guy in a so-called monogamous relationship looking to cheat. Nobody's got time for that. Then we've got the down-low guys who are partially into women, or the straight-up gay guys who admire and love us to death, but have no practical interest in women whatsoever. We can't get a break."

Erin and Kenya started going back and forth with so many male-bashing comments that Joel began to feel like he was in the middle of a tennis match.

Erin asked, "What about the brothas who think they're above dating sistahs and are out here wining and dining white women?"

Kenya wasn't done. "Girl, tell me about it. Please don't forget the brothas who want to be playas . . . out here running game on any woman desperate enough to fall for their bull."

Joel automatically thought of his buddies Dave and Greg.

As Erin spread crab dip on her bread she said, "I've only seen a few black guys our age with dates tonight. Look over there at that twenty-something girl with the fifty-something man."

Joel said, "That's probably her dad."

Before Erin bit into her bread she said, "More like her daddy . . . her sugar daddy. Look at his old tired ass trying to look young, wearing a Sean John short set with dress shoes and black knee high socks. That's so whack."

Kenya said, "He'll probably go home and overdose on Viagra trying to keep up with that young girl."

They all laughed.

"Leave that man alone." Just as Joel looked in the couple's direction the old man leaned in and kissed the young girl on her lips. Joel's eyes widened. "Oh damn, I guess you were right, Erin. That is her sugar daddy."

Erin said, "All right, just face it. There's definitely a shortage of decent black men."

Joel looked around again and said, "You might be right, but give us a break. Black men have had it hard since we arrived on this continent. We weren't allowed to be men for so long that now a lot of us just don't know how."

Kenya said, "We know there are still some good black men out here. Regardless of what we say, we still believe in y'all. I love black men, but sometimes it does seem like all of the good men are already taken."

Joel scooped up the last drops of crab dip with his bread and said, "Maybe you should broaden your search. I bet you're looking for somebody who is rich, intelligent, handsome, has good credit, a car, a house and so on. I'm not saying lower your standards, but at the same time be realistic. Work with a brotha."

Kenya said, "I already tried that . . . *working with a brotha*. Shoot, the average guy is intimidated by me because nine times out of ten I have more education and make more money than he does. I'm used to a certain lifestyle and some guys I've met in the past haven't even been outside of Baltimore. We compete with a lot of different obstacles to get to the good black men, and once we think we've found one . . . what does he do?"

Erin added with attitude, "He cheats on you."

"Say it again because I don't think the man heard you."

"He cheats on you."

Kenya said, "Excuse me, I need to run to the ladies' room." She looked over at Erin and asked, "You coming?"

"Yeah, you know I'm coming."

Erin asked Joel to watch their purses, gave him a kiss on the lips, and then followed Kenya to the ladies' room. He sat there and watched as Erin and Kenya strutted their fine asses inside, past the bar. Joel knew that the girls were headed off to strategize and gather more ammunition to complete their male-bashing mission. When they came back he planned to be ready for them.

Chapter 20

As soon as Erin and Kenya returned from the ladies' room Joel looked at Kenya and said, "A sistah cheated on me, Kenya. Now, whatcha saying?"

Erin didn't say a word; she just sat down next to Joel.

Kenya sat down and said, "I'm saying . . . look next to you. You were able to find somebody else, and to top it off . . . somebody who you seem to be very compatible with. We don't have it like that. I bet you could walk around and get at least ten phone numbers, in ten minutes or less, from black women who are full of potential. On the other hand, how long do you think it'd take for me to find the phone number of a brotha who would be willing to love me . . . respect me . . . and be my everything . . . forever, or at least until we both got tired of each other?"

Joel laughed and said, "Now that you put it like that, I guess black women do have it pretty bad. What do you suggest?"

Kenya said, "Hold on a second, here comes our food."

Drew Barrymore's look-alike placed a huge tray on a little folding rack. She sat each of their plates in front of them along with cocktail sauce and mustard for the crab cakes. She asked if there was anything else they needed and they all claimed to be fine.

They began to eat.

A few minutes passed and then Kenya said, "Joel, you asked what did I suggest since there is a shortage of black men. Have you ever heard of polyamory?"

Joel chewed his food slowly and looked at Erin out of the corner of his eye, as if to ask, *where the hell is she going with this?* He looked back at Kenya and said, "Yeah, I know what polyamory is. It's the practice of having more than one lover at the same time, with the full knowledge or agreement of the individuals involved. Basically it's a fancy term for sharing."

Kenya smiled and said, "Very good, I'm impressed. You seem to know a little something about everything."

"I try to do my homework, especially when it comes to love, sex and relationships. So, do you think that polyamory would cut down on cheating?"

"Yeah. With a polyamorous relationship everything is consensual. The people involved know who's going to be sleeping with who. It's not like swinging or recreational sex. It's not about being promiscuous or anything. To me it's about establishing a committed relationship with more than one lover, based on love and respect. Ideally, it can be two women and one man or two men and one woman."

Joel said, "The part about the one guy and two girls sounds fun, but the part about two guys and a girl is a little too freaky and sounds G-A-Y to me."

Kenya shook her head and said, "Freaky can be fun."

He asked, "Have you ever been in a threesome?"

"No."

They all agreed that they had never been involved in a threesome. For the most part Erin stayed quiet and let Kenya do the talking.

Kenya said, "So many people are unhappy or unfulfilled in their relationships that I bet that almost half of the couples you see out here tonight are cheating. Poly relationships are the thing of the future. The way I see it, we share our significant others unknowingly anyway. Why not just share them knowingly? All of us are nothing but recycled sex partners."

Erin finally decided to say something. "Yuck. Did you have to put it like that?"

Kenya swept her hair behind her ear and said, "I'm just trying to be real."

Erin said, "But you make that sound kind of gross, saying recycled sex partners."

"No matter how gross it sounds, it's true. All of us at this table have had sex and been cheated on, am I correct?" Erin and Joel both nodded their heads. "See, I thought so. Joel, do you believe in monogamy?"

Without even thinking he said, "Yeah. I'm not the cheating kind of guy. I've found everything I need in Erin. What's the point in cheating?"

Kenya laughed and said, "Give it some time and I'm sure the urge will hit you. Erin, can you honestly sit here and say that you are ready and willing to commit one hundred percent of yourself to Joel? I'm not even talking about marriage. I mean, as friends and lovers. Are you willing to be exclusive?"

Erin avoided answering Kenya and began to look around. "Where the heck is that waitress? I need another daiquiri."

Joel looked at Erin and said, "Go ahead and answer the question honestly."

Kenya said, "No, you don't have to answer. I'm not here to create a problem."

Erin moved her chair up to the table a little more and said, "I know, but I'll go ahead and answer. I'm very happy with you, Joel, but I can't say what I might do or how I might feel in the future. I don't know how realistic the concept of monogamy really is. We're constantly looking at other people and comparing. Attractions happen naturally. It might be unrealistic to be with one person forever."

He said, "I don't agree."

Joel started to think about his parents' relationship and then noticed a spark of light in the dark recesses of his mind. His mind opened and he began to understand a little more about where Kenya and Erin were coming from.

Kenya said, "Monogamy is possessive and insecure. Why should we be limited to one intimate partner? It's possible to love and be in love with more than one individual at a time. Polyamory is about freedom and sharing."

"You sound like a damn hippie or something," Joel added with a laugh.

Kenya said, "Shut up, Joel. Erin told me that you said your fantasy was to make love to two women at the same time."

Joel was shocked. He looked at Erin and asked, "You told her that?"

"Yeah, I didn't mean any harm. It was just girl talk."

Joel shook his head, sighed heavily and said, "It's okay." He paused for a second. "I did say that my fantasy was to make love to two women at the same time, but I also said that something like that actually happening is unrealistic. If you wanna know the truth, lately I've been fantasizing about going to Erin's classroom one day and making love to her on top of her desk. My other fantasies are about marrying Erin and having kids."

Erin said, "Awww, that's so sweet."

Erin and Joel kissed.

Kenya looked at Joel and said, "No . . . no . . . no. Okay, hypothetically speaking . . . what if I told you that I was interested in having a ménage à trois with you and Erin? What would you say?"

Joel lit up like a Christmas tree. He held back his excitement, scratched his head and said, "I'd probably say that sounded like a lot of fun, but I'd have to turn you down because I would never risk losing Erin. Stuff like that leads to so many problems and confusion. It's hard enough making a monogamous relationship work. Adding another lover triples the problems."

Erin took Joel's hand into hers. She looked him in the eyes and asked, "Joel, what do you think of Kenya? And I want an honest answer."

Joel looked puzzled. He didn't recognize this side of Erin.

"What exactly are you asking? I need to know if you're my girlfriend. Because before I answer that type of question I wanna know where our relationship stands."

"We're at a very interesting point in our relationship. I think it's time we expanded the boundaries and tested its strength at the same time. I can be whatever you need me to be. If titles are important to you then I'm your girlfriend."

Kenya smiled and asked in a sexy little voice, "Can I be your girlfriend, too?"

Joel ignored Kenya's question and said, "At first I thought we all were joking around a little, but it sounds like y'all are seriously interested in a ménage à trois. Am I right?"

Erin locked her arm around Joel's and said, "I'll answer that question honestly if you tell me whether you're attracted to Kenya or not."

Without hesitation Joel said, "Of course I am. She's beautiful. Looking at her is almost like looking at you."

Kenya smiled from ear to ear. "Thank you, Joel. I think you're drop-dead gorgeous." She took a deep breath and said, "You're so sexy to me. Everything about you is sexy . . . the way you talk, move, and the way you look. I can see your chiseled body through that shirt. Can I touch you?"

Joel didn't know what to say. He just smiled and mumbled, "Huh?"

Kenya had touched him earlier, but this was different. She slowly ran her hand up and then down the left side of Joel's muscular chest while Erin rubbed his right hand. His dick got rock-hard. People around them noticed the unusual display of affection. Kenya continued to touch Joel's chest with her left hand and placed her right hand under the table on his left thigh. She wanted to stroke his dick, but didn't want to move too fast.

The people who noticed what was going on looked like they wanted to know what Joel, Erin and Kenya had to eat or drink that made them act like that all of a sudden. Joel didn't resist Kenya's advances because it was so stimulating to be seated with his girlfriend while she allowed another woman to seduce him. The fact that they were in public added to his excitement. Erin and Kenya were two very sexually charged women who seemed to be in tune with Joel's erotic side. The sexual tension between them increased.

Erin said, "I'm glad you were honest because I knew you liked Kenya from the moment you saw her."

Kenya stopped touching Joel's chest but continued to move her hand along his thigh. She said, "I could tell you liked me from the way you kept staring at me and my titties."

Joel laughed and said, "Hold up. You might have to move your hand off my leg. You're making it kind of hard to maintain my composure in front of all these people."

In a seductive tone Kenya said, "I wanna make it hard."

Joel took a deep breath and said, "I'm not even gonna lie. I did take a few quick peeps at your breasts, but that was just a normal reaction. Look at them."

Erin continued to stroke his hand. "We understand. Nobody's mad at you for being a man. If you didn't look at Kenya's big-ass titties then I would have been worried."

Joel said, "All right, Erin, we're finished with my part. What about you wanting a threesome?"

"All I know is that I'd love to be around the two people who mean the most to me every day of my life, and it would be fun to share intimate moments together."

Joel asked, "Are you saying that you want to be intimate with a woman?"

"Yeah, but that doesn't necessarily mean sexually."

Kenya said, "Intimacy goes beyond sex. It's emotional and spiritual too, you know? Intimacy is just another word for closeness."

"Don't get offended by me asking this, but are y'all lesbians?"

Erin answered quickly, "No."

Kenya said, "We're not lesbians. We're just challenging the traditional roles of women in relationships and accepting ourselves for who we are by actively expressing our personal desires. What Erin and I feel for each other goes beyond sex or gender. I'm attracted to Erin the person, and not just Erin the woman. I've been around her so long that it feels like she's part of me."

Joel kissed Erin and said, "No, she's part of me. When I first saw her I knew she was special. When we touched, I looked down at our hands and it was like seeing an extension of myself."

Kenya said, "I'm not trying to outdo you, but when I first saw her it was like seeing a reflection of myself."

Joel laughed and said, "Oh my God, you've got a girl crush."

Kenya blushed. "So. I mean . . . I dunno." She bit her bottom lip, looked at Erin and asked, "Do I?"

Erin smiled and said, "Yeah. I think you do. We both have an emotional attachment to each other."

Kenya looked at Erin and said, "I love your personality and your spirit."

Joel shook his head and said, "I don't know what's up with y'all, but I kind of like it. Have the two of you ever done anything sexual to each other, like kissing or touching? And I have to ask . . . any licking, toy play or penetration?"

Erin said, "No."

Kenya replied, "Uh-uhh. None of the above."

Erin felt the need to clarify things. "We're both very attracted to men . . . incredibly attracted to you."

Joel said, "For a minute y'all sounded like lipstick lesbian or bisexual."

The girls felt kind of offended by Joel's remark.

Erin said, "I'm not willing to label myself as anything."

"Me either . . . no labels . . . I'm just Kenya. Don't try to categorize me. But honestly, I never knew that I could have feelings like this. Erin is the only woman I've ever felt this close to. Women are naturally more affectionate toward each other than men are toward each other. I have to admit that I do have a special attraction to Erin's sensuality and affection."

"So do I." Joel paused for a second. "All right, now I know

what you mean about Erin. She's easy to love and very nurturing, like a mother. It's something about her tender affectionate touch and those accepting and understanding eyes."

Kenya smiled and said, "That's exactly what it is. I couldn't have worded it that perfectly myself."

Erin moved her chair closer to Joel and said, "We're all the same. The three of us can have such a wonderful time together . . . sharing, learning and growing."

Joel shook his head and said, "I still don't know."

Now Kenya moved her chair even closer to Joel and said, "Just think of how much fun we can have . . . three becoming one, in every way imaginable . . . mentally, physically, emotionally and spiritually."

Erin said, "Our own little world of love, lust and sexual intrigue . . . with no one to label or judge us, because we'd make our own rules."

Kenya felt the need to set Joel straight. "But first Joel has to open his mind a bit more and stop seeing us with his eyes and start seeing us with his heart, the same way we see each other. Can you do that?"

In an understanding tone he said, "Yeah."

Erin stroked the right side of Joel's face and said, "Allow us to tap into your erotic side. You know I know all about it."

Kenya intertwined her fingers with Joel's and said, "I'm sure you know that Erin told me all about your amazing sexual skills."

Joel shrugged and said, "Yeah, I kind of figured that out on my own." Jokingly he added, "This is the exact reason why women shouldn't tell their girlfriends all of their business. So, is that what piqued your interest in having a threesome?"

"I guess so. From the way Erin described you and the way you make love, I can tell that you're special, Joel. You know you want and deserve to be with us. We're offering you the chance to join us on a journey of sexual exploration and discovery like you've never known. We're three rejected lovers who have the opportunity to be everything to each other in ways that our previous lovers failed to be. As long as we have each other we'll never be lost and lonely again."

"Give it a chance, Joel. We're talking about something deep and meaningful. This is an opportunity to spend time with two women who can do whatever you like, and make you feel whatever you wanna feel. We wanna learn about everything you like and why you like it. We know you'll do the same for us. We can take you wherever you'd like to go without even leaving the room. You can't put a price on that. Like the commercial says . . . priceless."

Kenya said, "Joel, look at me. I want to share so much with you. I just turned twenty-six, and I've never experienced sexual fulfillment with anyone . . . especially the way Erin described. The only orgasms I've ever had have been self-induced. I want you to be the first man to make me come. This isn't just about sex . . . this is about love, too."

Love is a powerful word that seemed to echo inside Joel's mind. It usually didn't take much coaxing to change Joel's mind when it came to matters concerning attractive women. Erin and Kenya were totally focused on Joel. The look in their eyes said, *the water is warm, feels great, so jump right into this loving threesome*. This was one of those find-your-life or wreck-your-life moments.

Joel thought, *I wanna live life to the fullest and this would be a heck of a start. But I don't wanna lose you, Erin.*

Erin seemed to read Joel's mind and said, "I know what you're thinking. I promise that you won't lose me. Things will only get better. We all can fall in love together and I know you'd like that."

Erin and Kenya's enticing ways proved to be too overwhelming and irresistible for Joel. He looked at them and said, "All right, I'll do it, but we'll have to take things a step at a time because we don't want anybody to get hurt along the way."

The fact that Joel didn't just jump at the idea of a threesome right away made him more desirable to Erin and Kenya.

He showed a level of restraint and maturity, and the fact that he was so cool and so concerned about the girls' feelings made him even more appealing. They lay their heads on his shoulders and he wrapped his strong arms around them.

People walked by staring, but the three didn't care. They closed their eyes, listened to Unity play their last song, and continued to cuddle.

Chapter 21

After dinner Erin, Kenya and Joel headed back to their building and decided to hang out at Joel's apartment for a while. The mounting sexual tension had eased up a bit during the ride home. At first it seemed like the three would rush home like horny coeds on spring break, but as soon as they got home they acted more like good friends hanging out on a typical Friday night. It was almost as if they hadn't even talked about having a ménage à trois.

The three probably didn't feel the need to rush into doing anything sexual. For them it was about timing and waiting for the perfect opportunity to jump in, almost like jumping double-dutch. The most important thing was fortifying their friendship as a threesome. But no matter how hard they tried to avoid the topic, sex kept floating around in their minds. With every passing second their energies naturally blended together in a way that none of them knew how to describe, because it was still so new and awkward but at the same time inviting.

The three sat in Joel's living room watching television. They sat close together and soon began to share all sorts of body contact. The girls rested their heads on Joel's chest and wrapped their legs around his. At first it was satisfying to be so close, until sexual curiosity eased its way into the picture. They wanted and needed to take things to the next level.

Joel was starting to get used to the idea of being sandwiched between two attractive women. They all seemed anxious because they sensed that they were on the verge of something amazing. The butterflies in Erin and Kenya's stomachs pretty much confirmed that something was about to happen, but still there wasn't any need to rush.

As Erin and Joel watched television Kenya went across the hall to get the gifts she had brought back from South Carolina for them. When she returned she handed them both gift bags. Erin and Joel looked surprised. Kenya explained that she had meant to give them the gifts earlier, but had completely forgotten.

Erin reached into her gold-colored gift bag and pulled out something wrapped in yellow tissue paper. She unwrapped it and found two bottles of flavored massage oil and a tiny box with a sterling silver toe ring inside.

Erin smiled, gave Kenya a hug and said, "Thank you. This is just like the toe ring I lost."

Kenya said, "Aw, it's not much . . . just a little something. I remember how upset you were when you lost the first one."

Joel laughed to himself because he thought this was a cheesy moment, with the hugs and gift sharing. He was hesitant to look inside his gift bag because he was afraid that he wouldn't be able to hide his facial expression if Kenya had gotten him something he didn't like.

Kenya looked at him and said, "Hurry up, Joel."

"Okay," he said as he reached inside his navy blue gift bag and pulled out a flat, rectangular object wrapped in light blue tissue paper. He opened the gift to find two African-American pornographic DVDs.

Joel smiled and said, "Thanks, Kenya."

She asked, "Where's my hug?"

They embraced.

Kenya said, "I want all of us to watch those together at some point. We should watch them right now."

Erin laughed at Kenya and said, "Are you still into porn like that?"

"Old habits are hard to break. I think I'm addicted. Sometimes it's the only way I can get to sleep at night."

Erin said, "I don't know what's worse—masturbating to porn to get to sleep or taking sleeping pills."

Kenya replied, "To me porn is definitely more addictive than sleeping pills."

Joel laughed and said, "If Kenya wants to masturbate then let her."

"Thank you, Joel."

Erin said, "Don't fall for that, Kenya. He just wants to watch."

"There's nothing wrong with that." Kenya looked at Joel and said, "I'll show you how I like to get myself off one day."

He flashed a mischievous grin and asked, "You promise?"

"Yes," Kenya said as she blew him a kiss.

Joel said, "I was just thinking that maybe we could make our own porno movie. I've always wanted to direct and star in my own movie."

Kenya asked, "Are you serious?"

"Yeah, I'm serious. My porn star name would be Will Harding, Rod Long or Mo Dixon."

Erin and Kenya laughed and reminded Joel of how crazy he was.

Kenya said, "I like those names, especially Rod Long."

Erin said, "I like that one too, but we could never do an X-rated movie."

Joel said, "Of course we couldn't, because our movie would definitely be a XXX flick. Y'all need to give that some serious consideration. What would your porn star names be?"

Kenya laughed and said, "I like Anita Johnson, Nikki Dix or Stunt Girl."

Joel nodded and said, "Good ones . . . I like those. Stunt Girl is sexy. What about you, Erin?"

She closed her eyes for a few seconds then asked, "How about Tasty Cakes, Cherry Cummins or Crystal Cox?"

Joel said, "I like all of those, especially Cherry Cummins . . . nasty . . . real nasty."

They all laughed.

Kenya leaned across Joel and whispered something in Erin's ear.

Erin said, "We have a surprise for you, Joel. We'll be right back."

Erin and Kenya went to Joel's bedroom to slip into something more comfortable. In the meantime Joel stayed out in the living room channel surfing. Within minutes he heard Corrine Bailey Rae's sultry voice coming from his bedroom. He couldn't wait to see what Erin and Kenya had in store for him. He was patient because he knew good things came to those who waited.

The time had finally arrived. The bedroom door opened and Corrine Bailey Rae's voice became even clearer. He noticed the unmistakable glow of candlelight. The bedroom overflowed with seductive energy as Erin and Kenya slowly made their way toward Joel, wearing nothing but their panties and his pajama tops, Erin in black and Kenya in blue. Joel gazed into their eyes for a few seconds and then looked them up and down. He was blown away by the two sweet and sexy women standing in front of him. The girls exuded confidence, feminine strength and beauty.

Erin and Kenya walked up to Joel without saying a word, took him by the hand and led him to their little secluded adult playground. Silence sealed their lips while their thoughts screamed with joy. The anticipation and excitement in the air were almost palpable. Once they made it to the bedroom they let their body language do all of the talking. This was so deep and meaningful that their souls were summoned.

Eyes glowed.

Souls talked.

Chemistry sparked.

Passion was ignited.

The new sexual revolution would not be televised, but instead distinctly memorized and savored—permanently etched into their minds because this was gonna be a night they would never forget.

There was no way to measure the heated atmosphere shared between the three lovers on this hot summer night. Joel, Erin and Kenya became mesmerized by each other. They had come so far in such a short time. Their fascination and infatuation went beyond a physical thing. They leaned in for a hands-free triple kiss that introduced them to the infinite possibilities and passion that could be shared among three.

The kiss that they shared was so exciting and satisfying that it made them feel like before that kiss they had never really been kissed. After that first kiss it was as if they were seeing each other for the first time. Their bodies were slowly drawn together until unknowingly they formed a love triangle. Their hands began to flow as free and easy as the wind while they kissed again. Erin removed her lips from the mix to allow Joel and Kenya to experience their first kiss. Joel repositioned himself to allow Erin and Kenya to share their first kiss as well. This was his way of showing his acceptance and understanding of the feeling Erin and Kenya shared.

The kisses that they all shared were so intense that no one could tell who was the giver or the receiver. They were all equal. They went back into a passionate triple kiss that was engaging and deeply engrossing. The three felt no need to rush because they had all night to enjoy the awesome feeling of togetherness and unity.

Being in a ménage à trois for the first time was somewhat like venturing into unfamiliar territory. The three remained calm, took a cautious approach and let nature take its course.

Joel looked at Erin and Kenya with a willing-and-ready-to-please expression.

Erin looked at Joel with a wanna-sex-you-up-and-down expression.

Kenya looked at Joel with a have-to-have-you expression.

Erin and Kenya looked at each other with a delightful expression that said, *This is our naughty fantasy come true.*

Joel smiled and asked, "Where are we going with this?"

Erin returned a seductive smile and said, "Everywhere. Where do you want it to go?"

Kenya answered for Joel, "Let our actions and not our words dictate how far we go."

"Sounds good to me," Joel said as he began to unbutton Kenya's top. "Don't be afraid. I won't hurt you."

Kenya blushed and said, "And I won't hurt you."

They paused for a few seconds, smiled, and exchanged sexy gazes. They had almost reached the point of no return. This was the last moment to make sure they all had the courage and desire to continue down this unexplored pathway to pleasure. All three seemed to be willing and ready. They let go of their inhibitions and trusted each other.

Erin sensed the synergy, but still felt the need to say, "Remember, jealousy doesn't exist here . . . can't exist here. This is about maintaining harmony, positive energy, making each other feel good and most of all . . . making love."

Joel unbuttoned Erin's pajama top, kissed her and said, "Trust me, everything is all right. I've never felt more excited than I am right now."

Kenya kissed Joel and then Erin. She said, "I want y'all to know that from this point on, nothing is forbidden or taboo."

"I know. From this point on, anything is possible and acceptable," Joel said as he stepped over and peeled back his cool blue sheets.

Chapter 22

Erin and Kenya made their way over to the bed. Joel lay them down on the bed one by one, starting with Erin. He tried to seduce them, but they turned the attention around on him. They wanted him to offer up some eye candy by removing some of his clothes. Kenya had already fallen in love with his muscular arms and legs and desired to see a whole lot more. Joel took off his shirt, and within seconds he felt the pleasure of two sets of soft hands all over his chest and abs. Kenya and Erin removed Joel's shorts and had him lying on the bed wearing nothing but his white Calvin Klein boxer briefs. Their hands explored the rest of his body and their lips delivered little kisses at the same time—making love to his flesh.

Joel was so hard that he was barely able to stay inside his underwear. Erin and Kenya didn't rush to remove his boxers. Kenya's eyes nearly popped out of her head when she saw the size of Joel's erection. At first she acted like she was afraid to touch him down there, like she was petting a snake for the first time. She wasn't accustomed to being with a man so well endowed. She played with his thing through his underwear and began to love the length, girth and rigidity of Joel's fully erect dick.

Joel couldn't believe how turned-on he was or how good

Erin and Kenya's hands felt. The next thing he knew the beast had been unleashed. Erin had pulled his thing through the opening of his boxers and began to please him with her mouth. She wanted to show Kenya how comfortable she was with Joel, and how good she was at giving head.

When Kenya saw Joel exposed she said, "My God, you're incredible." Her eyes scanned up and down his body. "Joel, you have such a beautiful body."

Joel and Kenya kissed, and then she made her way down below to join Erin. The girls moaned and groaned as they feasted on Joel's manhood at the same time. They turned their heads to the side in order to lick and nibble on his dick in perfect unison. Joel called this position the double down.

Erin and Kenya had their asses in the air, pointed directly at Joel. He managed to reach down to remove Erin's panties and then Kenya's. He played with their clits and then began to finger them. He motioned for Erin to come up top and straddle his face. As they moved into a sixty-nine, Kenya continued to satisfy him with her mouth and he continued to stimulate her with his index and middle fingers. She completely lost it when Joel found her G-spot. She hadn't been penetrated in a long time, and was almost too tight and delicate to handle his thick fingers. When she recovered she switched places with Erin and was quickly introduced to Joel's tongue thrusts.

After that they changed positions every few minutes. Their passion was so intense that they conjured erotic images from the past. In the vast ages of time nothing is old or new. Threesomes have been around since the beginning of recorded history. This was their version of the living Kama Sutra. It was all about three pleasing each other equally—that's how passionate and unselfish they were.

Soon the lines became blurred. Their flesh and spirits were closer and tighter than stitched seams. There was no way to tell where one body began or where the other ended. She, he and she—the three were now one. Pleasure was abundant and

continuously reciprocated. In no time they all had multiple orgasms from their prolonged foreplay. This was a deeply satisfying sensual experience and a sexual awakening for all three.

Being with Erin and Kenya was like a dream come true for
Joel. There was nothing cheap, crude or tasteless about what
they shared. Erin may have been right when she said that love
was dead, because what the three experienced felt like the re-
birth of love. They threw caution to the winds and did whatever felt natural.

Joel felt good about his decision to sleep with Erin and
Kenya. He felt he had seized the moment—taken hold of his
youth and maximized a once-in-a-lifetime opportunity. The
three of them had never felt more desired, attractive or self-
assured. Their bottled-up spirits had been shaken up, uncorked
and suddenly their unstoppable free spirits exploded all over
the place.

Joel and Kenya wanted to pleasure Erin at the same time.
They had her lie on her back while the two of them kissed
and touched her all over. It was as if Kenya mimicked Joel's
movements. As he caressed and sucked Erin's right breast,
Kenya did the same to her left breast. Pleasing Erin the way
they did was nourishment for their souls.

Joel ventured lower, around Erin's belly button, and Kenya
eventually joined him. A few minutes later he found himself
kissing Erin's inner thighs, and in no time he was slowly and
deliberately stimulating Erin's sensitive clitoris with his warm,
moist tongue. Kenya moved down the left side of Erin's body.
Joel sensed her there. He looked into Kenya's soulful eyes and
could tell that she wanted to join him. Erin appeared breathless, and fidgeted out of control. As if that wasn't enough, Joel
wanted to take her to another level. He penetrated her with
his middle and index fingers and moved them back and forth
toward her pelvic bone in a come hither motion.

Erin wanted to feel Kenya down there and Joel knew it. He
eventually moved his head over a little to make room for

Kenya to join him. They both ended up licking Erin's pussy at the same time, and she looked like she was about to explode. She grabbed them by the backs of their heads to help guide their dueling tongues. Intense sensations rose and fell as new ones were constantly created. Once Joel and Kenya had zeroed in on the right spots Erin let go and clenched the bottom sheet. She looked like she was completely breathless, letting out silent screams. She couldn't hold back any longer. She moaned loudly and then oozed with a silky smooth wetness that made Joel stop what he was doing so he could fuck her. He slid a condom on and Kenya grabbed hold of his fully erect dick and inserted it inside Erin.

Kenya was feeling really kinky. She felt like she was in the middle of her favorite porno movie, but this was real life. She was an active participant and that turned her on even more. She played with Erin's clit while Joel tried his best to wear Erin's ass out.

Joel's intent was to bring Erin to another orgasm and then he would get to Kenya. The more he looked at Kenya the more he wanted to be inside her. Within a few minutes Erin rolled right into another orgasm.

When Kenya's turn came she seemed more willing to provide pleasure than to receive it. Erin and Joel turned their attention on Kenya. She lay on her back with her legs slightly spread. Joel positioned himself between her legs and penetrated her for the first time. She screamed when she felt the pressure of Joel's huge erection.

Erin laughed and said, "You can do it. Go 'head and take all of that dick."

It hurt at first, but Kenya was able to adapt to the pleasure and pain. Joel was concerned and adjusted his rhythm. Kenya noticed the change right away. She was really getting into it and suddenly feared that he was about to stop.

She yelled, "Don't stop. I can take it. Give it to me. I need it. Fuck me, Joel. Fuck me hard." He went back to his normal rhythm and then she cried out, "Faster . . . faster! Yes . . . yes . . . yes! That's it!"

Erin held Kenya's legs in the air for a while and became more of a voyeur. A few minutes later she began to lick Kenya's erect nipples and played with her clit while Joel fucked the living shit out of her.

Kenya was very flexible. Joel watched as she pointed her toes like a dancer and then they started to curl. The next thing Joel knew Kenya's feet were up by her ears and then bent behind her head. The fact that she was so flexible turned him on even more and made him pound her harder. She clawed his back with her nails as her hands moved down to his ass.

Kenya went through an array of pre-orgasmic facial expressions and yelled, "Oh my God . . . ooh . . . aw yeah, Joel . . . I'm about to come!"

"That's it. Let it go," Erin coached Kenya, and touched her clitoris ever so gently, with just the right amount of alternating pressure.

Kenya's eye rolled back in her head. She tilted her head, arched her back and ascended to heaven.

Joel wasn't done. Fucking Kenya in front of Erin was exciting and made him want more. A few minutes later, when Kenya was ready and willing to continue, they changed positions so Kenya could see how it would feel to get fucked from behind. She got on her knees and lowered her head. Joel penetrated her from behind and she loved the animalistic appeal. He drove his hardness deep into her tight wetness. She oohed and aahed like a virgin and then out of nowhere she began to let out some deep moans. Then she came again—quick and hard. She collapsed on the bed and her entire body shuddered. Erin and Joel wrapped themselves around her. When they looked into Kenya's eyes they could see that she was in ecstasy.

An hour later the three started all over again. This time they changed the pace and made love to each other slower and softer. For the first time they were able to experience spirituality through sex. They grew spiritually and developed a higher consciousness—an extreme love high. It went beyond lovemaking because they combined their individual energies, and created a bold new energy and were able to control it. Together they rode waves of pleasure that lasted all night.

Chapter 23

The next morning the three slept in peace. They lay in bed naked, with their arms and legs intertwined like an erotic sculpture. The peace was slightly interrupted when Joel was awakened by an overwhelming urge to reposition himself. His neck and right shoulder were stiff as hell, and his arms and legs were asleep. His discomfort was just a part of the reality of sleeping with three in a bed—even a king-sized.

When he opened his eyes he saw Erin on his right and Kenya on his left. They were a beautiful sight to behold. Then he noticed that his bed was a mangled mess and so was the rest of his bedroom. Clothes, underwear and shoes covered the floor, but Erin and Kenya were his main focus.

He looked out his window and saw traces of morning dew. Birds flew high in the treetops and he listened carefully as they sang outside of his window. He heard the sound of the steady breeze as it flowed and resonated through the leaves of the trees. He was in a good mood. Besides some minor stiffness everything seemed perfect. The bold sky was so blue it appeared artificial. The clouds looked like shredded cotton balls. Love was in the air and to Joel, God smiled down upon him and the girls in the form of sunlight.

Joel stepped outside of himself for a moment and carefully studied the way he and the girls were positioned in bed. It seemed as if he was an artist or photographer, capturing a breathtaking image. He loved the way they looked together—naked and carefree with their brown skin shining in the morning sunlight. Joel saw them as a spectacular work of art that he titled, LUV4-3.

An acute case of stiffness along with numbness and tingling reminded Joel that he needed to reposition himself. He shifted to his left side where he was greeted by unlimited contact and access to Kenya's warm, sexy body. He smiled and automatically began to tease her skin with his lips. He was sure she could feel his warm moist breath, and then the cool gentle sensation of him blowing against her skin.

Within seconds Kenya was awake. She looked at Joel and smiled with her expressive eyes. Her eyes said, *Good morning . . . last night was absolutely wonderful. You did your thing. Woo!*

They kissed and then stared deeply into each other's eyes. Joel saw an unfamiliar look in Kenya's eyes—one that spoke of a budding obsession and a need to get closer to him. He had a funny feeling. In a way he knew it was a warning—maybe a sign of an impending heartbreak, but he chose to ignore it. He concentrated on the more familiar of the two expressions—brewing love. Kenya definitely had that look in her eyes. It temporarily took Joel's breath away and made him want to fall in love with her. This was nothing out of the ordinary for him. There he was again, falling hard and fast.

Joel kissed Kenya again. Then he turned toward Erin and used his mouth to create the same tantalizing sensations he used to wake Kenya.

The three lay in bed caressing and talking about what they experienced the night before. They showered each other with compliments. Their conversation was hot, and tempted them to start up something sexual again, but they didn't. They discussed their fantasies, favorite positions and how good their orgasms felt.

An hour later they got out of bed and headed to the bathroom. They seemed very comfortable being naked in front of each other. They showered together, and then the three of them stood in front of Joel's bathroom mirror to brush their teeth.

Erin and Kenya played around, making a combination of cute, silly and ugly faces in front of the mirror as Joel tried to be serious while shaving. They then took turns kissing him. He began to lighten up a bit and had fun smearing shaving cream on the girls. Everybody was a frothy white mess. When Joel was finished shaving he laid some kisses on Erin and Kenya that felt really good, and the girls got serious—serious about the art of kissing.

Erin and Joel exchanged deep passionate kisses.

Joel turned toward Kenya and gave her a long slow kiss.

As the three went back and forth kissing, they peeked at themselves in the mirror. They had never paid much attention before to how sexy or passionate they looked while kissing. They used a wide array of techniques, ranging from lips only, tongues only, sucking, biting, down to plain ole wet and sloppy.

The kissing continued for a while, until Erin looked at herself closely and then at Kenya and Joel. She saw the beauty in their new relationship, but somehow she knew that some, mostly religious and self-righteous people, would judge, condemn or read a whole lot more into what they saw when they looked at the three of them together.

The threesome's actions and undeniable attraction to each other did make them noticeably different. They had shed their protective layers and now Erin feared that the outside world would see them through tainted lenses instead of seeing them for the people they truly were—honest, open and realistic.

Joel looked at Erin and asked, "What is it?"

Erin quickly replied, "Nothing."

He knew that she was holding back and said, "No, tell me."

Kenya looked concerned. "What's wrong?"

Erin said, "Nothing's really wrong, but I'm just a little concerned about what people might think when they see the three of us together . . . I mean, after last night I don't think we'll be able to act like regular friends. It's obvious that we're much more than friends."

Kenya understood Erin's feelings. She knew that people were going to look at them differently. "I don't care. Forget what people think."

Joel said, "I'm happy, and I don't give a damn what people think or say about us."

Erin said, "You're both right. I don't think we have anything to worry about." She paused, then asked, "Do we?"

Joel and Kenya laughed and continued to kiss while Erin stared at her reflection in the mirror.

Later that morning the three went to the New Town Diner for breakfast. When they arrived there was a short wait. They were taken in by the wonderful aromas and the diner's retro appeal. The click-clank sounds of plates, glasses and silverware echoed in the background along with the rustling sound of newspapers. There was a steady buzz of conversation with an occasional outburst of laughter. The mood was light and cheerful.

The staff tried to keep everybody happy while keeping the customers flowing nice and steady, without feeling rushed. After about ten minutes the server escorted the three to their table. Just as they were about to sit down Joel looked over his shoulder and noticed a frightening but familiar face. His heart skipped a beat. He had to look again because he couldn't believe his eyes. He needed confirmation from someone to prove that he wasn't half crazy or hallucinating.

Joel asked, "Can y'all see that lady over there wearing the black and white outfit?" Erin and Kenya looked confused until he pointed and said, "The one with the big brown curly hairdo. I think it's a dried-out leisure curl or something."

Kenya laughed and said, "Oh, yeah, I see her."

Erin said, "I see her too. Who is that?"

"I think it's my ex's mother."

Just as Joel said that, the lady turned around and looked directly at him.

Kenya said, "She must have felt you pointing. Didn't your mother tell you that it was rude to point?"

Still in shock he said, "Uh-huh."

Within seconds Joel saw Renee's sister, Cheryl, exit the ladies' room and join her mother at their table. Sure enough, it was Renee's supposedly dead mother sitting at a table eating a hearty breakfast. She waved at Joel and he waved back.

Without any explanation Joel said, "That's Renee's mother. Excuse me, I'll be right back."

As Joel walked away, Kenya asked Erin, "What's going on?"

With a giggle in her voice she replied, "He said that's Renee's mother."

"I thought she was dead."

"So did I. Renee is crazy as shit. I would never sink that low just to get a man's sympathy or to get back into his life."

Kenya shook her head and said, "Tell me about it. That's sad and pathetic."

Joel walked up to Renee's mother and said, "Hi, Mrs. Rhodes. Is this really you?"

She stuffed a piece of sausage in her mouth and gave him a peculiar stare. As she chewed she said, "Yes it's me, Joel. Who else would I be?"

Her daughter, Cheryl, cleared her throat and gave Joel the same peculiar stare.

Joel turned toward Cheryl and said, "I'm sorry. Hi, Cheryl. How are you?"

Cheryl maintained her peculiar stare. She frowned and with plenty of attitude said, "I'm fine."

Joel said, "Be careful 'cause your face might get stuck like that."

She worked her neck, rolled her eyes and sucked her teeth. "What?"

He smiled. "Aw, nothing. I heard you were in the hospital recently. Is that true?"

"Yeah. And?"

"And nothing. I was just trying to be nice . . . making sure you were okay." Joel was turned off by their expressions and asked, "Did I do something to piss y'all off or something?"

Cheryl said, "My sister is a wreck, and if you had been doing what you were supposed to have been doing all along, she wouldn't be the way she is now."

Joel took a step back and said, "Oh, so it's my fault that she cheated? Plus, she walked out on me."

Out of Joel's sight, Renee exited the ladies' room looking numb, as if she didn't have a clue or care in the world.

Erin and Kenya watched everything unfold from their table.

Erin said, "Oh my God. Kenya, look, that's Renee coming out of the ladies' room."

Kenya did a double take and said, "Damn, she looks just like Beyoncé."

Erin said, "Shut up. C'mon, let's go over there. It's about to get real ignorant up in here."

Mrs. Rhodes saw Renee walking toward them and said, "Oh good, here comes Renee right now."

Renee didn't notice Joel right away, but when she did she stopped dead in her tracks. She covered her mouth with her right hand. Not even her hand could hide her reaction. Renee's jaw dropped so low that her bottom lip almost touched the ground. She looked like she wanted to run and hide. Instead she chose to face the consequences. She walked toward them slowly, like a four-year-old who had just gotten caught doing something awfully wrong.

Erin and Kenya walked up and stood next to Joel.

Cheryl overflowed with ignorance when she asked, "Who they supposed to be?"

Joel proudly responded, "These are my girlfriends, Erin and Kenya."

Cheryl repeated, "Girlfriends? What that supposed to mean?"

Erin knew Joel was about to expose their unique relationship. With caution in her eyes and in her voice she said, "Joel, no. Don't."

He smiled confidently at Cheryl and said, "Just what I said . . . my girlfriends . . . with an S. C'mon, you're a grown woman. You know what that means." Joel turned around toward Renee, knowing she overheard what he had just said. "Hey Renee, I was just about to ask about your mother's funeral arrangements."

Mrs. Rhodes almost choked and quickly asked, "My what?"

Renee was speechless and incredibly embarrassed. Her eyes held a familiar troubled expression, but this time it was more intense than ever.

Everybody braced themselves because they didn't know what was about to happen.

Renee started off with a subtle grin that turned into a giggle. The giggle quickly turned into an outburst of exaggerated laughter, and then out of nowhere came hysterical crying. A lot of the background noises ceased. Everybody in the diner stopped what they were doing and looked at Renee. She felt every set of eyes in the diner focused on her.

Renee's embarrassment magnified times ten. She stood her ground for a few seconds, looking trapped and helpless. She trembled.

Joel tried to help. "Renee, are you okay?"

Her mother said, "Honey, have a seat and take a sip of cold water."

Renee looked around and then fled out of the diner like she was running for her life.

Cheryl jumped out of her seat and headed out after her yelling, "Renee, hold up. Wait for me."

Things didn't turn out nearly as dramatic as they could have. The people at the diner lost interest in the drama as soon as Renee stormed out of the place. Most of the patrons shrugged and quickly turned their attention back to their food and conversations. They seemed to have had I-don't-give-a-damn or so-what-life-goes-on types of attitudes. This was a perfect example of how much society has been desensitized to other people's problems and despair. The breakout success of trashy talk shows, court shows and reality shows had completely changed people's views on the world. In order to get reactions out of most people nowadays there had to be a raw display of physical violence leading to bloodshed or death.

Joel, Erin and Kenya sensed the same thing. They thought of how much the world sucked and how perfect the world they had created behind closed doors was. They stood still looking very uncomfortable. They looked like they wanted to leave, but decided to stay. No matter what, the food looked and smelled too good to abandon.

Erin looked at Mrs. Rhodes and said in a comical way, "We're just gonna return to our table."

Kenya smiled and said, "Yeah, it was nice meeting you."

Mrs. Rhodes didn't say a word. She just shot them a mean look. She looked at Joel and said, "Please, sit down for a minute. We seriously need to talk."

Joel had his flaws, but bad manners wasn't one of them. He looked at Erin and Kenya and said, "It's okay. I'll join the two of you at our table in a few minutes."

They gave him smiles and nods of approval and then quickly cut their eyes at Mrs. Rhodes to let her know that they weren't pushovers.

As soon as the girls walked away, Mrs. Rhodes focused all of her attention on Joel. In a condescending tone she asked, "What are you doing with yourself? Better yet, I should be asking, what are you doing with those two?"

Without hesitation he said, "Having the time of my life . . . and I mean it. I've never been happier. Things are less complicated with those two than it was with that one out there." Joel pointed outside toward Renee's Escalade and said, "Look, there she is now."

When Mrs. Rhodes looked out the window she saw Renee crying and fussing at Cheryl. She tried to downplay the situation by saying, "I know Renee's a handful, but she still loves you. God loves you too, but I'm sure he doesn't approve of what you're doing with those two young ladies. And I'm using the term ladies very loosely. I can't believe you're sleeping with the two of them at the same time."

Joel cleared his throat and said, "I never said all that, but it's true."

Mrs. Rhodes looked up toward heaven and asked, "What's this world coming to?" She looked Joel directly in his eyes and leaned in toward him as if she had something important to ask. "Would you consider getting back with Renee?"

Joel raised an eyebrow and then asked, "For what? We were an awful mismatch. I'm into something new and exciting called happiness. Your daughter was never satisfied, and she's into too much unnecessary drama, chaos and confusion for me to deal with. She came to my apartment and lied to me. She told me that you died from a brain aneurysm."

Mrs. Rhodes frowned, then she lightened her tone and said, "I don't believe you. Did she really do that?"

"Did she really just have a nervous breakdown in front of all these people?"

She pressed her pouty lips together and said, "She's been through a lot. Renee and Robert broke up, and she's a little traumatized from going through two recent breakups . . . that's all. Renee is very resilient. She'll bounce right back in no time."

Joel said, "Maybe she'll bounce back after an extended stay in a psych unit at Sheppard Pratt." Mrs. Rhodes had no response. Joel's empty stomach growled as he continued, "Look, I'm not trying to be an insensitive jerk or anything, but I need to get back to my table and place my order. I'm starving."

Mrs. Rhodes's head began to ache. She closed her eyes and put her hands up to her face. "Is that it? I mean, you and my daughter lived together for a couple of years and that's all you have to say? You're starving."

"What else do you want me to say?" He paused for a second. "Okay, it hurts me to see Renee in the condition she's in, but that's the bed she made. I'm done catering to her needs.

I've moved on and now her problems are spilling over into my new relationship."

Mrs. Rhodes mumbled, "You call that a relationship?" She paused and repositioned herself in her seat. "Tell me one thing."

"What's that?"

"Are you still in love with my daughter?"

Within a split second Joel said, "No." Something jump started his heart. "But I'll always love her and the few good memories we shared." He stood up and said, "Good-bye, Mrs. Rhodes. I wish you all the best and wish Renee a speedy recovery."

Joel rejoined the girls at their table.

A few minutes later Mrs. Rhodes purposely walked past their table and said, "I just have one thing to say, and then I'm out of here." She sighed heavily. "From me to you, from the bottom of my heart . . . the three of you are freaks and I mean that in every sense of the word."

This was a defining moment, because Erin looked at Mrs. Rhodes and said, "I've gotta be real with you. Earlier this morning that may have hurt my feelings." She looked at Joel and Kenya and smiled. "Hearing something like that come out of your mouth means absolutely nothing. We all know that you want your daughter to be with Joel more than anything, but let me tell you that's never gonna happen. He's ours now."

Kenya laughed and said, "Sorry, Miss Lady."

Mrs. Rhodes appeared to boil over with anger. She looked at Kenya and said, "Fuck you." And then she addressed them as a group. "Fuck all three of you."

With laughter in her voice Kenya said, "Not even in your wildest dreams."

Mrs. Rhodes forgot that she was talking to three so-called freaks. Her ignorant comments had no effect on them. She huffed and puffed as she walked away.

Chapter 24

Joel could feel the underlying beat of a negative force that was determined to disrupt his rhythm. It began to play like that annoying music in movies when something bad was about to happen. He refused to acknowledge or give in to any negativity, because he was too focused on the positive. Renee and her family members were the negative force he didn't want to acknowledge. In her delusional state, Renee was determined to get back with Joel. She felt that they were destined to be together. Joel saw things a whole lot differently. He began to understand the law of attraction. He had rid himself of the notion that opposites attract, and was fully convinced that like attract like. Erin and Kenya were his destiny.

Joel, Erin and Kenya were on their way to Joel's favorite night spot, an upscale nightclub in downtown Baltimore called Club One. They were without a doubt dressed to impress. Joel had his swagger back and the girls looked sexy and sophisticated—together the three were blazing hot. Erin and Kenya added new dimensions to Joel's world, and he did the same for them. They were cut from the same cloth and were bound by a common thread. The three were at their best when they were together. When combined they completed each other and formed an exquisite life-sized tapestry.

As soon as they arrived at Club One they noticed that the bouncers were rejecting brothas at the door for violating the dress code. Why did grown-ass men want to show up at a club like this wearing athletic gear? They needed to grow up and stop shopping at sporting good stores for clothes. Even the NBA had a dress code. Club One was a place intended for a mature crowd to mix and mingle and have a straight-up good time. It wasn't a shabby pick-up or hangout spot for lowlifes to get drunk and cause trouble. Although the club had been around for years, some Baltimoreans still weren't used to having a club that rivaled the high-profile clubs of New York, L.A. and Miami.

Joel, Erin and Kenya wouldn't have any problems getting into the club. From outside they could hear and feel the bumping sounds of an original B-more club mix. The bouncers knew Joel and were glad to see him. They called him by name and gave him handshakes and one-armed half-hugs.

The exterior of the club was eggshell-white and pretty unimpressive, but the interior was all that and then some. It was like stepping into a futuristic world of hip-hop and house music. The club had four levels and each level had its own theme, based on the elements. The first level was earth, and of course its color was brown. There was a huge crowd standing around a custom-designed bar talking, drinking and laughing.

Joel wanted to show the girls around the entire club first so they could take in all of its energy at once. He felt good because everywhere he looked there was somebody coming up to greet him. Erin and Kenya were impressed—they had no idea he was so popular. He seemed to command more attention than anybody else, but remained cool and didn't let it go to his head. Erin and Kenya were thrilled to be in Joel's company.

The water level had cool blue and white tiled walls with portholes positioned throughout the entire level. Inside the portholes were images of women swimming. This level had the most laid-back social atmosphere of all. People sat on leather sofas, just relaxing and sipping their drinks. The three enjoyed a short stay on the water level and then made their way up a transparent staircase to the red-hot fire level. This is where the jam-packed dance floor was located, along with another custom-designed bar.

The three went to the bar and ordered wine for Erin, an apple martini for Kenya and rum and Coke for Joel. This was the level where he met Renee, and after their breakup where he had seen haunting images of her. The images were all gone now. Joel looked across the room at the catwalk, at the DJ, and then up a little to his right at the air level, also known as the VIP section. He couldn't believe his eyes. His buddies Dave and Greg had reserved a sofa for themselves. They were up there perpetrating real hard for two young girls with average-lookin' faces and big badonkadonk booties. Dave and Greg never cared too much about pretty faces or brains. Their one-track minds were constantly focused on thick sexy bodies. On the other hand, Joel liked women who offered the complete package—beauty, brains and body.

Joel laughed to himself because he knew that Dave and Greg had kicked out some major cash to be in the VIP section. To top things off, they had a bottle of champagne chilling at each end of their sofa. Whack-ass playas like them made Joel hate the playas and the game.

Dave saw Joel across the room and signaled for him to join them on the air level. He was excited to see Joel, mainly because he needed cash. It was still early and Dave and Greg had already spent a ton of money. They needed Joel's cash to help keep the night going strong.

Greg looked to his left and noticed Dave signaling for Joel. Greg had a glass of champagne in his hand and when he saw Joel looking at him he lifted his glass and nodded his head.

Greg stood up, walked over to Dave and spoke directly into his ear above the music level, "You signaling that nigga over here, you better make sure he's got some money to contribute toward this sofa and this expensive-ass champagne. He's been missing in action and probably forgot how we roll."

Dave said, "Don't worry, I got you. You know damn well Joel's stingy-ass keeps money in his pocket."

Greg noticed Erin and Kenya trailing right behind Joel. He said, "Oh shit. Are those two fine-ass honeys with him?"

The three maneuvered carefully through the crowd. As soon as there was enough space, Joel took Erin and Kenya under his wings.

Dave's eyes widened. "Damn sure looks like they're with him. I ain't never seen their fine asses in here before."

"Me either. Check them out. They're all up on him. If the three of them plan on sitting up here I know he's gonna have to come out his pockets for real."

As soon as Joel got close enough, Dave let Joel know that they had a code-one in progress. This meant that Dave and Greg were frontin' as doctors from Johns Hopkins Hospital. Everybody exchanged greetings and quickly introduced themselves. The guys excused themselves for some male bonding while Erin and Kenya sat on the sofa next to the two young girls, Meisha and Jazmeka.

Joel asked, "What y'all doing with those Similac babies?"

Dave said excitedly, "Oh, we got them . . . got 'em good. They're going home with us tonight."

Greg laughed and gave Dave a high-five. "No doubt, son. We're about to tear shit up as soon as we leave here. We just wanna get them a little bit more sauced up . . . let their minds marinate. You know what I mean?"

Joel shook his head and said, "Yeah, I know exactly what you mean."

Dave asked Joel, "Which one of those is yours?"

Joel caught himself downplaying the situation. "Neither one is mine. We're just real good friends."

Greg said, "Bullshit. Looks like y'all got that ménage à trois kinda thing going on."

Joel smiled. "We do, and I'm loving life. Love . . . love . . . loving it."

Greg said, "Ah man, I knew it. Goddamn pretty boys always

getting the hookup. Maybe I need to start working out and I get me two babes like that."

Dave said, "They're fine as shit. Are they sisters?"

"No. Just friends."

Greg looked back at the girls and then asked, "Can I borrow one of them or what?"

Joel quickly said, "Hell fucking no. It ain't like that. We're not open to other people. This isn't a one night kinda thing or a fling. We're in a committed relationship . . . meaning the three of us only."

Dave and Greg cracked up laughing.

Greg was kind of toasted and asked, "So, what, do they be fucking each other too?"

Joel looked serious and said, "Now you're getting too personal."

Dave laughed and said, "That sounds like a yes to me. You're the man, Joel."

Greg was envious. "Trust me when I say this. What y'all have won't last. You're living a fantasy. You're crazy if you think something like that is gonna last. I ain't never heard of black people doing nothing like that."

Dave said, "Man, black people have threesomes all the time, but trying to turn it into a real relationship is insane. Jealousy is gonna eat y'all alive. Man, I thought you had better sense than that." He turned toward Greg and said, "We gave him too much credit."

Greg said, "You ain't lying."

Joel sipped his rum and Coke, zoned out for a few seconds and then looked out over a sea of smiling faces. He noticed Renee's little drug dealing cousin Spanky and his boys in the crowd. He barely recognized Spanky without his fitted Atlanta Braves baseball cap. Joel thought, *How the hell did they get in here?*

Joel refocused his thoughts and said, "Well, so far things have been real good for me and the girls."

Greg said, "Yeah, that's nice to hear. We forgot to mention that we're gonna need one-fifty from you for your girls sitting their fine asses on our sofa."

"One-fifty?" Joel unintentionally sounded just like Gary Coleman when he asked, "What you talkin' 'bout?"

"Dollars. A hundred and fifty dollars. This is the VIP section. I know you like being up here with all the ballers and looking down on all these regular niggas."

"Shit, you must be crazy. I don't even think like that. We're outta here."

Dave grabbed Joel by the arm and said, "Seriously Joel. For one-fifty y'all can share the sofa and finish off one of our bottles of champagne. How's that sound?"

"Sounds like some bull to me. We're not staying here much longer." Joel reconsidered when he saw that the girls did look like they we're enjoying themselves. "All right. I'll give y'all fifty."

Greg said, "C'mon. Look how sexy your girls look all up in the VIP."

"They can look even sexier in the backseat of my Cherokee, for free." Joel reached in his pocket and pulled out three twenty dollar bills for Greg. "Here you go, Doctor Scott. That's for you and Doctor Johnson."

Greg looked down at the money and said, "All right, that'll work. But only two of y'all can sit on the sofa at a time, and that's good for another hour and a half. That breaks down to twenty dollars every thirty minutes."

Joel shook his head and laughed. "Your math is on point, but you sound dumb as shit. How the hell do those girls believe y'all are doctors?"

Dave said, "It's not like they asked to see our medical degrees. All they care about is being seen sitting up in the VIP section."

Greg added, "And they wanna see us keep pulling out cash for drinks."

Erin and Kenya stood up, walked over to Joel, and asked him to join them on the dance floor. They were too beautiful to be denied.

Joel turned toward Dave and Greg. "Keep our spots warm. We'll be right back."

Greg and Dave watched as the three made their way to the dance floor. They looked at Erin and Kenya, then behind them at the two gold-diggers on the rented VIP sofa. There was no comparison because they knew that Joel's cheap ass was enjoying all of that pleasure for free.

Greg saw how happy Joel looked on the dance floor, sandwiched between Erin and Kenya. He said, "That's one lucky son-of-a-bitch."

Dave stood there dreaming of being in Joel's position. His eyes looked dreamy when he said, "Tell me about it. I'm gonna have it like that one day."

Greg looked back at Meisha and Jazmeka and said, "I'm trying to have it like that tonight. Let me go over here and holla at these girls real quick."

Meanwhile, Joel was having the time of his life with Erin and Kenya on the dance floor. They were all over each other, dirty dancing to their own passionate vibe. Joel got caught up in the heat of the moment and kissed Erin. Then he just had to kiss Kenya because he couldn't kiss one without kissing the other. All eyes were on them—looking at them mostly with awe and admiration, but then there were the envious and condemning stares. The three danced so long and so hard that they began to sweat.

After being on the dance floor for almost an hour they headed back up to the air level. Meisha and Jazmeka weren't anywhere in sight. Greg was knocked out on the sofa and Dave was sitting next to him drinking straight from their last champagne bottle, looking like he had just lost his best friend.

Joel asked, "What's up, Dave? Where are the girls?"

He frowned and pointed at Greg. "This dumb ass right here ran them off."

Joel laughed and asked, "How?"

"He asked if they'd be willing to have a threesome with him tonight . . . they got offended and rolled the fuck out."

Erin and Kenya overheard what Dave said and they almost fell out laughing.

Joel laughed too, and said, "That's terrible. I'm not gonna use my last half hour on the sofa. Go 'head and keep that last twenty dollars."

Dave smiled and said, "All right, that's what's up. You're still the man, Joel . . . often imitated, but never duplicated." He stood up and did that half-hug handshake thing with Joel. He looked at Erin and Kenya and said, "It was a pleasure, ladies."

They waved good-bye and the girls followed Joel downstairs toward the fire level. Joel said good night to all of the familiar faces in the crowd. He got dirty looks from a few guys in the crowd. It's hard for haters to hide their emotions.

When they reached the earth level Joel heard a guy yell, "There he is right there, Spank."

Renee's cousin appeared out of nowhere and blocked Joel's path. Joel could feel the familiar underlying beat of that negative force that was determined to disrupt his rhythm. He wasn't too worried because nothing violent ever happened in Club One. Their security was tight. But Erin and Kenya were terrified. Kenya had been trained in self-defense, but that was in a classroom setting with friendly instructors, and these were thugs from the mean streets of Bodymore, Murdaland—the second deadliest city in the nation. It was kind of obvious that something was about to go down. There was frantic movement in the crowd. People started moving the hell out of the way.

Spanky looked at Joel with a mischievous grin and said, "What's up, Joel?"

Joel returned the same grin and said, "What's up, Spanky?"

Spanky's grin dissolved and was replaced by a troubled look. He mean-mugged Joel, looking him up and down. "Nah, I mean, what's really up with you, nigga?"

Joel didn't take Spanky seriously at all. He laughed in his face and said, "Man, get your little ass out of my way. Me and my girls are trying to get outta here."

"Y'all ain't going nowhere. You left my cousin for these bitches and you disrespected my aunt this morning. Don't nobody diss my fam like that and expect not to get dealt with."

Joel was serious now. "Yo, you better watch your mouth. Don't you ever in your worthless-ass life call these women out of their names." Joel paused for a moment and looked at the two guys with Spanky. They gave him looks that let him know that they had Spanky's back. Joel turned his attention back toward Spanky and said, "Look, you don't know what you're talking about. I'm outta here. C'mon y'all."

Joel walked right through Spanky just like he wasn't even standing there. Erin and Kenya followed Joel's path.

Spanky let Joel get away with knocking him out of the way, but when Erin and Kenya walked by he said, "You can go, but this one is staying with me."

Spanky grabbed Erin and everybody could see the instant look of fury in Joel's eyes. He was the nicest guy anybody could meet, but when somebody got on his bad side he was an unstoppable raging maniac. Within a second Joel unleashed a knockout punch that landed on Spanky's jaw. Everybody within twenty feet heard a loud crack and then saw Spanky fall to the floor.

Joel looked at Spanky's boys and yelled, "Now what the fuck are y'all gonna do?"

They looked puzzled. They wanted no part of Joel because he was obviously a good fighter. He took their boy out in a matter of seconds with one punch. And they didn't know how to fight without their guns.

For a brief moment everything came to a standstill and then the bouncers appeared. They grabbed Joel by both of his arms. Before Joel lost it again, one of the bouncers said, "Hold on. Calm down. It's okay, Joel. We got you, brotha." They took him aside.

The other bouncer said, "That was our fault. We never should have let their asses in here, especially the one you knocked out. Go home and we'll take care of him and everything else. He's going to jail tonight . . . believe that."

One of Spanky's boys was all up in the mix. He said, "That's bullshit. That nigga hit Spank. My man didn't even do nothing. Plus, he on probation . . . he can't go to jail."

The bouncer said, "He's going to jail tonight for assaulting that woman. And if you don't shut the fuck up you're going with him."

Spanky's boy said, "I'm leaving, but this ain't over. Believe that."

The bouncers were actually off-duty Baltimore city policemen. Joel didn't see the need, but the officers wanted to ensure his and the girls' safety by escorting them to the parking lot. They made it to Joel's truck safely and Spanky ended up in central booking with a broken jaw.

Chapter 25

The majority of the ride home was silent—no music or conversation. The silence amplified the sounds of the Jeep Cherokee's air conditioner, the engine and the tires. On a more personal level it was as if Joel, Erin and Kenya could hear their own heartbeats and breathing. Joel was still angry as hell and had a hard time cooling down. At one point he gripped the steering wheel so tightly that it seemed like he was about to rip it apart. At another point he pounded his fists against the steering wheel. He became increasingly frustrated the more his mind replayed the confrontation with Spanky.

Erin and Kenya had never seen this side of Joel before. They wanted to comfort him, but didn't know where to begin. An uneasy feeling moved between the three as their eyes drifted aimlessly back and forth. The pale green lighting of the dashboard's instrument panel gave each of their faces an unnatural, eerie appearance in the ashy darkness of night.

Joel noticed that his door was slightly ajar. He opened it while going sixty-five miles per hour and then closed it quickly. The sound of the door slamming startled Erin. Joel knew that he scared her. Somehow the incident changed his mood, and he tried not to laugh at Erin. Joel looked at Kenya, and they grinned. Then Erin smiled, too.

Joel laughed and said, "I'm sorry, Erin. I didn't mean to

scare you by opening my door like that." He looked over his shoulder and asked, "I didn't scare you, Kenya, did I?"

She made a funny face and said, "Not with the door. You scared me when you started beating up the steering wheel though."

They all laughed.

Joel said, "Sorry about that." He turned his attention toward Erin and asked, "Did you think I was about to jump outta here or something when I opened the door?"

Erin shrugged, smiled and said, "I didn't know what to think. You weren't acting like yourself. I guess you're better now, huh?"

"I'm all right."

Erin said, "I wasn't going to say anything about the way you were acting until we got home, and then I was going to ask you to take out all of your frustration on me." She reached out and touched his arm. "Oh my God, you're so sexy when you're mad."

Kenya laughed and said, "It's more like a scary, intimidating kind of sexiness . . . if that makes sense at all."

Erin said, "You got it right. That's why people should never underestimate guys with easygoing personalities. Y'all are the worst kind to deal with, because you take so much until you eventually boil over."

With a giggle in her voice Kenya said, "Tell me about it. Joel knocked that dude out cold."

Joel said, "I know, and he deserved it."

Erin said, "Yeah, he did. He had the nerve to refer to us a Bs."

"Yeah, that pissed me off. I kind of wish I could have handled things better and avoided feeding into his negativity. I don't regret what I did, but the whole thing is embarrassing when I think about it. All those people seeing me lose it like that. I can't ever go back to that club again."

Erin said, "None of us can go back there again. Do you have any idea how much attention we drew tonight?"

Kenya said, "A lot."

"I completely lost it when he put his hands on Erin. But I don't know what I was thinking because I put all of us at risk. Thank God everything turned out in our favor. The bad thing is that it might not be over. Y'all know how it is."

Kenya said, "It's over. They don't want any trouble from you."

"And I don't want any trouble from them. I ain't trying to get shot and end up being a damn murder statistic."

It was a serious topic, but they all laughed.

Erin said, "Don't even think like that. You create your own destiny with your words. What we focus on most, whether good or bad, eventually comes true."

Joel said, "You're right. I need to take my mind off of what happened with some music."

Joel had his iPod hooked up to his car stereo. He hit the Play button and then a bangin' beat seemed to come out of nowhere. The new Jay-Z song was playing, and the tempo flowed perfectly with the way Joel was cruising up I-83. Erin reached over and grabbed Joel's right hand. Kenya looked at their connection and felt a little left out. She took note of each of their positions and the significance. Joel was in the driver's seat. As usual, Erin was on his right side—his dominant side. Since Kenya wasn't able to assume her position on his left side, she was in the backseat. She refused to be left out and positioned her hand on top of Erin and Joel's. They unlocked their hands and wrapped their fingers around hers. Kenya played it cool because she knew that there would always be moments when Erin and Joel would unintentionally revert to their primary relationship.

Erin and Kenya practically ripped Joel's clothes off as soon as they walked through his front door. He managed to hit the light switch. A lamp came on, and its low wattage bulb provided dim shadowy lighting. Erin and Kenya continued to bombard Joel with attention. They removed his shirt and groped his muscular body like a couple of wild sex-starved groupies. They loved his smooth, dark flawless skin and let him know it by the way they kissed his body. Erin and Kenya treated him like a gladiator or a Zulu warrior who had just returned home from a victorious battle.

Erin said, "Joel, I'm so horny. I need to feel you inside me right now."

Joel kissed Erin and then kissed Kenya.

Erin said, "C'mon, skip the foreplay . . . I'm ready." She pulled up her dress, slid down her panties and stepped out of them. She leaned over the dinette table with her ass exposed. Erin looked back at Joel while touching herself and said. "C'mon and feel how wet I am."

Kenya smiled. She stood behind Joel, stroking his dick, getting him nice and hard for Erin. He took a few seconds to slide on a condom. His heart raced because he was excited and more than ready to please. He moved closer with his throbbing hard-on. He took Erin by surprise and plunged deep inside of her. She gasped for air and tried to move forward a little, but there was nowhere to go. He forced her to stand there and take every inch of him. He held steady for a minute so she could enjoy the deep penetration as well as the stretching sensation his big dick created. Kenya remained right behind Joel's remarkable physique, massaging his shoulders, back, buttocks and balls.

Erin loved the way Joel felt inside of her. She brought her legs together and eventually crossed them to make her pussy feel even tighter. Joel leaned forward and grabbed hold of Erin's breasts. He played with her nipples and kissed her on the back of her neck.

Joel was ready for a position change. He turned Erin around to face him. They kissed as he lifted her off the ground. She wrapped her arms around his neck and her legs around his waist. Erin felt Joel's hardness bump against her. She moved herself in an upward motion and then downward so he could penetrate her. She was so wet that she slid right down the shaft of his dick with ease. The stimulation from this angle was very pleasurable to both of them.

Being in the air was exciting to Erin. Joel began to walk around. He continued to fuck Erin as he carried her all the way to his bedroom. She loved riding his dick like this—it showed how strong he was and how much endurance he had. Joel thrust himself in and out while Erin bounced up and down. She rode him until she couldn't take it any longer. Her grip and entire body tightened as she gradually reached her climax.

Kenya stood aside, watching and masturbating. She hadn't even removed her panties. She just slipped her hands inside and let her fingers go to work. When Joel saw what Kenya was doing his erection intensified. Erin screamed out Joel's name and then let out a succession of beautiful orgasmic moans and groans.

Just as they finished, the neighbor who lived below Joel pounded on the ceiling and yelled, "Stop all that fucking noise."

Joel lay Erin down softly on the bed. He and Kenya laughed at the neighbor. Erin heard the neighbor's complaint and then again she didn't—she felt too much pleasure to care.

Joel kissed Erin on her lips. He removed his condom and wiped himself off with a towel. He was preparing himself for Kenya and she knew it.

With excitement in her voice Kenya said, "Erin, I'm gonna take Joel out into the living room. Do you wanna join us?"

Erin could hardly speak. She was so out of breath that all she could do was mumble, "No . . . go . . . ahead . . . without . . . me." She sighed heavily. "I can't move."

Joel said, "C'mon. We need you."

"No . . . I'm fine . . . right here."

With a little giggle Kenya said, "Okay, were gonna have fun without you then."

Erin's voice almost returned to normal. "Go ahead and . . . knock yourselves out."

Kenya said, "All right, we'll be back."

Tired of talking, Erin moaned, "Uh-huh."

Erin really wanted Kenya and Joel to stay by her side. She didn't want the two of them venturing off together, discovering something new without her. They were a threesome and that meant they were supposed to experience everything together. The three were beginning to make subtle mistakes. Erin held her tongue. She didn't want to seem jealous or insecure. Within a few minutes, nothing mattered because she was fast asleep. Joel had put it on her real good.

Kenya knew exactly what she was doing. She desired some alone time with Joel to please him with her body, using a more sensuous approach than Erin used. Kenya gladly took Joel by the hand and led him back out into the shadowy living room.

The temperature inside was about to match the steamy nighttime heat outside.

Kenya asked Joel, "You didn't come, did you?"

He laughed and said, "No."

She replied quickly, "Good."

"How did you know?"

"I know you and I love your style. You like to hold off on having orgasms."

"I always say ladies first, because if you're satisfied then so am I."

Joel meant that from the bottom of his heart. He was an unselfish and affectionate lover who had a deep understanding of the female psyche and physiology. He knew all about fulfilling a woman's intimate wants and needs and he was about to appease Kenya in every way possible.

One touch from Joel awakened millions of Kenya's nerve endings. He made her feel tingly all over. He put his right hand and then his left on her waist. He traced the skin around her panty line with his fingertips.

Joel whispered in her ear, "You're so sexy. You know that?"

Kenya felt a trickle of moisture between her legs. She was

so hot and bothered that she couldn't even think straight. All she said was, "Oh, God."

Joel removed her top and then her bra to reveal her big, beautiful, round breasts. Joel forced Kenya backward against the wall. His neighbor must have fallen asleep with his television on because they could hear it blaring next door. Joel moved his hands up Kenya's brown skin to her breasts. He squeezed them and nibbled on her nipples. Then he took both of his hands and gently slid them up to her neck. He brought his lips up to her neck as well and began to act like a vampire—kissing, biting and sucking.

Kenya said, "Oh, that feels so good. What are you doing to me?"

He caressed her face and said, "It's called seduction."

Joel's hands kept moving for a minute until he reached her earlobes and the back of her neck. He applied a gentle massaging motion as he kissed her left cheek. He sucked in a breath of air through his teeth that made a sexy hissing sound in her left ear and then did the same on her right side. He dragged his lips across Kenya's face and kissed her lips.

Kenya thought, *How is he able to do things so differently each time and be so good at it?*

Kenya was so sexy to Joel that he couldn't resist running his tongue across her teeth as they kissed. Toward the end of their kiss she sucked his tongue and wouldn't let go.

Joel mumbled, "Give it back."

They laughed.

Joel loved being with two women at once, but this was a welcome change. The only downside to being with Erin and Kenya at the same time was that he felt his attention pulled in different directions and worried about whether or not he was spreading it equally. That was just part of his attentive nature. The last thing he wanted was for either of them to feel neglected. Being with them separately meant that he could concentrate a little better on fully satisfying their individual needs.

Joel and Kenya were completely naked as they eased their

way to the floor. Kenya straddled Joel and he propped her up a little higher by moving his legs into an Indian-lotus position. They stared deeply into each other's eyes. Kenya placed Joel's hand on her heart and then she placed her hand on his heart. They synchronized their breathing and their hearts seemed to beat as one. This was a very intimate and powerful energy-sharing position. They kissed again, a kiss that felt eternal. When the kiss ended Kenya arched her back and put her big brown breasts and pointy nipples directly in Joel's face. He began to suck them with purpose and intention, and that really set things in motion. Their hormones, endorphins and neuro-transmitters began to peak and rage—creating a dreamlike atmosphere. Kenya hugged Joel's neck and wrapped her legs around him tightly.

They teased each other with their lips and kissed over and over again.

Kenya was dripping wet and Joel could feel the moist heat stirring between her legs. She shifted slightly. In an instant his erection rose and met with the tip of her excited clitoris. Joel had forgotten to bring a condom out to the living room. Their body heat was amazing. The sexy gaze that they shared was absolutely hypnotic. Joel couldn't bear to interrupt the magical moment. His dick was raring to go and Kenya's pussy was aching to be penetrated. Kenya started a slow sexy grind. And before they knew it Joel's dick was inside of her. She was getting it raw and loved the feeling.

Kenya had reached another first with Joel. This was a first that Erin hadn't even experienced. She continued to straddle him and grind until she found the perfect spot—a notch between the base of his dick and pelvic bone. It provided the perfect coital alignment, stimulating her clitoris and G-spot at the same time. Now she rocked back and forth until she and Joel were on the verge of coming. Kenya tightened her vaginal muscles around Joel's hardness and together they controlled the pace and intensity. They decreased the intensity a little and then gradually turned it up again. They played with the sexual energy for a couple of hours, until it got so intense that they couldn't do anything but let it go. Joel came inside of Kenya and she didn't even attempt to stop him. She loved the way it felt when he exploded and filled her up with his warm juices. This was an experience that they planned to keep hidden from Erin—a secret they planned on taking to their graves.

Chapter 26

Joel dreamed that he was naked and alone on a deserted island. In a way his dream seemed to have overflowed into reality, because the next morning he woke up naked and alone in bed. He imagined hearing his alarm clock go off and that was what woke him. In reality his alarm clock wasn't even set. His circadian rhythm was out of whack. He was getting used to staying up almost all night and then waking up closer and closer to noon.

Each morning his ear seemed to focus on the strangest sounds. He heard the distinct sound of a single bird singing a lonely song outside of his window. This was unusual. He wasn't as concerned about what was happening outside as he was about what was happening inside. He was alone in bed and wanted to know what was up with that. He heard the shower running and assumed that one of the girls was in there and the other must be out in the kitchen preparing coffee. But he didn't smell the refreshing and invigorating aroma of coffee.

It's funny how drastically things can change within a twenty-four-hour period. For the first time in weeks Joel felt alone. His deserted island dream had instilled in him a feeling of abandonment. He wasn't alone too long because guilt lay next to him in bed and made him worry that he may have done something to upset the balance of his relationship with Erin and Kenya.

The shower stopped and he listened as the shower curtain opened. The hooks slid across the metal pole. Joel lay in bed waiting to see which one of the girls would step out of the bathroom. Guilt was gone, and now Joel lay in bed with his new companion called mounting anticipation. Within minutes the door opened and Erin walked out of the bathroom wearing nothing but a plush beige towel and a smile on her face.

Joel sighed silently and smiled.

There wasn't a window in the bathroom and Joel thought that Erin had forgotten to turn off the light, but she hadn't. Kenya was right on Erin's heels, wrapped in a matching plush beige towel with a smile on her face that matched Erin's. She turned off the light just as she exited the bathroom.

Right away curiosity had stepped into the picture and it was killing Joel. He felt left out, not knowing what had just happened behind that closed door. His overactive imagination began to run through all of the sexual acts the girls could have possibly executed in his absence. His thoughts were vivid and amazing, but he knew that his imagination paled in comparison to seeing Erin and Kenya live in action. He felt cheated because he knew that he had missed out on one of the finest aspects of being in a female-male-female threesome—the amazingly beautiful girl-on-girl action. The passion that women share has intrigued men for ages.

Erin and Kenya smiled at Joel and said good morning.

He was kind of upset, but instead of voicing his complaints he just swallowed his words along with a portion of his male pride. His silence was far more dramatic than words.

It was obvious that the three had too much idle time on their hands. There wasn't much to do besides have fun and immerse themselves deeper into a smorgasbord of hedonistic behavior. That's pretty much what happens when three insatiable lovers attempt to live a reality based on fantasy and curiosity. Everything they did seemed to revolve around one main theme—sex. They began to make subtle mistakes that seemed to have become acceptable or seemed to become the norm.

Jealousy tried to make its way into the picture, but Joel wouldn't allow it inside. The three had reached a point where they had begun to experience moments of feeling left out, as interpersonal relationships developed within the threesome. Erin and Kenya had a warm and loving relationship established long before they met Joel. He began to wonder whether the girls had used the threesome concept as an excuse to explore their sexuality. Things were starting to get somewhat complex. Any relationship as eccentric as theirs was without a doubt susceptible to some degree of complication.

Joel tried to act unaffected. He looked at Erin and Kenya and said, "Good morning. What got y'all up so early?"

Erin casually removed her towel and began to dry off. "I don't know. I slept really good last night."

Kenya helped dry Erin's back and said, "So did I. And you obviously slept well because you slept right through the two of us moving around and talking."

Joel sat up in bed and asked, "What do y'all have planned for today?"

Erin said. "I dunno. Let's go to the mall."

Joel asked, "The mall? I know you're not a big shopper. So, what are you in the mood for . . . some socializing?"

"No, I'm in the mood for some shopping. I need something to make me look as good as I feel."

Joel raised an eyebrow and asked, "Did I miss something?"

Erin replied, "No. What do you mean?"

"You know . . . the action in the shower . . . you and Kenya."

Kenya removed her towel and began to dry herself off. "If you consider us showering together and washing each other's backs action, then you missed it."

Erin looked at Kenya and said, "Sounds like he's complaining to me."

Kenya said, "Sounds like that to me, too."

The girls giggled.

Joel said, "Maybe I am. What's so funny?"

Kenya said, "Nothing."

As Erin slipped into her underwear she said, "Well, you didn't hear me complaining last night when you went venturing off into the living room with Kenya."

Joel said, "But I'm sure you wanted to."

Erin twisted her lips and shrugged her right shoulder. "I dunno . . . maybe I should have complained."

Kenya made a strange face and said, "Since we're putting it all out there, Erin, I need to complain about all of the times you basically forced me into the backseat whenever we've ridden in Joel's truck."

Erin looked shocked and then confused. "Do I do that?"

Kenya replied quickly, "Yeah."

Joel nodded his head and said, "Yeah, you do."

Erin laughed. "Dag, listen to us . . . complaining."

Kenya put on her panties and said, "It looks like we need to make a few minor adjustments to help work out the kinks."

Erin said, "Things don't have to be complicated. We have a relationship with different modes of expression that offers a wide range of feelings and experiences. As a threesome, I don't think we should be preprogrammed or restricted to one mode like traditional relationships. We're better than that. If we need alone time with someone within the threesome, then it should happen. As long as we come back together and share, then everything should be okay."

Kenya and Joel looked at each other with an expression that said they needed to bury their secret even deeper. They quickly refocused their attention on Erin.

Joel said, "I agree."

Kenya took a deep breath and said, "So do I."

The telephone rang and Joel picked up the receiver and said, "Hello."

"Hi, Joel," his mother said.

"Hey, Ma. How are you?"

"Fine, and you?"

"I'm all right. What's going on?"

"Nothing. Just calling to remind you about my procedure in the morning."

"I haven't forgotten."

Mrs. Davis paused for a moment, then asked, "I already know the answer, but I'll ask anyway. You wanna join me at church this morning?"

Joel looked at his alarm clock and said, "It's ten thirty-eight and there's no way I can make it to church by eleven."

"We've got service going all day. Anytime you arrive for church is on time. God cares about your presence and not your lateness. He'll help you work on your timing once you put forth the effort. Our eleven o'clock service doesn't end until two. You can show up later this afternoon and stick around for our three-thirty service if you want."

Erin whispered something in Kenya's ear. They started acting silly, trying to make Joel laugh. When that didn't work they tried their best to distract him by dancing and shaking their butts like the video girls he loved to watch.

They had an obvious effect on him. He looked distracted and said, "Whew . . . I don't know. Ah . . . Ma . . . let me see now. Umm . . . shoot. What was I saying?"

Mrs. Davis said, "That's a shame. I remember when you wouldn't go a Sunday without going to church. Now everything else seems to come first. I hear that girl laughing in the background. Is that more than one I hear? Who is that?"

"Yes, ma'am. Those are my neighbors from across the hall."

"Isn't it kind of early for them to be in your apartment, don't you think?"

"Not really. We were just about to have breakfast."

"Yeah right, tell me anything. Are y'all in the kitchen or in the bedroom?"

Joel cleared his throat, but couldn't really clear his lie. "We're in the kitchen, of course."

"I pray to God you don't have them in your bedroom. Are you still fornicating?"

"C'mon, Ma. What kind of question is that? You know I am. I'm not married and I can't deprive myself of certain pleasures."

Erin and Kenya stopped acting silly and looked at each other, then at Joel, wondering exactly what the heck he and his mother were talking about.

Mrs. Davis said the same line she had been feeding Joel for years. "You need to learn how to find pleasure in other things besides sex."

"Please don't lecture me."

"All right, I'll stop. Since you can't make it to church, why don't you come here this evening for dinner? I'd be glad to have you. I won't stay for our three-thirty service. Instead I'll make you a good old-fashioned Sunday dinner. Does that sound okay to you?"

"Yeah, that sounds good. Can I bring my friends?"

"Sure, the more the merrier. Are they Christians?"

"Yes, ma'am."

"Good. That's a start. I gotta go. I've got a pot of greens cooking now and I'll fry the chicken as soon as I get back from church. Tell your friends I said hi."

Joel looked at Erin and Kenya and said, "My mother said hi."

Erin and Kenya sang out at the same time, "*Hi, Mom.*"

Joel asked, "Did you hear them?"

"Yes, I heard them. Okay Joel, let me go now. You be good and I'll see y'all later."

"All right. Enjoy church and we'll see you this evening."

Joel hung up the phone. He looked at Erin and Kenya. With laughter in his voice he said, "Y'all are soooo ignorant."

Erin looked at Kenya and asked, "Did you just hear him call us ignorant?"

Kenya replied, "Yeah, but I think it went beyond ignorant. He said we were soooo ignorant."

Erin said, "I think we're gonna have to kick some butt."

Kenya said, "C'mon, let's get him."

Erin and Kenya were full of child like energy. They dove on the bed and attacked Joel. He loved to play-fight and welcomed their kinky playful challenge. They were topless, wearing nothing but panties. The girls tried to grab hold of Joel to get him in a headlock, but they couldn't. He was way too strong, swift and agile for them to handle. He ended up tossing them around on the bed and roughing them up a bit—all in the name of fun. He piled them on top of each other, spanked their butts for a minute, and then began to tickle them half to death. He eventually gave in to the girls and let them pin him on the bed. Erin and Kenya celebrated their fake victory and then crashed on the bed on opposite sides of Joel.

Trying to regain her breath Erin said, "That was so much fun."

Kenya responded, "Next time we need to rough him up a little more."

Joel laughed and said, "That was fun. I think all three of us just had some type of fetish fulfilled."

Kenya said, "Especially you, with all of the tickling and spanking. We'll have to do some role playing some time."

Joel said, "That's fine with me. We can play sex slave, dirty cop busting two first-time prostitutes, or horny wife catching her cheating husband with his mistress, and so on and so on."

Erin smiled and said, "Mmmm . . . we can have so much fun together. The possibilities are endless."

With a mischievous grin Kenya said, "I know. I can't wait."

They lay in bed for a while watching television. A show about celebrity dream homes located in Miami caught their attention. Joel showered alone while the girls finished day-dreaming. They all got dressed and headed to the Owings Mills Town Center.

Chapter 27

B y noon it was hot and sticky outside. The temperature had soared to a miserable ninety-five degrees. All of the local news stations warned of the poor air quality and asked the public to go outside only if it was absolutely necessary. Not even the heat and humidity could tear Renee away from the hazy glass of Robert's bedroom window. She looked exhausted, and her body was drenched with sweat. She had been outside of Robert's house since eleven-thirty the previous night. Nothing mattered to her except exacting some sort of revenge for him dumping her so abruptly.

Renee had driven around for hours the night before, with nowhere to go and no one to see, until she happened to notice Robert and his new girlfriend, Tamara, coming out of the AMC movie theater in Owings Mills. They never saw Renee, and she ended up following them to Robert's house. He lived in a small two-bedroom ranch-style home located in the Wood-lawn section of Baltimore County.

Renee stood between a water hose caddy and some over-grown hedges on a mound of fresh mulch, watching Robert and Tamara make love. While standing there, Renee came to the conclusion that Robert was the most unimaginative man she had ever been with when it came to sex. He proved it by going through the exact same lovemaking techniques he used with her.

Tamara and Robert lay on the same sheets that he and

Renee lay on just a week ago. Renee figured that he probably didn't have the common decency to even wash those musty sex-stained sheets. The two of them looked like they were too much into the act of making love to even care about the condition of the sheets. More than anything Renee was a woman scorned and her mind was telling her all kinds of things regardless of whether they were true or not.

Renee had a flashback of the first day when things got a little heated and out of control between her and Robert. They had worked together for a couple of years and shared a mutual attraction. Renee considered him a hot prospect and often found herself fantasizing about him, especially on days she wasn't really feeling Joel.

Robert came into her office out of the blue and started some small talk, which led to them having lunch at a nearby restaurant. Actually he didn't come into her office out of the blue. He sensed her vulnerability a mile away. Robert was an extremely handsome, articulate and charismatic brotha on the surface. But beneath all that he was nothing more than a conceited, conniving and deceitful playa who loved to take advantage of unsuspecting women in unstable relationships. He used a calculated approach that totally blindsided Renee. She was completely taken by his alluring dark eyes. The subtle but unforgettable fragrance of his cologne captivated and delighted her sense of smell. The much needed friendly male-female conversation reminded Renee that she was desirable. Robert's ever-present boyish smile put her heart and mind at ease and paralyzed her defenses.

Eventually Robert got to the point. He told Renee how beautiful she was and confessed to being attracted to her since the first time they laid eyes on each other. Renee welcomed the attention from Robert and she fell right into his trap. She never wondered why it took him two years to confess to his instant attraction. The real reason was that it took a while for her turn to come around. He was only one man who had lots of women to serve.

Robert asked, "How are things at home?"

"Not good. I'm not happy."

Renee had no reason to tell him what was going on at home, but she sold her man out in a matter of minutes and let her personal business out, without even thinking of the consequences. She automatically trusted a man who she knew very little about. Renee really only knew two things about Robert for sure: she liked him a lot, and where he worked. That was all it took.

Robert calmly replied, "You deserve better. If I was your man I'd keep you happy . . . I'd provide pleasure like you've never known. You wouldn't have to ask for a thing because I'd make sure you had everything you've ever desired."

By five-thirty that evening they were making love on top of Renee's desk.

Sweat poured from Renee's forehead and tears poured from her eyes. No matter how much it hurt to watch Robert and Tamara, she just couldn't take her eyes off of them. She tried to disconnect her personal feelings from the whole situation, but instead became mildly aroused by what she saw. Robert did something that was all too familiar to her. He put Tamara in a missionary position and covered her with his warm body while working his hips to her pleasure. Tamara put her legs together real tight and Robert rode a little higher so she could get the right amount of clitoral stimulation.

It was as if Renee could feel Robert inside of her, she knew that position and his motions so well. For a moment she found herself wishing that she was in Tamara's place, just to have someone to kiss and hold her that close while being deep inside of her.

Tamara had her eyes closed and whined strangely, like she was going through different stages of orgasmic pleasure. Robert was about to climax when he thought he saw a vague image in his window out of the corner of his eye. His concentration was thrown off and so was his rhythm. He thought his eyes were playing tricks on him. When he looked again he clearly saw the top of a woman's head in the bottom corner of his window. He instantly recognized the honey-blond hair, the forehead and the eyes. His body already shielded most of Tamara's body. He quickly covered his ass with a sheet—as if Renee hadn't already seen it.

Robert and Renee's eyes locked. He yelled, "Oh shit, Renee!"

Renee burst out laughing because it was so funny to hear him call out her name in the middle of making love to another woman. Renee didn't care that she was caught. She just stood where she was and gave him the finger.

Tamara yelled, "What did you say? I know you didn't just call me by that crazy bitch's name."

Robert quickly replied, "No-no-no. There she is right there."

"Where is she?" Tamara asked as she looked around the room and then out the window.

Renee smiled at her and gave her the double-whammy— two middle fingers. She banged the glass real hard with her hand, turned around and walked over to her Escalade.

Tamara yelled, "Call the police!"

Robert knew that he had to nip Renee's insane actions in the bud. He wasn't the type of person who tolerated anybody trespassing on his property or trying to stalk him. He was wild and crazy enough to put an end to it himself.

Without even thinking, Robert's response was, "Fuck the police. I got this."

He jumped out of bed butt naked, slipped on a pair of beige see-through pajama pants and an old, worn-out Myrtle Beach T-shirt.

Tamara said, "Damn, do you have to put all that on? She'll be gone by the time your ass gets dressed."

"Shut the hell up," Robert said as he stepped into his flip flops and headed outside to confront Renee.

Robert knew that Renee had lost her mind because she was still parked a couple of doors down from his house. She sat in the driver's seat of her Escalade with the engine running, singing along with a new Beyoncé song. She had the window up with the air conditioner running.

Robert yelled through the glass, "You need to leave right now, and don't ever come back around here again. If I see you around here again I'm gonna take it as a threat and I'm not sure what I might do to you."

Renee saw and partially heard Robert, but she kept singing right along with the song. He knocked on the glass and Renee ignored him.

Tamara felt the need to come outside and let her presence be felt. She looked real special wearing Robert's oversized blue terrycloth robe and slippers. Renee noticed Tamara in her peripheral vision, but didn't react at all. Tamara marched right up to the driver's-side door, shoved Robert aside and opened it. Renee panicked when she looked down and saw Tamara standing there yelling obscenities.

Renee felt the need to defend herself. Her erratic behavior turned violent when she reached under her seat and pulled out an umbrella. All of a sudden she swooped down from her seat and started beating Tamara in the head and face with the umbrella's wooden and metal handle. The sight of blood didn't even make Renee stop. Robert's hand around Renee's wrist was the only thing that stopped her. Robert knew Tamara was wrong for confronting Renee and he kind of admired Renee's gangsta fighting skills. He felt that this was an ass-whipping Tamara brought on herself for opening Renee's door the way she did.

Within seconds Robert's neighbors came out of the woodwork to get an eyewitness account of the pure and unadulterated ass-whipping Renee put on Tamara.

Even though Robert found humor in the way Renee threw down on Tamara he was still pissed at her for bringing this kind of drama to his doorstep.

Robert said, "Renee, get away from here with all this. How could you embarrass me and yourself like this?"

"How could you embarrass yourself by putting on these nasty-ass see-through pajama pants?"

Little kids were outside eating ice cream and laughing at Robert's funny-shaped butt.

Robert ignored the fact that he was standing outside practically nude in front of his neighbors. He took off his T-shirt and applied it to Tamara's bloodied head and face. He didn't know what to say to Renee and just blurted out the first thing that came to mind.

He said, "Won't you go harass Joel and leave me and Tamara the hell alone? He's the one you're really mad at."

It was as if Renee's mind was open for suggestions, because hearing Joel's name made her feel that he needed to feel some of her grief, too. She looked around at all of the neighbors. A few of them were on their cell phones. Renee assumed they were calling for an ambulance or the police. She hurried back inside her Escalade. She threw it into drive and peeled out of the parking space.

Chapter 28

It's hard for most guys to go from store to store, rack to rack and then stand around for hours looking at women's fashions. Joel wasn't in the mood for holding pocketbooks while the girls tried on clothes. He knew the routine and decided to sit in the mall directly in front of Macy's entrance. The mall was bright and lively, with a whirlwind of different scents along with a kaleidoscope of colorful advertisements and displays. Joel adjusted to his surroundings and blocked out the obscure pop music that played softly in the background.

He planned to sit on the bench and play his NFL football game on his cell phone. Before he started playing his game, he did something completely out of the ordinary. He reached into his wallet, pulled out his rarely used Macy's card and told the girls to treat themselves to whatever they liked. He felt comfortable doing this because he knew they weren't the type to take advantage of his kindness. His gesture surprised the girls and made them smile.

Kenya asked, "Is this some kind of test to see where our heads are? I think you're trying to see whether we would take advantage of you or not."

Joel laughed and said, "No. That's not what this is about. I already know that I can trust the two of you."

Erin said, "You don't have to do this. We have our own money and credit cards."

Joel said, "I know I don't have to do it, but I just wanna do something nice for the two of you."

With laughter in her voice Kenya said, "Well, if you insist, I'll take it."

Joel handed her the card and said, "Go ahead . . . it's fine."

Kenya asked, "Is there a limit to how much we can spend?"

He said, "Use your own discretion. I'm not worried."

Kenya said, "All right, and you said pick out whatever we like, right?"

Erin said, "Yeah, he did say that. C'mon."

"I'll be right here playing my game . . . the Baltimore Ravens vs. the Cincinnati Bengals. See y'all in a little while."

Erin and Kenya thanked Joel and they both gave him quick pecks on his lips.

Joel sat alone on a bench playing a serious but imaginary football match-up on his cell phone. Some older married men sat across from him on the benches that surrounded the indoor fountain. Some of the men looked numb and exhausted. They just sat there guarding their wives' shopping bags. Joel laughed to himself.

A young couple and their little boy walked over to one of the other benches. The mother asked her son, "Are you going with me or staying here with Daddy?"

The little boy looked about three years old. He clearly stated, "I wanna stay with Daddy." As soon as his mother walked away he took off running behind her yelling, "I go with you."

Joel admired their little family. He found himself thinking about having a family quite a bit lately. He hoped to have kids one day. He always dreamed of having a Joel Davis Jr. who closely resembled him. He imagined having kids with Erin and Kenya. He imagined how they would look. He tried to figure out how the three of them would even integrate kids into their current relationship. He knew that people had done it, but deep down he knew that it would be confusing, weird, uncomfortable and possibly disastrous for a child to be raised in a poly relationship. His thoughts quickly shifted back to his game.

A few minutes later he was so engrossed in his game that it appeared as if he hardly noticed a steady stream of attractive women who walked by. He definitely noticed them, but didn't feel the need to acknowledge them with anything more than his usual brief eye contact and a subtle smile. Although Joel was into the game, he was well aware of everybody around him. As a matter of fact, he felt someone staring at him. He looked up and saw two guys who looked a whole lot like the rappers Baby and Lil Wayne staring at him from the opposite side of the mall. They walked by Joel without saying a word. A few seconds later he felt the same strange feeling. When he looked up he saw the same two guys again. This time he kept his eyes on the two of them. When they realized he was watching them, one of the guys headed toward Joel.

Joel was calm and took a couple of seconds to select the *save & exit* mode on his game.

The guy who looked like Lil Wayne approached Joel and said, "Yo, ain't you the dude who beat Spanky's ass last night at the club?"

Joel felt an instant adrenaline rush. His heart started beating out of his chest. Retaliation and bloodshed was all he could think of for the moment. He played dumb at first and said, "Huh?"

The guy nodded and said, "Yeah, you are the one. I remember you."

Joel was ready to take on whatever came his way. He stood up boldly and looked like he was ready to defend himself. With an intense look in his eyes he said, "Yeah, it was me. Why? What you want?"

The guy laughed and said, "Nah, I'm not trying to step to you like that. I just want you to know that the streets is lovin' you right about now. That nigga Spanky gonna be away for a while. He was on probation and I know they gonna make him serve out the last seven years he had left on his sentence."

Joel had a nonchalant expression on his face. "That's kind of messed up, but he brought that on himself."

"You don't even feel bad about that, do you?"

"Nope, I don't. Why should I?"

"Nah, you shouldn't. He wasn't a friend of mine. Me and my people hate him. You did him a favor and added a few more days to his life 'cause everybody was after that boy. They just gonna get him on the inside now. What was y'all fighting about anyway?"

"I used to mess with his cousin, and Spanky was mouthing off about stuff he didn't know nothing about. And then he put his hands on my girlfriend."

"I don't blame you for doing what you did. I would have knocked his ass out too, if he had touched my girl." The guy paused for a moment, gave Joel a look of respect, threw his hands up and said, "Aw-ight, that's it. I just wanted you to know what was going on."

"Yeah, thanks."

The two guys walked away, but Joel didn't trust them. He sat back down and felt like a stationary target sitting there. He continued sitting there, playing his game until it was interrupted by an incoming text message.

The text message was from Erin. It read, *I miss you!*

Within a few seconds another text message came through, but this time it was an *I miss you* from Kenya.

Joel replied to both messages, *I miss you, too!*

Forty-five minutes later, Joel saw Erin and Kenya walking toward him, each carrying two medium-sized shopping bags.

Kenya handed Joel his Macy's card and said, "Thank you. We didn't use your card. They had a nice sale going on and we decided to pay for our own clothes. We treated you to a couple of nice things . . . just to show you how much we appreciate you."

"You're both appreciated and that is why I offered to pay for your clothes. Now I definitely have to do something special for the two of you."

Erin said, "You've already done enough."

Kenya said, "Speak for yourself." Then in a sexy tone she said, "I know a few things you can do."

They all laughed.

Joel asked, "Did y'all get what you wanted . . . from the store?"

Erin said, "Yeah." She handed him one of the shopping bags and said, "This is for you from me and Kenya."

"What is it?"

Kenya said, "The simplest thing to do is to just look inside the bag."

Joel said, "I knew you were gonna say that."

Kenya said, "Just look inside, please."

Joel opened the bag and found two striped Ralph Lauren Polo shirts that were different from any of his others. He said, "Thanks. I love these. Just what I needed, a couple more to add to my collection." He paused for a moment and then asked, "So, what did y'all treat yourselves to?"

Before Erin and Kenya answered they were distracted by the little boy Joel had noticed earlier. He had returned with his mother. He walked up to his father and said, "We back, Daddy."

Erin and Kenya thought that the little boy was cute, but quickly turned the conversation back to shopping. They showed Joel their clothes. After that the girls wanted to go to Victoria's Secret and insisted that Joel come along to help them pick out something sexy. He agreed, because he loved looking at Victoria's Secret lingerie—what he considered gift wrap for breasts and ass.

The young married couple overheard Joel, Erin and Kenya's Victoria's Secret conversation. The husband envied Joel's situation with the girls and wished he could have traded places with him. The wife just stood still with a puzzled look on her face. She didn't know what to think of the threesome.

Chapter 29

Renee stopped by CVS Pharmacy on her way to Joel's apartment, to pick up her sleeping pills. Her mother had dropped off the prescription the day before. Luckily the medicine was ready for pickup because Renee wasn't in any kind of mood to wait. This wasn't the first time she had experienced anxiety and dramatic mood swings. For years she refused to go on antidepressants. Now she really needed a psychiatrist and some antipsychotic drugs, but she and her mother convinced her internal medicine doctor that she would be fine if she just got some sleep. Although the doctor knew Renee and her mother were in serious denial, he still followed their wishes.

Renee was on edge and hadn't slept in almost three days. Somehow she still felt revved up. The slightest thing made her irritable, like the stupid people around her complaining about the hot weather. Renee was in the middle of what she considered a really bad anxiety attack and the customers around her noticed the crazed expression that was plastered on her face, a mixture of shock and fear. Her heart seemed to beat out of control. Her chest felt tight and she had a hard time controlling her breathing. She couldn't think straight. She knew what she wanted to do, but there were just too many ideas in her head trying to surface at the same time. She wanted to go see Joel and go see her family. Something inside was telling her to go get a glass of ice water because she was dehydrated. McDonald's golden arches kept flashing in her mind, but her appetite was completely gone. Renee's stomach felt like it was filled with a million butterflies. The music that played over the intercom system seemed a lot louder than usual. She had a headache and kept feeling strange bursts of mental energy—crazy energy. It made her so anxious that she felt like she could break out into a high impact aerobic workout, do a tap dance routine, break through a brick wall and still have enough momentum left to run all the way home. She just wanted to take enough pills to finally get some sleep.

A few minutes later she got the pills and left the pharmacy. As she drove along the road she came to a red light. Out of nowhere she was struck by a strong urge to go through the red light and just plow right into oncoming traffic. She thought about driving her Escalade over the side of the closest bridge. Living felt painful and dying seemed peaceful. Everything was just so loud in her head and there was nothing she could do to settle things down.

Renee reached into her CVS bag and took out her pill bottle. She popped a couple of sleeping pills in her mouth and swallowed them down. She took one more and then another. The usual dose was one 10 milligram pill per twenty-four hours. When Renee reached Joel's development she parked two buildings down from his so he wouldn't notice her Escalade. She laughed to herself because she knew that nothing was going to stop her from getting inside of Joel's apartment. She had an extra key that Joel didn't know she kept in her change purse. As she made her way up to the front door she noticed Joel's nosey neighbor Ms. Benson exiting the building.

Ms. Benson recognized Renee right away. She liked Renee because she saw her as a troublemaker and a great source for gossip. In a lively voice Ms. Benson said, "Hey, honey. How are you doing?"

Renee gave her a strange look and said, "I'm fine."

Ms. Benson squinted and said, "You don't look fine."

Offended, Renee replied, "Well, neither do you."

Ms. Benson took Renee's response as a joke. "Aw, I'm up in age now, that's my excuse." She paused for a moment and then she realized that something really was wrong with Renee. She didn't know what to say next and asked, "You and Joel back together?"

Renee lied easier than she told the truth and this time was no exception. "Yeah, I'm back for good now."

"You know he's been running around with those two girls from upstairs."

With anger in her voice and in her eyes Renee said, "They're just friends."

Ms. Benson laughed and said, "Oh, you think so, huh? Those three are a lot more than friends. I heard they were having a threesome. Those girls been sleeping over there with him since the new one came home on Friday."

Renee snapped, "I don't care. Can you please leave me alone so I can go up to my apartment?"

"Well, I'm sorry. You go right ahead and take it easy . . . get some rest."

Renee kept walking and ignored anything else that may have come out of Ms. Benson's big mouth. She entered Joel's apartment without any difficulty. Right away she noticed how neat and clean his place was. She headed straight to Joel's bedroom so she could search through his personal belongings. The closet was her first stop. For some reason she checked all of his pants, shorts, shirts, and coat pockets and came up with nothing. The top shelf of the closet was lined with shoe boxes. Some contained shoes, while others contained paperwork. She pulled down the boxes and carelessly dumped their contents all over the place. Nothing was off limits. She looked under Joel's mattress and under his bed. When Renee didn't find anything significant she searched through his dresser drawers. Joel had cash tucked away in his underwear drawer and deep in the back of the drawer she found the note he had written in his classroom, titled "Free-flowin' Thoughts." Wrapped up inside the note was her one-and-a-half-carat diamond ring. She put the ring on her finger, but instead of putting it on her right hand she wore it on her left ring finger like an engagement ring. She sat on the floor and read Joel's note. His words touched her and the next thing she knew her tears had fallen onto the paper. They soaked into the paper's surface, making it easier for her to tear the paper into hundreds of tiny pieces that she tossed in the air like confetti.

Renee got up off the floor and turned on Joel's television. As soon as it came on she turned to a music video. She started dancing and jumping up and down on Joel's bed like she had completely lost her mind. All of a sudden Renee was struck by the urge to burn everything in sight like Lisa "Lefteye" Lopez did to Andre Rison's mansion. But Renee didn't want to risk the lives of the innocent people who lived in the building. She thought that vandalizing Joel's entire apartment would be more than sufficient. She began by kicking the lamps off of the nightstand. Renee wiped the dresser's surface clean with her hand, knocking Joel's little sculptures and designer cologne bottles to the floor. She punched holes in his painting and pulled down his wall-mounted flat-screen TV. She made her way out to the living room to break, crush and smash everything in sight. The other wall-mounted TV had to come down too.

Renee looked under Joel's kitchen sink and pulled out a gallon bottle of Clorox bleach and doused everything in sight, including most of Joel's clothes. She grabbed a butcher knife from the kitchen and sliced Joel's leather furniture to shreds. She vandalized the entire apartment.

On her way back to Joel's bedroom Renee stopped in the kitchen one more time and took out a bottle of wine that had been chilling in the refrigerator.

She sat on Joel's bed gulping down wine when she noticed two duffel bags sitting in the corner of the room near one of Joel's nightstands. She opened them and figured that they must belong to Joel's two girlfriends. These were their overnight

bags. Renee dumped their contents into one big pile. One bag
had a few sex toys inside. Renee wondered what kind of freaky
shit the girls were into. They had all types of lubricants, condoms and massage oils. Renee flipped the lid open on one of
their bottles of body wash, took a sniff, and instantly fell in
love with the fragrance. She began to undress and headed to
the shower with the body wash in hand. About ten minutes
later she got out of the shower and stood in front of the bathroom mirror. She studied her appearance for a while. Renee
was alarmed by what she saw. It didn't take a genius to see
that she looked insane. She was even more alarmed by what
she had done to Joel's apartment. In a moment of clarity, she
realized that he didn't deserve that.

She picked up her pill bottle and started taking a few more
pills. With each pill and every gulp of wine she began to feel
better and better. She eventually pulled back the covers on
Joel's bed and climbed inside. She felt right at home and enjoyed the comfort of his bed. Renee felt so much better that
she began to wish that Joel was there in bed with her.

Chapter 30

Mrs. Davis served a lavish and soulful spread that included her famous crispy fried chicken and mouthwatering buttery biscuits. On the side she had collard greens that were seasoned to perfection with smoked turkey, and potato salad with an even blend of chunkiness, creaminess and flavor. Joel and the girls had the ultimate pleasure of eating the cheesiest macaroni and cheese casserole in Baltimore. All of that was followed by delicious deep dark chocolate layer cake for dessert.

After dinner they sat in the living room relaxing with Mrs. Davis. They sat on her brown micro fiber sectional looking through old photo albums and talking about the past. The atmosphere was pretty relaxed. Their laughter mixed with the classic gospel sounds of Reverend James Cleveland playing in the background. Joel was sandwiched between Erin and Kenya and his mother sat slightly catercornered on Erin's right side. Joel loved that Erin and Kenya appeared to be getting along so well with his mother. On the other hand, Mrs. Davis had a problem sharing her son's attention. She felt that she couldn't compete with Erin and Kenya at all. It was obvious that they had completely won her son over.

Mrs. Davis showed Erin and Kenya a Christmas family portrait of herself, her husband and her two boys. She said, "That's me and Joel along with his brother and father."

Erin said, "Hold on, I didn't know Joel had a brother."

Kenya added, "Neither did I."

Joel put on a cheap smile and said, "Oh, that's Shawn. I thought I told y'all about him."

Erin asked, "Where's Shawn now?"

Kenya asked, "And where's your father?"

Mrs. Davis felt the need to speak up. "Mr. Davis just isn't home right now. And Shawn would have been here, but he thinks Joel is ashamed of him."

Joel spoke up quickly. "That's not true. I love my brother. I've never been ashamed of him."

Mrs. Davis said, "Is that why you talk about him so much?"

Everyone in the room sensed the awkwardness of the moment.

"Ma, stop . . . please." Joel had a photo album on his lap and felt the need to redirect everyone's attention. He pointed to a picture and said, "This was my first school portrait from kindergarten. Look at my nervous half-smile. I'll never forget that day. I was in the gymnasium with hundreds of noisy kids."

Kenya said, "This picture is so cute."

Erin said, "Yeah, you were cute in this picture, Joel. I have a picture with this same background. More than likely we were in the gym together and had no idea how many times our paths would cross in the future."

Joel replied, "That's funny. I wish we had been friends back then."

Erin smiled and said, "I know."

They kissed.

Kenya let out a fake laugh and said, "Wow, I know y'all aren't gonna sit here kissing and getting all mushy in front of Mrs. Davis."

Joel said, "My mother doesn't mind. From now on, each and every picture deserves a kiss."

Erin said, "That's fine with me. I think Kenya just wants a kiss too."

"Awww, does Kenya need a kiss too?" Joel said in a silly voice as he kissed her on her right cheek.

Kenya blushed and said, "Stop acting like this in front of Mrs. Davis." She looked at Joel's mother and asked, "You don't wanna see your son act like that, do you?"

Mrs. Davis made an uncomfortable face, shrugged and said, "I don't know. Don't pay me any attention. I'm just like a piece of furniture . . . just sitting here."

Actually she was doing a lot more than just sitting there. She watched closely how the three interacted with each other. What Joel didn't realize was that his mother sensed something out of the ordinary hidden under the superficial front they put up to disguise the truth. She knew that something wasn't quite right about the three of them being together so often and becoming such good friends in such a short amount of time. Being the same age and having common interests didn't make people act the way these three acted. There was a whole lot more going on. Mrs. Davis was trying her best to figure out the dynamics of their relationship and was determined to have an answer at some point before they walked out of her front door.

Joel gave himself away easily with his words and actions. Erin and Kenya's body language gave them away and also their expressive silent movie actress type of eyes. Mrs. Davis was observant enough to notice Erin and Kenya giving Joel the same adoring gazes that captured the appearance of being in love. Joel and Erin were supposed to be a couple, but Kenya seemed to be caught up in Joel's personal space quite often and nobody seemed to have a problem with it.

Mrs. Davis was jealous of the three of them. Their lives were just beginning and hers was in serious jeopardy of ending because of two malignant one-centimeter lumps in her left breast. She envied the fact that they were young and unstoppable. She studied Erin and Kenya's beautiful, smooth and supple skin.

With their gorgeous facial features and even more gorgeous bodies, the world was theirs to do whatever they wanted. It was so clear that her son would give the girls whatever they desired. Mrs. Davis felt like she had lost Joel, and she didn't like where he was headed.

Mrs. Davis grabbed Joel by his hand and said, "We need to talk. Can you two please excuse us for a few minutes? You're welcome to go to the kitchen and make plates to take home. Help yourselves and take as much as you'd like."

Kenya said, "Thank you. I was hoping we could take food home, but I was ashamed to ask."

Erin laughed and said, "Me too. Thank you so much, Mrs. Davis."

Erin and Kenya got up and headed to the kitchen.

Joel looked at his mother and asked, "What's wrong?"

"I'm worried about you and those girls."

"Huh? What's wrong with us?"

"I know what you're involved in. Are you sleeping with both of them?"

"Ma?"

"If you haven't, I know it's just a matter of time. Believe what I'm telling you." She looked at Joel and cut him off before he could open his mouth. "Don't say anything else because I don't like you lying to me. And I don't like what you're doing with your life. You weren't raised like this. I don't approve of it at all. I want you to know something else, too . . . God doesn't approve of it. There's something real strange about those girls. I know what it is, but I'm not even gonna go there. If you keep up what you're doing you're going straight to hell. That's all I have to say."

"Good, because I think you've said more than enough. I've never disrespected you and I don't wanna start now. So, I think we better go."

"That's fine with me."

Joel hid his emotions. He headed to the kitchen to get Erin and Kenya while his mother sat on her sofa, sulking. She had her head buried in one hand and pounded the sofa with the other. She wondered if she had done the right thing. Her righteous mind quickly reassured her troubled heart that she had done the right thing even if it meant hurting her son.

Mrs. Davis quickly hid her emotions as Erin and Kenya emerged from the kitchen, smiling from ear to ear, carrying plates loaded with food. Joel didn't want to take his mother's food. In fact, he didn't want to take anything else she had to offer. He had had more than enough from her.

Erin gave Mrs. Davis a hug and said, "Thanks again for everything, Mrs. Davis. The food was delicious." She paused for a second and then said, "I really admire you."

Kenya walked over to Mrs. Davis and gave her a hug and said, "And I think that you're such a beautiful person."

Erin added, "You're the type of woman we hope to become one day."

Their kind words broke through her bitterness. Mrs. Davis manufactured a smile and struggled to keep her emotions intact. She had so much weighing on her that she just wanted to fold under the pressure, but her faith was too strong to let that happen.

Joel gave his mother a hug and a kiss on her cheek. He said, "Thanks Ma, I'll see you in the morning."

Just that fast it seemed as if Joel had completely forgiven his mother. He remembered the stress that she was forced to deal with—her husband's infidelity and recent departure, being newly diagnosed with breast cancer, and the burden taking care of her drug-addicted son and his girlfriend.

At that moment Mrs. Davis felt so bad that she wanted to take back at least half of the hurtful things she had said to Joel, but didn't say a word. She simply stood in her doorway and watched Joel open the doors of his Jeep Cherokee for Erin and Kenya. She thought it was strange that Kenya was sitting up front with Joel. Then of course she thought the whole concept of a threesome was strange and incomprehensible.

Chapter 31

After returning from Joel's mother's house, the three decided to spend some time hanging out at Erin and Kenya's apartment. As soon as they entered their building they sensed something different in the air. It seemed fresher and lighter than usual. The air was free of the typical mixture of Sunday dinner aromas. On most Sunday evenings the hallways were flowing with the scent of soul food coming from almost every apartment in the building, along with the unmistakable scent of Caribbean cuisine coming from one particular apartment on the first level.

There weren't any signs of nosey neighbors roaming the hallways. The building was absolutely quiet—covered in an unusual calm. The drama mounting behind Joel's apartment door was perfectly disguised by peace and harmony. He and the girls were totally unaware of Renee's self-destructive behavior and the mess and mayhem she had created. They walked right past Joel's apartment without even looking in that direction. Renee lay unconscious in Joel's bed in desperate need of help. Someone needed to intervene as soon as possible because Renee was slowly fading into a deeper and deeper state of unconsciousness. Time was of the essence and meant the difference between life and death.

The three were in Erin's bedroom, stretched out across her bed trying to find something interesting to watch on television. As they dealt with petty issues, Renee was at serious risk of becoming the unfortunate victim of a successful suicide attempt. Her fate lay in the hands of three people that had no intentions of moving from the comfortable spots they occupied. After scanning through hundreds of cable channels they weren't able to find one decent program.

Joel said, "We might as well head over to my apartment. I've got some wine chillin' in the fridge along with a big container of fresh strawberries, whipped cream and about two pounds of grapes."

Kenya said, "Ooh, I love strawberries and whipped cream, but do you have any chocolate syrup to dip them in?"

Joel shook his head and said, "No, but I have a huge collection of black romantic comedies and dramas like *Love Jones, Love and Basketball, The Wood, The Best Man, The Inkwell, Brown Sugar* and a whole lot more. We can watch whatever the two of you would like to see."

Erin stretched, yawned and then asked, "Can't you just run across the hall and get all that stuff and bring it over here?"

Joel said, "I could, but it won't be the same. Over there we can watch the DVDs in high definition on my forty-two-inch plasma."

Kenya smiled and said, "All right . . . let's go."

It seemed like the three of them were about to move until Erin said, "Hold up a sec. We might have some chocolate syrup in our kitchen. Give me a minute to find it. Y'all know eating strawberries dipped in chocolate is so much sexier and sweeter than just eating them plain or with whipped cream."

Joel and Kenya laughed and agreed with Erin. They followed her to the kitchen and found an unopened bottle of chocolate syrup way in the back of their little pantry. Each of them seemed to be in a playful mood and didn't realize how urgent it was for them to get over to Joel's apartment before it was too late. Joel delayed things even more by kissing and fondling Erin and Kenya in the kitchen.

Finally they headed over to Joel's apartment. As soon as he

opened his front door they were greeted by the strong smell of bleach. Right away they could see that Joel's place had been vandalized. Everything was out of place except his largest pieces of furniture. Joel saw that most of his prized possessions had been destroyed. All of his time, effort and money that went into fixing his apartment up the way he wanted had completely gone to waste.

Joel yelled, "What the fuck?" He punched his door and said, "Aw, man. Look at this shit. They got me."

Erin's jaw dropped. She looked at the mess inside and all she could say was, "Damn."

Kenya stepped inside and said, "Oh no. Who do you think did this?"

Right away Joel replied, "Spanky. I know he had somebody do this. Damn, look at my stuff. They sliced up my leather furniture. Everything is ruined . . . everything."

Erin looked around and said, "Nah, you're giving that boy too much credit. This is probably just a random act of violence."

Joel replied, "I doubt it."

Kenya asked, "Did you leave your door unlocked?"

"No, you just saw me unlock the door."

Kenya thought for a second and said, "Yeah, you're right."

Erin said, "Whoever did this must have had a key."

As Joel picked up a pile of books he said, "No one else has a key. Maybe I did leave the door unlocked and whoever did this locked it when they left."

Kenya said, "I don't think so. It's highly unlikely for someone to break in and then lock the door behind them."

With frustration in his voice Joel said, "I dunno. I guess it doesn't really matter now anyway. All I know is that somebody destroyed everything I own. They even ripped my damn flat screen off the wall."

Kenya said, "Whoever did this did it just to piss you off because they didn't steal anything."

"Well, it worked because I am pissed off."

The kitchen trashcan had been knocked over and trash had been scattered everywhere along with old newspapers and mail. Joel walked through the rubble and made his way down the hallway to his ransacked bedroom. His attention was focused straight ahead at the lamps that had been knocked off the nightstands. The light from the lamps created large shadowy shapes along the walls and concentrated light away from his bed. Joel's room was such a mess that at first he didn't even notice Renee lying in his bed. As he turned one of the lamps right-side-up he saw her lying there, balled up in a fetal position. The sight caught him off guard and nearly scared the living shit out of him.

Angrily he yelled, "Renee, get your ass up. I can't believe you did this shit to me. Get up!" She didn't move. "I'm not playing . . . get up!"

There was an empty wine bottle next to her and Joel wasn't sure whether Renee had drunk it all or whether she had spilled most of it in his bed.

He assumed that Renee drank all of the wine and had vandalized his apartment in a drunken rage. He yelled, "Get your drunk ass up . . . right now!"

Erin and Kenya heard Joel yelling and came running. As they entered the room, they saw Joel shaking Renee. They shook their heads in disgust.

Joel sensed that something else was going on. He pulled back the covers and saw that Renee had a pill bottle near her hands. He also noticed that she had found the friendship ring he had given her. She wore it on her left ring finger. Everything added up to serious trouble, and the condition of Joel's apartment was the least of his concerns. He and the girls were obviously shaken by what they saw.

Joel picked up the pill bottle and realized that it was actually an empty bottle of sleeping pills. He cried out, "Aw, no!" It felt like the floor had dropped from under his feet and the room began to spin. He turned toward Erin and Kenya with a panicked look on his face and said, "I think she might have committed suicide."

Tears welled up in Erin's eyes when she said, "Oh my God, is she dead?"

Kenya said, "Please God . . . I hope she's still alive."

Joel feared the worst. He said, "I don't know . . . she doesn't look right. Call 911." He pulled back her eyelids and saw her distant pinpoint pupils. She looked dead, but Joel could feel that her skin was still warm as he scrambled to feel for a pulse. He said, "She's still alive. Her pulse is weak, but I can feel it."

Erin was so nervous that she forgot that she had her cell phone on her hip. She went looking for the house phone and seconds later realized where her cell phone was.

Kenya was so scared and upset that she looked like she wanted to run somewhere and hide.

All three of them were in a state of shock—this seemed so unreal. They had planned to watch a romantic comedy and had no idea they would become part of a real-life romantic tragedy. Everything happened so suddenly and unexpectedly. Joel had always said that Renee was as unpredictable as the weather, but this had topped anything she had ever done.

Kenya looked at Joel and said, "The ambulance is going to take forever . . . we've gotta do something."

Joel thought for a second and then said, "Grab me a towel."

Kenya had to think about which way to go and exactly where the towels were located. She had been trained in CPR and first aid, and within a couple of seconds she had gotten herself together. She reached inside the closet for a towel and handed it to Joel. She leaned over Renee and put her ear near Renee's mouth and nose to monitor her breathing.

Kenya said, "She's taking really slow, shallow breaths."

Joel replied, "I know. She's barely alive."

Erin had reached the 911 operator and relayed as much information to her as possible.

Renee's arms and legs flip-flopped as Joel repositioned her.

He placed the towel under Renee and held her head over the side of his bed. He stuck his finger down her throat in a desperate attempt to make her throw up the sleeping pills. Renee gagged and small amounts of clear fluid oozed from her mouth. She didn't seem to bring up enough stomach contents to make much of a difference.

Joel said, "Hopefully that will help, but I'm not sure how long ago she took the pills. She had the nerve to wash the pills down with wine. What was she thinking?"

Kenya read the label on the pill bottle and then yelled to Erin, "Tell the operator that the pill bottle has today's date on it and that she took the full bottle of sleeping pills." She read the rest of the label and said, "There might have been thirty pills in it."

Joel and Kenya kept calling Renee's name, trying to revive her, to no avail.

Kenya held Renee's hand and said, "I hope she isn't too far gone."

Joel held Renee's head steady and responded with a simple, "I dunno." Then he said, "This is serious. If she took thirty pills then she really wanted to die, and didn't just do this because she wanted attention."

Kenya looked at Joel. "I hate to say, but she must have wanted your attention. That's why she chose to come here and do all this."

Minutes later sirens could be heard blaring in the distance. The fire and police departments were the first to arrive on the scene. By the time the ambulance arrived the building was in a complete uproar. Neighbors were in the hallway and had eased their way into Joel's living room, trying to figure out what was going on. The police department tried to keep the onlookers as composed as possible.

The paramedics placed an oxygen mask on Renee and started an IV. Minutes later they placed her on a gurney and loaded her in the back of the ambulance. Most of the neighbors recognized Renee and jumped to all kinds of wild and crazy conclusions when they saw Joel get into the back of the ambulance and watched Erin and Kenya follow in Erin's little Mitsubishi Eclipse.

Ms. Benson had already contacted one of the local news station's hotlines to report the story. The reporter who answered the phone was anxious to get the scoop. Ms. Benson spilled her guts and embellished the truth by calling the incident a domestic dispute over a threesome. Once the reporter found out that Renee was still alive she didn't consider the story newsworthy. Ms. Benson was disappointed to lose her fifteen minutes of fame, but she still used the opportunity to be in the spotlight by spreading vicious rumors about the threesome and Renee.

Chapter 32

It was two in the morning and the emergency room's waiting area was full of strange characters. Every two minutes or so, a nasty cough could be heard. About a half-dozen patients were in tears from their intense pain. A couple of assault victims sat in the waiting area applying direct pressure to their bleeding wounds. Everybody in the waiting area looked liked they were tired of waiting. The overcrowding and treatment delays in the emergency room were caused by the majority of the patients being there for nonemergency complaints like colds, chronic joint pain and needing new prescription refills. The main people complaining about the long wait time were the ones who should have been seen at their primary care physicians' offices.

There were all types of sights and sounds to take in. A tall, slim, goofy-looking lady paced back and forth, scuffing her big yellow Sponge Bob Square Pants slippers across the floor. There was a guy sitting on the floor in between his girlfriend's legs as she braided his hair. No one wanted to look in their direction because the sight of his thick flaky dandruff falling like snow made them sick.

A loud ignorant woman sat in a wheelchair talking on her cell phone about how she hadn't paid any of her previous hospital bills and didn't plan on paying this time around, either.

She said loudly into her cell phone, "This hospital already

knows I ain't paying their asses. They know my history. Shit, the way I see it, health care should be free in this country anyway."

People around the lady smiled and agreed about free health care. She was ignorant, but at least she realized something that the government didn't.

The waiting room's television was tuned to CNN, running the same stories over and over. A teenage boy had his headphones turned up so loud that his music, laced with offensive rap lyrics, could be heard throughout the waiting area. Some people felt like reporting him to hospital security, but they didn't. Maybe they didn't because he wore a T-shirt with a big stop sign on the front that read *Stop Snitchin'*.

The air inside was cool and crisp until a new patient sat down smelling like a hot nasty cheesesteak sub with extra onions.

Erin, Kenya and Joel sat in one corner of the waiting area looking sad and uncomfortable while Renee's parents and sister sat in the other corner looking tired and annoyed. Renee's family barely spoke to Joel. All they wanted from him were the facts about what happened to Renee. They acted very insensitive and inconsiderate toward him. It didn't bother Joel too much because he was used to them treating him badly. He just didn't like the dirty looks Renee's mother and sister kept giving Erin and Kenya.

Joel and the girls stayed around because they wanted to make sure Renee was going to be okay. Once they got confirmation of her status they planned to leave. The longer they sat in the waiting area the more tired and uncomfortable they became. The three decided to go around the corner to a small, dimly lit canteen. The area was actually closed, but that didn't stop them. They sat alone at a tiny cafeteria-style table.

Joel thought that this was the perfect opportunity to share what was on his mind. He said, "I'm so tired of other people that I don't know what to do."

Erin smiled, nodded her head and said, "Tell me about it."

Kenya said, "It's so much better when it's just the three of us alone." She paused for a second and said, "I'm going to slap the shit out of the next person who gives me a dirty look."

Erin said, "Yeah, I'm getting tired of getting those dirty looks too."

Kenya said, "Renee's family looks at us like we're a wild balancing act that they can't wait to see fall over and come crashing to the ground."

Joel said, "Fuck them. I don't really care what they think because I'm happy to have the two of you in my life. I don't know what I did to deserve y'all, but I'm thankful."

Erin smiled and said, "I feel the same way about you. God brought us together for a reason."

Kenya said, "He brought us together because He knew that we needed each other." She reached for their hands and said, "And I'm so glad He brought us together."

Joel gave each of the girls a quick peck on the lips. Then he felt the need to apologize and explain his mother's actions from earlier.

Joel looked at Erin and Kenya and said, "I wanna apologize for the way my mother acted earlier this evening. I know that y'all picked up on her attitude."

Erin said, "Of course we noticed something strange was going on with her, but overall she's a sweet lady. No need to apologize. Your mom was fine."

Kenya said, "Yeah, don't worry. I knew she would have a problem with us." With a giggle in her voice she said, "Mrs. Davis kept giving me funky looks all evening and I was on my best behavior."

Joel said, "Sorry about that."

Kenya shook her head. "It was nothing."

Erin laughed. "Oh, I caught a few of those funky stares too. Your mother is a very religious woman so of course I knew she would frown upon everything we stand for. I had already prepared myself for scrutiny and rejection. To be honest, she handled things a lot better than I had expected."

In an apologetic tone Joel said, "She's dealing with a lot of issues right now. I should have mentioned it before, but I didn't want to bring myself or anybody else down by dwelling on so many depressing issues."

Erin asked, "What's going on?"

"My mother was diagnosed with breast cancer. Her doctor found two one-centimeter lumps in her left breast."

Erin said, "Oh, no. I'm so sorry to hear that, Joel."

Kenya said, "Awww, poor thing. I feel so sorry for her. Is there anything we can do?"

Joel looked drained. "Yeah, just keep her in your prayers. I think she'll be fine . . . I know she'll be fine. My mother is scheduled for surgery here later this morning. Her doctor plans to perform two lumpectomies instead of a mastectomy."

Erin said, "I feel bad. Breast cancer is so common nowadays. My grandmother and two of my aunts are breast cancer survivors. So far my mother has been blessed and remains cancer free. Because of my family history I'm at risk and I know I'll have to start getting mammograms a lot earlier than the recommended age of forty."

In a soft tone Kenya said, "No one in my immediate family has been diagnosed with breast cancer, but that doesn't mean they don't have it. For the most part, I think my mother has been avoiding mammograms for years because she heard that they're painful. And I think she's afraid to be examined because she fears that they might actually find cancer. She said just finding out that she had cancer would kill her."

With a serious expression Joel said, "Not knowing could kill her even faster. That's exactly why black women are dying at a faster rate from breast cancer than any other group." He paused for a brief moment and said, "Well, my mother is dealing with a lot more than cancer. My father wasn't home when you visited because he left her for another woman . . . some young girl with two kids."

Kenya's eyes watered and she appeared too choked up to say anything. She shook her head and then lowered her face into her hands.

With tears in her eyes Erin said, "That's too much to deal with. How could your father leave her at a time like this?"

"She never told him about the breast cancer. I guess she didn't want his pity and wanted him to do what felt natural."

Kenya thought about how healthy Mrs. Davis looked and said, "Oh my God, she's strong."

"To top all that off, my brother and his girlfriend moved in with my mother and are completely taking advantage of her kindness. I'm sure the two of them are still using drugs and that's why they can't afford to pay her." He let out a heavy sigh and said, "My mother is dealing with too much stress. The woman that y'all met this evening is nowhere near the real Mary Davis."

Erin said, "I know this sounds crazy, but is your mother's illness the hardest thing you ever had to deal with?"

Without even thinking Joel said, "Yeah. Dealing with my mother's diagnosis and all of this unnecessary family drama is hard. There's never a dull moment. My father is in a midlife crisis. He just wants to feel young again, or feel like he's still got it. But that's gonna wear off sooner than later. Everything that I've ever known about love and relationships stems from what I learned from my parents. And now they're getting a divorce after all these years." Joel paused for a moment as he remembered something that he hadn't thought about in a while. He said, "I've had to overcome a lot in the past. I wanna tell y'all about something."

With a curious look on her face Erin said, "Go ahead."

Kenya looked up and asked, "What is it?"

"You can't really know me without knowing my past. I've never shared this with anyone besides my parents. I feel really close to the two of you and that's why I feel the need to tell y'all about a huge obstacle I had to overcome." Joel took a deep breath. "Back when I was eighteen I started dating the daughter of our church's pastor. Her name was Nia and she was my first real girlfriend. To make a long story short, I got her pregnant and her parents forced her to have an abortion.

Then they moved her down South to make sure we never saw each other again. I didn't think moving her away would have worked, but eventually our interests drifted in other directions and we lost contact. We never saw each other again. The whole incident kind of scarred me. I was heartbroken, mostly because these so-called religious people took the love of my life away and helped murder my child. I always felt that Nia was carrying my son . . . my namesake, but I never got the chance to see or hold him."

Erin and Kenya came around to Joel's side of the table and laid their heads on his shoulders.

Erin whispered, "I never would have imagined you experienced something so traumatic at such a young age. No wonder you're so passionate about everything you do."

Joel said, "Sometimes dealing with loss has that kind of effect on people."

A few minutes passed, but Joel's story was still swirling around in Kenya's mind. With a spaced-out expression in her eyes she said, "That was probably one of the saddest stories I've ever heard. I think we all have secrets. I have something I want to share." Kenya paused. "If y'all really knew me you'd know that I had it rough growing up. When I was little my mother didn't live in a big expensive house in the suburbs or drive around in a Mercedes-Benz like she does now. To be honest, she struggled throughout most of my childhood. She suffered years of physical and mental abuse from my biological father until he decided to walk out on us when I was five. I barely even knew him, but I knew that he was mean to my mother and caused her a lot of pain. Some things you just don't forget. For some reason I still have vague memories of a caring father figure too. Don't ask me why I've held on to those memories for all these years, because he never really did anything for me. Maybe I wanted him to be caring so bad that subconsciously I created a caring fatherly image to make myself feel better. When he walked out on me and my mother we had to move out of our house and were forced to move into subsidized housing. I've been terrified of rats and roaches since I can remember, but that's what we were forced to live with. As the years went by, my mother worked the nightshift full-time at a nursing home, and attended nursing school full-time during the day. I admired her for that. When I got a little older I had to stay in our apartment alone, sitting in the middle of my bed, too scared to move because of the rats and roaches running free. Eventually I got a little better, but I never grew accustomed to living in a rat- and roach-infested apartment. We were so poor back then." She let out a heavy sigh. "My mother finished nursing school years later, got married, and my stepfather moved us to a much better place. I've always tried to forget about the horrors of my childhood. I pretended that my stepfather was my real father and that I always lived in a pristine environment. I'm not a phony or anything . . . I just wanted to escape my painful and ugly memories. Maybe that's why I work so hard now, so I'll never have to live like that again."

Erin said, "Girl, if anybody understands, you know I do."

Joel said, "So do I. You turned out pretty good to have had such a rough start."

Kenya smiled and said, "Thanks. It was weird hearing myself say something aloud that I've been holding inside for so long."

Erin said, "Well, I have a secret that I'd like to share too, but I'm just not ready to share right now. I don't think this is the right time or place."

Joel shrugged and said, "That's fine. Whenever you're ready to share I'll be ready to listen."

Kenya said, "I feel the same way. You know Joel and I are here for you. Take your time because we're not going anywhere."

Erin said, "Thanks. I'm glad y'all understand." She paused for a second and then said, "Since everybody's sharing their deep dark secrets I guess the least I could do is share mine too."

Kenya said, "If you want to share then we're here to listen."
Joel nodded and said, "Go ahead and open up. Just say exactly what's on your mind."

Erin said, "Okay." She closed her eyes and began to rock back and forth a little. Her slow, gentle rocking motion seemed to relax her as she prepared to share her secret. Joel sat close to Erin to provide extra comfort and support. Kenya repositioned herself on the opposite side of Erin because she could tell that whatever was on Erin's mind was heavy. Erin said softly, "It was summertime, about two weeks before the start of my senior year. I was supposed to spend the night at my best friend Nicole's house. Her parents had gone out for the night, to a party all the way down in Annapolis and we were home alone. It was no big deal for two seventeen-year-old girls to be home alone on a Saturday night. We were in her bedroom listening to music and dancing. All of a sudden Nicole left her bedroom without saying a word. I assumed she was going to get us a snack and something to drink because she had mentioned that earlier." Erin paused for a moment. When she continued, the canteen area appeared to have gotten colder and darker. Joel and Kenya were caught up in Erin's story and relived her experience right along with her. "The entire house was dark and quiet, except for Nicole's bedroom. I remember feeling cold. Cool air filled the house, thanks to their central air-conditioning unit. After dancing for a few minutes I began to warm up and the cool air didn't bother me as much. Before long I was into my own little world, just enjoying the music. The next thing I knew I heard Nicole's bedroom door open. I had my back to the door and was so preoccupied and zoned out that I didn't even notice her older brother Teddy standing right behind me until I felt someone breathing on the back of my neck. I looked up and was startled by his reflection in the mirror. He startled me so much that I stopped dancing and screamed. He just laughed. That's when everything turned really weird. He asked, 'Did I scare you, shorty? Don't stop dancing because of me. Who taught you to dance like that? I know you ain't trying to turn into one of them freaky-ass girls from around here, are you?' I said no. He made me show him how I danced again, and then he danced with me, pressing himself all against me. He was aroused and I could feel it. I stopped dancing and he forced me to continue. He started feeling on me. I called for Nicole, but there was no answer. That's when I realized that she thought she had done me a favor by hooking me up with her brother. I always said that Teddy was cute, but I didn't want to be alone with him." Erin began to sob a little, but was able to continue. "That song called 'Bump and Grind' by R. Kelly started playing. Teddy said, 'I'm gonna see if you can handle me.' At some point it seemed like he was being kind of playful, but then he got aggressive. I knew that he had been drinking because he smelled like beer. He got real rough and held me tight and forced me to dance again. He said, 'I like you a lot now that you got bigger tits and a fatter ass. Bet you think you're a woman now. You been fucked yet?' I didn't say anything. He said, 'Come on, you can tell me. I'm like a big brother to you and I have a right to know. You better tell me the truth.' I said no, I'm still a virgin. There was a strange look in his eyes. He said, 'Oh, yeah. You better not be lying to me. Let me check you out to make sure.' I screamed, no. He picked me up and slammed me on Nicole's bed. He put his hand up my dress and all of a sudden he snatched off my panties. Then he pinned me on the bed. He was strong . . . a whole lot stronger than I was." Erin began to cry. "I felt his fingers moving around down there as I squirmed from side to side. I felt his finger penetrate me and I screamed. He pressed his body against me even harder. He kissed me as I tried to scream louder. I kicked, hit and bit him. He was way too strong for me. He said, 'I'm gonna see if you really can handle me now.' I remember feeling a strange pain between my legs and then he applied more force. I could smell and feel his hot beer breath against my skin. Sweat dripped from his forehead all over me, and then he rubbed his coarse facial hairs against my face. When he was done he just lay there holding me as tight as he could. Then he started giving me kisses and telling me how sorry he was. I just lay there lifeless, like I had been murdered. He might as well have taken my life. I was breathing, but I didn't want to. He left me lying there with the bottom half of my body exposed. I couldn't move, so he pulled my dress down and told me to go into the bathroom and make sure I washed. He begged me repeatedly not to tell anyone about what he had just done to me. I cried, but I was too messed up to even wipe my own tears. He wiped my tears and said, 'I know you don't want me to tell your mother how hard you made me. You're a nasty little thing. You started this by dancing around like that.' I never said a word to him. He kept telling me to remember what he said. I got up and ran all the way home. When I got there my mother was fast asleep and I was so thankful because the last thing I wanted was for her to see me looking like that. I made my way to the shower and washed myself over and over again. No matter how much I washed I still felt dirty. I felt and smelled him on me for the longest time. It felt like he had stained my soul, but over time I found the strength to get beyond that night and I eventually got myself back on track. I never reported Teddy to the police. For all these years I acted as if that incident never happened. I guess that's why I had so many sexual hang-ups. Well, if y'all didn't know me . . . hopefully you know me a little better now."

Erin looked so vulnerable that Joel felt the need to hold her and make her feel safe. But Kenya put her arms around Erin first, and their prolonged hug made Joel feel momentarily excluded.

A couple of minutes later Kenya and Erin allowed Joel to share their embrace. This was an emotionally charged moment. There was a long period of silence. Renee's suicide attempt had helped bring a lot of pain, sadness and honesty to the forefront. The three had opened up and flowed with honesty. They had let each other inside to face issues they usually faced alone. Their weaknesses and vulnerability made them even closer. The three were naked—stripped down emotionally, but flawless and beautiful to each other. Their exuberance for life made them so strong—too strong to let the past beat them down.

Chapter 33

A few minutes later Joel said, "I guess we better get back around to that crazy-ass waiting area and see if the doctor has an update on Renee's condition."

As soon as Joel and the girls stepped into the waiting area they noticed that Renee's mother and sister were crying their hearts out.

Joel stopped dead in his tracks and braced himself for the bad news. His stomach felt like it was tied up in knots. He looked at Erin and Kenya and said, "I don't wanna go over there because I don't wanna know...I don't wanna hear whatever they have to say because I know it's bad news."

Erin said, "It's obvious that they just found out something. Hopefully it's not as bad as you think."

Kenya said, "You need to find out what happened."

Joel said, "All right, give me a second." He took a deep breath, prepared himself for the worst and said, "I'll go, but I'm still not ready."

Erin said, "It's probably best that Kenya and I stay over here. I'm sure Renee's family doesn't want us in their business. If you need us we'll be right here."

Joel gave her a little smile and said, "All right."

Mrs. Rhodes and Cheryl were so upset that they didn't even notice Joel walking in their direction. When Mr. Rhodes noticed Joel he stood up and greeted him with much more re-spect this time. Mr. Rhodes seemed incredibly humble.

With a worried look on his face Joel asked, "What's going on?"

Mr. Rhodes said, "Things aren't as bad as they seem. Victoria and Cheryl are just upset because the nurse let us go in the back to see Renee and they had her on a ventilator."

"Is she okay?"

"I think she's going to be fine. The doctor is supposed to come out and take the family into one of the conference rooms to discuss Renee's case. You're welcome to join us if you'd like."

This made Joel feel a little better. He nodded his head and said, "Sure."

"Look, I'm sorry for the way we treated you earlier. It's just kind of unsettling seeing you with your girlfriends . . . to-gether . . . like that and all. Victoria and Cheryl didn't want you or them here at first, but now we realize that you didn't do anything wrong."

Joel felt so many emotions raging inside of him that he was about to explode. He managed to stay composed and said, "I've always treated your family with respect, especially Renee. It's not like I really wanna be here . . . she got me involved in this. I thought the two of us had moved on, but evidently not. She's the type of ex-girlfriend that just won't go away." Mr. Rhodes gave Joel a funny look, as if to say his comment was inappro-priate. Then Joel said, "You know what I mean."

"Of course, I know what you mean."

Joel sighed loudly and said, "I'd love to be home in bed right now, but your daughter destroyed my apartment and then attempted to take her life in my bed. Can you imagine how that made me feel?"

"No . . . I can't," he said evasively.

"My girlfriends and I tried our best to save Renee's life and instead of y'all thanking us . . . everybody treated us like we tried to kill her."

"I understand what you're saying. Again, I apologize for what happened. I'll pay you for any damage she caused."

"We can talk about that later. Right now I just want Renee to make a full recovery."

A few minutes passed, then a nurse gathered Renee's family and Joel and they all headed to a conference room. Mrs. Rhodes and Cheryl were civil, but gave Joel the silent treatment. As they sat there in complete silence a doctor entered the room wearing light green scrubs.

With a mild Latin accent he said, "Hello family, my name is Dr. Richard Diaz. I've been taking care of Ms. Rhodes tonight and she has shown some minor improvements. Her heart rate and blood pressure are normal. We did a gastric lavage and administered a medication to counteract the effects of the sleeping pills. She's still in what we call a medication-induced coma. Luckily for all of us they don't make sleeping pills like they used to. She took a new class of pills that are less potent than the old benzodiazepine class. The new class can be lethal when taken in large amounts. We assume she took the full bottle of thirty tablets."

Mrs. Rhodes cried out, "Oh God."

"Ms. Rhodes experienced some respiratory distress earlier and I felt the need to put her on a ventilator . . . temporarily . . . just to give her system a break. I expect her to sleep for hours, but she should recover within the next twenty-four hours. However, we're going to admit her so we can observe her for the next couple of days or so. I had the chance to review her records and speak to her primary physician. Has she been acting strange lately? Been depressed? Trouble sleeping? Mood swings? Increased energy and restlessness?" Dr. Diaz watched as everyone nodded their heads in agreement. Then he asked, "Did any of you know that she suffers from bipolar disorder?"

Mrs. Rhodes said, "I knew it."

Dr. Diaz asked, "Does anyone else in the family suffer from bipolar disorder?"

A dead silence fell over the room.

Suddenly Mrs. Rhodes broke out crying and said, "Me. I'm bipolar too. I've known for years. I was diagnosed with manic depression when I was in my twenties, but I have been in denial the entire time." She cried so hard she could hardly talk. "I saw the same symptoms in my daughter . . . the deep sadness, helplessness and then the euphoric moods. She jumped from one idea to another and could hardly sit still. The poor thing spent all of her hard-earned money . . . shopping for all kinds of things. Her judgment was impaired. I tried my best to cover it up and now look what that led to. She tried to kill herself." Mr. Rhodes put his arm around her and handed her a couple of tissues. She continued, "The only time she was truly happy was when she was with this wonderful young man sitting right here." Mrs. Rhodes paused for a second and Joel looked completely blown away. Mrs. Rhodes continued, "My daughter's illness started to get the best of her and made her do all kinds of things, including break Joel's heart." She looked at Joel and said, "I'm so sorry we never told you what was going on with Renee, but we were ashamed. She never meant to hurt you."

Joel had a huge lump in his throat and could barely speak. With tears in his eyes he said, "It's okay. Now I understand exactly why she did the things she did."

Dr. Diaz said, "You all have to work together as a team and recognize what triggers the depressive and manic episodes in Ms. Rhodes. From now on it is critical that she take medications and see a psychiatrist on a regular basis. With bipolar disorder she will experience ups and down that are too much to handle on her own. There is no cure for bipolar disorder, but it can be treated."

After the conference with Dr. Diaz, Renee's family headed out to the waiting area and allowed Joel time to visit alone with Renee.

Joel hated seeing Renee in the condition she was in, so he

tried to keep the visit as short as possible. He took Renee by the hand and whispered in her ear, "Renee, I know you can hear me and I want you to hurry up and get better." Something inside of Joel made him say, "I love you." He kissed her on the cheek and then headed back out to the waiting area.

Chapter 34

The aroma of fresh brewed coffee drew Erin, Kenya and Joel back to the canteen that had served as their confessional during the wee hours of the night. It was officially open for business and had lost most of its intimate appeal. The area was now well lit and flowed with employees and visitors looking for a quick Monday morning pick-me-up.

This time the three sat at the same cafeteria-style table with lightly sweetened black coffee for Joel and mocha lattes for Erin and Kenya. Each of them had bran muffins. Erin didn't have much of an appetite. She split the top of her muffin and spread butter into its warm center. As the butter began to melt she sampled the goodness by eating a small piece. Erin assumed her nurturing role. She broke her muffin into smaller pieces and hand-fed the rest to Kenya and Joel.

Joel seemed distant. He tried his best to ignore the morning paper that sat inches away from him. He caught a quick glance at something about Baltimore's 190th murder of the year and the stock market plunging. Joel actually turned the paper facedown to avoid reading the depressing headlines because he already had enough on his busy overloaded mind.

At six-fifty, the three switched themselves into overdrive and headed upstairs to the operating room's registration area to meet up with Mrs. Davis, whose surgery was scheduled for nine o'clock. Joel went straight to the registrar and asked if his mother had arrived. She was an attractive plus-sized sistah who kept giving Joel goo-goo eyes. Erin and Kenya noticed, but got a kick out of seeing other women sweat their man.

The registrar hadn't seen Mrs. Davis. To be on the safe side she double-checked with a couple of the nurses before giving Joel an answer. After a few minutes she told him that Mrs. Davis hadn't arrived yet. Joel was tempted to call his mother, but he decided to give his mother a little more time.

As the minutes passed everybody began to worry that something might be wrong, especially when Mrs. Davis hadn't arrived by seven. A few minutes later the registrar called Joel to the desk and informed him that he had a call. He looked confused for a second and then quickly figured that it had to be his mother.

He picked up a phone at the farthest end of the desk and said, "Hello."

"Good morning, Joel."

"Hey, Ma. Good morning. Where are you?"

"Home."

"Home? Did you forget about your procedure? They're waiting for you. You were due here by seven."

Erin and Kenya looked at Joel with concern and curiosity in their eyes. He looked back at them with total confusion in his eyes and simply shrugged his shoulders. They shook their heads in disbelief. It was obvious that it was his mother and she was being stubborn.

Mrs. Davis said, "I know what I was supposed to do this morning. Last night I prayed harder than I ever prayed in my life. When I woke up this morning I felt a change. God healed my body. I'm telling you . . . today is a blessed day."

"Okay. Now you just have to get here as soon as possible for the surgeon to do his thing."

"You don't understand the change I feel. I've never felt so good. The lumps are gone. I don't have any aches or pains and my mind is clear. I'm not having the surgery."

"What?" He let out a heavy sigh. "There's nothing to be

scared of. I'm on my way over there to pick you up. I'm going to see if they can still do the surgery as long as I can get you here before nine."

"Please listen to me, Joel. Whatever I have right now is what I plan to leave here with . . . my cancer included. Nobody's cutting on me. The biopsy was enough. I know what I have and what it will eventually do to me, but I'm okay with it. It's in God's hands now."

"Do you understand what you're saying? I'll ask the staff to reschedule the procedure. You just need a little more patient education. I'll come over later today and review the patient information packet with you. I'm sure we can have your doctor or one of his nurses review the information with you. Would that make you feel better?"

"No . . . I'm already better. You don't understand. I don't want the surgery. All I want to do right now is go on that pilgrimage to the Holy Land . . . get baptized in the Jordan River . . . walk the same path my Savior walked before He made the ultimate sacrifice." She paused for a second to praise God and then continued. "I'm ready to move on to a better place. I know that God has already prepared a home for me. I put a down payment on my heavenly home when I gave my life to Christ a long time ago. My debt has been paid. Yes, I've been redeemed. God is so good to me. I've lived my life. I've had my share of good days and my share of bad days. And you know what? God has given me the strength to bear it all. This is my sunshine after the rain. The storm is over and now I can clearly see the path that I've chosen and it's the right one. I'm going to heaven and I'll see you when you get there. Oh Joel, I know you're gonna make it there one day and we'll both share the glory. I'm so sorry for saying the hurtful things that I said to you yesterday. I just know that God is trying to tell you something. If you just take the time to listen I'm sure you'll figure it out. He's trying to make a change in your life too. Don't forget who you are and where you came from. Most of all, don't forget God. You were raised in church, and I want you to start going again on a regular basis."

"I know. I will. I haven't forgotten about God. I still pray every day."

"It's time to get closer to Him. Choose the right path. We all fall along the way, but you have to get up again. You've fallen . . . get up Joel . . . get up. Tomorrow is a brand new day and all of your sins can be washed away. Do you understand what I'm saying?"

"Yes."

"It's so true. Do me a favor and tell those people to give somebody else my slot because I don't need it."

"I hope you know what you're doing. What can I do to change your mind?"

"Nothing. I know what I'm doing. Don't worry about me. I'm fine. I'm not depressed or crazy. I'm just tired of this world. I love you, Joel."

"I love you, too. What are you going to do?"

"I'm about to make arrangements to go to Jerusalem as soon as possible. I'll leave today if I can. This is something that I need to do for myself. Don't come here looking for me because I won't be here. It's time that I do something for myself for a change."

"Call me and let me know that you're all right when you get to wherever you're going. I don't know what else to say. You might be making a huge mistake."

"Well, it'll just be my huge mistake. I don't have any babies or a husband to worry about anymore, do I?"

Joel closed his eyes and said, "No. Maybe you can reconsider the surgery when you get back home."

"Okay . . . if that makes you feel better."

Joel began to realize that his mother was being guided by a stronger power and that resisting it was useless. At that moment he felt a strange sense of calm. He felt himself gradually letting go of his mother and giving her and her problems to

God. She had chosen her path, just like his brother and father had chosen theirs. Joel opened his eyes and looked directly into Erin and Kenya's eyes. When he looked at them he saw love and knew that he couldn't go wrong. He accepted his fate and chose to continue down his current path side by side with Erin and Kenya.

Mrs. Davis was a lot sicker than anyone had suspected. She knew that her health was failing, but didn't want to admit it to Joel. The battery of diagnostic tests she had undergone failed to pick up on certain uncommon characteristics of her cancer. The type of cancer cells she had didn't have the common proteins or receptors that made them treatable or responsive to chemotherapy. She had an aggressive form of breast cancer that had already begun to rapidly spread to her surrounding organs. There was a good chance that she wouldn't even make it back home from the pilgrimage. Actually, she didn't want to come back home and had given in to the idea of visiting the Holy Land and then dying. Joel said goodbye to his mother and they both knew that this was possibly the last time they would speak to each other.

Chapter 35

So much had happened in such a short amount of time. On the way home he talked to Erin and Kenya about the details of his mother's decision to forgo any type of cancer treatment. Their hearts went out to Mrs. Davis for making such a life-altering decision. They looked at Joel in amazement because they couldn't believe how strong he was. He seemed to be carrying on with his life as if none of this family drama or relationship drama from his ex even existed.

Erin knew that the pressure had to be building up inside of Joel and would eventually come to a head. She asked him, "What are you thinking right now?"

"I'm thinking about a whole lot of things. I've always had this I-can-save-the-world mentality, but I can't even save one woman . . . my own mother. It hurts."

In a sympathetic tone Erin said, "Awww, don't think like that. You can't do everything. You try so hard, but it's impossible to be everything to everybody."

Kenya added, "She's right, Joel. It's too much for one person to bear."

"I'm used to it. As a teacher I always feel obligated to save all of my students. And y'all can't begin to imagine how overcrowded my classroom is. Everybody wants to be in Mr. Davis's class. Those kids need to be saved from all of the adversities they face. Most of them look up to me because they know that

I grew up in the same neighborhood, went to the same school and sat in some of those same seats."

Kenya said, "You talk about me putting too much pressure on myself. You can't save the world . . . not by yourself anyway."

When they stopped at a red light Erin took Joel by his hand and said, "The crazy thing is that you have so much pressure on you and not once have you shed a tear. It's okay for you to cry. As a matter of fact, it's healthy."

Joel shook his head and said, "I don't wanna cry. Crying won't do me any good."

Erin asked, "Do you think crying is weak or something?"

He said, "Kind of."

Kenya asked, "Why is it that most men don't cry in real-life situations, but when it comes to sports y'all just let the tears flow? I see athletes cry like babies whether they win or lose."

Joel said, "I don't know how to explain it. I'm just trying to figure out what's gonna come out of all this. Trust me, it's gotta be something good." He yawned and said, "Hopefully all of this despair is going to broaden my perspective on life and stimulate some kind of growth."

Erin laughed and asked, "What? I'm sorry for laughing, but what are you talking about? Poor thing. You're drained. We all are."

Kenya laughed too and said, "I know, right. I'm so sleepy I can hardly see straight." She nudged Joel and asked, "Are you all right, man?"

Joel smiled and said, "I'm okay. Just trying to stay awake and be as optimistic as possible. Don't worry, I'll be all right."

Joel's cell phone rang. He looked at the Caller ID and saw his mother's home number pop up. He said, "Hello."

"What's up, Joel? It's Shawn." There was a long awkward pause. "Your brother, Shawn."

Joel was so shocked he could hardly talk. "Yeah . . . hey . . . I know . . . what's up . . . Shawn? I was just wondering how you got my cell number."

"I got all of your numbers. Is that a problem?"

"Nah, not at all. I just haven't heard your voice in a while."

"I really haven't had the need to call you until now. You should be glad you haven't heard from me because that means I'm doing all right. I always try to save you as a last resort in trouble situations."

"Uh-oh. What do you need, some money?"

Shawn laughed and said, "Ain't that some shit? See what you think of me. Nah, I don't need none of your damn money . . . not right this minute anyway."

"What's going on then?"

"It's Momma. Something ain't right with her."

"What do you mean?"

"She gave me a hug, a kiss on the cheek and then told me that she loved me. She left out the front door with some bags and didn't say where she was going or when she was coming back. Now check this shit out. Daddy just called looking for her and told me to get the hell out of his house because he and that girl broke up. He said he was on his way back home and my black ass better not be here when he comes home. I need to know what the hell is going on around here and what I'm supposed to do. Momma said I could stay here. I need a roof over my head and I feel like Daddy is seriously trippin'. I'm gonna have him call you so you can help me straighten this out."

"Don't have him call me because I don't have nothing to say to him . . . nothing. Do you understand?"

"I hear you, but I don't understand."

"Look, Momma is sick. She was supposed to have surgery done this morning, but she refused."

"What's going on with her?"

"She has breast cancer."

Shawn had difficulty trying to process what he had just heard. "Aw, shit." He lowered his tone and couldn't get his thoughts together. "Aw, shit." Shawn lowered his tone even more as Joel's words sank in and he repeated, "Aw sssssssshit."

"Is that all you have to say?"

"What I'm gonna do? I mean, is she bad off?"

Joel shook his head because he knew that his freeloading brother was thinking of himself more than their mother. "I think she's pretty bad off considering the fact that she won't let her doctors do anything." Joel paused for a second and said, "I know you're worried about yourself, but you're just gonna have to be a man. Keep your head up and try your best to stay clean."

Shawn moaned, "I haven't had anything in me in a while."

"What's a while?"

"I'm gonna be honest. It's been a few days now."

"Well, at least that's a start. Maybe you should go to a Narcotics Anonymous meeting or something."

Shawn laughed and said, "I don't need no meeting. I said I haven't used in a few days. I can do this on my own. The urge is gone."

"Yeah, for now."

"You don't even know what it feels like, so stop trying to talk about something you can't relate to."

"I just call myself trying to look out for you, big bro. If you need me, you know my number. Don't call me for no dumb shit though. Do me a favor and stay out of Daddy's way because he's gonna feel real guilty when he finds out about Ma. His guilt is gonna turn into anger and I know you don't want him to take it out on you."

"She didn't even tell me she was sick," Shawn said, in tears. "See how y'all treat me," he cried. "Damn."

"Be a man, Shawn. Do you have a job?"

"No."

"Do you want a job?"

Shawn paused for a few seconds and then said, "Yeah, I want a job. I'm trying. Stuff like that takes time when you have a record. Nobody is in a hurry to hire somebody like me. You think you can bring me an application from your job?"

Joel laughed and said, "I'm sure you've heard that old saying, *you gotta get up . . . get out and get something.* Show some initiative and do it for yourself. You gotta see it, believe it and want it. The future is right now. Don't let another moment or another opportunity pass you by."

Shawn got offended by Joel's little speech. "Hold up a minute. Who you think you're talking to . . . one of your students or somebody? I don't even know why I called you anyway. Fuck you, Joel."

The phone call ended with an abrupt click. Joel wasn't surprised that Shawn hung up on him. He had come to expect just about anything from his unstable brother. Joel continued to act unfazed, all the way to Erin and Kenya's apartment. As soon as they made it to Erin's bedroom they all crashed in her bed and slept for hours.

Chapter 36

Later that evening, Renee awoke to the muffled sounds of roaring, hissing and beeping machines. As her hearing became clearer, she began to recognize the familiar voices of her family members. The head of her bed was elevated at a thirty-degree angle. She slowly opened her eyes to a dimly lit room, but was blinded by the bright lights from the hallway. Her vision was blurry, but gradually she was able to focus clearly on her sister on one side of the room and then her parents on the other.

Cheryl was the first to notice that Renee's eyes were open. "Look, Renee's eyes are open." She stood up and moved closer and said, "Hey, girl. Welcome back. Look at you. You're doing just fine now."

Renee's parents moved in closer. Her family tried to be supportive and acted as natural as possible, even though Renee looked like she was in pretty bad shape.

Mrs. Rhodes said, "Oh God, look at you . . . so precious." She kissed Renee on the cheek and said, "God can do all things but fail. I knew He'd bring you back."

Mr. Rhodes said, "Hey, Renee. How you feeling, baby?" He smiled. "I know you're all right."

Renee returned a blank stare. She realized where she was and became incredibly sad and frightened. She felt lethargic and momentarily confused. Her eyes watered and she began to cry. She didn't know what day it was or why she was in the hospital. She assumed that she had been in a car accident. This was a dramatic scene—a profound moment that Renee and her family would never forget.

Mrs. Rhodes said, "Don't cry, baby. You're gonna make me cry again. You're fine. Everything is gonna be okay."

Mr. Rhodes was about to break down himself. He acted strong and said, "I'm gonna let the doctor know that Renee is awake."

Mrs. Rhodes answered, "Good." She looked at Renee and said, "You're such a fighter. You know that?" Renee returned the same blank stare. Her mother smiled and said, "I know you know."

Cheryl and Mr. Rhodes couldn't bear to see Renee looking so incapacitated. A big part of the problem was that they both had unrealistic expectations about her recovery. They assumed Renee would awaken and instantly be just like her old self. The two of them looked deflated, but tried to hide their real emotions. They quietly exited the room to notify the doctor of Renee's status.

Mr. Rhodes never guessed Renee would end up in a crisis like this. She was so beautiful that he had imagined she would be happily married by now and her strong youthful husband would bear most of her burdens instead of him—a burned-out, over-the-hill father of two overly dependent adult daughters. He had always wanted sons, but wouldn't trade his girls for anything in the world.

Mrs. Rhodes stayed by Renee's side. She felt as guilty as ever, seeing her child in such a compromised condition. She wanted to exchange places with Renee because Renee had inherited this unforgiving mental disorder from her.

Renee lay there, trying her best to assess her situation. She looked down at her toes and wanted them covered because they were cold. She tried to speak, but realized she couldn't because she had an endotracheal tube jammed down her throat. With every passing second she became more aware of her body and surroundings. She wanted to rub her nose, but couldn't because her hands were restrained to keep her from pulling on any of her tubes, lines or drains. She struggled to piece her thoughts together, but everything was a blur. She was sorry that her family had to see her like this because she knew that she looked awfully pathetic lying there.

One face that she longed to see was noticeably missing. She wondered where Joel was and why he wasn't at her bedside. In an instant her thoughts of Joel triggered an eruption of images inside her mind. It was hard to figure out whether the images were real or imagined.

Mrs. Rhodes noticed a panicked look in Renee's eyes and asked, "What is it, baby? Relax yourself and go back to sleep. You gotta get your rest."

Mrs. Rhodes feared that if Renee remembered what happened it might hinder her recovery. She applied a cool compress to Renee's forehead. She held Renee's hand and stroked her face gently.

Renee was caught up in a brief flashback. She began to remember the bottle of sleeping pills, the cold wine and the unbearable feeling of worthlessness. She slowly pieced the main elements together and knew that she had done something to hurt herself. Everything else was a blur. At that moment she realized that she had survived a suicide attempt. She worried about what the future held for her, and wondered whether she had done any permanent damage to herself. Suddenly, Renee wished that she had died.

The walls were closing in on her. She felt like she was suffocating and began to breathe against the ventilator. That caused an alarm to sound. Mr. Rhodes and Cheryl had returned to the room along with Renee's nurse. Her family panicked, but the nurse quickly reset the alarm. The problem had already been corrected because Renee was unconscious again. It was normal for a person in her condition to slip in and out of consciousness. Being awake in this condition was entirely too much for her to deal with. She was mentally and physically exhausted.

Renee reentered la-la land and soon began to relive vivid, sweet memories of being with Joel. She immersed herself so deeply into the memories that she created images of moments that had never actually happened. This was like a priceless form of virtual reality. The new images were so real and beautiful that they gave her an overwhelming sense of peace and calm.

Chapter 37

The threesome had willingly gone into seclusion, away from the unrelenting and scorching summertime heat. They stayed inside Erin and Kenya's comfy apartment eating, sleeping, bathing and making love together almost all week. Nudity had become the norm, and spine-tingling sex had become a regular part of their daily ritual. They were temporarily cut off from the outside world that didn't really understand or appreciate a relationship like the one they shared. They seemed to feed off of each other's energy and showered each other with lots of affection. Being together like this confirmed that they possessed the power to turn the ordinary into the extraordinary. The intense nature of the world they created on the inside changed their view of the outside world. To them everybody else was an outsider.

Although sex played a major part in their relationship, the emphasis began to shift more toward love and belonging. All three seemed to have found their niche. They welcomed the change and embraced it. More than anything, they began to develop a better understanding of the subtleties and nuances that went into making a successful polyamorous relationship.

Joel spent a couple of days planning what he considered a much-needed two-part surprise getaway.

On Friday morning the threesome woke up in Erin's snug queen-sized bed looking like they were in the middle of playing a game of naked Twister. They missed Joel's apartment and his king-sized bed. They had carried out a series of clean-up and recovery efforts in his apartment, but for the most part the place remained in a shambles. Joel came to the conclusion that it was time to give up his apartment. Since he had a month-to-month lease, Erin and Kenya planned to move Joel and his king-sized bed into their apartment.

The moment had almost arrived for Joel to reveal the first part of the surprise he had planned for Erin and Kenya—what he called the ultimate date. He asked them to dress in evening gowns because a limousine was scheduled to pick them up later that evening. As the hours passed, Erin and Kenya knew that they were in for a treat. All that day there was something extra special about the way Joel looked at them, held them and kissed them.

A white Lincoln Navigator stretch-limousine arrived at five-thirty that evening. The driver was a heavyset middle-aged white guy named Chuck. He parked the limousine and made his way up to the apartment to meet his clients.

As usual the three were dressed to impress. Joel exited the building first, looking very formal. He was decked out in his fresh-to-death black Hugo Boss tuxedo with a crisp white dress shirt and an extra-thick black silk necktie. The two-button peaked-lapel jacket accentuated his athletic physique. Joel held the door as Erin exited wearing a stunning celery green silk gown with an embroidered bust and thin spaghetti straps. Kenya followed close behind wearing a sexy chartreuse silk chiffon gown with halter straps. Erin and Kenya purposely chose to wear shimmering summer-colored gowns with styles that showed off their individuality. Their gowns were made by a well-known African-American designer named Rudy Alston. His fashions were known to accentuate black women's coca-cola figures—plump bottoms, ample bust and narrow waist-lines.

A lot of their neighbors were just arriving home from work. They stopped and stared as Erin, Kenya and Joel got into their limousine. Ms. Benson stood frozen on the sidewalk simply admiring how handsome Joel looked in his tuxedo and how dazzling Erin and Kenya looked in their elegant gowns. The neighbors thought of the three as weird and very hard to figure out. In reality they were just bold, daring and different.

Joel made sure that there were two dozen long-stemmed roses along with a chilled bottle of champagne waiting for Erin and Kenya inside the limousine. They thanked Joel for their surprise, but had no idea where they were headed or what else he had in store. They just sat back, relaxed, cuddled up with their man and enjoyed the ride.

It took about thirty-five minutes for the limousine to arrive at the Joseph Meyerhoff Symphony Hall. A crowd of well-dressed classical-music enthusiasts moved at a snail's pace toward the main entrance. A few black concertgoers were scattered throughout the predominantly white crowd. Chuck parked his limo and then made his way around to open the door for Joel and the girls. Joel stepped out first and took Erin on his right arm and then Kenya on his left arm. Heads turned, smiles gleamed, eyebrows raised and there were some double-takes.

Joel had the pleasure of hearing the Baltimore Symphony Orchestra perform live during a school trip, and had always promised that he would return. He just never imagined he would return and make such a grand entrance with a beautiful woman on each arm.

Erin and Kenya had never heard the BSO perform live. They had always dreamed of dressing up and attending what they thought of as a high-society cultural event like this. All their lives they had seen people on television going to operas and ballets. This was an exciting chance for them to dress up and rub elbows with some of Baltimore's elite. It definitely lived up to the hype.

Joel was different from any man Erin or Kenya had ever dated. Most guys they dated in the past would have been too intimidated to attend this type of concert.

The BSO created music that sounded like heaven on earth. No other venue in the area matched the Meyerhoff. Every instrument could be heard, and conveyed as much feeling as any vocalist. The music was dramatic, emotional and uplifting. Joel had achieved his goal—he could clearly see that Erin and Kenya thoroughly enjoyed themselves.

After the concert Chuck drove the threesome around downtown Baltimore for a little while. Joel had him drop them off at a park called Rash Field where they could enjoy the breathtaking view of the inner harbor and the city's skyline. They stood atop a grassy hilltop on a wide sidewalk surrounded by lush greenery, watching Baltimore unwind from a busy week. The passing cars roared while the city lights created a somber glow in the darkness of night.

A warm gentle breeze began to stir and made the leaves on the trees shimmy. There were several couples sitting on benches or walking along taking in the romantic atmosphere. A saxophonist sat under a lamppost playing his heart out for dollars or loose change. The night sky was so clear that the stars looked like a million sparkling diamonds set against a coal-black velvet background.

Erin looked at Joel and said, "This is really nice and I'm all for strolls in the park, but I'm hungry."

Kenya laughed and said, "So am I. As a matter of fact, I'm starving. We need food."

Joel was calm and cool. He took off his jacket, loosened his necktie and said, "Just keep walking and I promise y'all a meal you won't forget."

As the three walked along the sidewalk they noticed a white canopy set up next to a white truck with the company's name Ready-set Gourmet painted in fancy red lettering on the side.

As they got closer to the canopy Kenya said, "I smell something good." She pointed toward the elegant table, took a deep breath and said, "Look at all this. God, this is so romantic."

Soft glowing candlelight lit the scene. There was a large

sterling-silver candelabrum in the middle of the table. Four mixed bouquets of white, yellow, pink and red roses sat on white columns at each inside corner of the canopy.

Erin exhaled loudly and said, "This sure is romantic. I wish this was for us."

Joel smiled and said, "Yeah, this is nice. Somebody kicked out a lot of cash to make this happen." He stepped in for a closer look and was very impressed. "One day I might surprise y'all and do something like this."

A middle-aged black couple emerged from the rear of the truck dressed like chefs. They noticed Joel and the girls and walked toward them. The man looked at Joel and said, "Hello. How may I help you, sir?"

Joel chuckled and said, "I'm Mr. Davis and these are my lovely guests, Erin and Kenya."

Erin and Kenya's eyes widened and their hearts skipped a beat. They blushed and then turned into two giddy little schoolgirls.

Erin looked at Kenya and whispered, "What's he doing?"

Kenya looked puzzled. "I dunno. Is this for us?"

Erin smiled and said, "I think so . . . I hope so."

Erin and Kenya were blown away by Joel and his extravagant surprises.

The guy who was talking to Joel said, "All right, Mr. Davis. I'd like to welcome the three of you. I'm Lawrence Connors and this is my wife Lori Connors and we're the co-owners of Ready-set Gourmet."

Lori smiled and said, "Good evening everybody, and welcome to Ready-set Gourmet. Come right this way." She directed them to their table.

It was a round table, so quite naturally Joel sat with Erin on his right side and Kenya on his left.

Joel had contacted Lawrence earlier in the week and reserved everything. Usually a dinner like this had to be planned weeks in advance, but there was a last-minute cancellation and Lawrence was able to accommodate Joel. Joel pre-selected shrimp cocktails for their appetizers and jumbo steamed lobster with a steamed vegetable medley and seasoned mashed potatoes for their dinner entrées.

Within a few minutes their appetizers were served. Their entrées followed and the three talked and joked around while dipping their lobster in warm butter. They spent about an hour eating dinner and drinking champagne.

After dinner Joel looked at Erin and Kenya and said, "I kept saying that I wanted to do something special for the two of you and this is it." Though he already knew the answer, he asked, "How did y'all enjoy everything?"

Erin said, "Thank you so much. Everything was beautiful. All I can say is that you're a man with a lot of style."

Kenya said, "Thanks so much for showing us a different side of life. The concert was nice, but having dinner out here like this is absolutely incredible."

Joel smiled and said, "I wanted to do something that was a little over-the-top and I'm nowhere close to being finished."

Erin said, "This is enough. I'm sure you put out a lot of money to make this happen."

"I did, but the two of you are worth every penny."

Kenya said, "I keep asking myself, all this for us?"

Joel said, "You're worth it."

Kenya laughed and said, "We know it, but the fact that you know it means everything."

"I told y'all it doesn't stop here. We're all interested in an exotic getaway, right?"

Erin said with a giggle in her voice, "Yeah. We can leave tonight if you're ready."

With a straight face Joel asked, "How does next week sound?"

Kenya's eyes widened. "Oh my God. Are you serious?"

Erin said, "He sure looks serious."

Joel couldn't hold back his smile. He pulled out some paperwork. He unfolded the flight confirmation and reservation information for the Atlantis Resort in the Bahamas.

Erin looked at the dates and confirmation numbers and said, "He is serious. Awww, I can't wait. Thank you . . . thank you . . . thank you."

Kenya said, "Thank you, Joel. You're so sweet. What would we do without you?"

Joel asked, "What would I do without the two of you?" He paused for a second and said, "I've had a lot on my mind lately. I've been through a whole lot too. The good thing is that the two of you have been by my side the entire time and I love y'all for that."

Out of nowhere Erin said, "I love you, Joel."

Kenya added with sincerity, "I love you too, Joel."

Joel appeared to be blown away by Erin and Kenya's affectionate words. "This is wild. Hearing those words come out of your mouths is mind-blowing. I love you, Erin." He gave her a long, slow, passionate kiss. Then Joel looked directly into Kenya's eyes and said, "And I love you, Kenya." He gave her an equally passionate kiss. "There's so much going on inside of me right now. I keep hearing my mother's voice. She's guiding me . . . leading me closer to God. I've been praying like crazy, asking God to help me make a change in my life. I wanna do things the right way without compromising who I am, but honestly it's hard trying to lead a Christian lifestyle living in this sexually charged world that we live in."

With a worried expression on her face Erin asked, "What exactly are you saying?"

Kenya noticed that Joel seemed to have had trouble finding the right words. She said, "Go ahead and just say exactly what's on your mind."

"Okay. I feel like God is watching me . . . every little thing I do. I'm trying to find a healthy balance between spirituality and sexuality without feeling guilty. I want us to get closer to God even though people think that He won't understand or approve of a relationship like ours. But I think He will . . . I pray He will."

Kenya smiled and said, "We're spiritual beings and we

know God. We don't need any religion or any hypocritical peo-ple telling us how God wants us to express our love for each other. No matter what, God is inside of us. Trust me, we're al-ready close to Him."

Erin said, "I agree with Kenya."

"So do I." Joel paused and then asked, "I've come up with a way for us to get even closer to God.

Erin asked, "How?"

Joel stood up and moved his chair out of the way. He posi-tioned himself between Erin and Kenya and then got down on one knee. He reached into his pocket and pulled out two ring boxes. "I'd like to know if the two of you would be willing to commit your lives and your love to me because I'm willing to give the two of you my life, my love and anything else I have to offer."

Joel slid a two-carat diamond engagement ring on Erin's fin-ger. He turned toward Kenya and slid a two carat diamond en-gagement ring on her finger. They were both filled with excitement and nervous energy.

With tears in her eyes Erin said, "Yes, I'm willing to give you everything I have."

Kenya's eyes watered. She reached over and took Erin by the hand. She looked at Joel and said, "I love both of y'all and I'm willing to commit to the two of you for the rest of my life."

Joel said, "I was thinking that we could make this as official as possible and have a commitment ceremony in the Bahamas."

Erin said, "That sounds like a beautiful idea. Wow . . . I don't really know what to say. When we first met I tried to block my emotions because I was afraid to love again. But now I can't do anything else but love you, Joel."

Kenya said, "This was the surprise of a lifetime." She held her ring next to Erin's and said, "Look at these rings. Joel, you are the epitome of true love and seduction. I've never met a man like you before."

Erin said, "Neither have I. You really know how to make us feel special."

"Both of you make me feel special. I need the two of you in my life."

Erin said, "Joel, you satisfy my innermost needs and so does Kenya. That's what makes it so easy for me to sit here and say yes to spending the rest of my life with the two of you."

Joel asked, "What more can I ask for? We're friends . . . we're lovers . . . and most of all we're one, and nothing can change that."

They joined together and shared a passionate triple kiss.

The three took a moment and had a serious talk about what it meant to commit to each other. They discussed the importance of honesty and trust. They spent the majority of the discussion talking about the compromises and sacrifices that needed to be made in order to have a successful polyamorous relationship. One of the biggest issues that came up was kids. Erin and Kenya admitted that they had no desire to have kids. After some deep thinking, Joel came to the conclusion that although he wanted kids, he would be willing to give up the idea if that was what it took to be happy and spend the rest of his life with Erin and Kenya. They were learning to see life in new ways and knew that they had to ignore certain outside influences that only stood to harm them in the long run.

When the three got home they made love to each other like there was no tomorrow.

Chapter 38

The next morning Renee woke up with the realization that nobody could or would ever love her the way Joel did. All night she dreamed of the good times they used to share. She felt sorry that she took Joel for granted and wished that their relationship could have lasted forever. She overflowed with indescribable emotions that made her long for and need him like air, water and food.

Renee was determined to make a rapid recovery. The doctors put her through a battery of mental exams and were impressed with her results. She answered questions with appropriate responses during her psychoanalysis sessions. Renee was clever and her I.Q. was well above average. She wanted to straighten herself up as soon as possible because she felt that was the only way she could get Joel back. There was a tiny voice of doubt in the back of her mind telling her that Joel no longer belonged to her and would never be hers again. The voice reminded her of the vicious and destructive things she had done in his apartment. She asked herself over and over how she could possibly compete with two attractive women who gave Joel so much attention. She couldn't even begin to answer that question. She simply planned to take things day-by-day.

As a result of her quick recovery and cooperation Renee was released from the hospital a day earlier than originally planned. She took a major step when she accepted the fact

that she had bipolar disorder. Renee agreed to take antipsychotic medications and to see her psychiatrist regularly.

Mrs. Rhodes never remembered seeing Renee look happier. Whenever Renee mentioned Joel's name she seemed to
glow even more. Her mother realized how much Joel meant to
her daughter and decided to give him a call to see if he would
be willing to pay Renee a quick visit. She thought it would be
a good thing if he could see how calm and sensible her daughter was. More than anything she wanted Joel to see how beautiful Renee looked.

Joel decided to visit Renee without Erin and Kenya. When
he arrived at the Rhodes' home Mrs. Rhodes greeted him
with a warm embrace. Joel wasn't sure whether he trusted this
new friendly version of Mrs. Rhodes.

She said, "Thank you so much for agreeing to see Renee.
She's upstairs in her bedroom. She has no idea you agreed to
come here."

Joel seemed somewhat hesitant and asked, "Do you think
it'll be okay with her that I came here unannounced?"

"Sure, she'll be excited to see you."

"How is she?"

"She's doing fine. Wait till you see her. Come on and I'll
take you up to her room."

Joel followed Mrs. Rhodes upstairs. Renee's bedroom door
was closed. Her mother knocked, but there was no response.
Joel looked worried. Mrs. Rhodes assured him that everything
was okay. She opened the bedroom door. From where they
stood they could see that Renee was fast asleep.

Mrs. Rhodes said, "Go right inside. It's fine to wake her.
I'm sure it'll be a pleasant surprise."

Joel said, "Okay."

Mrs. Rhodes closed the door and Joel walked toward Renee's
bed. He stopped and stared at her for a moment. He never remembered seeing her look more natural and beautiful. She
looked like a black version of Sleeping Beauty, waiting for her

prince to awaken her with a kiss. Instead of kissing Renee, Joel touched her right shoulder and shook her gently.

"Renee . . . Renee, wake up."

Renee stretched and rubbed her eyes at the same time. She opened her eyes and looked at Joel sideways. She smiled, sat up in bed and said, "Hey Joel, where did you come from?"

"What do you mean? Where did I come from? I appeared out of thin air."

Renee laughed and said, "You're too smart. You know what I meant. I just dozed off. I didn't expect to wake up and see you standing there, but I'm so glad you're here." She moved her legs over and said, "Sit down."

Joel sat on the side of the bed and said, "You look well."

Renee said, "Dag, thanks." She gave Joel a funny look and decided to mess with him a little. "I thought I looked better than *well*."

"You do." Joel acted like he didn't really want to look at Renee for more than a second at a time. The last thing he wanted to do was to give her the wrong impression or start something he didn't want to finish. He avoided eye contact as much as possible because he could feel Renee staring at him. He mumbled, "You look . . . pretty."

"Thank you."

"I've got something for you." Joel took out Renee's friendship ring and slid it on her left ring finger. "I thought you might have wanted this back."

Renee lit up and sounded almost breathless. "Yeah, thanks. Did you mean to put it on that finger?"

Joel responded quickly, "No, I wasn't thinking. That's where you had it the other night when I found you in my bed."

They shared a moment of awkward silence.

Renee said, "I need to apologize for all of the things I did in your apartment. I was completely out of my mind, but I'm okay now . . . I'm back to normal. I'm so sorry for what I did to your things and I'm going to repay you."

"Good, because you really wrecked my shit." He smiled and said, "But it's okay for now, we don't even have to talk about that. Actually, I'd rather not talk about it. I'm just glad you're doing better."

"You saved my life and I'm so thankful."

"I didn't do it alone. Erin and Kenya helped me."

Renee rolled her eyes and said, "Oh yeah . . . them. They saw me like that?"

"Yeah. No big deal."

"Maybe not to you. I never thought about them finding me. I only thought about you."

Joel frowned and asked, "What were you thinking?"

"I wanted to die. And I wanted to hurt you for not being in my life. I felt totally rejected that day."

Joel noticed tears welling up in Renee's eyes and said, "Please don't get upset."

"I can't help it. Now I realize how stupid and selfish I was being. I was spinning out of control and had no idea what I was really doing. I couldn't control my impulses."

"Just don't scare us like that again."

"Did Erin and Kenya make fun of me?"

"Not at all. All they wanted to do was to help you."

"I feel so stupid. But tell them I said thanks."

"You shouldn't feel stupid. You couldn't help what happened. You were sick. That could have happened to anybody."

"Why are you being so understanding?"

"What do you want me to do, kick your ass while you're down? Because I can if you want."

They both laughed.

"No. I want you to hold me for a second because that would make me feel a whole lot better."

"I don't think that's a good idea."

Renee looked dazed and confused—she couldn't understand why Joel didn't want to touch her. She worried that he no longer found her attractive. "I promise not to bite."

Joel laughed and said, "Okay."

He took Renee into his arms and he could feel her melt. Actually she felt really good to him because just a few days ago he thought that she was gone for good. Their embrace seemed to go on a little too long and Joel's arms began to loosen.

Renee held him tighter and whispered, "Don't let go . . . don't ever let me go again. I'm sorry for everything I did to you. I missed you so bad that it hurts. I still love you, Joel."

"Stop. I can't go there again."

Renee felt herself clinging and slowly peeled herself away from her sweet obsession and said, "Don't treat me like a stranger. I'm sure you still remember what we used to share. You can't tell me that things like that don't run across your mind from time to time."

"That's all in the past now."

"Deep down inside I know that you still love me. You still love me, don't you?" Joel didn't respond. "Something's different." She prepared to ask a question that she really didn't want answered. "When did you stop loving me? I need to know."

"I don't wanna answer that."

"Because you still love me."

"I'll always love you, but I'm not in love with you. I realized I wasn't in love with you the day I met Erin." Joel paused and said, "I've said too much and the last thing I came here to do is to hurt you. I would never want to hurt you. The best thing I can offer you right now is friendship. As far as I'm concerned we'll always be friends."

"You don't understand. Friendship isn't enough."

"Nothing is ever enough for you. That's one of your biggest problems."

She let out a heavy sigh. "You're my biggest problem. Why can't you understand me? The pain I feel right now runs almost as deep as the love I feel for you . . . it hurts so bad. I've been waiting for this moment to be face-to-face with you again, but this conversation isn't going like I had planned. I'm pouring my heart out and you don't understand a word I've said. I've never felt like this about anyone and I don't want to be without you."

"I understand what you're saying. You just need more time to clear your mind. You've been through a lot."

"I'm still going through a lot. Stop treating me like I'm crazy."

"I know you're not crazy."

"Well, you're treating me different. You used to love me and treat me like I mattered."

"You still matter."

"I wanted to die, but you saved me. Save me one more time. Let's get back together. That's all I'm asking you."

"We can't. I didn't want to tell you, but things between me, Erin and Kenya are more serious than you probably think. We're having a commitment ceremony in the Bahamas next Friday at four o'clock. We're renting a spot on the private island where they filmed that movie *The Blue Lagoon*."

Renee pressed her lips together and fought to hold her tears back. With sarcasm she said, "That's lovely, but I can't imagine you with those lesbians like that. What do you see in them and why do you think y'all have a future together?"

Joel laughed and said, "Don't call them lesbians."

"That's exactly what they are. And you avoided my question. Why do you think y'all have a future together?"

"I'm in love with them and the three of us just belong together. Everything is so smooth when we're together. I'm in love with them—"

Renee cut him off. "You're not in love with them. Don't be stupid. It's called infatuation. It won't last."

"If it ain't love then I don't know what love is."

"You don't."

"You're bitter."

"No, for once in my life I'm being real. My heart is aching and excuse me for saying this, but I'm horny as hell too. We could be having sex right now and nobody would know." Renee turned on her side and said, "Don't you miss this ass and being inside me?"

Joel had never heard Renee talk dirty and tried to hide the fact that he liked it. He looked at her and said, "Come on, how are you gonna ask me something like that?"

She touched herself and asked, "Remember how tight and wet it used to feel? I know you remember. I remember how good you used to lick me down here. You used to fuck me so hard. But I liked when you took your time and made love to me real slow, like nothing else mattered in the world but me. I had the best orgasms that way. It felt like something was building up inside of me and then out of nowhere I'd have the most intense orgasm. You used to be my man and I need you back so bad . . . oh, so bad."

Joel put his finger up to Renee's lips and said, "Shhh."

Renee had an unexplainable effect on Joel. He took her in his arms again. He used the heels of his feet to take off his tennis shoes. The next thing Renee knew she was lying in her bed wrapped up in Joel's strong affectionate arms. He knew that he was sending mixed signals, but he just couldn't help himself. To Renee it felt like heaven being in Joel's arms.

Joel had incredible willpower. He was in control, knew his limits and how far he would allow things to go. Joel watched as Renee's medicaton began to take effect. He held Renee until she fell asleep. He gently kissed her on her forehead and then eased his way out of her house and, he hoped, out of her life.

Chapter 39

The following Monday morning Erin, Kenya and Joel boarded a nonstop US Airways flight to Nassau. Their four-hour, fifty-minute flight was smooth and relaxing. The whole time they were filled with excitement and anticipation of spending passion filled days and nights together in paradise.

Joel had booked an ocean-view suite at the Atlantis Resort on Paradise Island. Bright and lively Caribbean colors filled their suite. From their balcony they had a breathtaking view of the Atlantic Ocean. On the opposite side of the building was an incredible view of the Nassau Harbor and the Atlantis Marina. The resort had its own water park, aquarium, and a host of other attractions. This was the type of place that could keep the threesome busy with activities or they could enjoy themselves doing nothing at all.

They spent most of their first day sightseeing and getting familiar with their surroundings. At all times they were surrounded by unimaginable beauty. The broad horizon was where the blue sky and turquoise water met. The turquoise water faded into crystal clear water along an enormous stretch of beachfront that was covered in hot white sand.

The threesome developed a daily routine. They began each day with an early morning swim, breakfast and then a walk along the beach. Their afternoons were spent hidden away amongst the resort's lush tropical greenery. They spent hours relaxing and swaying on a hammock under two huge shady palm trees with nothing but the peaceful sounds of the ocean and the gentle Bahamian breeze flowing through the trees.

All of the romantic alone-time had the three in perfect sync. They were far removed from the stresses and strains of the real world. They managed to pull off a few late night rendezvous, making love in secluded spots along the beach. This was just an introduction to passion, fun, excitement and relaxation because they still had their ceremony and honeymoon to look forward to.

The next day they found time to go over to the public beach to mingle with the natives and the other tourists. There were cabanas set up along the beach for chaise lounge and umbrella rentals. Small groups of Bahamian women braided female tourists' hair. Two or three women worked together on one head at a time. One of the ladies noticed Erin and Kenya walking in her direction and asked, "Braid the pretty ladies' hair?"

Erin and Kenya smiled and said in unison, "No thank you."

Every few minutes a man walked along the beach carrying a cooler filled with ice, milk, juice, fruit, coconuts and rum yelling, "Who wants to get hammered? Drink all day for ten dollars . . . Bahama Mamas and Pina Coladas."

The idea of tropical drinks all day for ten dollars caught their attention. They spent hours relaxing in the water or on the beach, sipping Bahama Mamas and Pina Coladas from hollowed-out coconuts. Erin and Kenya decided to get their hair braided so they could fit in with the other tourists.

Joel got hammered for real. He didn't even remember walking back to their suite. He woke up in bed alone at one-thirty in the morning. A tiny glow of light could be seen under the door. When Joel listened closely he could hear the sounds of feminine moans and groans. He was fully awake now and full of excitement to see Erin and Kenya in action. He took off his T-shirt and swim trunks and headed to the living room butt-naked with a raging hard-on, hoping to join the fun.

Joel was quiet because he wanted to catch the girls in action. The first thing he noticed was their neatly braided hair and then their glistening brown flesh. What he saw next wasn't at all what he expected to see or how he dreamed Erin and Kenya would look when they made love. He imagined that they would look extremely beautiful and passionate, but instead they looked like they were part of a pornographic lesbian fuckfest. He wondered what happened to all of the gentle touching, caressing and slow passionate kisses.

Erin and Kenya had bottles of lubricant and their devices laid out in front of them on towels. Kenya was on the floor lying on a huge beach towel with her legs spread-eagled while Erin jabbed her to death with a big black dildo. Erin used her free hand to stimulate herself with a multifunctional motorized dildo. They looked like they were having the time of their lives. Joel was shocked, amazed, intrigued and disappointed at the same time.

Kenya tapped Erin's arm to let her know that it was time for a change. Things really got out of hand when Kenya reached into her duffel bag and was about to put on a strap-on when she noticed Joel standing there looking at them. Then Erin noticed him too. Their hearts stopped. They instantly tried to hide their embarrassment and their sex toys. They felt weird and uncomfortable with Joel watching them during one of their intimate girls-only sex sessions. They had thought he was drunk and completely done for the night. They never guessed that he would come sneaking up on them, disturbing their precious alone-time the way he did.

With a look of disappointment on his face Joel said, "Damn, it looks like y'all don't even need me anymore."

Before Erin and Kenya answered Joel all they could do was breathe heavily and look at him with dazed and confused expressions.

Chapter 40

On Friday morning Renee was on her way to her weekly therapy session with her psychiatrist when she was struck by an irrepressible urge to be with Joel. She thought to herself, *At four o'clock the lesbians win.*

Out of nowhere she started talking to herself. "I can't let them win and just take my man without a fight."

The next thing Renee knew she had made a U-turn. She was speeding down the street, headed away from her therapy session and was on her way to BWI Airport. She knew that she was being impulsive again, but didn't care. All she knew was that it was eight-fifteen in the morning and she needed to get to the Bahamas before four o'clock, by any means necessary.

Usually Renee would have parked her Escalade in the $8 per day long-term parking lot and caught the courtesy shuttle to the terminal. But she was in such a hurry that she parked her truck in the $65 per day garage attached to the terminal.

The airport was overloaded with summertime travelers. Most of the passengers already had reservations and their boarding passes in hand. All Renee had was a crazy impulse and an almost maxed-out Visa card. She didn't even have a clue what airline flew to the Bahamas. It was as if her female intuition or something guided her directly to the US Airways terminal. She looked at a monitor for departure times and destinations. Her eyes nearly popped out of her head when she saw a flight departing at nine-forty to Nassau. She was nervous and excited. Her emotions seemed to overpower the effects of her medication. She fought like hell to stay composed.

"Please God ... please God ... I gotta make it," Renee kept mumbling to herself.

The last thing Renee expected was a line at the ticket counter. She broke out in a sweat. Somehow she managed to stay calm even though it seemed like the line wasn't moving at all. Within ten minutes she had made her way to the head of the line.

A lady with long red hair signaled Renee over to the ticket counter and asked, "How may I help you, ma'am?"

"Hi, I need one ticket on your next flight to Nassau."

The lady asked, "One way or round-trip?"

Renee thought for a second and then said, "Round-trip."

"Will you be returning to BWI?"

"Yes, I think on Monday."

The lady looked at Renee like she was crazy and said, "So, you think Monday or you know for sure Monday?"

Renee gave the lady a look that said *I know you're not giving me attitude because I will slap you.* She remained calm and said, "On second thought, I better make it a one-way ticket. My fiancé is already there. He might surprise me and decide to extend our trip or something. You know how guys are."

The lady said, "Sure. Wait please, while I check the availability." She paused for a minute while the information popped up on the computer screen. "Our next flight leaves at eleven twenty-five."

Renee yelled, "No! I need to be on the nine-forty flight."

"I'm sorry ma'am, but that flight leaves in approximately forty minutes and I don't think you'd be able to make it. We'll have to check your bags, and you have to make it through that long security check-in line over there."

Renee shook her head and said, "I don't have any bags."

The lady looked confused. "You're going to the Bahamas and you don't have any luggage?"

Renee smiled and said, "I told you my fiancé is already there. He's got everything I need."

The lady returned a soft smile and said, "Oh, I'm glad to hear that because I was getting kind of suspicious . . . last minute flight . . . no luggage . . . one-way ticket, and you look kind of nervous. You know, ever since 9/11 we have to take everything seriously. I mean, you wouldn't believe some of the people who come through here. One day—"

Renee was about to snap because she didn't have time for small talk. She interrupted the lady and asked, "Could you please speed up a bit? I'm really in a hurry."

The lady put on a fake smile and said, "I'm sorry. I don't know where my head was. I'll need your identification and I'll try to book you on the nine-forty flight, but there's no guarantee you'll make it in time."

The airfare was a little over seven hundred dollars. Renee didn't think twice about paying it. The butterflies in her stomach had taken flight and were doing loops and nosedives. She looked down at her watch and mumbled, "Please God . . . please God . . . I gotta make it."

When the lady handed Renee her boarding pass she felt like she had cleared a major hurdle, but she still had a few hurdles left. Getting through the Transportation Security Administration check-in was a major obstacle in itself. There was a check-in line that snaked around five times before she could even reach the line that led to the metal detectors and x-ray machines.

Renee freshened up her lipstick and began to ask people to let her up in line. To her surprise people allowed her to get ahead of them.

Renee mumbled, "Please God . . . please God . . . I gotta make it." She looked at a little old white man who had a kind face. He was one person away from the TSA security guard who checked the IDs and boarding passes before the metal detectors and x-ray machines. Renee tried to look pitiful and said, "Excuse me sir, my plane is boarding right now and I was wondering if you would let me in front of you so I won't miss my flight?"

The old white man looked at Renee and said with a raspy voice, "I'm sorry. You'll just have to wait like everybody else."

Renee accepted the old man's rejection and simply said, "Thank you anyway."

The old man began to feel sorry for Renee and said, "Miss, if these other people don't mind me letting you up, then I guess it's okay if you go ahead of me."

Most of the people in line were an hour-and-a-half to three hours ahead of schedule and couldn't care less whether one teary-eyed woman who was about to miss her flight went ahead of them or not.

Renee made it through security and ran down to her gate barefooted, with her shoes in one hand and her open Coach bag in the other. By the time she made it to the gate the last passenger was headed down the corridor toward the plane. It appeared that she had made it just in time.

During the flight Renee was too worried about making it to the Bahamas in a timely manner to even remember that she had a terrible fear of flying. Her plane touched down in Nassau at two fifty-five. She couldn't believe that she had made it to the Bahamas. She wasn't too sure about where to go or what to do. She remembered Joel saying something about the Blue Lagoon. Renee knew that she had come too far to mess up or to give up now.

Hundreds of tourists rushed past Renee as she stood in the middle of the airport. She was momentarily at a loss, but something guided her to a full-figured black woman with a round glowing face and a tiny afro-style hairdo.

Renee said, "Hi, can you please tell me how to get to the Blue Lagoon from here?"

The lady said, "Oh honey, that's another island. You need a taxi to the Paradise Island Ferry Terminal. It's about a half hour from here and Blue Lagoon Island is a twenty minute boat ride from there."

Renee took a deep breath and then asked, "Can you please show me where I can get a taxi?"

The lady smiled and said, "Okay. Come this way." She led Renee outside to a big blue van and said, "Wait here while I get the driver. He won't leave till he has a full load of passengers ready to go. It costs five dollars to get you there."

Excitedly Renee said, "If you find the driver I'll give you twenty dollars and give him fifty dollars if he can take me right now."

"You'll have to give him sixty dollars because this is a twelve-passenger van."

"Fine. I'll do it."

Within a few seconds the lady returned with a big sweaty black man wearing sunglasses. He walked over toward Renee, wiped his forehead with a handkerchief and asked, "Ma'am, you ready to go?"

Renee smiled and said, "Yeah." She looked at the lady who helped her, handed her a twenty-dollar bill and said, "That was fast . . . thank you."

The lady said, "Thank *you*."

The taxi driver looked at Renee out of the corner of his eye with a curious expression and asked, "You'll pay me sixty?"

"Yeah, I'll pay. If you can get me there in less than a half hour I'll even throw in a small tip."

The taxi driver smiled and said, "Okay ma'am, let's go."

They sped down the left-hand side of the road. At first that caught Renee off guard. She had forgotten that they drove on the opposite side of the road in the Bahamas. She was fine as long as she didn't have to drive. It was hot as hell inside the van. The air conditioner felt like it needed to be recharged. Now Renee was sweating from her nervousness and the heat.

Renee looked at the busy weekend traffic and asked, "How long do you think it will take to get to the ferry terminal?"

"It's hard to say with this kind of traffic."

Renee mumbled for the third time, "Please God . . . please God . . . I gotta make it."

The taxi driver asked, "What did you say?"

"Nothing. I was praying."

He raised both eyebrows and said, "Oh, praying is good."

The next thing Renee knew the taxi driver started talking about church, sin and salvation.

Twenty-five minutes later they arrived at the ferry terminal. Renee had no idea which boat was headed to Blue Lagoon Island. She saw a bunch of commercial boats. One boat had the words *Glass Bottom Boat* painted on the sides and another had *Dolphin Encounter* painted on its sides. Then she noticed a party boat blasting reggae music and displayed a bunch of liquor and beer advertisements.

Renee walked along the pier under the hot sun, wasting valuable time and looking lost.

Out of nowhere a male voice with a heavy Caribbean accent asked, "Hey, where you need to go?"

Renee shouted, "I'm trying to go to Blue Lagoon Island."

The man said, "That's where I'm headed."

Renee looked closely at the man's unmarked beat-down rust bucket of a boat. She looked at the three strange-looking guys aboard and they all smiled and waved at her.

Renee quickly said, "No, that's okay."

The man motioned with his hand and said, "C'mon."

Renee laughed and said, "I'm crazy, but I'm not that crazy."

"Whatcha scared of?" He looked over his shoulder and said, "That's my crew. This is the last ferry to the Blue Lagoon today. I can get you there quick and cheap . . . six dollars."

Renee looked at her watch and realized that she didn't have any time to spare. She thought, *I can't let those lesbians win.* She stepped aboard the rust bucket and said, "Please God . . . please God . . . I gotta make it."

Chapter 41

Joel had hired a company to coordinate the commitment ceremony. The coordinators had done plenty of weddings and commitment ceremonies, but this was the first one they had ever done where there weren't any guests. It was kind of sad that no one was present to witness the threesome's special day. A few chairs were set up just in case someone arrived and wanted to witness the ceremony. A non-traditional wedding cake sat on a small table next to the empty chairs. The thing that really made this cake stand out was the groom standing between two brides.

Erin and Kenya looked beautiful in their white linen dresses. Erin's dress was strapless and Kenya's had her favorite halter strap design. Joel was dressed in white linen too, a short-sleeved shirt and long pants. The three of them looked like they belonged together. They had purchased their clothes a couple of days earlier from a lady at a local craft market. Once she said that the outfits were cut from the same cloth, the three knew they had chosen the right clothes for their ceremony. The bright sun made the soft white linen glow in the tropical setting.

This ceremony wasn't legally binding or recognized as a marriage. It was more or less a personal expression of love and commitment between three people. More than anything it was a way of asking for God's special blessing on their lives and their relationship.

Erin, Kenya and Joel took this ceremony seriously. To them it carried the same weight and meaning as a traditional wedding. They walked hand-in-hand toward the minister, who stood at an altar on a small bridge that extended from one end of the lagoon to the other. The minister was dressed in white as well.

Reverend Gamble opened his Bible, read a few scriptures from I Corinthians and then he said, "This is a beautiful day that the Lord has made in order to bring three special individuals together to publicly declare and affirm their love and to commit their lives to each other."

After a short prayer Erin and Kenya began to exchange vows. Joel was bothered and confused by the order of service because the girls knew he was supposed to recite his vows first. He couldn't understand why the girls decided to exchange vows first, but he didn't complain.

Renee arrived safely on the island. A female employee from the Blue Lagoon's gift shop guided Renee to where wedding ceremonies were usually held. She took off her shoes and nearly killed herself running as fast as she could, past colorful canoes, picnic tables, coconut palm trees and volleyball nets. It was a couple of minutes past four o'clock when she made it to a huge pavilion. She almost lost it when she saw that it was empty. All she could do was jump up and down and mumble, "Shit . . . shit . . . shit."

It was after four o'clock and Renee knew exactly what that meant. She refused to give up and let Erin and Kenya take her man. Renee took off running again, calling Joel's name.

Just as Joel began to recite his vows to Erin and Kenya he heard someone calling his name. He stopped, looked around and saw Renee running full speed across the white sand in his direction. Erin and Kenya stopped breathing. They looked angry and completely baffled.

Erin asked, "What the hell is she doing here?"

Joel hunched his shoulders and said, "I dunno."

Kenya said, "We better keep an eye on her 'cause y'all know she ain't right . . . damn mental case."

Renee was out of breath by the time she reached the altar. Joel look stunned. Now Erin and Kenya looked mad as hell because Renee's unexpected arrival brought the ceremony to a screeching halt.

Breathless, Renee said, "Hi, everybody. Sorry to interrupt things, but I really-really need to speak to Joel."

Erin said angrily, "No!"

Renee looked confused and repeated, "No?"

With much attitude Kenya said, "That's right, no! You can't just come up here trying to ruin our special day like this. You need to sit down over there and be quiet so we can finish what we came here to do."

Joel looked at Erin and Kenya and said, "Wait, it's okay." He turned toward Renee and said, "Look, Renee, I'll give you a couple of minutes to get out whatever you have to say, but after that you have to promise to go away and leave the three of us alone."

Erin said, "She's not gonna do that because something is wrong with her. She's crazy."

Joel said, "Erin, stop. Don't do that."

Kenya said, "I don't feel safe with her being here like this. No telling what that bitch has in her bag. Somehow we need to put an end to this because she's never gonna go away."

Joel said, "Excuse me, Reverend Gamble. And please excuse Kenya's mouth."

Reverend Gamble said, "It's fine. No harm. Do whatever you need to do, son."

Joel walked away from the altar with Renee. As soon as they got about fifty feet away he asked, "What the hell are you doing here?"

Renee looked him in his eyes and said, "I'm here for you . . . here for us."

Joel didn't really know what to say because it was crazy, but also impressive that Renee thought enough of him to come so far. He softened his tone and asked, "You came all the way to Nassau for me?"

Renee teared up. "Not just for you, but both of us."

He exhaled and said, "Damn, you're persistent. Are you feeling okay? You're not well, are you?"

Renee said, "I've never felt better." She stepped closer to Joel and took him by the hand. Erin and Kenya watched from a distance as Joel allowed her inside his personal space. "Listen Joel, we're both at a crossroads and we need to choose the right path."

Joel shook his head and laughed. "You sound like my mother."

"Think about what you just said. That has to be a good thing." She put his hand up to her lips and said, "I need you in my life. Can't you see that we're meant to be? Being without you is unnatural. All this time your love has held me captive and won't let me go. With you I find peace of mind. I need you. You've always had my back and been there to pick me up. You saved me, now allow me to save you."

"What's that supposed to mean?"

"You know exactly what that means." Her eyes shifted over to Erin and Kenya. She frowned at them and then looked into Joel's eyes again. "I can't live without you. I refuse to turn around and just walk away without you by my side where you belong. I'm not leaving here without you. If you want me to beg then I'll beg. Please don't walk away from me and make a big mistake. I know what you're trying to do. I know you better than you think I do . . . I know you . . . I know your heart. I see the real you and I want you to see the real me. It's me . . . the old Renee is back . . . the one you first fell in love with. Can you see the real me?"

"Yeah, I see you. But I have an obligation that I need to fulfill. I belong with Erin and Kenya."

"You belong with me. I know you can feel it. God is here

right now. He wants us to be together, to get married and raise a family. Can't you see us together with a pretty little girl and a handsome little boy?"

Joel saw a brief vision, but forced it out of his mind. He said, "I can't see it." He pulled his hand away from Renee as rejection knifed its way through her heart. He looked into her eyes and said, "I'm sorry. I gotta get back over to the altar. Some things are just meant to be and others aren't."

"Sorry I can't erase the past, but I'm offering you a future . . . a real future. You don't have a real future with them. You don't even know them. After all I've gone through today I can't believe you're just gonna walk away from me."

Renee stood still and watched her best friend and former lover walk out of her life. She felt like her heart had stopped beating and the air had been sucked out of her lungs. Reality began to sink in. She had traveled by plane, taxi and boat to be with the man of her dreams and was now forced to live a nightmare. She didn't have a place to stay, a way back home or a decent change of clothes. She had traveled thousands of miles for nothing.

Joel rejoined Erin, Kenya and Reverend Gamble at the altar. He picked up where he left off and began to recite his vows. He said, "I . . . I," and then he paused as a gentle rain began to fall from a sunny, cloudless sky. Joel knew that it was a sign from God because he felt His presence. He looked over at Renee and she had her teary eyes focused directly on him. She just stood there crying her heart out.

Meanwhile, Joel looked at Erin and Kenya holding hands. He looked at the expensive diamond rings he had bought, gleaming in the sunlight. The money he spent and the rings were meaningless to him at that point. The fantasy he had tried so hard to believe in was over. Erin and Kenya had created a new bond and Joel was no longer one of them. The love he thought he had for them faded. He could clearly see now that the whole threesome thing had been about the girls all along. He came to the realization that they had used the threesome and the sexual experimentation as a way to bring the two of them together. It was hard to admit, but Erin wasn't able to love him until Kenya stepped into the picture.

Joel said, "Hold up . . . wait a minute. I can't do this. I just realized that God doesn't want us together like this. Living a Christian lifestyle isn't as hard as I thought. When I do things I'm used to doing them wholeheartedly, and I refuse to be a lukewarm Christian. The whole time we've been wondering why God brought the three of us together. Now I know why. He brought the three of us together to make me see where I really need to be. I hope the two of you will be happy together."

Erin and Kenya didn't say a word as Joel walked away. They just held each other tightly and rejoiced in the fact that they had each other.

Erin came to the realization that Joel and Renee truly belonged together. Deep down inside she knew that Renee didn't exactly come between the threesome because Renee had been there all along—in Joel's heart. Erin knew that she and Joel could have had something incredible together, but she jeopardized it all by allowing Kenya into their relationship. Above everything, Erin came away with the person she had been closest to most of her life.

Kenya came to the realization that she and Erin were lesbians. At that point she was willing to be labeled or categorized just as long as she and Erin could be together. Kenya also realized that there was a good chance that she was pregnant with Joel's baby. If that was the case she planned to explain the situation to Erin and they would raise the child as their own.

Joel walked over to Renee and could clearly see that she had a need to love and a need to be loved—a need to touch and be touched—a need to hold and be held. He took her in his arms and tried his best to love the hurt away. He wanted to raise the family he had dreamed of with Renee and wanted them to grow old together.

Joel said, "I'm still in love with you, Renee."

She whispered, "Marry me . . . let's get married."

Joel smiled. "I'd love to make you mine, to have and to hold, for better or for worse, through good times and bad times, for richer and poorer, in sickness and in health, to love you and to cherish you, from this day forward until death do us part."

They kissed. This wasn't just any kiss, but it was one that said, *Our love is infallible. I promise to love you forever and a day.*

Renee and Joel were overwhelmed with joy. They had built something special in the past and watched it fall apart. Now they had the opportunity to rebuild their lives together and share something even more special. What started out as *the beginning of the end* was now *the start of a new beginning.*